W9-CIJ-540

War Against the Animals

Also by Paul Russell

FICTION

The Salt Point
Boys of Life
Sea of Tranquillity
The Coming Storm

NONFICTION

*The Gay 100: A Ranking of the Most Influential
Gay Men and Lesbians, Past and Present*

War Against the Animals

Paul Russell

St. Martin's Press ☙ New York

WAR AGAINST THE ANIMALS. Copyright © 2003 by Paul Russell. All rights reserved. Printed in the United States of America. No part of this book may be used or reproduced in any manner whatsoever without written permission except in the case of brief quotations embodied in critical articles or reviews. For information, address St. Martin's Press, 175 Fifth Avenue, New York, N.Y. 10010.

www.stmartins.com

Library of Congress Cataloging-in-Publication Data

Russell, Paul Elliott.
   War against the animals / Paul Russell.—1st ed.
      p.   cm.
   ISBN 0-312-20935-5
   1. AIDS (Disease)—Patients—Fiction.   2. Dwellings—Maintenance and repair—Fiction.
3. New York (State)—Fiction.   4. Brothers—Fiction.   5. Boys—Fiction.   I. Title.

PS3568.U7684W37 2003
813'.54—dc21

                                         2003040617

First Edition: August 2003

10 9 8 7 6 5 4 3 2 1

For Raye,
with love

ACKNOWLEDGMENTS

With heartfelt thanks to my editor, Keith Kahla; my agent, Harvey Klinger; trusted readers Christopher Bram, Tom Heacox, Ralph Sassone, Chris Bagg.

To those others who have helped make life and work possible: Eric Brown, Mike Rhodes, Karen Robertson, Bill Pinch, Eric Lee, Dean Crawford and Darra Goldstein, Judy Nichols, the Proust Reading Group, Boris Petrov, Adam Potkay, Frank and Holly Bergon, Stewart Strunk, Keith Scribner, Alton Phillips, Benjamin Brust, Randy Cornelius, Rob Tatum, Michael Silverman, James Michael Aldrin, Evan (and Casey!) Lacon, the Eleanora Foundation, Ehren Hansen. . . .

In loving memory of: Christopher Canatsey, Rod Sorge, Ronnie Cox, Holden McCormack, Michael Stremel, and Mr. Romeo.

To Daisy and Paintbrush in what is no longer the first of their nine lives.

We are what we look upon, and what we desire.

—Plotinus

PART ONE

Et in Arcadia Ego

ONE

He had promised to have Max and Perry over for dinner as soon as Dan was gone. Nothing elaborate, only a quiet commemoration, wake, celebration, exorcism—whatever might best describe the occasion. Thus, on a bright evening early in June, Cameron Barnes watched as his two best friends left in the world made their way across his lawn to the front porch where he stood waiting.

"Hiya, beautiful," said Max, kissing him on the lips. "I have to say, you're looking awfully well."

"And I'm feeling awfully well," Cameron allowed as Perry, in turn, embraced him, pecking him lightly on the cheek and enveloping him momentarily in sweet cologne. "In fact, I'm feeling rather extraordinary these days."

But perhaps "extraordinary" should be explained, he thought. He didn't want to alarm anyone.

"I mean," he continued, "extraordinary in a good way."

"We brought you this," Perry said, unwrapping from a soaked towel a bottle of wine. "I tried to keep it cool on the way over."

"Of course, we had to have a fight about it," Max said.

"He thought we should just bring red. I told him no, we'd stick it in a bucket of ice water and that'd keep it cold."

"Now we have water all over the backseat."

"Honey, nobody drinks red wine in the summer. Please. Summer's for white wine, gin and tonics, mint juleps . . ."

"You hate mint juleps," Max reminded his boyfriend.

Cameron found the sheer ordinariness of their bickering oddly pleasing. "Actually, I don't know a single southerner who likes mint juleps," he ventured, accepting from his fellow southerner the perspiring bottle and motioning both his guests indoors.

Their entrance startled a black cat crouched on the dinner table, amid plates and silverware and candlesticks. "Diva," Cameron said sternly. *"What* are you thinking?"

The creature paused for a second, then leapt down from the table and disappeared soundlessly into the kitchen.

"She's just living up to her name," Perry purred after her.

"Never make the mistake of adopting a female cat," Cameron said. "Unless, of course, something happens to me. Then she's all yours. Casper too, of course."

"Nothing's going to happen to you," Max said.

"Well, I want *something* to happen. Anyway, I should have timed all this better. I haven't cooked a dinner in so long. Everything's ready already. I hope it's not too gauche just to sit down and eat."

"Shall I open the wine?" Perry suggested. "Cameron, will you have some?"

"Of course. My doctor says I can have a drink from time to time, no problem."

"Excellent," said Perry, who did not need to know that Cameron resorted, on occasion, to Stoli and orange juice to help the pills go down.

From the kitchen Cameron brought roasted chicken, cold asparagus vinaigrette, mashed potatoes. In the old days, Dan would sometimes spend a whole day preparing a dinner for guests. He'd been a master of intricate menus: Cameron still shuddered to recall the *mousselines de grenouilles*. Even when it was just the two of them, Dan would commandeer the kitchen, relegating Cameron, who'd always rather enjoyed cooking, to chopping an occasional vegetable or tossing the salad.

"Lovely," said Max. "I don't think I've tasted your cooking in years. Remember our supper club way back when—you and Toby and me and Roger? God, that was a lot of fun." Max poked an asparagus spear at Perry. "Way before your time, youngster."

4

"Yeah, yeah, I know. I missed out on most of the fun in life."

"Well, alas, in a way you did. I wouldn't have skipped the seventies for the world. Remember jug wines? God, those could give you a hangover. But that was okay. We were usually too stoned to notice. How did we ever manage to live like that?"

"I think we were much younger," Cameron told him. "And much, much stupider."

"Oh, not stupider," Max said. "I've been getting stupid ever since. I was at the very pinnacle of my intelligence around 1978. And you—you made a mean spaghetti with meatballs back in 1978, never since equaled."

"Spaghetti with meatballs. I'd never make such a thing anymore. Dan spoiled me, I guess. He took very good care of me, you know. Through everything. He richly deserves his freedom."

"You must be furious with him," Perry said.

"Not in the least. I know you won't believe me, but it's true. We had our run together, it was a good run, really, in spite of everything. If ever there was a perfect time for a parting, it's now. My T cells are way up, my viral load's practically undetectable. I couldn't have a better prognosis if I asked for one. Did I tell you I'm going back to work? I talked to Jorge, who seems delighted to have me back."

"Of course he's delighted," Max said. "He owes you everything."

"Still, I'd understand if he felt a little cramped having me around."

"Please," Perry interjected. "Have you seen what he's been doing to Chuck and Peter's garden? It looks truly hideous."

"That's coleus," Cameron told him, feeling he should defend his protégé. "It's all the rage this year."

"It's still hideous."

"I'm glad you're going back to work," Max said. "It's important to be out in the world. You've been in a stalemate way too long. You and Dan both."

"I was pretty sick there."

"Don't remind me. But now—what an extraordinary position you're in. Don't you see? This is life saying to you, 'Cameron, you thought it was over, but it's not over.' Endless Surprise. That's what life is."

"Is he always this inspirational?" Cameron asked Perry.

"There's a reason we call him Mr. Motivation Man."

"Just don't be too disappointed in the new me, okay?" Cameron told his

5

friend. "I'm still the same middle-aged queer with AIDS and a lot of qualms about just about everything. I'm not complaining, mind you. I'm thrilled to still be on the planet. But I'm also realistic about just where things stand in my life. All I want right now is to take care of my health and, maybe, if I feel up to it, do another garden project or two before I fade gracefully into the sunset. The rest I'll take as it comes."

"That's fine. I love your gardens. I wish I could afford one. I just don't want you to set your sights too low. I want you to be proactive. It's scary, I know. But the great love of your life might very well be waiting out there for you right now. Even as we speak. You never know."

Cameron had to laugh. "I love you, Max. You never give up."

"No, I never do." Max spoke with fervor. "Remember what you said to me about Toby Vail? Back when you two first got together? You said, 'This is crazy. This is never going to happen.' And did it happen?"

"Yes. And was it crazy?"

"Well, yes, I think it probably was. But it was the high point of your life."

"It gave me AIDS."

"You don't know that for sure."

"No, I don't," Cameron admitted. "Anyway, I got over any regrets a long time ago. And, yes, you're right. Toby was the high point of my life. In spite of everything. Or, no—I should say, *because* of everything."

"See? And who's to say life doesn't have an even higher peak in store for you? You can't know—none of us can know, and that's my point."

Cameron was on the verge of saying something, he could never afterward remember what it was, when all at once, from the road, came the shriek of tires clutching asphalt.

"Oh my God," Perry said.

Cameron felt a spike of adrenaline—where were Casper and Diva? He always imagined the worst when it came to that treacherous stretch of road in front of his house. Leaping from the table, he tried to peer out the window, but the drapery of wisteria along the porch made it difficult to see much of anything. The whole house would come down, Dan used to warn, unless they got rid of that vine.

Max was already out on the porch. "There's a truck stopped," he said as Perry and Cameron joined him.

A gray pickup had skidded halfway onto the gravel of the road's shoul-

6

der—one of those pumped-up muscle trucks Cameron despised. Music, heavy on the bass, boomed from the cab. No casualties lay in sight, no cat or possum or deer.

"You weren't expecting anybody else for dinner, were you?" Perry wondered.

From the passenger side of the truck a young woman emerged; once free, she leaned into the open door and shouted, as if lobbing a grenade into an enemy bunker, "Fuck you!"

"Well, ouch," Max murmured as the three of them leaned out over the railing (the floor slanted; the porch was gradually pulling away from the house). "I always did think you lived on an awfully exciting road."

The young woman waited there by the car, hands on hips. Acid-washed jeans fit her like a second skin; she sported a bountiful head of straw-berry-blond hair; her peach blouse had been tied off to reveal a diet-flat midriff.

The driver's door swung open and a young man climbed down. Look-ing across the truck's bed (the whole thing jacked up so high he could barely see over it), he ordered flatly, "Get back in the truck, Leanne."

"I don't love you anymore," Leanne informed him.

"Get back in the fucking truck."

"Go fuck yourself for me, okay?"

They hadn't the slightest idea they were being observed. They were twenty, twenty-two—desperate and clueless, Cameron thought, then reproached himself. Who was he, of all people, to think that?

"Do you want me to put you in the fucking truck myself?" the young man asked Leanne ominously. "Because I will do that."

He was not unbeautiful. His thin face tended toward gaunt, his small nose turned up appealingly, his close-cropped hair could almost pass for a military cut. He wore camouflage fatigues and a white, sleeveless T-shirt that revealed his perfectly sculpted upper arms.

With a sudden yelp Leanne turned and fled into the woods—Cameron's woods, twenty acres he and Dan had purchased some years back as a hedge against a convenience store or trailer park going in across the road. Leanne's flight caught the young man off guard; he shook his head in astonishment or disgust. He spit on the pavement. Leaving the car's engine running, the steroidal music pumping thunderously, he sprinted into the undergrowth after her.

"If he comes back dragging her by her magnificent hair, I'm going to pass out with joy," Max announced. "I adore redneck drama."

The truck sat empty and abandoned, its hazard lights flashing, the hectic message of its music unheard by any who might be able to decipher it.

A thrashing about in the underbrush heralded the couple's return. The handsome redneck grasped Leanne by the elbow and steered her roughly toward the truck. Noticing, for the first time, the three witnesses on the farmhouse porch, she yelled, a little halfheartedly, "Help. He's abducting me."

"What the fuck're you looking at?" her companion called sharply their way.

"Let's go inside," suggested Cameron, who tried to avoid incidents with the locals at all cost. He and Dan had had a couple of nasty confrontations with kids trespassing in the woods on their ATVs that he'd feared might lead to his house getting torched.

Despite his taunt, the young man didn't seem to mind an audience. He held Leanne against the truck and kissed her fiercely. "Everything's under control," he announced cockily. "Everything's just fine down here."

Leanne kicked him hard in the shin.

"Ow," he yelled. "Asshole."

"You're the asshole, *asshole,*" she corrected him.

"That's it. In the truck." He wrenched open the door and hoisted her inside. "Stay," he ordered, then slammed the door shut.

Surprisingly, she didn't try to bolt, sitting subdued as he sauntered around to the driver's side. Had his kiss stunned her into submission? Or was this exactly what she'd wanted all along?

The pickup's engine roared full throttle, and in an impressive spray of gravel the truck shot off. He should have written down the license number, Cameron thought—just in case. But in case of what? Whose business was it, after all, what happened between consenting adults? He imagined their whole lives to be nothing but a series of such episodes—blind, passionate, satisfying. Didn't most of human existence operate at the level of dreary farce?

Though how reluctant, when faced with the alternative, one was to give any of it up.

"Heterosexuals," Max sighed. "Ain't they a riot?"

"Anybody who needs a truck that size," said Perry, "has got a tiny penis. Trust me on that one. I grew up with boys like that."

"Come," Cameron urged his friends. "Let's finish our supper."

The last of the spring peepers' sweet cacophony filled the warm air. Against the shadowy mass of trees, fireflies pulsed. His friends had gone, finally, and Cameron felt unexpectedly relieved as he sat out on his back steps and contemplated the darkness that claimed his garden.

He should have known they'd have to talk about his future without Dan. He missed Dan enormously—after eight years together, how could you not at least miss the habit of daily companionship? But at the same time, he'd felt these last weeks an exhilaration accountable only in part by the return of his health. He was grateful that Dan had been willing to speak the sorry truth about that stalemate Max, all too accurately, saw they'd wandered into. When he'd met Dan, eight years his junior, he'd been thirty-eight, recovering from a long season of grief and resigned to all sorts of things—not least among them the prospect of spending the rest of his life living in Manhattan and successfully, if rather joylessly, designing school playgrounds. Their attraction had been mutual and powerful, but the half-life of all that radiant energy had proved surprisingly brief. Still, their life together had taken him places he'd never expected. It was Dan who'd encouraged his dream of forging romantic gardens in the country rather than utilitarian pockets in the city. It was Dan who'd suggested leaving behind neighborhoods too haunted with ghosts of the recent dead. It was Dan who'd rented the car that had brought them, one winter afternoon, to the hinterlands west of the Hudson, where they'd gotten pleasantly lost among forsaken hamlets and bankrupt family farms.

How well he remembered that drive: a small river, now placid, now rushing, accompanied them as they entered a narrow valley; between the dark, scouring stream and the steep hills there remained barely room for the road and a sleepy scattering of wooden houses that coalesced into the main street of a village. They drove past a stone church, a languishing luncheonette, the red-brick Excelsior Hotel. He'd had the clearest, strangest sense that this place had been waiting for him his whole life. Most of that life, up till then, had been indecipherable to him. Only now and again had he been seized by a moment of such great clarity: on waking from a dream one morning when he was sixteen to discover, to his utter, everlasting surprise, that he'd fallen helplessly in love with Mitchell Johnson, the handsome boy who played trumpet in the high school band; or a summer afternoon long after Mitchell had faded into unrequited memory, when he found himself alone in the ancient ruined theater at Termessos in southern Turkey, Toby Vail having wandered off to look for the famous rock tombs, leaving him alone with nothing but the sun, the mountains, the ravishing sky, suddenly ambushed by what he told himself must be no less than Being itself.

Poor Dan too must have felt, as they crept along the main street of Stone Hollow, his own sense of certainty. "One day," he'd told Cameron, "you and I are going to live here."

"Do we really want to live in a place like this?" Cameron had asked cautiously. "I bet they eat gay men for breakfast here."

"Oh, I'm sure they do. But it's nice to dream. Anyway, we'll never be able to find it again. It's probably not even on any map."

But they *had* found it again, and not only on a map; against Cameron's better judgment they'd ended up sinking all their money—his money, really—into a 160-year-old farmhouse they'd found lingering precariously on the brink of no return. Friends had been skeptical, even alarmed. "You two are going to disappear," Max had warned. "We'll never hear from you again." But that hadn't happened. Instead, their friends had ventured up from Manhattan in droves to assist in, or in some cases merely to appreciate, the house's steady progress (as a restorer, Dan had turned out to have a touch of genius about him). Perhaps they had all thought of the house, in those early years, as a life raft that might carry anyone to safety. Only some of them, it turned out, would not be so lucky. Already Toby—charmed, beautiful, doomed Toby—had been swept away. Then, one after another, Ken and Jamie and Roger had plunged into the raging torrent. Cameron had realized, one day in the early nineties, that nearly every man he'd loved in the seventies and eighties was now dead.

A stirring in the lilacs interrupted his musings; a white form burst forth and scampered toward him. With a single fluid motion Casper leapt into his lap. Cameron stroked the creature's luxuriously arching spine; he listened with gratification to the motor of its purr. Did Casper remember anything of his life with Jamie and Roger, before illness had forced them to give him up? Without warning, a great wide ache of longing came over him—but for what? He was forty-six. He'd been shipwrecked, left for dead, only, unlike the rest of them, he'd been given a second chance, at least for the moment, and now found himself alone and well-nigh defenseless against the island's magic, waiting for whatever strange new adventure proposed to befall him.

Past Casper's steady purr, another sound caught his attention. He listened. Quiet, persistent, coming from the dark beyond the porch light's glow, it was as if someone stood in the bushes and methodically tore a sheet of paper into strips. He had never much minded the solitude of the country, its pitch-dark on cloudy nights, its diamond show of stars on clear; lately, though, he'd been aware of just how isolated he was. On one side of him lay the Rural Cemetery, with its several acres of graves both old and recent. On the other, back toward town and buffered by former fields grown up thick with saplings, a housing development from the mid-sixties kept out of sight and mostly, except when kids decided to run their ATVs through his woods, out of mind.

Listening to that methodical, perplexing sound—first one strip, then another, carefully shredded—he was aware of the great looming night beyond the house, how it swarmed among the flowers of his garden, flowed in like a steady breeze through the window screens, how it would hover over his bed through the long hours till the noisy flock of crows scavenging the compost heap signaled dawn. The thought crossed his mind that the handsome redneck in the gray pickup had somehow decided to come back, looking for trouble, but that was of course absurd. He and his friends had barely registered, if at all.

As if somehow aware of his attention, the noise persisted. He listened intently, in something of a quiet panic because he could not make out what it was in the dark. Then he glimpsed movement; a camouflaged shape came into focus.

A deer was browsing among his hosta. He almost laughed in relief. A young buck with tentative antlers looked at him, eyes bright disks of light, then lowered its head to take in another mouthful of expensive, ornamental leaves.

For a moment he had the strangest impression that if he spoke to the deer, the deer would speak back. "Hey," he said, but the buck seemed oblivious to his presence. Of course it must know he was there, but it must not care. The Camerons of the world were no threat. So it chewed leisurely. June so far had been dry; perhaps that was why the creature had ventured so uncommonly close to the house. From Cameron's lap, Casper watched with interest as the sleek, beautiful animal continued its methodical grazing, till after several minutes, and of its own accord, it turned and wandered off into the dark where peepers and fireflies broadcast again and again their shimmering seasonal question: *Will you have me? Will you have me?*

"That's all she wrote," Cameron told Casper with a yawn. "Time for bed." The evening had exhausted him. Still, it was a good exhaustion he felt, not like that persistent, debilitating fatigue of old. What a strange thing, to know with reasonable certainty that he would give other dinner parties. That he would seek out old friends and make new ones. That perhaps—and this was an idea—if he could manage to renovate the neglected flowerbeds and encourage the rosebushes, he'd even throw a garden party on the grand scale he and Dan used to manage back in the days before he got so sick. A start would be to repair the old shed at the back of the garden; last winter's snows had nudged it from quaint dilapidation to outright eyesore.

Indoors, dirty plates cluttered the kitchen counter, but he would save those for tomorrow. From the cabinet he took down his bottle of Stoli, then decided to forgo that indulgence. He poured himself a tall glass of springwater from the plastic jug in the fridge and headed upstairs to face his nightly ritual of pills.

TWO

In the parking lot of the Benedictine Hospital, Jesse waited for his brother to come down. He hadn't meant to leave the room like that, abruptly and without a word, but the sight of his old man had undone him. He kicked the front tire of his brother's truck repeatedly—an action he knew was perfectly pointless, but he couldn't think what else to do.

Dr. Vishnaraman had been matter-of-fact, taking him and Kyle aside in the hall and explaining how Pop's liver was failing: a large tumor had completely enclosed the main blood vessel. "If he's lucky," Dr. Vishnaraman told them, "he'll slip peacefully into a coma." In the dead fluorescent light of the hospital corridor, Jesse had tried to regard the small, dark man without bitterness.

Kyle wasn't so forgiving. "If he's *lucky,*" he said, spitting out the word like it was hateful. "What the hell does that mean?"

Dr. Vishnaraman, of course, didn't know Kyle. He spoke soothingly. "Dying is sometimes not so easy. Or, perhaps I should say, dying itself is in fact absurdly easy. But getting there—that sometimes is very hard. It can be a great relief when it's over."

Kyle rocked back and forth on his feet; he clasped his elbows. "There must be something you can do," he said ominously.

The doctor looked pained. He glanced down at his expensive gold watch. "I'm very sorry," he said, "but I must tell you boys truthfully. I'm afraid there is nothing."

"Does he know?" Kyle cocked his head to one side to indicate the patient beyond the door.

"The body knows," Dr. Vishnaraman said. "So, yes, he can hear what his body is telling him. I'm sorry for you boys." He reached out sympathetically to touch Kyle's arm. Kyle flinched noticeably and pulled back, though the doctor didn't seem to take it amiss. "I know it is very difficult. You can go in and see him now. Savor this time with your father."

They'd put Pop in a single room; he was too ill to share a double anymore. The antiseptic smell barely masked the room's sickly odor. Bill Vanderhof gazed up listlessly at the television where Sunday-morning politicians ran their mouths. He hadn't shaved in several days. His cheeks were sunk in and hollow, but his belly had swelled up something terrible. His skin had a greenish yellow cast to it.

"Hey, guys." He turned and smiled weakly. "Looks like your old man's hit a bit of a rough patch."

He wasn't an old man, really, only forty-seven.

"You're gonna be fine." Kyle touched him on the shoulder of his hospital gown. "That Buddha-head of a doctor don't know his ass from an elephant."

Pop laughed at that. He showed his gold incisor with his grin. "You bet I'm gonna be fine," he said. "I'm still counting on winning the damn lottery one of these days."

"I picked you up some tickets like you said," Kyle told him.

One moment Jesse was standing by the door; the next, he was half-running down the corridor, past the nurses' station, down the fire stairs. Before he knew it, he was standing in a cold sweat in the warm, reassuring sun of the parking lot. The sky overhead was flawless blue except where the brazen sliver of a jet marred it. Even now he could turn and walk back up to that room, could explain, "I got the cramps. I went to find a rest room." But he couldn't move from where he stood. If I wasn't such a fucking coward, he thought, kicking again at the tire of his brother's pickup.

The glass doors opened but it wasn't Kyle. A family strolled out, done up in their Sunday best. Spanish words, quick and blurred, sprang from their mouths. They walked directly toward him, almost like they knew him, almost like they could claim him, the parents chattering away, the three children quiet, their smiles dazzling, two small boys and a teenage girl.

14

With feigned indifference he glanced aside as they passed close by, feeling nonetheless a fleet spasm of longing. His brother would go for that little señorita, he thought. He'd enjoy laying eyes on her.

But what could Kyle be doing up there that would take so long? Pop wasn't much of a talker; neither was Kyle, for that matter. It was the women in the family who chattered away—his mom, his sister. He tried to imagine the little señorita in her bright white dress pouring a dark torrent of words over his brother. He tried to imagine Pop and Kyle just sitting there looking at each other, helpless, letting the minutes tick by. *Savor this time with your father.* He heard Dr. Vishnaraman's voice in his head, the last thing he wanted to hear, but there it was. What a very weird thing to tell somebody, Jesse thought, kicking once again at the tire, hating the dark little doctor, families of Mexicans, the whole fucking universe, basically.

The exercise burned off a little of the fear, but still the fear kept coming back in waves, able like water to find its way in anywhere. Pop hadn't been sick a day in his life except for the appendicitis scar below his belt line; then one day this spring he just took to bed. He itched all over, he said, it was driving him insane. He had a fever that wouldn't go away. He couldn't eat. Overnight, it seemed, the whites of his eyes colored up yellow. Hepatitis, Uncle Roy had surmised, but it wasn't hepatitis, it was much much worse.

How long had this been lying in wait?

You look just like your daddy did when first I met him, his mother had told him not long ago—told Kyle too, since people sometimes mistook the two of them for twins, they looked so much alike.

What else had Pop handed down to them besides his looks?

The glass doors opened again, and this time, finally, it was Kyle. He walked forth confidently, the picture of health and strength and courage—all the things that were good in the world. It made Jesse ashamed, the way he'd let all those fearful equations loose in his head.

"That was some stunt you pulled back there," his brother said with a frown. "Where the hell did you go? I was waiting for you to come back."

"I'll come back tomorrow," Jesse said truthfully. "I wasn't feeling too well. I think it was those fluorescent lights made me dizzy."

His brother looked him over coldly, then looked away.

"So how is he, do you think?" Jesse asked when they'd climbed in the truck.

"Our old man's a fighter," Kyle said. "If anybody's going to pull through, it'll be him." He paused for a moment, then added, like he needed to reassure himself, "He's a Vanderhof."

It was another thing Jesse'd heard his whole life. Vanderhofs are old as stone around here. Vanderhofs stick together like the local cement. Nobody or nothing can knock down a Vanderhof and keep him down. But as they pulled out of the hospital parking lot, Jesse Vanderhof felt only the clammy grip of terror. We're doomed too, he thought wildly, me and Kyle both.

But Kyle didn't seem to have such thoughts. He drove steadily, one hand on the wheel, the other hanging comfortably out the window.

Dr. Vishnaraman had put Pop on tranquilizers—sedated him for the ride downhill. But what about the folks on the sidelines, innocent bystanders who might share those same rotten genes? Surely there should be pills for them too—only Jesse Vanderhof would never be able to go to Dr. Vishnaraman, or any other doctor for that matter, and admit, a perfectly healthy nineteen-year-old with all his life ahead of him, "I'm nowhere near there yet, but already I'm fucking scared to death of dying."

He held out his hand, experimentally, and could see it trembling before him. He tried to hold it steady, but couldn't.

Kyle looked over from behind the steering wheel. "What the fuck are you doing there?"

"Nothing."

"Don't go weak on us, man. We got to pull together in this. We're family. We're strong."

The day was ridiculously beautiful. They headed out of Kingston, past the traffic circle and onto the long, straight stretch of road that ran south toward Stone Hollow. On either side, fields shin-high with corn stretched into the distance. This was where he'd grown up, lived his whole life. Those fields in the distance his uncle owned. His own family too had farmed once upon a time after settling in the valley of the Schneidekill sometime back in the 1600s, or so said his mother, who was a Bondurant, another of the old, old families. The name Vanderhof was scattered throughout these hills and hollows; he had cousins everywhere. There were the Kerhonkson Vanderhofs and the Krumville Vanderhofs and the Rosendale Vanderhofs. At family gatherings—the Fourth of July, Christmas, Easter—he sensed a whole thicket of history lurking just beyond the screen of his relatives' conversations, tantalizing, only now and then revealed. In school, once, the teacher had given them the assignment of drawing a family tree. He'd sat with his grandma at the kitchen table one winter night and listened to her spin tales that had been handed down for generations: a girl taken prisoner by Delaware Indians, a daring rescue, the old stone house, the very one where they still lived, attacked with flaming arrows during the Second Esopus War. On the chart the teacher had given him, she filled in grandparents and great-grandparents he'd never known, Vanderhofs and Bondurants and de Hulters and Schneidewinds that nested in the tree branches like strange, colorful birds.

The old stone house sat a ways outside of town, atop a hill overlooking the fertile valley: the tiny original house, now the kitchen and bathroom, attached at right angles to the larger, later farmhouse to form an L. Moss grew thick on shingles that had needed replacing forever. The Gothic gables were coming apart one by one. Under the profusion of accumulated stuff—old trunks, bottomless chairs, a defunct wringer washing machine, many, many jugs and bottles—the front porch sagged. Pop had never seen a piece of junk he didn't bring home; likewise he never liked to see anything thrown away. The big attic was piled to the rafters with outworn clothes, chests of old letters or tools or toys, furniture and lamps and dressmakers' dummies and guns put out of sight and out of mind; the swaybacked barn too held rusting plows, tractors, hay balers, the walls hung with hoes and rakes and shovels no one except boys at play had touched in Jesse's lifetime. (Afternoons after school, armed with scythes and pitchforks, he and Kyle used to put whole villages to torture and death.)

Kyle floored the accelerator and the Ford roared aggressively up the drive in a scatter of gravel; then he braked the truck to an abrupt halt next to Jesse's own ailing pickup, their mother's Crown Victoria, their sister's low-slung Mustang, the ancient panel truck on whose sides BILVIC CONSTRUCTION: NO JOB TOO LARGE OR SMALL had been carefully stenciled. Jesse watched for a moment as Kyle knelt and received the frantic attentions of Poke, the crazy black mongrel. Beneath Kyle's rough handling, Poke rolled on his back in ecstasy. Anyone else, he'd bite.

Leaving his brother to all that affection, Jesse lurched into the house.

Home from church, his mother and sister were finishing their lunch. They sat at the kitchen table eating egg salad sandwiches and smoking

17

cigarettes. "I wish you'd called us before you left," his mother said. "We were just fixing to go up to the hospital right now. We figured you were still there. You and your brother want something to eat?"

"I'm not all that hungry," Jesse told her. "I'll just have a glass of water. I think we're going swimming."

He lifted a glass from the cupboard and held it under the faucet.

His mother took a final drag on her cigarette and ground it out. "The doctor—I can't ever pronounce his name—"

"I just call him Dr. Vish," Patti said.

"Well, Dr. Vish, then, he said we might want somebody there with him round the clock. I thought I told you that. He said your daddy could go at any time."

"He told us," Jesse said between long swallows of cool water. "Not that he knows his ass from an elephant."

"Jesse," his mother admonished him, though he pretended not to hear. He finished his glass and refilled it.

"I'll do cot duty tonight," Patti proposed.

"We'll do shifts," his mother agreed. She took out a cigarette from her macraméd holder and lit it, though not without observing—to Patti, he thought; not to him—"I should take a hint and quit these things. The last thing I want to do is blame your daddy for his ills. I'm not against drinking, everything's got its time and place, I guess. But any man who takes to drinking in the morning is just asking for trouble. But he wouldn't listen to nobody but himself on that one. I know that doesn't sound too charitable, I'm aware of that. I'm just speaking the facts."

Their mother didn't touch alcohol. When they were growing up, whenever Pop wasn't around, she used to say, trying, Jesse supposed, to educate them, "Don't beer look an awful lot like piss? I can't imagine drinking anything looking like that, can you?"

"The doctor never said it was drinking," Jesse ventured. "It could of been any number of things. It could of been handed down."

But what if it was just the drinking? What if there wasn't any invisible doom except of your own making? Then he and Kyle could go scot-free.

Setting his empty water glass on the counter, he stepped inside the bathroom and shut the door.

"I might never have married your daddy," he heard his mother tell his sister, "if I'd of known from the beginning he had that particular weakness. But I didn't know for years and years, till I came on his empties in the cellar. He was being so clever, he thought—stashing them in the old chimney where nobody'd ever look. Well, I was never one for having secrets kept from me, and I let him know that."

"It's just a bad situation," Patti said. She had a way of making thoughtful pronouncements. She was in her last year at the community college and everybody agreed, of the three kids, she was the one bound to go farthest. For whatever that was worth.

Standing in front of the washbasin, Jesse scrutinized the whites of his eyes in the splotched mirror of the medicine cabinet. They weren't exactly white, but not jaundiced either—bloodshot was the worst they could be accused of.

Kyle and I don't hardly ever drink, he reassured himself.

He moved to the toilet and pissed a nice clear stream that drowned their talk. Pop's urine these days was dark, his stools white as paste. Jesse didn't want to know that, but he did. I'm fine, he told himself, zipping up. I'm completely healthy. I got years and years still to live.

Weed's Mill Falls was a collection of some fifteen wooden buildings clustered along the narrow road; on Sundays parked cars lined both sides, BMWs and Jeep Cherokees, weekenders who flocked from their country houses to hang out at the Onion Café—BRUNCH ALL DAY SUNDAY promised the sign out front—or browse the flea market for "finds" to haul back to the city.

Kyle whipped the truck into the lot behind the volunteer fire station, and in the loose gravel they skidded to a stop. He pulled down the seat and rummaged among oil quarts and stray tools, but then seemed to think better of it. Pushing the seat upright, he grabbed his towel, and together they headed down the path to where the leisurely Schneidekill abruptly plunged thirty feet over a broad stone lip. A clot of large tree trunks, bone bare, hung at the top of the falls; it'd be next spring before high water finally sent them over. At the base of the falls, the roofless stone walls of the old mill, long since overgrown by trees, loomed four tall stories; nearby, a squat modern hydroelectric station, a seamless concrete bunker except for its metal door, tapped what modest fund of power was to be had from the rushing water. Below the falls the Schneidekill, no longer useful, ran amid low, flat sheets of rock. Stone piers on either side of the stream, the only remaining traces of the old aqueduct that had once carried the canal across, were perfect for diving from.

Two large dogs bounded their way, accompanied by their owner's shouted assurance: "They're friendly, they won't bite." Kyle knelt and let them nuzzle him excitedly. "Atta boy," he kept repeating to one and then the other as he roughed up their ears. Dogs loved Kyle. Jesse watched his brother and felt a sudden shadow of sadness fall across everything. He wondered, did Kyle despise him for being afraid? But Kyle, rising, releasing the dogs to romp back to their owner, was all smiles.

"We should of brought Poke," he said.

"Poke gets himself in trouble," Jesse reminded him.

"Too true. That's why he's the best."

They climbed the path to the top of the aqueduct pier. Behind them, the slumping trough of the old canal led back through the woods toward a defunct lock whose dressed stone walls, still intact, rose majestically out of the mossy water of the canal bed. On the pier, two junior-high-age boys in microscopic swimwear were daring each other to jump, but neither would. Jesse wondered who they could be: only guys on a swim team wore suits that skimpy. They weren't from around here, he concluded, and the arrival of the kids' parents, moments later, confirmed that.

"Oh my God," said the boys' father. "That's insane. Don't even think of trying to dive from there."

Jesse saw how Kyle, removing his T-shirt and sneakers, looked at the group with barely disguised contempt, but the family seemed utterly unaware they were being so critically observed. They moved in their own world. The father had skinny white legs; he wore sandals and a ridiculous straw hat. The mother was more like the boys, slim and tan, maybe a swimmer herself. Jesse felt an ache go through him, but why? He too despised them, he thought.

"Let's go back down to the water," the mother urged her sons. She had a stern, slightly horsey look to her.

"People were jumping from here," one of the boys argued. He rocked back and forth impatiently and crossed his arms over his bare chest.

"Some people are crazy," the father said. With his middle finger he pushed his horn-rimmed glasses up his nose. He was a lawyer, Jesse thought, a stockbroker; he had wads and wads of cash stashed away. "It's not safe," the father went on, his voice high and nasal. "They should really have some kind of lifeguard here. Somebody's going to get hurt." Why, Jesse thought, would anybody in their right mind want to sound like that? His money, though, must be a serious consolation.

The boy relented without putting up a fight, and Jesse could see he'd grow up to be just like his dad. The mother touched the small of her son's back, just above his suit, to urge him along the path, and for some reason it made Jesse remember the Mexican girl back at the hospital. He tried to visualize her beauty, but already she'd faded. All he could see was her white dress.

"It's not safe," Kyle mocked the family once they were barely—or not even—out of earshot. He was excellent at voices. "Here's your fucking safe," he said. With scarcely a pause he stepped to the edge of the pier, flung back his head, spread wide his arms, and disappeared with a whoop. Danger diving, they called it. If you knew what you were doing, it was completely safe, though last summer some knucklehead from New Jersey had split his head wide open and drowned. But he and Kyle had dived here forever; never once had they had even a close call.

Still, Jesse held his breath for the two seconds it took before the percussive sound of Kyle's splash signaled he was in the water. He peered over to see Kyle's sleek head and shoulders bobbing in the deep pool; with both hands Kyle cleared the streaming water from his face and looked up. "What're you waiting for, wuss!" he yelled up.

Jesse wouldn't be hurried. He pulled off his T-shirt and folded it carefully, setting it on top of his rolled-up towel. Balancing on one foot, then the other, he took off his sneakers and set them side by side. He felt no fear, though he was, he reminded himself, sort of taking his life in his hands. A few feet to the right or left and you'd go out like a light, never feel a damn thing ever again.

Like slipping into a coma.

He jumped. He felt adrenaline flood his body as he hung for a millisecond in air and then plummeted. The slap of the water's surface on his body was satisfying, the rough way it resisted and then received him. He came up gasping.

Kyle had already remounted the pier. He loomed there, a shadow against the dazzle of sunlight, waiting for Jesse to clear the pool, and Jesse obliged, hauling himself up on the flat rock to catch his breath. His brother soared and fell.

"Nice one," Jesse called, but Kyle didn't hear. From across the way came the pleasant smell of pot. A guy and two girls were passing a joint back and forth. Closing his eyes, wishing he hadn't left his towel up on the pier but too lazy to fetch it, he stretched out on the flat rock and felt how it gave back into his body the healing light of the sun. He basked in the radiant heat as it stripped his cells bare of flaws. In a hospital room in Kingston, Pop might be slipping right now into a coma, but that was another life, one parallel to this one, where everything was twisted and painful. Beneath all the other noises—the screams of little kids, laughter, a radio playing—the Schneidekill sluiced between boulders and everything was at some kind of peace. The world would never end.

With an enormous splash, a body entered once again into the pool of deep water.

"Well done," he heard a voice proclaim. "Very Thomas Eakins."

"The old swimming hole," said another.

The weekend fags were out. He opened his eyes to see a gaggle of them a dozen or so yards away, men in their late twenties wearing sunglasses with colored frames, Hawaiian shirts open over smooth chests. Their bodies had the plastic look of those guys you saw in perfume advertisements. One sported bright yellow hair teased up in spikes. Another wore turquoise trunks. Jesse couldn't begin to imagine the kind of lives they must lead.

They'd hauled low-slung beach chairs onto the shelf of rock to claim it as their own private stretch of beach, and they sat fanning themselves and sipping pink-colored drinks one of them poured out from a thermos.

Kyle emerged from the water and sat next to Jesse, legs drawn up, arms clasped around his knees. Water droplets glistened on his calves. Jesse thought about observing, casually, "The fags are out in full force," but his brother could see that as well as he.

"I wish I had my cigarettes," Kyle told him.

From the pier, another diver plunged into the Schneidekill. The water swallowed him in a gulp, then spit him back out. He clambered up the rocks toward them, his dark hair slicked down, his body streaming water. He tugged at the waist of his black trunks, and for a split second Jesse

22

didn't recognize who it was. Then Kyle said, "Hey, Brandon," and reached out his hand for his buddy to slap him greetings. They went way back, Kyle and Brandon Schneidewind; there'd even been a time when Brandon had lived with them off and on, sleeping on the floor when things got rough at home and he was working for Pop.

"About your old man," Brandon was saying, settling himself down next to Kyle. "That really sucks."

Some queasy emotion wandered through Jesse.

"Yeah, well . . ." Kyle looked off into the distance, at some space above the heads of the fag pack. "He's gonna pull through," he added after a long pause.

"We're all in his corner for him, man," Brandon said. "Besides, your old man can get himself out of anything they throw at him. Remember when he got in so much trouble for clearing that swamp?"

Kyle laughed. "He's still mad about that."

"He should be. Fuck! The look on those clowns' faces: 'He's ruining the swamp! He's ruining the swamp!'" Brandon cried out in mincing tones. He too was good with voices; the two of them used to clown all the time.

"Like you can ruin a fucking swamp," Kyle said.

"You're forgetting—it wasn't a fucking swamp, man: it was a *wetland.*"

"Wetland my ass. It wasn't even wet most of the time. They should of paid him money for the way he improved it."

"They don't want you to touch nothing these days," Brandon said. They all knew what he meant. Improve a falling-down old house with aluminum siding, some idiot was going to yell at you for ruining it. Blaze a trail in the woods with your three-wheeler, some asshole was sure to threaten you with trespassing—one weekender had even brandished a gun ("He's getting himself in way over his head," Kyle had said darkly). And that wetland: the clowns at the DEC had wanted Pop to fork over a $4,000 fine, but fortunately he'd gone to the town clerk's office and settled it for $200.

They sat for a few minutes in silence and honored the memory. What had been a patch of muck was now a sparkling little lake where mallards floated and three white geese patrolled the shore and sometimes a great blue heron stalked the shallows.

"Hey." Brandon broke the silence. "You seen Alice and Leanne? They said they might be coming down here."

Jesse glanced his brother's way, but Kyle had perfected a look that was impenetrable.

"Haven't seen them," he said tersely.

"Me neither," Jesse added, then instantly regretted having spoken. He tended to speak way too much, he thought. It was something he was working on.

A shriek went up from the posse of fags. One of them had stood up and was flapping his arms like a chicken. The others pointed at him and laughed.

"She's staying away from me," Kyle said. He sighed profoundly. "There's something real fucked there."

"She's freaked about your old man, is all," Brandon told him. "I know for a fact. She told Alice she felt so bad."

"And she can't tell me that herself?"

"I'm not disagreeing. It's just . . ." Brandon paused, searching for a word. "It's hard."

"I wish people would stop being so fucking down about everything," Kyle said with a gust of anger. "It's not over, not by a long shot. Everybody seems to fucking think it is." He stood up abruptly.

"Hey, man," Brandon said, "I didn't mean to . . ."

Kyle was already striding off. He didn't look back.

Brandon looked at Jesse for support.

"It's hard," Jesse told him, pleased to feed Brandon's words back to him. "For everybody," Jesse added, watching as his brother skirted the fag posse and tore up the slope to the pier. He waited for Kyle to appear at the top, to danger dive into the deep pool, but he didn't.

Brandon seemed to know Jesse hated him. He stirred uncomfortably, but spoke nonetheless.

"I guess him and Leanne are having some problems, huh?"

Jesse tried to seem impenetrable. "You'd have to ask Kyle about that."

"Yeah. You don't ask Kyle about that kind of thing, do you?"

"I don't," Jesse said. His brother ran through girlfriends like a fox in a chicken coop. Jesse's own girlfriend he'd had for nearly two years. Eventually he and Donna would get married, he supposed. Settle down and have kids. He hoped Brandon knew that.

"He's a deep one, your brother," Brandon said. "How long have I known him?"

Too long, Jesse wanted to say, but didn't. He could feel Brandon watching him, and he was determined not to give his brother's best friend a thing. He kept his face frozen.

"Well"—Brandon stood and ran his fingers through his black hair—"I gotta go, I guess." He looked down at Jesse and shook his head. "Oh, man, this is all so fucked."

"Get outta here," Jesse told him.

"You keep me posted on your old man."

Jesse only nodded. He watched Kyle's buddy lope away and thought that, yes, it was true, he really did hate Brandon Schneidewind, and Brandon probably hated him too, but nobody except for the two of them ever need know that.

He wondered if he should go look for Kyle. You never knew what Kyle was going to do next, and though most of the time that was exciting, sometimes it could be alarming. Jesse felt that alarm now: he really had expected him to danger dive, to work off his grief and anger that time-tested way. He stood and surveyed the riverbank, but it revealed no trace of his brother. The sun that had been warm and healing now felt oppressive on his skin.

"Girl, you do *not!*" screamed one of the fags.

"You tell her," said another. Involved in their antics, they didn't look his way at all; still, he felt self-conscious walking by their encampment.

Go away, he wanted to tell them. We didn't ask you to come here.

But from the look of it, they were here to stay.

He climbed up the rise to the pier. His clothes lay folded where he'd left them, but Kyle's were gone. He slipped into his sneakers, enfolded his T-shirt in his towel, and walked back toward the fire station lot. He thought again about the Mexican girl from the hospital, and how, when he saw Kyle, he'd tell him about her.

Kyle was standing by the truck. The driver's side door was open, and the seat pulled forward. Jesse saw him take a swig from the bottle and put it back behind the seat. His brother looked up and saw him. Jesse walked slowly his way, careful not to look like he'd seen anything. Kyle wiped his mouth with the back of his hand. He spit on the pavement. "Hey, little brother," he said, like nothing at all in the world was anywhere near wrong.

THREE

With a double beep of its horn, the panel truck pulled into the gravel driveway. BILVIC CONSTRUCTION: NO JOB TOO LARGE OR SMALL read the hand-stenciled sign on its side. *Bilvic*—was that a Serbian name? Cameron wondered. As for the quaint stencil, he very much liked hand-lettered signs, holdouts against the relentless corporate drive toward uniformity. Max had recommended the fellow—"colorful, probably alcoholic, did perfectly fine work for me" had been his description. Cameron thought he rather looked forward to the cantankerous, rough-edged old codger.

He was surprised, then, to see instead two strapping young men clamber down from the truck. "Hey, guys" he said as they approached, conscious how his voice settled an octave lower than usual for the sake of the locals. In his youth, such a reflex had meant nothing less than survival; as an adult, he might have thought he'd shed that old mode of camouflage, until Max pointed out one day, as they walked out of a hardware store, "Darling, you were butching it up back there like somebody trying out for the rodeo."

That had been before he got sick. Now, don what protective coloration he might, he was just one more faggot with AIDS. All it took was a look in the mirror to see how his skin had that tight, stretched look that was a dead giveaway. But did the uninitiated—these two young men, for instance—even notice?

Still, *I'm not what you think,* he wanted, irrationally, to tell the two as they stopped before him. But then, what exactly was he? Rather than attempt an answer, he stuck out his hand, only to realize, as first one and then the other young man firmly grasped his palm, that he'd seen the two before, or at least one of them, though it took him a moment to recall exactly when and where.

"So you're the guy who needs some work on his barn?" said the one who'd identified himself as Kyle. They were brothers. They might almost, for that matter, be twins. Cameron wasn't entirely sure, looking from one to the other (the younger wore a plum-colored baseball cap), which was the bully with the muscle truck and the rebellious girlfriend he'd witnessed a few nights back. And neither gave any indication they'd ever seen *him,* or that anything the least bit memorable might have occurred on that stretch of road that ran past the white farmhouse with green shutters.

"Not really a barn," Cameron said. "More of a shed, actually. It hasn't been used in years, but I think it was some sort of chicken coop for a while. It's in terrible shape, maybe unsalvageable."

"You should trim that vine off your porch there," Kyle told him.

"I know," Cameron said, feeling reprimanded, though he had no intention at all of getting rid of the wisteria, which reminded him of his grandmother's house in Tupelo, Mississippi. As to the young man's identity—of course, he thought, he might be mistaken. His brain wasn't as sharp as it used to be. He got all sorts of little things wrong he'd never have tripped over in the past. It was distressing. Still, he was sure it had been one of them. That upturned nose, the quasi-military haircut, short on top, almost shaved on the sides. Remarkable how alike they looked, though on closer scrutiny he could tell they weren't in fact twins, that Kyle was at least a year older than his brother—whose name, in the distraction of the handshake, the stir of recognition, Cameron realized he hadn't caught. He wondered if he should ask him to repeat it, but was afraid of somehow sounding too eager. But eager for what? he wondered as Kyle, clearly the spokesman for the two, commanded, "So let's go see the damage."

It was always dramatic how the garden opened up once you rounded the corner of the house—a vista of flowerbeds and rose bushes in wanton June bloom, the bluestone patio with its ornate Indonesian teak benches, the low wall that framed another level beyond, to which obscuring shrubs

27

and conifers lent an air of mystery, an invitation to explore. And, of course, the great, spreading, two-hundred-year-old red oak that had been one of the main reasons he and Dan had fallen in love with the tumble-down property.

"Pretty nice," Kyle observed, though it was possible he was just being ironic.

"Thanks," said Cameron, trying a vaguely dismissive tone, as if he'd just happened to make such a garden but wasn't excessively invested in it. "A bit neglected, I'm afraid."

"You made this all by yourself?" inquired the younger brother as they strolled past showy pots of agapanthus, the raised herb bed with its silvery lavender and gray-green thyme, the sad, deer-devastated hosta. "I mean, like, wow."

"I used to do gardens for a living," Cameron admitted, trailing slightly behind, observing with a trace of disappointment how they both wore those baggy blue jeans that were all the rage these days among the young. Whatever happened to nice tight-fitting denim? "Landscape architect," he told them. "I'm retired now."

"You don't look hardly old enough to be retired," Kyle said.

For an instant Cameron debated telling them everything. But why? Did he feel somehow guilty that he knew what he knew about Kyle's girl-friend troubles? For it was Kyle he'd witnessed in the road, he was sure of that now (it was the peremptory way he'd said, "Let's go see the dam-age"). Odd to know about this complete stranger a melodramatic little item Kyle's own brother probably didn't know.

"I didn't retire, exactly," Cameron explained. "I suppose you could say I moved on to other things." Then he added, for the sake of the younger brother's blurt of enthusiasm for his garden, "But I certainly enjoyed myself at it while it lasted."

To that, however, neither brother made any reply, and they proceeded in what seemed, suddenly, an awkward silence. Had he been too familiar? He was conscious of being alone with two young men who might very well hate his kind with a vengeance.

At the garden's edge, in the shade of the great oak, sat the yellow shed, paint peeling, roof pitifully swaybacked, the glass of its windowpanes broken out. Obvious rot afflicted the lower boards of its siding. He felt vaguely ashamed at having neglected its health over the years.

"So," he said as he unlatched and flung open the double doors. A scatter of disused and broken things greeted them—rusting, unidentifiable farm implements, two defunct lawn mowers, various odds and ends he and Dan had moved out there from the attic, or picked up over the years at tag sales and auctions and found they had no use for.

Kyle laughed abruptly, more a snort than a laugh.

"What?" Cameron asked guiltily.

"You got nearly as much junk as we do back home," the younger brother explained. He scratched the back of his head, behind his baseball cap, as if to dislodge some recalcitrant thought. "Our old man's a pack rat, big time."

"Oh?" Cameron found himself oddly touched by the confession, as if it were some quaint gesture of friendliness on the younger brother's part. He reminded himself that these two were, after all, barely more than kids. It was even possible—amusing thought—that with his stately farmhouse, his opulent garden, *he* was the one who intimidated *them*.

"Was that your dad I talked with on the phone?" he asked, thinking it odd that Max hadn't mentioned old man Bilvic's vibrant assistants.

"He'd of been here today, only he's a little under the weather," Kyle said as he stepped over a pile of junk and into the shed.

"He's in the hospital," the younger brother added.

"I'm sorry to hear that."

"Yeah, well," Kyle said, "it's one of those things. You know, these are in pretty bad shape." He scrutinized the rafters of the sagging roof. "All this is gonna have to come down, I expect."

"He ain't making it out," the younger brother mentioned, so quietly it seemed the information was meant for Cameron's ears alone. Kyle heard it, though. Later Cameron would think it possible, had he not been there, that something violent might have happened, the look Kyle threw his brother was so unaccountably fierce. But that was only for an instant, and in the next instant Cameron was no longer sure he'd witnessed anything at all pass between them. Kyle continued, coolly, to inspect the beams, the joists. "Real two-by-fours," he said.

"I imagine this was built in the thirties," Cameron told him.

"Can't be much later than that." Kyle slammed a stud with his open palm to test the frame's integrity. "She's still pretty solid on her foundations." He crossed his arms over his chest and appeared to think. "I'll call you tomorrow. I'll get you an estimate. We could start next week."

"That sounds just fine," Cameron told him. Then, turning to the younger brother he said, "I'm sorry, I'm afraid I didn't catch your name."

"Jesse," the young man told him. "And my brother's Kyle."

Cameron nodded. "I'll expect to hear from you," he said to Kyle. He nodded to Jesse as well. He could see how it was; he felt a momentary impulse of pity for the brother who made no impression on people, whose name everyone instantly forgot in the glare of his brother's presence.

He watched them as they sauntered back to their truck and climbed in, as Kyle revved the engine and aggressively threw it into reverse. Tires engaged the asphalt of the road with the shriek of a wounded animal, and they were off. He hated the way rednecks drove their trucks, as if speed and recklessness might assuage the dead-endedness of their lives. Asshole, he thought to himself, surprised at the sudden vehemence of his emotion. Something about these two made him vaguely nervous, and he told himself he'd have undoubtedly preferred the steady, alcoholic old man.

"Guy back there," Kyle said as they made their way slowly down Main Street. "Wouldn't you know? They should really think about changing the name of this place to Fag Hollow. It's getting so you can't stir 'em with a stick."

"Who'd want to?" Jesse said.

"That's funny," Kyle told him. "Sometimes you're funny, little brother. You know that?"

Jesse decided to take it as a compliment.

"Fag," Kyle said, pointing to the little café that had recently opened up. "Fag," he said again, as they passed the bicycle store. "Fag, fag, fag," he counted off, gesturing to this house or that. Jesse always wondered why Kyle was so obsessed with knowing where the fags of Stone Hollow worked and lived. He wondered if he'd have ever noticed any of that if it weren't for his brother.

"As long as he pays us," Jesse said, "and keeps his hands off our butts."

"True enough. Live and let live. I won't suck your cock if you don't suck mine. That's my philosophy." Kyle laughed abruptly, and Jesse, feeling Kyle glance his way, laughed as well, somehow pleased they could share this joking between them.

"Actually," Kyle said, "kill 'em all. Every last fucking one."

For some reason Jesse remembered, with a strange sense of despair, the abundant riot of color in their new employer's garden, its bounty and opulence. But why, he wondered, should that depress him? Why should he think of it at all?

They had turned from Main Street onto the state highway and began to climb the hill out of the narrow valley. Up ahead, a small foreign car toiled on the steep grade. "Move it, buddy," Kyle said. He pulled the truck so close he was almost nudging the rear bumper. "Move it, asshole," he demanded again, leaning on the horn. There was something about Japanese cars that pissed Kyle off, especially ones that got in his way. For an instant Jesse was sure Kyle was going to give that little car a tap, but he managed to muscle up without touching it.

All at once they'd attained the crest of the hill. With the road leveling off, any reasonable automobile would have picked up speed, but the driver was clearly pissed now too. If anything, he slowed some more. It put Kyle in a rage.

"Motherfucking asshole," he said, pulling out a long one on the horn, followed by several sharp bursts as he swung the truck out into the other lane, across the double yellow line. Up ahead some little distance, a Trailways bus lumbered toward them, but Kyle wasn't about to let things drop so easily. He pulled even with the Toyota.

"Give him the fucking finger," he commanded Jesse, and Jesse, feeling a little ridiculous, obliged. Clearly it was the right thing to do, for Kyle seemed no longer angry but exhilarated—there was a fine line he could cross in an instant, the way on a cloudy day the sun can suddenly come out.

A little balding man in glasses glanced their way nervously and hit the brakes. They shot on ahead of him and cut in just as the bus and its angry horn bore down on them.

Jesse's heart was thumping. He looked over at his brother. "Going to the hospital sure puts me in a fucking bad mood," Kyle said in an ordinary tone of voice, like all his rage had been suddenly expelled and he was looking back on it calmly. It occurred to Jesse, hardly for the first time, that everything somehow meant a lot more to his brother than it did to him. He envied him that. Sometimes he felt like he was just going through the motions, numb as an arm or leg that's fallen asleep.

Kyle interrupted Jesse's thoughts. "Oh, fuck!" he said.

His brother was looking in the mirror. Jesse craned around to see the police car, lights flashing, coming up on them fast. "Now where the moth-erfuck was *he?"* Kyle said, slowing and pulling off onto the shoulder.

It wasn't the first time they'd ever gotten stopped, and Jesse knew the routine. As Kyle fumbled in his wallet for his license, Jesse uncocked the glove compartment and rummaged for the registration. It was one piece of advice Pop had always given them: whatever you do, keep the damn reg-istration up-to-date. And never, ever give the cops a hard time.

"Good," Kyle said under his breath as the cop approached.

A burly fellow with a crew cut leaned in the window.

"Hey, Kenny," Kyle said. "What's up?" Kenny was one of the Ker-honkson Vanderhofs. They'd grown up together, though he was three or so years older than them. They always saw him at family get-togethers.

"Kyle, Kyle, my man," Kenny said wearily. "What were you thinking back there?"

"I'm sorry, man. Did you see how slow that guy was going?"

"I don't care. You got to watch it, Kyle. You weren't thinking back there. Got me? You weren't *thinking."*

"Okay," Kyle said amiably. "I wasn't thinking."

Kenny stared at him seriously. "Look, buddy, you're my favorite cousin. I don't want to go scraping you off the road someday. Or anybody else. You hear what I'm saying?"

"I hear you," Kyle said. He was like a little kid being punished. Jesse knew his brother hated that.

Kenny kept looking at him for another half minute, as if gauging this weighty thing and that. Then he asked gently, "How's your dad?"

"We were just going up to the hospital. He's hanging in there. Fighting like a trooper."

"I always looked up to your dad. He's a good man. Had some hard times, but a real good man."

"The best," Kyle said.

"Well, you take care." Kenny touched Kyle's arm warmly. "Give my best to the old man. And, hey there, Jesse." Kenny threw off a loose salute.

"Hey," Jesse told him.

"You keep this brother of yours out of trouble."

"I try." Jesse made himself grin, as much to show Kyle he was joking as to show Kenny he was serious. He remembered Kenny as sort of a bully

32

when he was a kid. He'd gotten in trouble at school for throwing sand in somebody's eyes; there're been a big to-do about that, but that was a long time ago. He'd done well for himself. He was half of Stone Hollow's police force these days, though they were looking to hire a third part-time. Kyle talked about taking courses, but of course he never got around to it.

"One of these days," Kyle said as he started up the truck, "I ain't going to be so lucky. I know that. In case you're thinking I don't."

"I'm not saying anything," Jesse said, though it amazed him the things Kyle could get away with.

He, on the other hand, was the kind of person who was sure to get caught at every single thing he tried.

The hospital room was bleak and filled with light. Next to the folded-up cot where she'd spent the night, Patti sat in the chair in the corner and read the *Reader's Digest*. Pop was sleeping, though the difference these days between sleeping and waking with him didn't seem too clear. All Jesse knew was, he dreaded the moments of Pop's waking.

"It's fucking ninety in here," Kyle observed.

"Do you have to say *fucking* all the time?" Patti asked him. "And, yes, it feels like ninety 'cause the air conditioner's broke and I got about fifteen minutes of sleep last night, thank you."

Pop lay on top of the covers, the skimpy hospital gown barely concealing his swollen belly. Kyle sat down beside the sick man and stroked his hand just above where the IV tube went in; Jesse sat on the floor at the foot of the bed, his back to the wall. Bill Vanderhof's thin legs were spread apart, and Jesse tried not to stare up the open hospital gown at the long snake of the catheter emerging from his dad's cock. From fear or shock, that member had shriveled down to a tiny size, like it couldn't even remember its other life as that length of dusky flesh Jesse used to take curious stock of whenever his old man stood naked at the washbasin and shaved or, since he never believed in wasting water on a shower, toweled himself dry after his sponge bath. He never shut the bathroom door when it was just family around, not even for pissing and shitting. "I got nothing to hide," he used to tell Jesse and his brother. "And neither should you fellows. Women," he added, "are different that way."

It looked so painful, that belly, bloated up like a dead raccoon by the side of the road. The thought was horrible, but like so many horrible thoughts that stuck in his brain, Jesse couldn't wish it away.

In the heat of the noonday sun, sometimes the pressure was too great; the drum-tight skin burst open, the guts blew out. He'd seen red innards splattered with bright green flies.

"I thought I died," Pop said quite clearly. Their entrance must have disturbed the shadows that were filling him. At the sound of their old man's voice, Jesse and his sister joined Kyle by the side of the bed. "Oh, God," Pop said, his voice cracked by a sob. "I dreamed I was dead."

"Pop, we're here," Patti said. "We're with you. Everything's okay."

But that didn't seem to reassure him much. He looked at them all with his yellowed eyes, like he was trying to figure out something he couldn't get to the bottom of.

"Pop," Kyle said, stroking the back of the old man's needle-punctured hand, "you find yourself going back there, you stop yourself. You got me?"

Pop looked at Kyle like he didn't quite recognize this fellow who was holding his hand. "Mister," he said in a formal tone of voice, "if you see my boys, would you tell them to come see me?"

"Your boys are right here," Kyle told him. "Look what we brought you." From his pocket he drew out a wad of Lotto tickets.

Pop ignored him. He turned his head from Kyle to gaze out the window. "Tell them they don't need to hide from their old man."

"Pop," Kyle said. "It's me. I'm right here."

Their dad sighed a deep, defeated sigh. "Oh," he said, turning back to Kyle and studying him for a minute. "Kyle and Jesse. My two boys. For a minute there I thought . . ." He grimaced; a low moan escaped his lips. "Jesse?" He beckoned, and Jesse squatted down by the side of the bed, his face close to the old man's grizzled cheek. "Let me ask you something, Jesse. Did you ever marry that girl?"

"Not yet," Jesse told him.

"I forget her name."

"Donna," Jesse prompted.

"Donna. Didn't you used to go with some girl named Donna?"

"That's the one, Pop. I'm still going with her."

"You going to marry her?"

"Maybe," Jesse told him, thinking about it for a moment, then changed his answer to a firm "Probably."

"You promise me that. I got to have seventeen grandchildren before I die. You hear what I'm saying?"

Jesse nodded, not trusting himself to speak. *Seventeen?* Patti mouthed to Jesse from across the bed. He'd always thought he'd have kids—in the Lord's good time, as their mom was fond of saying. He'd always figured Donna DuBois would likely as not end up being their mother.

Bill Vanderhof was silent for some moments—he seemed to be mouthing numbers, maybe counting his way toward seventeen, following those numbers like signposts leading him back to wherever it was he went when he went away from them, some deep woods he wandered out into, the way he used to in the fall, with just his rifle and his whiskey to keep him company. Did everybody have a trackless place in them like that, or did finding it spell your own doom? It made Jesse wonder, looking around that room at his brother, his sister, their own selves both entirely visible and at the same time inscrutable. He felt himself, oddly, moving away from them, though he took scarcely a step in any direction. He had his own deep woods, though in the next moment he was securely back in that brightly lit room, watching Pop—the part of him anybody knew—fade away before his eyes.

FOUR

His chin set firmly in a metal restraining stirrup, Cameron told his handsome young ophthalmologist, "I keep seeing these brown spots. They float around. I mean, when I turn my head quickly, they sort of float to catch up. It's very annoying."

Dr. Vosper nodded noncommittally and continued to shine his astoundingly bright light first in Cameron's dilated right pupil, then his left.

Actually, Cameron thought, but dared not say, the brown spots did not so much annoy as terrify. Of all that lay in wait for him, the possibility that he might one day go blind panicked him the most. I'd rather lose my mind than lose my sight, he told himself, though of course the former possibility wasn't particularly pleasant to contemplate either.

Dr. Vosper laid his instrument on the counter and took up his clipboard. "What I'm seeing here is a relatively common complaint. Nothing to do with HIV. It just happens as you get older. Bits of vitreous matter detach themselves from the retina to float free. It's absolutely nothing to worry about."

"Will it go away?"

"Sorry." Dr. Vosper smiled the sympathetic smile of a man who'd never had a serious malady in his life. "But you'll get used to it. Right now you're probably obsessing with the spots, but after a while, well . . . Let me put it this way. Human beings have this amazing capacity, you know, to make adjustments. Keep tapping somebody on the head with a hammer, eventually they won't even notice it anymore."

"Tell me about it," Cameron said.

Dr. Vosper was in his early thirties; from his perfectly trimmed dark hair to his crisp white shirt and chinos, everything about him was immaculate, and Cameron allowed himself the luxury of imagining, for one idle moment, his ophthalmologist courting dishevelment and worse in the arms of another man. But who? The Bilvic brothers sprang instantly to mind. Now there was an arousing little scenario. Absurd, really, but that had never stopped him. His high school years had been redeemed by unlikely but really pleasurable mental couplings.

What did stop his unruly imagination was a sudden sense of surprise, amusement, mild shock. Perhaps it was the new medicines, or an aftereffect of Dan's leaving, or perhaps only a cruel somatic trick—but how truly strange, how deliciously inconvenient to have recovered, in the last few weeks, something very like that old accomplice, the sex drive he thought he'd lost for good.

Only to what end?

"How're you feeling these days?" Dr. Vosper was asking him.

"Amazingly well," Cameron told him disconsolately.

"I'm very glad to hear that." The doctor shook his hand warmly. "Come back in another three months. Unless, of course, something comes up. But I think you have plenty of reasons to be cautiously optimistic."

"Thanks," Cameron told him, though cautious optimism seemed, all of a sudden, not quite what he needed.

The pert young receptionist processed his credit card and then handed him a pair of dark, wraparound glasses. "You're all set, Mr. Barnes," she told him. "Your vision probably won't be back to normal for a few hours. Do you have somebody here to drive you home?"

"That would be me," Max said from the waiting room. He laid aside his *National Geographic* and rose from his seat. "That was quick," he noted as they emerged into dazzling sunlight. "So what's the prognosis?"

"I'm fine, apparently," Cameron told him, a little unnerved by just how blurred the world around him seemed. "I'm just getting old."

"Aren't we all. But that's good news."

"Yes. Funny when that's the good news."

In the noontime traffic of Broadway, he could bring nothing into focus. The words on traffic signs, storefronts, billboards, refused to come clear. Without warning he found himself in the midst of a quiet panic. Despite Dr. Vosper's sunny assurances, maybe he really was beginning to go blind.

To divert his mind from that abyss, he said impulsively, "So your old man Bilvic turned out to be quite a surprise."

"What are you talking about?"

"The guy you recommended to me. The reliable alcoholic."

"You mean Bill Vanderhof?"

"I thought his last name was Bilvic."

Max laughed. "That's funny. It's Bilvic Construction. His name is Bill, and his wife is Vicky. Short for Victoria. Bill-Vic. Get it?"

"Oh." The information unsettled him. He had the nagging feeling he'd been getting too many things wrong recently. "I think I called him Mr. Bilvic when I talked to him on the phone. How embarrassing."

"He's probably used to it by now."

Had he called those two boys by the wrong name too? Not that it mattered. Still—he didn't want to seem a fool.

"But what surprised you about him?" Max was asking.

"You never mentioned he had two hunky sons."

"I never knew."

"Well, now you do, because they're the ones who're going to do the work on my shed. Turns out the old man's in the hospital. Apparently he's not doing too well at all."

"I'm sorry to hear that," Max said. "Bill's the brother, you know, of Roy Vanderhof. Part of that whole clan."

"Your bêtes noires."

"You bet. They're not unbeatable, you know. They're very vulnerable on the nepotism issue."

Cameron wouldn't ever say it in so many words—even to think it seemed vaguely disloyal—but he desperately wished Max weren't so dead set on running for mayor in the fall elections. It seemed the very embodiment of futility: the Vanderhofs were as unalterable an aspect of the local landscape as any geographical feature; they'd run Stone Hollow for generations—highly inbred generations, as Max liked to put it. Max's political urges went far back as well. In 1972 he'd run for president of the sophomore class at Oberlin on the "Gay Vegetarian Trotskyite" ticket and barely lost. In the late seventies, at the University of Michigan, he'd organized a Gay Law Students Caucus consisting of himself and two lesbians. Cameron remembered a cold morning in 1986 when Max had dragged him along to a mock funeral being held in front of City Hall, and he'd somehow found himself next to Larry Kramer, helping to shoulder the empty, surprisingly light coffin in a sea of raised fists. Toby was in the hospital then, barely able to speak, and Cameron had had a heart filled with righteous rage. How long ago all that seemed. He hadn't been to a demonstration in nearly a decade. The war's objectives, once so clear, so imperative, suddenly ceased to matter that much once he'd gotten his own diagnosis. His resignation had surprised him even as it angered people like Dan and Max, who'd accused him of withdrawing without a fight. How to tell them it felt like an honor to follow someone as exhilarating as Toby Vail down into darkness? That would have sounded like craziness. But in his heart, he knew it was how he'd felt, and even now he resented, a little, his friends for making him live.

"I wonder sometimes," he said as they passed the wooden sign welcoming anyone who could see clearly to Historic Stone Hollow, settled in 1696, "whether the trouble you're going to stir up is worth it."

"We live here too," Max told him adamantly. "It's our town as much as it is theirs."

How eager he and Dan had been at the prospect of Max and Perry moving up from the city. "It'll be fun," they'd all said conspiratorially. "We'll make a little gay enclave in the woods. We'll start a trend." Did he sometimes regret that trend? Already, in the five years since his friends' arrival, enormous changes had taken place. His Trotskyite days long gone, Max had opened Zanzibar, a funky and popular vegetarian café, was partners in an art gallery located in the old stone church, and had brought in Damien, a pal from Manhattan, to start a bookshop—Liberation!—an incongruous mix of bestsellers, books about the Hudson Valley, and gay and lesbian videos; twice already its front window had been shattered. The semi-derelict gauntlet of old buildings that had so enchanted Cameron that long-ago winter afternoon was all spruced up now. Even the welcome sign hadn't been there when he'd first moved to the area; Max's brainchild, the Main Street Business Association, had put it up. So it was, in a sense, Cameron considered as they made their way down that spruced-up but blurry Main Street—past Liberation!, past the Spiritus Gallery, past Zanzibar—his own damned fault.

But Max was his very best and oldest friend. They'd met their first day at Oberlin; still dazed after the twenty-four-hour bus ride north from Memphis, he'd stood in the door of his new dorm room and stared with some consternation at the dark, curly-haired, distinctly unprepossessing boy who sat on the bed smoking a joint and reading a dog-eared copy of *Thus Spake Zarathustra*. A month earlier, an envelope had arrived to inform him that his roommate would be Max Greenblatt from the Bronx. The information had given him momentary pause. Max Greenblatt. The name was so unlyrical, even ugly, an old man's name, and he realized how much he had secretly depended on a beautiful, enchanting roommate he would fall in love with at first sight.

Sounds Jewish, his father had mused. Will you like rooming with a Jewish fellow?

Cameron had never met a Jewish fellow before, though the Jews were a favorite theme of his grandfather Lucius Barnes, who could sit on the wisteria-curtained front porch of the old house in Tupelo, Mississippi, and hold forth for hours about their diabolical machinations.

The Jewish fellow had put his book aside and smiled a smile full of crooked teeth and said, "Hiya. So you're a southerner. Well, if we don't get along, I guess we can always apply for a room change."

Twenty-eight years ago that was. Without Max Greenblatt, Cameron told himself, he'd be utterly lost.

"About those brothers," he said. "You've at least *seen* one of them before. Dinner last week. The young fellow with the muscle truck and the reluctant girlfriend."

"Leanne!" Max said. "Yes. We were quite taken with that tableau, weren't we? So that was one of the Vanderhof boys. Figures. The whole clan's about as smart as a box of rocks, as far as I can tell. I always suspected they dragged their women around by the hair."

"I thought your platform was to represent *all* the people of Stone Hollow," Cameron teased.

"Of course. Every last one of them. Is our redneck Romeo as hot as I remember him?"

"He's not too bad," Cameron admitted. "He and the brother both. If you go in for rednecks, that is."

"I know. Not your type. Pity."

They'd climbed out of Stone Hollow's narrow valley to the plain above town where Cameron's farmhouse stood. He was surprised to see the BIL-VIC CONSTRUCTION truck in his driveway—not that he could make out the words. But of course, even when he'd been able to see them clearly, he'd misconstrued their meaning.

He hadn't thought the brothers were starting till next week.

"So," Max said, "let's go take a look at these Vanderhof hunks. Who'd have guessed? Nature's always so surprising that way."

"Don't ogle," Cameron warned.

"Never," Max promised. It made Cameron suddenly anxious, but what could he do? Max would be Max, whatever the circumstances, and all Cameron's attempts at concealing the truth about himself would come to naught.

We live here too, he thought defiantly as they made their way around back, through the garden suddenly gone late Monet. With hammers and crowbars, the Bilvic brothers, newly magnified into Vanderhofs, were tearing the roof off Cameron's shed. They'd removed the contents and piled all that collection of antiques and outright junk on the grass beneath blue plastic tarps. In the generous warmth of the afternoon sun they'd stripped to the waist. Kyle and Jesse Vanderhof might be about as smart as a box of rocks, but their smooth, bronze chests gleamed magnificently, their slim, muscular forms graced the shed's roofline like nature's own ornament—a vision, to Cameron's unfocused eyes, more vague promise than detailed fulfillment, but oddly stirring nonetheless.

In no time at all the horrible routine had settled in. Somebody or other had to be there; Jesse's turn usually came late afternoon and early evening. He'd find his mom sitting in the chair beside Pop, who was usually asleep, or what passed for asleep. Sometimes she'd be holding his hand, and Jesse imagined she might have been sitting that way for hours, neither of them saying a word, Pop maybe not even conscious anybody was out there gripping his hand, but still holding on for dear life.

The TV was on. The curtains on the windows were pulled shut against the hot afternoon sun. He came over and she turned her cheek his way so he could give her a kiss. She held a *Reader's Digest* in her lap, folded open to "Laughter: The Best Medicine."

"How's it going?" he asked.

"He was complaining about gas," she told him. "They put this tube in to relieve him. I don't think it did anything, and it was making him real uncomfortable, so they took it out."

"Put the tube in where?"

"Where do you think?"

"Oh, man."

His mom looked around for her bag. "Alright, I'm out of here. You and Patti got everything figured out for later?"

"She's coming by at ten. And Donna said maybe she'd stop by."

"I wouldn't tire him out."

"He won't even know she's here. Besides, Pop likes Donna."

"What's not to like?" Did his mom always have to find something snide to say? Though she'd deny it every time. There was the evening she'd asked Kyle at the dinner table (he was fifteen, Michelle de Hulter was the first girl he'd gone out with), *What do you want with that little old thing?* Words out of the blue. *Vic,* Pop warned, *leave the kid alone for God's sake.*

I'm not saying a thing, she'd said. But Jesse'd never forgotten. Never forgiven, either, he thought.

Now his mom stood in the doorway. She looked crushed and old, and he had no idea how she was taking any of this. "Have some of your pop's supper when they bring it," she said. "He sure ain't going to touch most of it. It's a shame to let it go to waste. I ordered him some Salisbury steak. It was real tasty last time. Not undercooked."

"I'll make out just fine," he told her. "Now go."

The vinyl chair seat, as he settled in, was still warm from her bottom. She'd been watching *Oprah.* He clicked through a dozen channels till he found ESPN, but they were showing golf. Another sports channel had skateboarding; he watched for a while as guys his own age went back and forth on a U-shaped platform made of plywood sheets. A more pointless sport he couldn't imagine.

With a fresh sting of resentment, he remembered what his mom had said. What *wasn't* to like about Donna? When he tried to think about her, though, she went blurry on him. There were things about her he could never recall when he was away from her: the exact color of her eyes, what she smelled like. Her voice, though, could talk endlessly in his head sometimes, a low, mumbling drone saying nothing in particular. He clicked off the TV and went to the window. Pulling back the curtains, he let the sun warm him. The room wasn't too high up, only the fourth floor, so there wasn't much to see, just the parking lot, a few people walking to or from their cars. In the distance you could see the gray-green Catskills.

On the table by the bed lay a fresh wad of the Lotto tickets Kyle was good about bringing by, though Pop mostly didn't care anymore. What was he going to do now with a million dollars? Jesse felt that familiar emptiness open up inside him, almost a kind of nausea. Pop had always been a kid, he thought; he'd never grown up. Christmas or birthdays, he always made a show of opening presents, holding them up to his ear and shaking them and then whistling out the side of his mouth, like a canary was inside the box. He loved that trick. And once he made a jazz band out of different sizes and shapes of bottles, then played them with spoons. He'd make up songs with words that didn't make any sense.

Bill, their mom would say. *You're acting like a kid.*

He'd look at her and make his eyes bug out. He could make all sorts of faces, mimic all kinds of voices. Kyle had picked up the talent from him. *I'll say one thing,* their mom would tell Kyle, shaking her head and pursing her lips: *You're your daddy's own son, that's for sure.*

And what was the joke Pop used to tell? He'd gotten it from his own old man, whom he used to fight with.

Watch those swinging doors, Son, he'd say in a deep voice.

Then, in a high-pitched squeal: *I'm looking for my daddy!*

Who's your daddy? the deep voice would bellow.

Fluke McGook.

I'm *Fluke McGook.*

Daddy!

Son!

They all liked that joke.

Sometimes Pop would reverse the voices, and they liked that too.

Bill, I swear, their mom would say.

It wasn't all jokes, of course. Once, when Jesse and Kyle were horsing around in the barn, Kyle broke the mirror on an old bureau that was stored in there. It wasn't worth anything; the glass was splotched and silvery. But a few days later, Pop must've noticed. He made trips out to the barn a lot—just to check on things, they supposed back then. He called them out and pointed at the broken mirror. *Who did that?* he asked.

Kyle shrugged and looked away.

Look at me, said Pop. *Did you do this?*

Kyle nodded his head yes.

Did you know about it? Pop asked Jesse.

There was no lying to Pop. They both knew what was coming. They watched as Pop went into the woods and cut birch switches with his pocketknife; then he lashed them till the backs of their thighs and calves were crisscrossed with thin lines of blood. That wasn't too often, but it was sometimes.

Another time they'd found some empty bottles in a chest, under a musty old blanket. Kyle had an idea. He mixed powdered ice tea and filled the bottles and screwed the caps back on tight; he brought them up to the house and set up a bar on the kitchen table.

They were both upstairs when Pop came in.

Get your sorry asses down here, he shouted up to them.

He was standing in the kitchen holding up one of their bottles. *Where'd you find this?* he asked them.

Find what? Kyle played innocent. They both did.

Pop twisted off the cap and took a sip.

What the fuck! he said.

That was another time they got a switching. And maybe it happened then, or yet another time, Jesse couldn't remember, but Kyle had lowered his pants and Pop had his fresh-cut switch ready to go when Kyle looked back at the old man and said, calm as anything, *Mister, just what do you think this is gonna prove?*

Pop loved that. Afterward, he told that story on Kyle all the time.

At Mama Florella's, across the street from the hospital, Jesse stood at the counter and ordered a slice of cheese pizza to go. He hadn't been able to bring himself to touch the food they'd brought Pop: a disk of unidentifiable meat smothered in congealed gravy, chewy mashed potatoes. He'd hoped Donna would come by, but when he'd called her house, her mom said she'd gone to the mall with friends.

When he heard someone call his name, he turned. At a booth in back sat a couple of guys he'd gone to high school with.

"Hey, dude. Long time no see."

"Wanna join us?"

He didn't know them too well. Dave Powers and Rusty Schlickeisen had been in his shop class. They were cutups, not bad guys; these days they both worked for the highway department. He saw them around from time to time, shoveling asphalt or hacking roadside brush. The third, facing away from him, turned around to look.

Jesse hesitated. He and Gary Dunkel had been great pals once, for about six months—but that was a couple of years ago. Since then they'd barely spoken.

"Hey, Jesse," Gary said, which decided him. Grabbing his slice and his can of Coke, Jesse strolled over.

"What brings you up to the big city?" Rusty asked.

Jesse slid in next to Gary, who didn't flinch. "My old man's laid up in Benedictine."

"No kidding," Rusty said. "What's he in for?"

"Cancer," Jesse told them, amazed how effortless that word was becoming.

"What kind?" Gary asked.

"Liver."

"Oh, man, that's bad shit."

"Tell me about it," Jesse said. He ate his slice in silence, feeling the three watching him. "So what're you guys up to?" he asked in between bites.

"Just hanging out," Rusty told him. "Same old same old."

Jesse tried to think of something to say. He remembered how chosen he'd felt when Gary had decided to take him up as a friend. "You still got that Taurus?" he asked. Gary used to give him a ride home from school sometimes.

"Nah. I got rid of that, like, a year ago."

"So what you got now?"

Rusty erupted in a loud guffaw.

"What?" Jesse asked.

"Toyota," Gary explained.

"Japanese? That stuff's crap," Jesse said, though he had no idea whether that was true. Pop always said it was.

"See?" Rusty said. "Everybody knows it."

"You guys are something else," Gary said. "God damn."

Jesse remembered how, at first, he'd thought Gary was making fun of him. They didn't have any classes together. Their paths hardly ever crossed. Gary played on the football team, the basketball team. He wrote for the student newspaper. All that put him far outside Jesse's orbit. But they talked sometimes, mostly on line in the lunchroom; it was always Gary who spoke to him first, usually to make some corny or amusing crack about the food. Sometimes they'd sit at the same lunch table—it just happened that way. And that had been all, really. Still, he'd felt . . . well, he didn't know how he'd felt, except that he looked forward to running into Gary. Then one day Kyle asked him, "So who the fuck's your new pal there?" Was it so obvious? Jesse'd wondered—like there was something wrong with hanging out with Gary Dunkel. "There're things you don't know shit about," Kyle warned. "Trust me."

Kyle always knew more than he did. So he let Gary go. Nothing dramatic; he told himself Gary probably never even noticed. Then in the spring Donna had come along. Life was like that.

"So what you been up to?" he asked. It wasn't like they'd fought about anything. They'd just been friendly and then not so friendly.

"Gary's a college dude these days," Rusty said. "Romancing the coeds."

"Get out of here," Gary told him, grinning and swatting at Rusty, who leaned back to avoid the back of his hand. "I'm at Ulster Community," Gary explained to Jesse. "Thinking about maybe transferring over to Marist next year."

"Really," Rusty insisted. "You oughtta see the babes this guy brings home."

"My sister goes to Ulster," Jesse said. "Patti? You ever run into her?"

Gary thought for a moment, shook his head. "Don't think so. People kind of come and go over there. How's your brother? I heard you and him were doing some carpentry work around."

"Whatever we can get. I didn't know you knew my brother."

"Everybody knows Kyle. He still going with Leanne?"

"Far as I know," Jesse told Gary. Told them all. He could see that hungry look in their eyes, even before Dave said, "Your brother's sure the lucky son of a bitch."

But Jesse didn't want to talk about his brother. You move on, he thought, sliding out of the booth and standing. "I gotta be getting on home. Good running into you guys."

"Stay cool," Gary told him. But it was strange; he felt some sadness charge the air between them, that hollow, aimless feeling of might-have-been.

It was nothing he couldn't shake as he walked out into the humid night air. Broadway at this hour was nearly deserted; if you didn't know better, you could almost think the whole world had died. For a minute, looking up at the brick pile that was Benedictine, he tried to figure out which lit window might be Pop's, till he realized Pop's room faced completely the other way.

FIVE

The Rudds, Bernard and Barbara, lived with their prize-winning bichon frise, Ariadne, in a luxuriantly hideous stone manor that had been built in the 1880s by Anton Clouser, the cement baron who'd owned many of the mines and quarries that still dotted the landscape around Stone Hollow, and who'd committed suicide, barely a decade after the house's completion, when the local cement industry's collapse took his fortune down with it. As Cameron parked in the magisterial circular drive, a feeling of queasy anxiety ambushed him. Ariadne's frantic yaps from a screened-in balcony alerted the house to his approach, and he took in the overgrown yews and rhododendrons lapping at the foundations, the scattering of aged maples and Norway spruces, the dull expanse of lawn in the middle of which a colorful box kite lay wrecked and abandoned. "She's been asking for you, and no one but you," Jorge had told him; they'd both agreed it was the perfect way to ease himself back into the profession his illness had forced him to abandon.

"Barbara Rudd. So pleased to finally meet you in person." Languidly she extended her hand to him. Tall and stately, she reminded him more than a little of a magnificent horse. Her gaze passed through him and into the distance. A little nonplussed, he turned to see what she watched so intently.

"Boys," she said, shaking her head. "I told them to put that kite away.

They just went off to two-week swimming camp this morning. It looks broken already. How can that be? They only got it yesterday."

Growing up, he'd known the wealthy by the stained and blemished clothes they brought in to have dry-cleaned—tuxedos and gowns, silky dresses and linen suits. His dad had managed a One Hour Martinizing franchise in affluent East Memphis; many afternoons after school, and always on Saturday, Cameron had stood behind the counter of Barnes's Kwik Kleen and received, with a fixed smile, those bundles of expensive, dubiously soiled clothing; with the same smile he returned magically renewed, neatly pressed items on hangers, the whole order swathed in filmy plastic that could perhaps be used to suffocate someone, should the need arise.

Dirt is dirt, his father always said—not so much out of bitterness as fine-tuned gratitude.

He never imagined he'd still be smiling that same smile, albeit exquisitely fine-tuned itself over the years.

"I was so devastated when I heard you'd gone into retirement," Barbara told him. "You did such beautiful work for the Cosgroves. Also the Friedmanns. That pavilion on the pond. Truly magnificent. Ever since we bought this house, I've so longed for a Cameron Barnes garden."

His "sabbatical," as his temporary retirement was now officially described by Paradise Designs, had made his work even more coveted. Well, dirt is dirt, he reminded himself. And rich people had been extremely good to him over the years—none more influentially so than Mrs. Uma Waddeston, with whom, at a B&B in a small village in Oxfordshire, he'd fortuitously shared a breakfast table one summer morning in 1971. He was nineteen, she close to eighty. He could no longer recall how, over eggs and blood sausages and fried tomatoes, their conversation had unfolded, only that, improbably, they'd hit it off. When, at the end of the meal, she'd mentioned she'd be making a day trip to Hidcote and would he have any interest in accompanying her, he'd instantly said yes, having learned, over the past several weeks of backpacking, all the pleasures and advantages of improvisation. As for Hidcote itself, he had no preconceptions whatsoever. A garden, as far as he was concerned, was the plot in the backyard where his dad tended tomatoes and pole beans and okra in his scant spare time.

Wandering Hidcote's swooning rose borders, Cameron felt he'd stepped into paradise, only later learning from Mrs. Waddeston, who wisely and immediately sensed her young American's enchantment, that *paradise* was in fact the very word, in Persian, for "garden." Together they admired the topiary doves in the white garden; they strolled together on graveled paths among formal clipped hornbeams and emerged into the vast theater lawn, hauntingly austere within its enclosure of high yew hedges. In the herb garden Mrs. Waddeston identified lavender and rosemary and santolina, subtle plants unlike any he knew. She'd lost her husband six months before; determined not to recede into life's background, she was spending the summer driving about the British Isles in her battered Austin. If he enjoyed gardens—and he did, he did!—she'd be delighted to convey him to many more.

Stowe, Sissinghurst, Stourhead: in a single month those harmonious landscapes had changed his life. Mrs. Waddeston, whose own lovely garden in Bromley marked the terminus of their rambles, was an encyclopedia of fact and anecdote, introducing him to luminaries he'd never heard of—William Kent and Capability Brown and Gertrude Jekyll—as if she'd known them all personally. When he returned to Oberlin in the fall, he found himself procrastinating, while writing papers, by browsing the library's collection of books on gardening, where he had occasion to learn, first to his consternation, then later to his amusement, that Mrs. Waddeston had not hesitated to fill out her gaps in knowledge with a bit of invention every now and then. But his education had begun. He spent hours poring over color plates of monastic cloisters, Zen sand gardens, the exotic effusions of Roberto Burle Marx in Brasília. Gazing out the library window, he'd dream of transforming snow-blanketed Tappan Square, devastated by the recent demise of all its stately elms, into a place of beauty, serenity, contentment. Surprising nearly everybody, he applied to—and was accepted by—the master's program in landscape design at City College. The rest, as they said, was history—his own history, written in dozens of pleasing rearrangements to the landscape over the last quarter century.

They had moved around to the back of the house. At the bottom of stone steps badly in need of repair, which Ariadne raced madly up and down, stood a handsome, mostly ruined pergola. Once there'd been a border of roses, he could see; now orange daylilies ran rampant.

"It's all pretty much a blank canvas," Barbara told him, gesturing grandly. "Do with it what you will. Ariadne, stop that. Come here."

To Cameron the canvas seemed not so much blank as disfigured. He liked, though, the challenge of retrofitting neglected gardens.

"What kind of a budget are we looking at?" he asked.

Having scooped Ariadne into her arms, Barbara looked at him down her equine nose. "Oh, there is no budget. Whatever it takes. My husband may be a genius when it comes to software, but with anything that's not virtual he's a complete Philistine. So where the garden is concerned, all decisions are up to me. I put myself completely in your talented hands."

"In that case"—Cameron smiled his much practiced smile—"I think we can come up with some ideas that will please you a great deal."

He'd been worried he no longer had the necessary energy, that his libido had died in more ways than one. But now that he was on the site, now that he'd been given carte blanche, he felt the old, subtle exhilaration. In all respects, it seemed, he was coming back to life. He might reserve for Barbara and her class a small, secret disdain, but that would hardly prevent him from presenting her—and her silly, altogether adorable dog—with the most splendid arrangement of horticultural pleasure he could manage.

His first impulse, on returning home, was to call Dan immediately and tell him the happy news, so it was with regret that he remembered, as he walked into the house, their agreement to refrain from any contact at all, at least for the time being. *Let's let things settle down a bit,* Dan had said. *Let the air clear.*

That had seemed entirely sound advice at the time. Dan's leaving had been in neither anger nor haste, but instead methodical, even-tempered. They'd both known full well that the time had come to go their separate ways, and their last couple of months together had been more wistful than anything else. Even so, the many-stemmed question of their failure together—what had gone wrong?—continued to haunt him. He remembered reading once, in college, that the ancient Greeks believed the gods knew all the words that mortals spoke, but also knew the secret meanings of each of those words, meanings that were withheld from mortal knowledge.

One minor incident—ridiculous, unfathomable, emblematic—from fairly late in their breakup: he'd been out on a brief errand, and when he returned he noticed, placed on the banister post at the top of the porch steps, three flat stones. He remembered taking off his coat, hanging it on the peg in the mudroom. Dan was in the kitchen playing solitaire, as he often did when he was alone. Beside him sat a half-finished glass of iced beer—a habit of his Cameron had once found endearing and now, in this late stage of their relationship, thought merely odd.

"I'm going to ask a very Cameron question," he said.

"Go ahead," Dan told him without looking up. "Shoot."

"What are those stones doing there?"

"What are what stones doing there?"

"On the back porch. I'm assuming you put them there."

"I don't know what you're talking about." Dan laid one card on top of another (Cameron had no head for card games of any kind).

"You do too know what I mean. Look, I'll show you." Cameron opened the back door.

Dan didn't move. "You're letting in the cold air."

"I'm trying to show you what I'm talking about."

"I know what you're talking about."

"Well, then . . ."

Dan moved another card. "Well, what?"

"I asked you a question. Why did you put them there?"

"You really want me to tell you?"

"Well, yes, that's why I asked." Already Cameron could see how this perfectly simple conversation had gotten out of hand—but there was no going back, for either of them. That was what was so infuriating.

Dan said, "Does everything have to have a meaning?"

"I just wanted to know. I was curious."

"Well, don't be."

"Are you trying to drive me crazy?"

"Nobody needs to do that." Dan took a sip from his beer. He hadn't once looked up from his game.

"What's that supposed to mean?"

"Give it up, Cam, okay? Just give it up."

"I just asked a simple question. Why can't you give me a simple answer?"

With a single gesture, Dan swept the cards off the table.

"What?" Cameron asked, feeling a small terror in his heart.

"You're impossible. This whole thing's impossible."

"I didn't do anything."

"No." Dan finally deigned to look at him. "You never do anything. It's never you."

"I don't understand."

"No, you don't." Without another word Dan got down on the floor and began gathering up the fallen cards. For a moment Cameron had stood there, wondering if he should help, then decided, perhaps fatally, that such a gesture would only provoke Dan further.

Remembering that episode now filled him with rage—not at Dan, not even at himself, but just the stupid folly of it all. Even if he were to defy Dan's sensible injunction and pick up the phone, what would they have to say to each other that hadn't already been said to death? That was really the worst of it—that everything had been talked out long ago.

When Toby died, Cameron had felt a sense of relief he could barely admit to himself. Not just relief that Toby had ceased to suffer, but that he wouldn't grow old, wouldn't become mediocre or tedious or predictable, wouldn't lose his way in life's confounding maze. The disease had ravaged him, it had taken his beauty, his continence—even, at the very end, his coherence. But it had left one thing intact: that shimmering, never-to-be-sullied promise for which one had loved Toby so very much.

Monstrous thoughts. To go on living, Cameron knew, was much the harder thing. Nonetheless, on this afternoon in the middle of June, he did not pick up the phone.

Animals surrounded Jesse. They perched on pillows, lined the headboard above him, marched across the top of the dresser, where the mirror reflected each one—bears, lions, monkeys, happy-looking dinosaurs, unicorns in all the colors of the rainbow.

He lay on Donna's bed and tried not to feel like he was drowning. Picking up a plush, purple unicorn and setting it on his chest, he warned, "He's a lot worse than when you saw him last. He mostly just stays in a coma now."

She looked at him seriously from where she sat on the edge of the bed. "That doesn't matter. I still want to go see him."

He addressed himself to the unicorn, which had big brown eyes and ridiculously long eyelashes. "You don't have to. He ain't gonna know who you are. He don't know anybody these days."

"Your dad's always been really nice to me."

"He always liked you," he said, still gazing at the unicorn. No matter how many times he adjusted it, the stuffed animal's single horn kept flopping over to one side. He wouldn't tell Donna what Pop had said about getting married. Maybe when it was all over—then he'd tell her. He had too much on his mind right now. ("She'll make you a pretty nice wife," Kyle had conceded on the way home from the hospital that afternoon. "But, man, I'd play the field more if I was you.")

Donna touched his knee, let her hand rest there. After a while she commenced rubbing gently in little circles. He stared at the purple unicorn and tried to let her touch relax him. *Why do you like unicorns so much?* he'd asked her once. *Because they're imaginary,* she'd told him. It seemed like such a strange thing to say, but he'd never forgotten it. For two years they'd been together, a time that seemed like forever. She never put any pressure on him.

He spoke for the sake of speaking. "He was awake for a little stretch yesterday. He thought he was on vacation. He kept wanting to know where the beach was. 'We won that free ticket to Hawaii, didn't we?' he kept asking. Man, it'd be funny if it wasn't so fucking sad. Sorry."

She'd been trying for years to get him to clean up his language, and mostly he'd been doing a pretty good job.

"Your dad always loved the Lotto," she told him.

"He never won a dime. He must've fed twenty bucks a week into tickets, and I don't think even one cent ever came back his way."

"I know you're hurting a lot inside. I know your whole family is."

Jesse thought she was going to make him cry if she kept on like that, tears of frustration more than anything else.

She stopped rubbing his knee and took the unicorn from him gently. Things are never going to be the same, he told himself. Like a seed pod, everything had split open to scatter to the winds. They were all of them adrift, waiting to land on rich or stony ground. He remembered that from Sunday school, years ago.

Donna crawled up next to him and put her arms around him. Her hair smelled of shampoo. He'd noticed recently she was getting heavy, like her mother.

He could lie there all day, he thought, just staring at the ceiling, feeling her arms anchoring him. There wasn't any reason not to marry her. They'd have kids. They'd buy a little house like this one. Her room was painted pink, the warm, stifling color of flesh. It was a tiny room, really, in a tiny house. Suddenly queasy, he pushed his girlfriend off him and made himself get up from her bed.

"Let's go," he told her, adding, though he knew it was hardly the truth, "We don't have all day."

In the darkened living room, her brother sat watching TV. He'd stare at the flickering screen for eight hours at a stretch, the way other people worked jobs. He'd drink his way through a twelve-pack before he passed out on the sofa, soft rhythmic snores defecting from his open mouth.

Four years older than Jesse, Sean DuBois had been a star basketball player at Feverskill; his three best buds from the team had died in the car wreck, and for a long time nobody expected him to make it either. But he did, though he was nothing like he once was. Still, it was a miracle he was even alive. In Donna's parents' bedroom hung a picture of the Virgin Mary with seven swords stuck in her blood-red heart. Her mom said a prayer before that picture every single day.

"Hello . . . Jess," Sean greeted in his hollow, mechanical way as they crossed the shadowed living room to the front door.

"Hey, Sean, how's it going?"

"Like p's and q's," Sean said mysteriously, the same exchange they always had whether Jesse was coming or going.

He knew the neighborhood kids called Sean "Boo." That and other things Jesse knew made him feel sorry—even ashamed—for the DuBois family.

"Sean, sweet," Donna said. "Mom's making Mexican casserole tonight. Your favorite."

Sean nodded without saying anything. Otherwise he remained motionless, slumped on the sofa flipping nonstop through TV channels like somebody anxiously looking for something important he'd misplaced.

The parking lot at Benedictine Hospital was full. There was Kyle's gray pickup; his mom's boxy Crown Victoria. Jesse made a full circuit twice, then had to park his own limping truck in a metered space on the street. He'd just dropped a dime in the slot when he saw a car ease out of a space up close to the hospital's glass doors.

Donna took his arm as they walked, and though it irritated him when she clung to him like that in public, he didn't say anything.

"Jesse." A voice spoke his name, almost like it was in his head. He looked around. Some dozen yards away, in a little fenced-in plot of stones and bright flowers that abutted the parking lot, his mother sat on a bench and smoked a cigarette. How could he have heard his mother speaking in an ordinary voice like that, from such a distance away? Behind her, a concrete statue of the Virgin Mary spread its arms. He was always a little suspicious of Virgin Marys. His mother used to take him to the Abundant Life Fellowship, where they didn't believe in statues or saints or blood-red hearts stuck through with swords. It was years since he'd been, though his mom and Patti still went all the time.

THE HOPE GARDEN said a sign beside the metal gate.

"It's nice out here," his mother observed as he and Donna approached. "Peaceful." She pointed to the flowers, the statue. A birdbath was off to one side, full to the brim even though it hadn't rained in weeks. Jesse wondered who'd taken the time to plant and tend the flowers, to keep the birdbath full, just to make this a nice place for people to sit.

His mother wasn't actively crying. Tears seeped down her cheeks like the bright trails slugs leave behind.

"Mom," he said, feeling a hole open up inside his gut.

She smiled a hard, fixed smile.

"When?" he asked.

"A little while ago. Your daddy just slipped out on us, Jesse, when nobody was looking. I went up to the nurses' station for an aspirin, and when I came back, he was just gone." She looked off to the distance and bit her lip. Her cigarette had burned down to nothing, but she didn't seem to notice. "Your brother's up there with him now."

He would not cry, even though he felt Donna grip his shoulder sympathetically. *Never cry in front of a girlfriend,* Kyle had told him once. *They'll never respect you afterward.*

Donna kneaded his shoulder like she wanted to milk tears from him that way. He wondered if she had ever respected him.

"You two go on up," his mother said. "I'm going to stay down here for a bit. Collect my thoughts." Flicking aside her spent butt, she opened her macraméd case to fetch a fresh cigarette. "I called Patti, and your uncle Roy, and I left a message for Doty. She'll call everybody else. Roy's going to talk to the funeral home."

"How's Kyle?" he asked.

His mom drew deeply on her cigarette. It was amazing, he thought, how composed she was. It was hard to admit, but Pop had irritated her in so many ways. Disappointed her. Still, she'd done her duty. It didn't make him love her any more, though. "You know how your brother is," she told him. "He was so close to his daddy. You all were, but Kyle . . ." He waited for what she would say. "Kyle's just got such a big heart."

He wouldn't wait on the elevator, but took the fire stairs two at a time. Donna he left far behind. In that single room on the third floor, his brother stood at the big window, gazing out at the Catskills ranged in the distance. He didn't turn around when Jesse bounded in, out of breath. On the windowsill a pot of chrysanthemums offered up its sunny blossoms. GET WELL SOON! encouraged a shiny, heart-shaped balloon somebody'd brought up from the hospital gift shop downstairs.

The adjustable bed had been lowered so the mattress lay flat. Pop looked asleep, only with one difference: it was like somebody had gone and smoothed out all the furrows in his brow. Jesse hadn't ever considered how careworn Pop had looked in life, but now he could see it clearly.

They'd unhooked him from the IV tubes and the catheter. Now he was just a body. Already the flesh of the corpse was cooling. Already the work of decay had begun. Jesse felt a peculiar sweat break out all over him.

In the doorway, Donna appeared. She'd had the good sense to take the elevator.

Without turning from the window, Kyle said, "Leave us alone with our old man."

Donna hesitated. She looked at Jesse.

"Do that for us, Donna. Okay?" Kyle went on.

Jesse could see her stiffen. He knew she was a little afraid of Kyle. *Marry that girl,* Pop had told Jesse. But now he secretly allowed himself to hate Donna DuBois. Rearing out of nowhere, the ugly emotion shocked him; but he couldn't pretend. Go away and leave us alone, he wanted to tell her. Get the fuck away from me and my brother.

"I'll be down in a bit," he said to her reassuringly.

"I'll be with your mom." Never taking her eyes off his brother—had Kyle sensed her by smell or, like rattlesnakes, by heat?—Donna backed cautiously out the door.

Now everything would have to start. The relatives would come around, the garrulous Rosendale Vanderhofs and the reserved Kerhonkson Vanderhofs, people Jesse hardly ever saw, aunts and uncles and cousins from the hills and hollows all over Ulster County. They'd shed their fair share of tears, offer awkward heartfelt condolences. They'd get blurry drunk and tell stories about Bill Vanderhof. Brandon Schneidewind would tell the story about the swamp.

He pushed the image of Brandon Schneidewind out of his head. It was a kind of blasphemy even to consider Brandon in this room, at this moment, in the presence of his dead father, who'd always liked Brandon, who'd considered him, truth be told, a kind of third son in the family.

For the dead man cooling on the bed in front of him, Jesse felt nothing—like the end of a movie, when the credits roll, and there's nothing else to do but leave the theater. Rather it was Kyle who seized all his attention. His brother remained motionless at the window, his back to Jesse. Grief had turned him to stone. He was impenetrable to light and shadow alike.

The television ran with the sound off, some soap opera Jesse recognized as being a favorite of his mom and Patti. There'd been a bond between Kyle and Pop nothing could break. It was Kyle the old man took hunting on the old Bondurant property in Greene County, Jesse trailing along, a shadow in the pale winter light. It was Kyle the old man offered a shot of whiskey to from the pint bottle in his hip pocket, never thinking to tempt Jesse with its forbidden sting. When Kyle got hauled in for trespassing on weekenders' land, the old man just grinned and spit.

"So I guess you were right," Kyle said slowly. All the emotion had drained out of his voice, like a shallow pond in August where the fish are suffocating.

"What?" Jesse asked carefully. "What was I right about?" His heart hammered painfully in his chest. Somebody's got to get hurt, he thought. We don't get out of this without somebody getting hurt.

He'd never loved anybody the way Kyle loved Pop, and that thought made him feel sick and empty. Was it the mountains in the hazy distance his brother watched so intently? Maybe the Mexican girl was walking with her family through the parking lot and he'd spied her beauty. Leanne had broken up with him—of that Jesse was all at once quite sure.

Turning suddenly from the window, Kyle said, his voice breaking a little, "It was like nobody wanted him to live, Jesse. Like everybody just resolved to let him go."

Jesse braced himself. "Nobody wanted to let him go," he said. "But, Kyle, like the doctor said, you got to face facts."

Kyle stood there, his back to the abundant, awful light streaming in from the window. Gazing down at Pop stretched lifeless on that bed, he ran his hand back and forth through his close-cropped hair. After a long moment he said, his voice low and certain, "I don't know facts."

SIX

Cameron sat at his usual table, near Zanzibar's front window, sipping his morning latte and paging through the weekly *Stone Hollow Reporter*. The Town Council had voted funds to repair the aging recreation center. Murcheson's Electrical Supply Company was applying for a zoning variance. A two-page spread covered the high school's graduation and featured, among others, a photo of two smiling senior boys, one with his arm around the other. An article on page nine profiled a citizens' committee that had been formed to protest the widening of rural roads. "Simply put: we cannot afford to stand by and let this kind of wanton destruction take place," he read. "Two-hundred-year-old trees have been cut down. Stone walls built before the Revolutionary War have been brutally dismantled. This is an outrage, and I urge everyone who loves Stone Hollow's beauty and tranquillity to send a message to the politicians in November, particularly Highway Supervisor Otto Vanderhof and his brother the mayor, that we're absolutely sick and tired of incompetence and nepotism in town hall."

Even before he reached the attribution, Cameron could recognize Max's passionate—some might call it strident—voice. He put down his paper and gazed out the plate-glass window at the pleasingly dreary little luncheonette across the street, where he and Dan used to have lunch from time to time in the old days, the two of them sitting in a booth, flirting amiably with Marlene the waitress, who knew exactly what was what, and listening to the rough banter, the put-downs and the rude asides, that passed for conversation between Tony at the grill and the huge-gutted locals who lined the counter, their buttocks nearly engulfing the round stools on which they perched.

"I gotta go down to Pennsylvania next week," one guy would say.

"Don't they call that extradition?" Tony would call out.

Cameron missed all that, even though he was never a part of it, only a kind of benign voyeur. He wished Max hadn't chosen to open right across the street. He'd love to be able to sneak into the Main Street Luncheonette now and then for a nice, greasy grilled-cheese sandwich without feeling too conspicuously disloyal.

He wondered if Zanzibar had hurt the luncheonette's business any, though from the number of pickup trucks in the little lot beside it, that didn't appear to be the case. Stone Hollow was two parallel worlds, hardly ever touching, though acutely aware of one another nonetheless.

Returning to his paper, he saw that Otto Vanderhof had used a letter to the editor to speak up in his own defense. "To the misguided and uninformed citizens who impute my motives, let me say: The safety of our children and firemen are of the paramount importance. So is our Duty to modernize our roads. The Lord is my Shepherd, I shall not want. God Bless America."

Feeling a hand on his shoulder, he looked up. "Hiya, sweetie," said Max, bending down to kiss him on the cheek. "Mind if I join you?"

"Of course not. I see your roads campaign made it into the *Reporter.*"

"Did you read Otto's letter? What a moron."

"He seems to have the Lord on his side."

"Fuck the Lord," Max said. "Do you know what Abe Gorecki told me? Otto's ordering his road crews to do overtime, so that when he loses the election in November, the damage'll already be done. And who's going to stop him? His brother the mayor? We're screwed in this town. Screwed royally. I can't stand it."

Cameron certainly sympathized with Max—he'd seen some of those "improved" roads and they were truly alarming; he dreaded waking up one day to find the road crews improving his own stretch of pavement. Still, Max's agitation gave him pause.

Max seemed to sense that. "Enough about politics. Just make sure you sign the petition on your way out. What I really came over to talk to you about is far more interesting. It's about your love life."

Cameron suppressed a laugh. "Isn't it a little early in the morning to talk about that? Or a little late in the day, depending on how you look at it?"

"Don't be ridiculous. Perry and I've been talking it over, and we think we've got just the man for you."

"Oh, please. I haven't even begun to recover from Dan yet."

"And you never will if you keep on like this. Your friends think you need to get out more."

"I thought Zanzibar was Stone Hollow's place to see and be seen."

"You know what I mean," Max told him. "So listen. Elliot Shore. Heard of him?"

"I don't think so. Like you say, I haven't been getting out much."

"He's new to the area. Just bought a weekend house. I met him up at Broken Rock."

Cameron pretended disapproval. "And what were *you* doing at Broken Rock, pray tell?"

"Nothing, unfortunately," Max said cheerfully. "Just looking. But you never know what might happen. This pack of college boys descended. It was like a vision. Six or seven of them. They all stripped down to their boxers and went in for a dip. They pretended I wasn't even there. Probably for them I wasn't. Just part of the scenery. The old troll who comes with the rocks."

The secluded spot—a shelf of rock where a mountain stream broadened into a swimming hole—certainly had its memories. Dan had even gotten arrested there two summers ago—at the time, a peculiar relief for Cameron. He'd been feeling guilty about Dan's fidelity to a partner prematurely on the twilight side of sex.

"I've been thinking of driving up some afternoon," Cameron said. "Not to cruise, of course. I want to see the mountain laurel. It should be in bloom pretty soon. Dan and I used to make a little pilgrimage every year."

"The mountain laurel's not the only thing in bloom. Believe it or not, the place is hopping. Just like the old days. So I was walking along the edge of the stream and there's this guy sitting on a rock, reading a book. He seemed very attractive, and I thought, 'Why the hell not?'"

"Your motto."

"So I went up to him and asked, 'What are you reading?' And he looked at me and said, perfectly serious, *'Ivanhoe,* by Sir Walter Scott.' I thought it was enchanting, especially the 'by Sir Walter Scott' part. Then he said, 'You should know, I'm HIV-positive, and if you aren't, you shouldn't even think of thinking of anything.' And I thought, 'Well, that's pretty admirable.' So we just sat there and talked. And I couldn't help but start thinking about you. He's smart. Very kinetic personality. I think you might like him. And vice versa."

Cameron felt something very much like dread come over him. "Max, are you serious?" he asked.

"Absolutely. He's interested in meeting guys who are positive. So I mentioned I had a dear friend."

"You're trying to set me up on a date?"

"Think about it, sweetie. You're not locked up in a prison. That's maybe what they want you to think, but it's not true. We've had to fight for everything, remember? It's no different now. I'm not going to let you give that part of yourself up."

"It's scary," Cameron said.

"I know," Max told him. "But in your own way, you've always been just about the bravest person I know."

Pop hadn't wanted nothing fancy, and they took him at his word. Kyle made the arrangements—a plain coffin, plainest of the plain, but even so it cost a small fortune. Uncle Otto wasn't too happy when he saw Pop laid out in it at Bondurant's Funeral Home. That's the kind of coffin Jews are buried in, he told them, though how he'd know what kind of coffin Jews were buried in was anybody's guess.

Vanderhofs from Rosendale and Kerhonkson and Krumville came out for the service, as well as a bunch of Pop's buddies from the Main Street Luncheonette, where he liked to stop in for coffee and scrambled eggs. Jesse chided himself for looking around for Gary Dunkel, of all people; there was no reason for Gary Dunkel to be there. Donna had come with Leanne and wore a light blue dress that made her look all right.

In the little memorial chapel, Uncle Roy stood at a podium in front of the coffin, flanked by two flower wreaths, and said a few words—how Pop always kept his word, no matter how bad the chips were down; how he always provided for his family, who were the apple of his eye; how he'd be surprised and pleased by all the people who'd come to say good-bye to him here in this room. Then the preacher at the Abundant Life Fellowship where Patti and their mom went got up and spoke for several minutes like he'd known Pop pretty well, though Jesse couldn't figure out how that would be, since Pop had never darkened the doorway of his or any other church. Jesse sat in agony, in dress pants and a jacket he'd grown too big for in the two years since he'd worn them last, but they were all he had. The preacher finished by saying, "A good, good man has gone home to the Lord." Then Patti played a tape of "Amazing Grace," which had always been Pop's favorite tune, the one he'd sing out loud sometimes when he led Jesse and Kyle tramping through the woods. Pop had been especially fond of the line "that saved a wretch like me," and he'd draw out the word *wretch* in ways that made them all laugh.

Besides Jesse, Kyle, Uncle Roy, and Uncle Otto, the pallbearers were their cousin Kenny from the Stone Hollow police, and Brandon Schnei-dewind, who Kyle insisted on including because, as he said, Pop had took to him. Jesse hated the thought of it, but what could he do? Hoisting the casket, they carried it out to the waiting hearse. Jesse was surprised how light it was; he'd have hardly believed Pop was in there at all.

Not too many followed them out to the cemetery—maybe out of respect for the immediate family. Hot sun blazed down as the preacher led them all in saying the Lord's Prayer. Jesse realized, halfway through, he'd forgotten most all the words. When the prayer was finished, their mom unpinned her corsage and laid it on the top of the casket. The funeral director and his assistant lowered the box into the hole a backhoe had scooped in the ground. There it stood, a few dozen yards away, a big yellow machine cooling along with its operator in the shade of an old tree, just waiting to fill the dirt back in.

And that was all. Or supposed to be. Uncle Roy hugged their mom. Then Uncle Otto did the same. Both men shook hands with Jesse and said, "See you on back at the house." Relatives had brought casseroles, potato salad, a cooked ham. Leanne and Donna stood together talking. It always relieved Jesse to see them friendly with each other; sometimes he half wanted to thank Leanne for being nice to his girlfriend, for treating her like an equal, but he knew it wouldn't sound the way he meant it. Besides, he hardly talked to Leanne much. She made him nervous. All his brother's girlfriends made him nervous, though he hadn't ever hated any of them the way he'd hated that first one, Michelle de Hulter.

Everybody moved slowly—maybe reluctantly—to their cars. Kyle alone remained by the grave. Pulling a pint of whiskey from his jacket, he cracked it open and held it high.

Their mom saw him. "Kyle," she warned. He'd already gotten in trouble with her back at the funeral home for trying to stash the bottle in the casket next to Pop's body.

Kyle paid her no heed. "See ya, hombre," he said. "Meet you on the other side." He turned the bottle upside down and let the gold liquor empty out onto the coffin lid. Next to him, Jesse could feel Patti flinch. "Why does he have to be like that?" she said under her breath.

Later, he figured Kyle must have had the whole thing planned. Brandon tossed him a shovel, took another for himself. Kyle didn't hesitate. He dug right into the pile of dirt and flung a shovelful into the open grave. Then another and another.

Nobody moved. They all just stood and watched as Brandon joined in, the two working together without a word spoken between them. Everybody could hear the dirt drumming down on the casket. Sweat glistened on Kyle's face—or was it tears? You couldn't say. Kyle paused to take off his jacket and toss it onto the ground, and Brandon did the same. The back of Brandon's dress shirt was soaked through. He wiped his brow, leaving a smear of dirt. Looking straight Jesse's way, he held out the shovel in a silent summons. Jesse looked at his mom, who told him, her voice uncertain and pleading, "Honey, we need to get on back to the house. Folks'll be expecting us there."

He only shook his head, not trusting himself to speak. It felt good to grip the handle, wood worn smooth from use and sweat. Next to him, Kyle had sunk to his knees, seizing big, stony clods of earth and heaving them into the hole as Brandon too continued to work. Now dirt completely covered the casket. Their mom's corsage lay buried. Jesse wondered what it'd sound like inside that box, the hollow thuds as dirt landed on the wood. But of course Pop was deaf to everything down there. They weren't going to see him again.

Wielding the shovel, he was battling the enemy, claiming back the man who'd played tunes on empty bottles and told funny stories in different voices and was regularly laid up with those damn migraines.

The adults watched, expressionless, like they knew it was best to stand aside.

Ten minutes turned into half an hour. Brandon handed his shovel over to Kenny and stood with his hands on his hips, shirt open, breathing hard. Leanne took a short turn from Jesse, then passed the shovel to Kyle.

Leaning against his machine and smoking a cigarette, the backhoe operator watched them from the shade. Had he ever seen anything like it?

Soon enough Jesse and Brandon were back at it, facing off over the pile of dirt, staring at each other as they dug their shovels in and heaved more loads into the grave. Jesse dared himself not to look away. Brandon's hooded eyes held not a glimmer of anything. It always pained Jesse that Pop thought so highly of Brandon. But there were things Pop couldn't know, things for some reason Brandon seemed able to carry so much better than Jesse.

Then Brandon abandoned his shovel to Kyle, and just at that moment somebody, Jesse thought it was maybe Leanne, started singing "Amazing Grace." Like fire catching in dry brush, the ragged tune went around the group, and he and Kyle joined in too, practically yelling out the line "that saved a wretch like me," sweat or tears or whatever it was coursing down their dirt-streaked faces, laughing at the joke of it, their dead Pop's high spirits singing from out of the grave, "that saaaved a *wretch* like meee." The preacher didn't understand at all. He looked perturbed, maybe even insulted. Jesse didn't care. Besides, how were you going to stop him and Kyle? That was what Jesse felt most of all—the sense that once they got going, him and his brother, they were fucking one hundred percent unstoppable.

He thought it was just the kind of funeral Pop would've wanted his boys to give him.

SEVEN

Sometimes Cameron would watch them for a bit. Standing at an upstairs window, he could see the Bilvic brothers, as he privately persisted in calling them, at the far end of the garden as they went about their work in the late-afternoon heat.

The faint sounds of their radio wafted his way. The brothers' tastes were surprisingly catholic: a bedrock of country music, just as he'd expect, but sometimes they tuned in a pop station and even, on occasion, subjected themselves for a while to a ponderous dose of rap.

This afternoon, they were sticking with country. Mostly they worked without speaking, though now and then he could hear Kyle's humorless staccato laugh. He wished he could make out their conversation; he wondered what Jesse said from time to time that his brother found so amusing.

He wanted nothing from them but the proximity of their health and youth and watched them as a ghost might watch the goings-on of the living. They had all their lives ahead of them, a future to squander heedlessly. The luxury of it nearly made him weep.

He knew next to nothing about them, of course. Their observable presence was but a slender portion of whatever real lives they led, and remembering his initial glimpse of Kyle as the enraged, bullying young swain, he found himself curious about the submerged regions of those lives. What had ever happened, he wondered, between Kyle and that young woman of his? And the old man their father, who was sick in the hospital, who perhaps, if he'd heard Jesse right, was dying. They were a strange pair, reminding him a little, he'd come to realize (hence the nervousness, the vague attraction), of certain boys he used to fear in high school, one boy in particular, Tommy McCalla, an ingenious bully who'd mysteriously had his number before even he himself had been aware of it, who used to sidle up to him in gym class and murmur threateningly, "You know you want to blow me. Meet me after school or I'll tell everybody all about you." Feeling terrified and confused, he *had* met Tommy after school—it had seemed, at the time, the only way to escape the older boy's taunts. For three months of his sophomore year, several times a week he'd knelt before Tommy in his tormentor's musty garage with a mix of excitement and loathing. Afterward, with a look of complete disdain, Tommy would zip up without a word. At the end of the school year he and his family moved away to Georgia.

Cameron could still hear Tommy's seething, whispered refrain—"Faggot, faggot"—as he moved relentlessly to climax. He heard it even now with sweet, angry arousal.

Done for the day, the Bilvic boys had come down from the roof and were ambling through his garden. They'd put their shirts back on. Around his waist Kyle wore a nail pouch; off one hip hung his hammer. Jesse had taken off his maroon baseball cap and rubbed his hand through the stubble on his head. Kyle walked in front, and Jesse playfully swatted him on the shoulder with his cap. "Cut it out," Kyle told his brother without bothering to look back. "Fucking dirt monkey."

The words made Cameron smile. He felt sorry for them. Despite their bravado—Kyle's especially—they were really just lost, clueless kids. He stepped back from the window and realized, with regret, that their stint with him was coming to an end. Another week at the most and they'd be done. He'd never see them again, or if he did—what would it matter?

From the back door came a peremptory knock. "Cameron," Kyle called out. He'd insisted they not call him Mr. Barnes.

"Coming," Cameron told him, already halfway down the stairs. The two brothers stood at the screen door. All at once they seemed awkward, uncertain.

"Yes? Come on in." He'd never had them in the house before.

As usual, Kyle spoke for the two of them. "Um, can we ask you about something?"

"Okay," Cameron ventured warily. Had they somehow seen him watching at the upstairs window?

Kyle's eyes darted around the kitchen before settling on him. Jesse's gaze was roving as well. He remembered why he hadn't thought it a wise idea to let them in his house.

"We were wondering if maybe you could do us a big favor." Kyle's voice was humble, deferential, and Cameron felt suddenly not so much wary as strangely stirred. What had taught this young redneck such cautious tact?

"If I can," Cameron told him, eager now to be of whatever help he could.

"I'm sorry to ask you for this," Kyle said hesitatingly, "but could you maybe front us some bucks?"

So that was it. Cameron sighed with a perverse twinge of disappointment. "Did I not give you enough for materials?" He tried his best not to sound too stern, only inquiring.

"No, materials are fine. We got everything we need. We were just hoping, like, we could maybe get an advance on the rest that you owe us."

Cameron had paid them a third of their projected wages at the outset. Surely there was nothing wrong in paying them another third, he calculated quickly. "I don't see any problem with that," he said.

"Thank you, sir."

Suddenly Cameron found himself detesting the sound of this young man's wheedling politeness. Didn't he realize how easily it could backfire? But of course, no, he wouldn't realize that.

Cameron rather liked Jesse for remaining mute, for standing awkwardly just inside the screen door, as if ready to bolt should anything go wrong. Kyle might have the greater presence, but there was something to be said for failing to be an operator.

"I don't have the cash on me," Cameron said. "If you want it today, you'll have to take a check."

"We can deal with a check," Kyle told him. "No problem."

"My checkbook's upstairs. Do you want a glass of water or anything?"

"We're fine."

As he mounted the stairs, Cameron could hear them talking to each other, Kyle saying something, Jesse answering, their voices low and unintelligible, then Kyle's humorless staccato laugh. His checkbook lay on his desk, and he started to sit and write it out, but then thought it best not to leave the Bilvic brothers to their own devices for too long downstairs. Not that he didn't trust them. Of course he trusted them. They weren't *that* stupid, after all.

When he returned to the kitchen, it was as if they hadn't moved—except they both held half-empty water glasses.

"We were thirstier than we thought," Kyle told him.

Cameron resisted the momentary urge to feel he was somehow, in a way he couldn't quite put his finger on, being taken advantage of.

"Did you get some bottled water from the fridge?" he asked automatically.

"Just the tap."

"Next time," he told them, not that there'd necessarily be a next time, "help yourself to the good water. The stuff from the tap's undrinkable."

"We drink it all the time," Kyle said. "There ain't nothing wrong with it."

Cameron might, he thought, say something about the town's lack of a proper filtration system, how the turbidity made the water dangerous for a person with a compromised immune system. But he wouldn't. Why would they want to hear something like that?

"Well," he explained, envying wildly their pitiable lot as he sat at the kitchen table to write out their check, "it just tastes bad to me, is all."

He'd barely finished his meal of broiled fish and rice when the phone rang. Expecting either Max, who usually called around dinnertime to check on him, or one of those telemarketers on whom he regularly hung up, he was instead confronted with a young voice saying, "It's Crazy Jamey again, my friend. How'd you like to suck my dick?"

Instantly Cameron clicked off the phone, regretting even as he did that he hadn't had the presence of mind to say, "Okay, Crazy Jamey, I'll suck your dick if you suck mine." But he knew that was stupid, perhaps even dangerous. Every now and again he and Dan had gotten a call from this Crazy Jamey—some kid in the housing development down the road, he suspected, perhaps one of the various delinquents he'd yelled at for trespassing on his property, sullen, defiant boys Dan always worried might come back and burn their house down.

The phone rang again. Best to ignore him completely, Cameron counseled himself, though at the same time he felt a sudden spurt of anger: How dare this kid harass him? Against his better judgment he picked up the receiver and said, as calmly as possible, "Fuck off, you little shit, before I call the police."

"Cameron? Are you okay there?"

"Oh," Cameron told Dan.

"Maybe you'd rather not talk."

Cameron's laugh was a little hysterical—he could tell by the sound of it. For weeks he'd imagined getting this very call and had wondered what he'd say. "I didn't know it was you," he apologized. "Honest."

"Well, you've certainly gotten more aggressive since I left. Didn't I use to accuse you of keeping your feelings bottled up?"

"It was this stupid prank call I just got. Crazy Jamey. Remember him?"

"It's been a while, hasn't it? Or is he a regular again?"

"I was hoping he'd forgotten all about us."

"They never do," Dan said. "That's why I always said you should go easy on the ATVers."

"You know me, I've been friends with Max too long. I believe in fighting for my rights."

He could hear Dan sigh. There was so much they should be talking about. He didn't know at all where to begin. And neither, apparently, did Dan.

"So I just thought I'd call and see how you're doing," Dan told him. "I hope you don't mind."

"No, not at all. I'm fine. I went to the doctor last week. Everything's great. He was very pleased."

"That's terrific."

"Yeah, I suppose it could be much worse," Cameron told him, thinking, My boyfriend could have left me, or something like that. My life could have fallen apart. A fierce swell of nostalgia overtook him. All their sweet, unbearable life together.

"And what're you up to?" he asked, trying his best to sound steady, even a little perfunctory. He really wished Dan hadn't called. Now he was going to be in a funk all evening.

"Nothing much. I'm still staying at Robert's. I've been lazy. I've barely even looked for an apartment. It doesn't really make sense to. Tony's going away for six weeks in July and August, so I'm going to house-sit for him. Look after his cats. How are Casper and Diva, by the way?"

"The cats are fine," Cameron said, trying not to feel betrayed. Robert was one thing—he and Dan had gone to college together—but Tony had been Cameron's friend long before Dan ever came on the scene. But of course, Tony was now *their* friend. Not everybody was going to be as fiercely protective of his wounds as Max and Perry.

"Diva brought a vole in this morning," Cameron went on, hardly listening to himself. "I found it in the kitchen."

"Oh, good."

He'd tried hard, over the years, to make his friends like and accept Dan. He had only himself to blame.

"And the job front?" he asked as disinterestedly as he could.

"I've got some leads here and there. I was talking to this guy I met who designs Web sites."

Who? Cameron wanted to ask. Who? Who? But he didn't ask. Dan had always been talented with computers; he used to sit for hours in the upstairs study and search the Web for pornography or hang around in chat rooms comparing notes, Cameron supposed, with other HIV-negative men whose partners were positive. He hadn't ever asked; he hadn't wanted to know. He'd kept his feelings bottled up. Life in that house had been hell for Dan.

The strangest thing, he wanted to tell his former lover. My sex drive—you know, that pesky old thing I once lived for?—well, it seems to have come back. Isn't that a hoot? Too late in the game for us, of course, way too late, but I thought you'd appreciate the cosmic irony there.

"You'd be good at doing Web sites," he told Dan.

"I guess. We'll see what happens."

"Good luck."

There was an awkward pause, and Cameron realized his words had probably sounded dismissive.

"Well," Dan said at last, "like I said, I just wanted to see how you were doing. Give my love to Max and Perry."

"I'll do that."

"I miss you," Dan told him.

Please don't say that, Cameron thought. Don't say anything charming or affectionate or moving, or I'll have to send somebody down to Manhattan to kill you.

"I miss you too," he said.

"Is it all right if I call again?"

"Yes, of course. I'd like that. Just don't ask me to suck your cock."

"I wouldn't dream of it," Dan said wryly. "Bye now." And with a click he was gone.

Why had he said that last stupid bit? Or more to the point, he thought, why had Dan's meager observation "I miss you" given him the stirrings of a hard-on? Could his own words, he wondered forlornly, have had the same effect on Dan?

The weather had turned humid over the last several days. Stowing his empty plate and milk glass in the sink, he ventured out into the evening. It had become his habit, after supper, to walk in the cemetery up the road. He didn't like negotiating the road's narrow shoulder on foot—cars came around the curve much too fast, and tonight a squirrel lay in its own gore—but once he'd entered the cemetery proper, all was quiet and welcoming. Beneath huge silver maples and Norway spruces, the earliest tombstones dated back to the beginning of the nineteenth century, limestone markers etched faintly with a willow tree or clasped hands, their elegant script recording down to the month and day the exact duration of a life. By midcentury, granite family markers replaced the limestone ones, great patriarchal shafts surmounted by grief-draped urns and surrounded by a circle of individual graves. All the oldest families of Stone Hollow slumbered there: the Bondurants and Vanderhofs and Schneidewinds and de Hulters, their enchanting first names long ago gone out of fashion: Silas, Lavinia, Viola, Jeremiah, Augusta.

The prospect of lying here himself someday appealed to Cameron enormously, though he'd instructed Dan—and, more recently, Max and Perry—to cremate him and scatter the ashes beneath the lilacs in his garden, alongside Hermione and Brutus, beloved cats lost to the treacherous road.

Dan's phone call had both thrilled and depressed him. Face it, he reminded himself lest he get any foolish ideas: the relationship died a long time ago. It died when you got sick and Dan stayed healthy. It died when Dan's drinking got out of hand. It died when you looked at the man you'd fallen for a decade before and saw only a loser quietly squandering one opportunity after another. Undoubtedly he should have done more, Cameron chided himself, he should have cared more, only his own sur-

73

vival had so preoccupied him that he'd had neither the spiritual nor physical capital to invest in anything but that single goal. And now that he was surviving better than he'd dared hope—what next?

Beyond the old graves moldering in their glade, a host of more recent markers jutted starkly from the manicured lawn. He found this part of the cemetery depressing. Why didn't anyone plant trees here? Even real flowers had been banished in favor of plastic ones. He hated all this sterile rage for neatness that was overtaking the world (The Chaos Garden, tidy Dan had once dubbed their own lushly planted patch of ground). Despite its bleakness, however, the treeless lawn did offer a commensurate expanse of beautiful sky above. Low in the sultry west the sun appeared dilated, crimson, almost cool to the touch, and suddenly Cameron was grasping for a memory. It was as if, beneath this sunset, lay another, and by some accident of haze or heat, the two resembled one another entirely. He was sixteen and had only recently learned to drive; after dinner, he'd borrow the family car to wander aimlessly the streets of Memphis, full of lonely longing—for what, he didn't exactly know, but he often ended up on the bluffs overlooking the Mississippi, where sunsets the very color of longing beckoned to him from beyond the Arkansas floodplains.

Mitchell Johnson had meant everything to him in those days, though by any objective measure theirs had been nothing more than an ordinary friendship between schoolmates. All the great gusts of emotion had wreaked their violence within, invisible to the unsuspecting boy who was their cause.

Cameron remembered now, thirty years later, the two of them taking a walk in the late summer, and a puddle of water where a swarm of cobalt butterflies had gathered to drink, and how they all fluttered up as he and Mitchell approached. What had they been talking about? Of their long, earnest conversations he could remember scarcely a word. Mitchell had been a devout Pentecostal, an Eagle Scout, a member of the school's math club. He'd been on the tennis team, though Cameron, for some reason, never once saw him play.

Strange, the little things you could regret after so many years. It seemed impossible he could have let someone like that simply disappear from his life, and yet that was exactly what had happened. He'd gone away to Oberlin, he'd met Max Greenblatt, he hadn't looked back. Had he resented Mitchell for never returning his love? Though how could he have blamed poor, sweet, clueless Mitchell, to whom he'd never so much as breathed a word of his secret?

At forty-six, what might Mitchell Johnson be like? Impossible even to imagine. At seventeen he'd been handsome, a little shy. Vastly dull, if one were to be completely honest with oneself. Nevertheless, he'd broken Cameron's heart every time he'd walked into the bandroom, begun unpacking his golden trumpet from its battered case, then looked across the room and smiled his friendly hello.

Cameron realized he had stopped walking. He was simply standing, contemplating the enormous inviting sun, wishing suddenly, hopelessly, amidst all that haunted light, that his life had been entirely different, and that in that different life he still knew Mitchell Johnson, they were still friends.

In that different life it would have been Mitchell and not Tommy McCalla before whom he knelt worshipfully on the concrete floor afternoons after school; it would have been Mitchell's sweet seed he had gratefully received.

Perhaps Dan was right, he thought, resuming his pace as the sun swooned past the treeline. Perhaps it wasn't such a good idea to spend too much time in cemeteries. Dan had always preferred regular hikes in the woods, the views from ridges. They'd had a terrible argument once, in Italy, because Cameron had wanted to picnic in a cemetery outside Urbino.

At two modest, side-by-side graves he paused to pay brief silent tribute: Mike and Larry, lovers he'd known only a little—funny, affectionate, unlucky young men who'd died barely into their thirties. It pleased him, somehow, that they lay next to each other, slipped in undercover, as it were, amongst all these inviolable family plots.

The evening sun had gone down completely; nonetheless a last surge of color charged the sky overhead. Regaining his health, he'd regained a certain sense of wonder he'd lost through the gray days of his illness. Still, it troubled him to realize he'd probably never again feel longing—or anything else—as intensely as he'd felt it when he was a teenager. The scar tissue thickened. Books, music, friendship, sunsets—about none of those things did he care the way he had once cared.

What would he say to Mitchell, were they to meet again after all these years? Confess the truth—I never loved anybody the way I loved you?

But that was ridiculous. It had all been in his head. Or, no—it had all been in his heart. Either way, it was gone as if it had never been.

A little beyond the graves of Larry and Mike, a bier of flowers marked a fresh burial. Cameron strolled out of his way, across the grass, curious, as always, who it might be—not that he imagined he'd know him or her. A temporary metal tag had been stuck in the ground to mark the site till a proper headstone could be put in place. William Vanderhof, he read.

So Kyle and Jesse's dad was dead. They'd said not a word to him about it. Were they stoic or merely unfeeling? What they thought about anything, he hadn't the slightest clue. With some surprise he remarked the dates that enclosed their dad's life with such finality. In his imagination, he'd somehow granted Bill a good two decades the "old man" would never live to see.

So this was yet another thing he'd been mistaken about. Bill Vanderhof had been scarcely a year older than he.

EIGHT

Jesse's truck, that total piece of shit, had stranded him at the D & Dee convenience store. The key turned with a dull click and nothing happened. It wasn't the battery; it was going to be the fucking starter, and the fucking starter was going to cost him way more than he had to spend.

"Fuck this shit," he said. "Goddamn fucking piece of motherfucking shit."

Donna had asked him to keep his language decent. He was trying.

The parking lot was deserted except for some woman pumping gas. Sometimes he wanted to punch everything in sight. He wasn't like Kyle, who could take a piece of junk and keep it running indefinitely. This was his second truck, even worse than his first one.

He tried to start her a few more times but knew it was pointless. She was stone dead. Climbing down from the cab, he walked over to the pay phone only to realize he had no quarters. He had nothing. He'd spent his last dollar bill on a soda.

Fetching the unopened can from the truck, he reentered D & Dee's air-conditioned haven.

"Hey, can I return this?" he asked the girl behind the counter. LORI said her name tag. He didn't know her.

"What're you talking about?"

"Can I get my money back?"

"No," she said, drawing out the *o* and sounding like he'd somehow offended her.

"It ain't been opened." He held the can up in front of her face. "See?"

"I can't give refunds on food items. Sorry."

"I'll put the soda in the cooler. Nobody's gonna know."

"Are you crazy? I'm going to call the manager."

He hated dealing with people he didn't know. "Look, I just need to make a phone call and I don't have any money. My truck's broke down out there."

"Larry," she called out. "This guy's hassling me."

He didn't know Larry either. Usually he went to the Stewart's across the street.

"What's the matter?" Larry was forty with a belly. He held a mop.

"This guy wants his money back on the soda. I don't know what he's up to."

"Okay, guy," Larry said. "I don't have time for you. Outta the store."

It occurred to Jesse that maybe Larry was mistaking him for Kyle. That happened sometimes, and when it did, there was no talking around it, that story was over before she got wrote.

He turned on his heel and walked out.

The warm air outside was a relief from the air-conditioning and fluorescent lights. He stepped off the curb and saw a car bearing down on him.

"Whoa," he said. But the car wasn't going to hit him. It eased to a stop and he found himself looking, through the windshield, at the guy who was paying his salary these days.

Cameron Barnes smiled through the glare of the glass, and Jesse stepped aside to let him pull on in.

"How's it going?" the older man asked as he emerged from the silver-gray BMW. It wasn't the kind of car Jesse would ever want to own, exactly, but he and Kyle had definitely admired its sleek, expensive presence in the drive.

He felt oddly nervous being spoken to by this man. Jesse had hardly ever said much of anything to him, Kyle being the one who did most of the talking. Without his brother there, he felt at something of a loss.

"Not too bad," he said, though of course he couldn't be doing any worse. The last thing he needed was for Cameron to think he was some loser who couldn't get his pickup truck to start. But then he thought, *Why* do I care? I hate your name, he wanted to tell Cameron. It was just one more thing he and Kyle had poked fun at on the sly. Whatever was your mom thinking, giving you a name like that?

But Cameron wasn't about to wait for stupid questions from the likes of Jesse. "That's good," he said briskly, then marched on past him like Jesse was somebody barely worth noticing.

Trying to think what to do next, Jesse watched through the window as Cameron went to the cash machine. He slid his card in and punched his code, and then, as he waited for the machine to give him his money, he gazed out the window to where Jesse stood watching him. Jesse looked away quickly, chagrined to be caught staring. He hadn't been staring, had he? He'd just been thinking. All at once misery overtook him. A guy like Cameron never messed around with a piece of shit that wouldn't drive. No, a guy like Cameron took care of himself. He bought the best. He wanted something done, he hired you to do it. Fix the shed, mow the grass, tend the flower garden.

Stuffing bills in his wallet, Cameron emerged from the store.

"Hey," Jesse said tentatively, still standing by his dead truck. Cameron stopped and looked at him. There was something superior about him that Jesse despised. For an instant he wished he hadn't spoken, but then he plunged ahead anyway. "You're probably going to think I'm some kind of idiot, but my truck quit on me. I need to make a phone call or something but I don't have a penny on me right now."

Cameron just looked at him, one eyebrow raised, like he didn't understand what Jesse was saying to him.

"Do you have like a spare quarter I can borrow? I'll pay you back."

Cameron continued to regard him, though he reached in his pocket and pulled out some coins. He held them in his palm and extracted a quarter.

"You need more?" Cameron asked, the way he probably talked to any panhandler.

"No, just a quarter. I need to call my brother."

"What's wrong with your truck?"

"Won't start. I think it's the starter."

"I guess that makes sense." Cameron's face lightened in a smile. "What's your brother going to do?"

Jesse felt another wave of misery. He had no idea what Kyle was going to do other than poke fun at the sorry excuse for a truck Jesse drove. What he needed was a tow, but he sure didn't have money for that. Or, down the road, for a starter.

He was fucked, and fucked grandly.

It made him a little angry to admit the truth to Cameron. "I got to get this thing hauled, and I know this sounds stupid, since you just loaned us a bunch of money, but Kyle and me both are bone dry." He hesitated, then added, "It's been a rough couple of weeks."

Cameron spoke in a quiet, level way that almost made Jesse jump. "I was very sorry to hear about your dad. I saw the marker up in the cemetery. Otherwise I wouldn't have known."

There wasn't a marker, of course, just a flimsy metal tag. When they might be able to afford a regular stone was anybody's guess, though Uncle Roy had said he'd do what he could.

"Keep a stiff upper lip. That's my brother. He didn't want us talking about it. He and Pop were real close. I mean, we're all a close family, I was close to my dad too."

He knew he was saying too much, but Cameron's words had caught him off guard.

They really were a close family, he assured himself, though he wished there was a way for Kyle not to know about any of this—not about the truck or the money or what he'd said about Kyle just now to their employer.

Their employer, he reminded himself, was a fag.

"If you're in a bind," said their employer, "I can always advance you a little more cash. You've got it all coming from me sooner or later, right?"

That was true enough. "Are you sure?" he asked.

"Of course. Look—I'll run you out to Al Bosco's garage. We'll get you fixed up in no time."

It occurred to Jesse that somebody like Cameron probably had no idea what a new starter would cost—and stranger still, just might not care.

He'd never ridden in a BMW before. He tried to pretend he was the kind of person who was used to riding in one—but what kind of person would that be, exactly? He'd always imagined being rich someday; Pop always told them Lotto was a boat that'd come in for them one of these days, and when he was a kid, he'd believed just about everything Pop had said.

"By the way, the shed's looking good," Cameron told him as they headed up the hill. "You guys are doing a nice job. I'm sorry I never met your father. My friend Max always said he did really good work."

"He was good at what he did," Jesse agreed. He wondered what Pop would make of him riding in a car with the likes of a rich fag like Cameron Barnes. Pop used to complain how a perfectly good town was going to hell because of people like that moving in, buying up, taking over. *I'm happy to take their money,* he'd say. *That don't mean I have to like them.*

Jesse watched the woods flash by beyond the car's tinted windows, surprised by how numb he felt to everything.

"He wasn't that old. What did he die of? If you don't mind my asking."

Jesse thought maybe he did mind a stranger asking such a thing, but he answered anyway. "Cancer." He hated that word. "Liver cancer. It came on sudden." He paused for a moment. "You think something like that's maybe genetic?"

He didn't know why he thought this guy who drove a BMW might be able to lay to rest the nagging feeling he might be programmed to walk in his daddy's shoes.

"I think there're probably lots of causes," Cameron said. "Genetic, environmental, behavorial. It's probably a mix of all those. Like most diseases."

"I see," said Jesse, hardly satisfied. He wondered if he'd ever stop worrying that hard little knot of fear inside him. "It didn't take him hardly any time to go. He wasn't in the hospital more than a couple weeks. My mom says that's good, in a way. I mean, he didn't have no medical insurance, so we got the hospital bill to pay on top of everything else. You know how much it costs just to fucking bury somebody?"

He shouldn't have said *fucking,* he thought. It just slipped out.

Cameron didn't seem to take offense. "Tell me about it," he said. "And what's the alternative? Even cremation's not cheap. It cost my friend Roger nearly a thousand dollars to get himself cremated last year."

Cameron laughed. He was peculiar, Jesse thought.

"Called around from his deathbed to compare prices," Cameron went on. "Always one for a bargain. Some of us thought he might have better things to do, but Roger said, 'Look, I'm a detail man.' Can you believe that? Three days before he dies, he's still micromanaging everything. Though I guess he was lucky. Still had his wits about him. Actually, I admired Roger a great deal. When my time comes, I've told my friends, just compost me in the garden. Spread me under the lilacs."

The outburst made Jesse a little uncomfortable. He wondered who this Roger was.

"I really like your garden," he ventured, thinking maybe to change the subject, but Cameron paid him no heed.

"And about health insurance. Don't even get me started. It's ridiculous this country doesn't have universal coverage. Look at a family like yours. I mean, what're you supposed to do? Sell the house?"

"No," Jesse said with certainty. "We ain't about to do that. It's our house. We've been in that house near to three hundred years."

"Really?" Cameron seemed genuinely surprised.

"It's the truth."

"What kind of house?"

"Old."

"I like your sense of humor," Cameron told him. "You're funny."

"Well, it *is* old. It's made of stone."

"Whereabouts?"

"You go out Route 314, it's kind of on a hill. There's a little lake at the bottom."

"I know it exactly. I pass by that house all the time. Wonderful old house."

"My dad dug the lake," Jesse said with a touch of pride as they pulled into Big Al Bosco's Towing and Repair. Cameron steered them slowly through the lot of used and junked vehicles, including a beauty of a Trans Am Kyle had had his eye on for some time. He'd have to let Kyle know she was still sitting pretty in the lot, not that they could spare a penny for her right now.

They'd already sold Pop's old panel truck for next to nothing, and their mom seemed eager to get rid of all sorts of other stuff of his. She and Patti were planning a tag sale to try to disperse all Pop's junk he'd squirreled away over the years.

Holding a can of beer, Big Al ambled out to greet them. In the dim light behind him, Jesse could see the enormous pyramid of empties in the corner. That worried some people, but Pop had always been loyal to Big Al. All the Vanderhof vehicles ended up here sooner or later.

But just what did it look like to be riding in a car with somebody like

Cameron? Jesse glanced over at his benefactor to try to gauge the answer to that question and decided, to his alarm, that it couldn't look worse.

Still, the guy had saved his ass. Sometimes you found yourself in a situation you just couldn't do that much about.

"So, we're all set?" Cameron took out his thick wallet. "I hate how the cash machine only gives you twenties."

The exchange of bills embarrassed Jesse; he wished Cameron had loaned him the money in the privacy of the car, but there was no going back. Cameron counted out bills on bills.

"That should do you for now," he said briskly. "It was good talking to you. I enjoyed it. I certainly hope the rest of your day goes better." He reached out his hand and Jesse, a little surprised, hesitated a moment before taking it in a loose handshake.

He knew Cameron was looking him full in the face, but the last thing Jesse wanted was to meet his eyes. He looked instead to where Brandon Schneidewind stood watching him from the shade of the garage. Of course it'd be his luck Brandon was working today.

"What's up?" Brandon asked as he sauntered over. He was grinning broadly and carried his own can of beer. The three of them watched as Cameron clumsily backed his car out of the lot.

"Man, you are sure riding in style," Big Al observed.

They might have his sorry ass trapped, Jesse thought, but he could still throw a good offense. "Today it sure looks that way, now don't it?" he said, giving them both that steely Vanderhof look he'd copped from his brother.

He found Perry's car in the drive and Perry in the garden, crouched before a pot of agapanthus, adjusting his camera lens.

"The garden looks like crap these days," Cameron apologized.

Perry continued to hone in on the dark blue blooms as if they were his delicate prey. "Your garden never looks like crap," he said. "It has fabulous dignity to it. It's like those temples that were built to be great-looking ruins."

"What temples are those?"

"Oh, I don't know. You see them all over the world. You just know they look better now than they did when they were new."

"I see," Cameron told him. Perry had a whimsical way about him that made some people decide he was a little bit of a fool. An odd combination of fool and prodigy, Cameron thought as Perry clicked, advanced the film, clicked again. Also a great beauty, at thirty-three even more handsome than he'd been when he came into their lives nearly a decade ago. "The face of Antinoüs," Dan used to say, not entirely as a joke.

From its earliest beginnings Perry had been taking portraits of Cameron's garden, in love with its shaggy profusion, its romantic neglect, the suggestion of good intentions gone to seed—all the things Dan had disliked in a garden and come to embody in his own life. Strange that box-wood parterres and conical yews and acres of emerald lawn had been Dan's idea of horticultural order. What did that reveal about his ex's inner life? Cameron had always wondered. And what did his own penchant for The Chaos Garden attest to? For he had to accept, however reluctantly, that he'd found Jesse's plight at the convenience store shamefully arousing in all its haplessness and rank disorder.

"I've been thinking," he told Perry, "and I've decided to go ahead and give my garden party again this year. At first I thought, no, without Dan it won't be any good, but then I just decided, why not? What the hell."

Perry wiped long, dark strands of hair from his eyes. "Excellent," he said. "What's a summer without one of your garden parties? Can we start on the guest list immediately? Nothing but hot, hot boys. My lucky camera will love it."

Perry's lucky camera, with which he'd been all over the world, was a 1952 Leica. If his professional shoots for the Met, Storm King, the New York City Ballet, paid the rent, other more private photos fed the soul. The walls of his and Max's house were hung with prints of dark-eyed boys sprawled languidly on carpets, or eating apricots beneath a tree, or diving from a rocky promenade into the ocean. A gallery in SoHo and another in Key West sold his work; a German publisher had issued a handsome volume in black and white, and if some who gazed on his pictures worried that he skirted certain taboos a little too closely, Perry remained steadfast in asserting that everything was in the eye of the beholder, and in his lucky camera's eye was only sweet, sweet innocence.

They strolled past old-fashioned roses coming into first flush of bloom—Madame Hardy, Comte de Chambord, Madame Legras de Saint Germain, their names nearly as redolent as their blossoms.

"I wish I'd gotten out here one last time before you started redoing the shed," Perry said. "I rather liked its dilapidation."

Its present incarnation did look awfully raw and new. Cameron thought he would have to take care in choosing a paint that would ease it back into its verdant surroundings.

"Also," Perry went on, "I was hoping to catch sight of your workmen. Max told me to keep an eye out for them. Are they playing hooky today?"

"They tend to keep somewhat irregular hours," Cameron explained evasively.

"Too bad. You know how yummy I find laborers of the youthful persuasion. All that glistening sweat, those hot muscles, the je ne sais quoi of raw, unexamined physicality. Are they really as hot as Max promised? Do they have tattoos?"

"I really haven't noticed," Cameron said, feeling unexpectedly protective, any temptation to recount the afternoon's rather pleasing adventure with Jesse prudently quelled. "They're a bit young for me, I'm afraid."

"Besides, you don't like them too rough, do you?"

"I guess not. Was Toby rough?"

Perry laughed. "Are you kidding? Toby was a prince. He had the blood of Cherokee nobles in him." He took a couple of quick steps, then turned and shot Cameron at close range. "Perfect."

("Stop buzzing me," Toby used to complain, tired of Perry's endless photographing of him, enough to fill dozens of now cherished albums. They had in general regarded one another somewhat coolly, though that hadn't prevented them from falling into bed together one stoned night in Manhattan. Afterward Toby had been wistful. "I usually don't go in for doing that," he confessed. "What on earth was I thinking?"

"So how was he?" Cameron had had to ask.

"All things considered—unremarkable. But don't ever tell Max I said that. He and Perry were made for each other. Just like you and me. It's something Perry and I had to get out of the way.")

"Don't waste film on me," Cameron chided Perry lightly. "Save it for your next victim." Cameron wasn't entirely sure, besides a steady stream of inspired chatter and that flirtatious smile of his, how Perry managed to talk young men and boys, more or less complete strangers, out of their self-consciousness and into varying states of undress as often as he did. Afterward those impromptu sessions could sometimes cause his subjects second thoughts. As long as he'd captured what it was he was after, Perry seemed not to care, despite an unpleasant incident in Istanbul once, and another in Passaic, New Jersey.

The thought that Kyle and Jesse could be coaxed into some striking tableau in the midst of his garden was certainly stirring, and Cameron imagined them there, rough grace in the dappled sunlight, fauns in the woodland, the spirit of Pan made visible. But what was Pan but that feeling of nameless dread, that panic that comes upon the solitary wanderer in the dells of Arcadia? Cameron thought he was, on the whole, rather glad Perry had missed his young men—or that they had missed Perry, whose rare brand of beauty they would probably not have appreciated in the least.

In any event, he reminded himself, they weren't *his* young men. Far from it: Kyle and Jesse belonged to nobody but themselves.

NINE

Music to his ears, the sound of their three engines thundered in the open air. It made Jesse think of movies like *The Road Warrior*. It made him feel fearless, invincible.

They crossed the fields behind the house, cut through a stretch of woods, dared the cops by shooting down the county road for a couple hundred yards (nobody was around to see), then veered abruptly into another stand of trees. It was cool in there, and they stopped momentarily to rip down the yellow NO TRESPASSING signs some asshole had put up since they'd last come through. Only a couple years back, you never saw any NO TRESPASSING signs; now they were everywhere you turned.

Steep banks shaded a narrow slough that already, the beginning of July, was drying up. The lack of rain was starting to hurt all over; the handful of folks he and Kyle mowed lawns for were all calling to say they had no need for them right now.

Kyle shredded the signs into small strips and let them flutter to the ground. When they started their machines back up, the noise startled a doe and her two fawns, who bounded away in long, graceful leaps. The hunting was good back in here, deer and turkey and squirrel; this had been one of Pop's favorite haunts. He'd spend hours in the fine November rain in a blind he'd built up a maple tree, sipping blackberry brandy and waiting, watching, listening. Jesse himself didn't have the patience or concentration for hunting; unlike Pop and Kyle, he got no pleasure from being damp and chilled to the bone. Still, he told himself this was one of his memories of Pop—tramping with him through the gray woods at dawn—and he should hang on to it.

Out in the woods, Pop had been a different man from the one they knew around the house. The woods didn't irritate him the way people did. The truth nobody liked to say was that deep down Pop had always been a loner, happiest when off by himself, whether drinking or hunting or just whiling away the time.

Kyle wouldn't be too happy to read some of his brother's thoughts, Jesse knew. Family had always meant a lot to him.

They'd come to the clearing where the sandy trail crossed the abandoned railroad bed. Black raspberry brambles grew in profusion, the red berries still ripening, though the dry spell had stunted them. Kyle called a halt, and Brandon yelled over the throb of their engines, "Which way, man?"

Kyle considered for a moment, then pointed down the rail trail. Jesse wasn't crazy about riding the rail trail. It was posted NO ATVS, and people walking or on bicycles gave you a dirty look. But his brother never let things like that stop him, Brandon either, and the last thing Jesse wanted was to look like a pussy. Besides, what harm were they doing? As Pop always said—and Pop had gotten a few dirty looks in his time as well, and from people not worth half what he was—they could be off doing drugs instead of good clean fun.

The trail this afternoon was more or less deserted. They overtook a couple of guys on bikes, dudes in spandex and plastic helmets they left to eat their dirt, but that was about it. Up ahead, a spur led off the main rail bed toward twin silos that rose out of the middle of the woods. His first time here—he'd have been eight or nine—they'd been ranging through the woods with Pop and just stumbled on it. Of course, Pop had probably been there a dozen times, but he pretended it was something they'd just discovered. What is it? they both asked, tugging at his sleeve, alert to the spooky feel of the place. Even now Jesse found it hard to believe the great hulk of stone and brick and rusting iron wasn't the ruins of some castle built by ancient Iroquois kings, which was what Pop had told them it was. Now he knew it was only a hundred or so years old, the defunct Clouser cement mine and kilns and storage silos. It was the coolest thing he'd ever seen, him and Kyle rock climbing on the huge tumbles of cut stone. Best was the mine's big open mouth, now filled with turquoise water, a hole who knew how deep. Pop hinted, when they were older and needed more than Iroquois kings, how he knew about a body that had been dumped there back in 1969, weighted down with chains and stones, and Jesse, peering into that unfathomable water, was inclined to believe him to this day.

If Pop had been making it all up, now nobody would ever know.

The flooded mine opening might've been a fine place for swimming, but word was something in the water made you sick.

They drove slowly all around the ruins, dodging in and out of the rubble. Something about the place provoked thoughts. Under the shade of some pines, where ashes marked the remains of a campfire, they came to a stop. The only person around was some guy taking pictures off in the distance.

Kyle pulled from his back pocket a pint of whiskey and shared it with Brandon, then handed it over to Jesse, who took the bottle and contemplated its amber contents. Kyle was walking in his daddy's shoes, no doubt about it. Since the funeral he'd been racing through about one of these a day, and Jesse wanted to tell him, Slow down there, you probably got Pop's liver, we probably both do, but of course there was no telling Kyle any such thing.

"If you're looking for the worm, monkey fuck, it ain't there," Brandon said.

Startled, Jesse threw back his head and took a bitter swallow. It warmed his throat going down; he thought he could feel it tickle his liver like a little electrical spasm.

He handed the bottle back to Kyle, who was looking at him with narrowed eyes.

"What?" he said.

"Nothing," Kyle told him, taking a long, steady drink and keeping his eyes on him till Jesse looked away in confusion. He held the half-empty bottle up to the light. "I gotta say, I really love this stuff. But it's fucking eating all my goddamn money."

"Thank God for our great friend Boo," Brandon said. *"Boo,"* he added, making a face to scare children.

"Yeah." Kyle laughed dryly. "Jesse, you better not be thinking about ditching that girl of yours anytime soon."

"Not likely," Brandon answered for Jesse. "Them two's for life. You can just tell."

You don't know the first thing about me, fuckhead, Jesse warned silently. "At least somebody here *has* a fucking girlfriend," he said.

Kyle looked a little disbelieving. "You little fuck," he said ominously.

Jesse knew when he'd scored, knew also when to beat a hasty retreat. "I'm just shitting around," he told his brother. "I don't mean nothing by it."

"I should beat your fucking ass for that," Kyle explained to him.

"So, Kyle"—as always, Brandon saw his opportunity and took it—"what happened with you and Leanne anyways?"

"Nothing happened."

"Shit happened," Brandon taunted him. "Shit always happens with the females."

"I'll fucking show you how shit happens."

They were best friends; it was how they were with each other. Jesse'd never had a friend like that.

Did Kyle lunge first, or Brandon? Anyway, they were wrestling now. "Wait," Kyle urged, and handed Jesse the precious pint. "Okay. Let her rip."

Brandon came at him, head down, and Kyle sort of received his butting head into his hands and held him there. Brandon put his arms around Kyle to try to shake himself loose, but Kyle was holding tight. Back and forth they contended, locked together, till Brandon hooked his leg behind Kyle's knee and they both went down in the dirt, rolling over and over, clinging to each other and whooping with surprise and maybe pleasure whenever the other landed a punch. Jesse stood by his three-wheeler and watched enviously. He knew better than to join in. In fact, he didn't want to join in, not with that fight—some other fight, maybe, somewhere, with somebody. Suddenly, strangely, he felt so empty he thought for a second he might pass out. He uncapped the bottle and lifted it to his lips and took a Kyle-sized gulp. The whiskey went almost instantly to his head, and he wasn't sure whether he felt better or worse.

Kyle and Brandon had tumbled to a halt. Breathing heavily, they lay together on the gravel that stretched down to the poison-blue water of the mine. "Shit," Brandon said about nothing in particular.

"You fucker," Kyle told him kindly. "You need a fucking haircut." He grabbed at Brandon's dark hair and yanked hard.

"Get your hands off me. You want me to look like a fucking jarhead. Like you and your brother."

"Better than looking like a faggot," Kyle said. "Jarheads kick butt."

"Jarheads eat pussy."

"Ain't nothing wrong with eating pussy, my friend." Kyle raised himself on his elbow. "Keeps you strong and manly."

"Well, if I can trust my calculations, only our man Jesse here's eating any pussy these days," Brandon said sadly.

Aware the two were scrutinizing him, Jesse held out the bottle. Kyle hauled himself to his feet and came up the slope. "Thanks, little brother." He took a deep swallow and pledged, "Swig Heil," as he liked to do when he was being grateful.

Jesse pointed mutely to the smear of blood on Kyle's elbow.

"You fucking wounded me," Kyle told Brandon. He held his arm up to study the gash.

"You'll survive," Brandon diagnosed. "Go wash it off in the water."

"Yeah, then I'll fucking glow for sure."

"You won't need a night-light."

"I don't need a night-light. It's Jesse who's scared of the dark."

"I am not," Jesse said, wondering what he'd ever done to make Kyle think he was, or if Kyle was only fooling with him.

"Jesse's not scared of nothing," Brandon said, looking his way boldly, with a shit-eating hint of a grin on his handsome face. "I'd say Jesse's the bravest motherfucker I ever met."

"And a world-class pussy eater," Kyle said, laughing that laugh of his that never sounded much like a laugh. "Aren't you, little brother?"

Jesse tried to think what to say, but Kyle, suddenly, had gone and turned serious. "I think you should get to know him better," he said in a flat tone of voice.

It knocked Jesse off guard. "Who? What the fuck're you talking about?"

"He gave you a ride," Kyle said.

"Who gave me a ride?" Jesse challenged, though all at once he knew. Kyle and Brandon had been talking. Brandon had told him what he'd seen.

He knew he should've mentioned it to Kyle, but he hadn't, he didn't know why. He'd felt vaguely ashamed, like it was some weakness he'd showed. That must've been it. But not telling his brother had made it that much worse, he saw now. Never try to keep anything from your brother.

"He must like you," Kyle went on.

"Fuck you," Jesse said. He'd taken a ride from Cameron Barnes; it was no big deal.

He'd also taken money—had Brandon seen that too?

Kyle only smiled. He held up the empty bottle to the light, examining it sadly, then like a seasoned pitcher tossed it against the rocks on the far side of the mine entrance. The shatter was clear and brilliant and satisfying. Jesse also knew it could be a warning.

"Hey, Jesse, your brother's crazy," Brandon said by way of explanation.

The afternoon had turned sultry. Some lazy thunderheads bloomed in the west, but you just knew they wouldn't come to anything. While Jesse rang the doorbell, Kyle waited in the truck. With both Donna's parents working day shifts at the correctional facility out in Napanoch, when Donna was working too it left Sean alone in the house. Jesse could see the TV's flicker in the darkened living room. He rang again and waited, idly studying the brown, treeless lawn, the empty birdbath a disappointed mockingbird sat peering into. All that stuff at the mine had put him in a mood, even though Kyle had told him, "You know us, little brother. We're just fucking around." Well, he hadn't liked it much, no matter what his brother said. He still felt vaguely accused of something, though for the life of him he couldn't say what it was, exactly. I didn't *do* anything, he wanted to insist, but he figured that would probably make things worse too.

He banged a couple of times on the door and called, "Hey, Sean, it's me."

Kyle had the truck radio playing loud; it came booming across the lawn, some hot-sounding girl promising love, love, love. The door opened a crack, and Sean stuck his head out warily.

"Oh. Jesse. Hey."

"How's it going?" Jesse asked, trying to ignore that Sean had buttoned his shirt up wrong.

"Like p's and q's. Want to come in?"

"I thought maybe you'd like to go for a little ride. Nice day out."

"I was watching the television."

"It'll be there when you get back. How about it?" Jesse punched Sean lightly on the arm. For some reason Sean liked that—maybe it reminded him of when he was on the team, before the accident. Donna said he'd used to be a big kidder, everybody'd liked him, though now, five years later, nobody came around much anymore. There wasn't too much to come around for, Jesse supposed.

"I got to put my shoes on," Sean told him.

"Okay. You go put your shoes on. I'll be right here." Jesse hesitated a moment, then added, "Oh, and fix your shirt." When Sean had disappeared inside the darkened room, Jesse turned and gave Kyle the thumbs-up, but his brother wasn't watching. He was staring off distractedly into space, his head slightly moving to the beat of the music. Without meaning to, Jesse felt a sudden warm rush of feeling, some emotion he had no name for, but it encompassed everything—his brother, Donna's brother, the parched lawn and sad little house, the sky filling with thunderheads.

"Okay," Sean said. "All ready." Jesse caught Sean's powerful unwashed odor as he lumbered past and cautiously negotiated the three brick steps down to the sidewalk. Usually Jesse sort of liked the smell of an honest sweat, but Sean's wasn't an honest sweat. It was a fat person's sweat, meaty and rancid, the sweat of flesh mushroom pale from sitting in that dark, closed living room watching television day after day.

He followed several paces behind as Sean made his hesitant way toward the truck. He hadn't known Donna's brother in the days when he'd been more nimble-footed than any of them, and as he gripped Sean's elbow to help steady him, those days seemed hard to imagine. Breathing heavily, Sean hoisted himself up into the cab and slid across to the middle of the seat; Jesse moved in beside him and shut the door.

They headed out toward the little plaza on the edge of town with its pizza parlor, video store, and Stone Hollow Wines and Liquors. Jesse had never wanted to be any part of what he was doing; the whole thing was Kyle's bright idea, cooked up one desperate dry afternoon several months ago, but then Kyle always had a way of talking you into just about anything, and once you were in, you were in. When Jesse'd made it clear that Donna couldn't ever know, Kyle just nodded and said, "Obviously." It hadn't taken Jesse too many seconds to see he was caught.

They parked at the far end of the plaza, over by the Dumpsters. "Here," Kyle said, reaching for a slip of paper on the dash and handing it to Sean. "Just give this to the guy. And this'll more than cover it," he said, as he slipped him a twenty. Kyle had gotten his ass busted one too many times with a fake ID, not only in Stone Hollow's only liquor store, but in all the stores around as well.

As Sean shambled toward the liquor store, the two brothers watched in silence. Kyle felt no shame; Jesse was sure of that, and he wished, at moments like this, he could be more like his brother. His whole relationship with Donna, solid and dependable as it was, seemed to him a kind of secret weakness, even a lie. But if it was a lie, then what was the truth? Jesse suspected his brother had loved Leanne, and Brenda before her, and Michelle, and any of a dozen others, ten times more than he himself had ever loved Donna, and yet Donna was the one he was going to marry, and if he married her, he was going to have to keep things like borrowing her brother a secret from her for the rest of their life together.

It made him nervous to wait—and Kyle, despite everything, was drumming his fingers on the steering wheel, though that was just impatience, not nervousness. After several minutes, Sean emerged from the store, pausing to blink in the bright sunlight, disoriented maybe, forgetting for a second or two what he was there for.

"We're over here, you dumb fuck," Kyle said under his breath as Sean looked this way and that, and Jesse suddenly had the most vivid memory: he was fifteen, running upstairs to get something from the bedroom, not pausing to think why the door might be shut, not bothering to knock, just opening it wide to find Kyle and Brenda LaVoto lying not on the top bunk but the bottom one, Jesse's bunk, Kyle with his shirt off, that gold chain she'd given him glinting against his smooth, bare chest. They weren't doing anything, just lying there together, except for Kyle's shirt both of them fully dressed, and Kyle was looking into Brenda's eyes and stroking her strawberry-blond hair. Their mom strictly enforced the No Girlfriends Allowed in the House Rule. At the time it didn't matter one whit to Jesse, in fact he secretly approved, but it was a policy he knew Kyle chafed under. Still, he hadn't thought his brother would dare defy their mom like that, and he wasn't defying her, exactly, since they all knew she'd gone off for the afternoon to Rosendale to see a cousin who was ailing; but two things shocked Jesse in the instant before he shut the door and fled back down the stairs: first, that Kyle had brought Brenda not to his own mattress but to Jesse's, which might have been more accessible, but still it was both defiling and exciting to find his brother there; and second, that Pop was down in the yard burning some old lumber, and he had to know exactly what Kyle was up to, must even be giving his approval in complete defiance of their mom's wishes, all of which the old man confirmed, as Jesse confusedly stumbled past him, by reaching out and catching him by the arm, pulling him momentarily into his orbit, the flames from his fire suddenly hot on Jesse's face as Pop winked and told him, whiskey burning on his breath, "You don't have to go and say nothing, now do you?"

"Excellent," Kyle was telling Sean, who'd come around to the driver's side to hand over the loot. Sean looked on neutrally as Kyle quickly made sure he'd gotten the right number of bottles. "Well done, my man. Now we better get you some ice cream and move you on home pronto. How's that sound, old buddy of mine?"

The Family Market was practically empty. Wearing her regulation blue smock over her pink sweatsuit, Donna stood at the cash register talking to C.J., the bag boy, a high school kid with a sly smile and short, spiked hair Jesse figured he probably dyed that coppery color. Jesse always wanted to wipe that smile off C.J.'s face; how Donna could stand him, he didn't know, but she didn't seem to mind. She was stuck with him four afternoons a week.

Her eyes narrowed as he came up to her. She'd let him know she didn't like him visiting her at work, and he wasn't too sure why he'd come. He hadn't been home two minutes before hopping in his newly repaired truck, which was still, when all was said and done, as big a piece of shit as ever.

"Can you take a cigarette break?"

She looked around the deserted store. "Cover for me," she told C.J. "I'll be back in five minutes."

"No problem," he said, still smiling that smile. He wore little gold hoop earrings in both ears. Jesse could never get over his suspicion of guys who wore earrings, no matter what you saw on MTV.

They were hardly through the automatic doors when Donna took out a cigarette.

"Let's go around back," Jesse told her.

She looked at him but said nothing, only paused to light her cigarette. Then she followed him to the loading dock. Stacks of empty six-packs awaited pickup. The odor of garbage was powerful, that smell of spilled ice cream on a hot summer's day that made Jesse faintly sick to his stomach. It smelled even worse than Donna's brother, if that was possible.

95

ONION 47—that was what some kid had spray-painted in blue and silver across the concrete block wall.

"Here, let me have a puff." He took the cigarette from her and slid it between his lips. His lungs were weak, which was why he'd never taken to smoking. Still, a nice long drag from time to time was refreshing. The nicotine went right to his head.

He felt a cough, though, form somewhere in his lungs, an insidious little tickle, and he handed Donna back the last of her smoke burned down almost to the filter.

When she stubbed out the butt against the graffitied wall, he moved in and kissed her hard on the mouth, slipping his tongue in and probing. Usually he hated the stale taste of cigarette in her mouth, but today, for some reason, it excited him.

After a minute she pulled away, but then leaned her head on his shoulder.

"Why'd you do that?"

He was a little out of breath and had the sudden ache of a woodie down his jeans. "I don't know." He wiped his mouth with the back of his hand. "I felt like it."

"You come down here just for that?"

"I guess."

"You're funny. Is that why I like you?"

"Beats me," he told her, leaving unsaid whatever else he might have said: that Kyle's taunts had put him in an evil funk; that his brain was swirling with anger toward his brother, toward Brandon, toward Sean, most of all toward Cameron Barnes, whose favor had put him in this mess. Never trust a stranger who does you favors, he told himself fiercely. You don't know where it'll land you.

I hate you, Cameron Barnes, he vowed, feeling at the same time vaguely ungenerous toward the man, who after all had meant him no harm.

Donna was looking at him strangely.

"What?" he said. (Never trust anybody, he thought, not even yourself.)

"You had such an expression on your face just then."

"Oh," he said with a shrug—or was it, in the sultry sunlight, a shiver? "It stinks back here something awful. Can't you smell it?"

TEN

"Such a gorgeous day," Max had called him to say, "and you wanted to see the mountain laurel in bloom. How about I come by and pick you up in half an hour?"

Cameron felt grateful for the interruption, having spent half the morning sitting at his drafting table, filling in the last details of the site plan for Barbara Rudd's garden. Years ago he'd devised an innovative way of indicating the individual plantings within a border; hence, his colorful pen-and-ink designs invariably looked handsome on the page, collectible as minor works of art in themselves. The current plan was no exception. Still, a certain dissatisfaction gnawed at him.

He confessed as much to Max as they drove past fields of stunted and browning corn.

"I don't know what it is, but I'm not doing my best work. The project's not difficult—the challenges are all unexceptional, but so are my solutions. Nobody needs to know this, of course. Jorge's got his own projects he's working on. And Barbara—well, Barbara just chirps with enthusiasm every time I walk her through my latest ideas. But *I* know, and I don't like it. It's like something's come loose in my brain."

"Have you talked to your doctor?"

"He's not concerned. He seems to think there're all sorts of reasons why I might be having trouble concentrating. He suggested meditation."

"Oh, good. I can just see Mr. Skeptic here meditating."

"Do you think I took a wrong turn somewhere in my life?" Cameron asked.

"What do you mean? When you stopped believing in God?"

"Hardly. But I was just thinking—maybe I made a mistake giving up my practice in New York. Maybe I sold out, and that's what's taking its revenge after all these years. Part of me looks at the trophy garden I'm doing for Barbara and her filthy rich husband and wonders, 'What's the point?'"

"Please. Leaving New York was the best thing that ever happened to you. If Dan ever did anything right, it was getting you away from Toby's ghost."

If only Max knew. But then no one knew. No one had to know.

"Dan was certainly all for the country-garden thing," Cameron admitted. "Even if it turned out he didn't much like the results. But you're right. I was dying back there. But I still wonder if I betrayed something."

"Like what? Fighting city hall for piddling little grants? Scrounging for shitty projects nobody else would even think of taking on?"

"I was thinking more about my old lofty ideals. I mean, I thought I could change the world."

"Well, you *were* an Oberlin graduate, after all."

"Plus I knew you. I'd been so thoroughly indoctrinated in all that socialist optimism. But I really did think that things like good urban design—playgrounds for the inner city, that kind of thing—could actually, possibly, maybe make a difference."

"Cameron, hello? The seventies are finished, sweetie. Kaput. We've all changed, and changed again. We're sailing into a new century. If I had my way, Bill Clinton would be president forever. Surprising, I know. But guess what? If I'm a Volvo liberal these days, it's because I actually happen to like my Volvo."

"That still doesn't make me happy with this fucking garden. I wish I could make something like that garden Derek Jarman built. The one in the shadow of a nuclear power plant. Just stones and rusted metal and driftwood, beachcomber stuff, and whatever tough native plants would grow. But it was so beautiful. Just stark and elemental. I'll never do that kind of garden."

What would've happened, he wondered, had Mrs. Waddeston taken him to Dungeness instead of Hidcote that fateful day? But that garden hadn't existed then. Jarman had only begun it after he got sick with AIDS, and there'd been no AIDS that lovely day Mrs. Waddeston had taken Cameron to Hidcote.

"Dan and I've been talking fairly regularly, by the way. I thought I'd mention that. He says he's going to come up for my garden party. I'm thinking that'll be a good thing."

"I hate the thought of him continuing to torment you."

"Actually, I enjoy his phone calls."

"You don't have to lie to me," Max said.

"If I'm lying," Cameron told him, "then I don't know it."

He had the vague sense that Dan had started seeing someone in New York, though he hadn't asked. He had no desire, these days, to torment himself unnecessarily with anything.

"Oh," Max said as they rounded a curve, "those are absolutely the best kind of lies." Ahead lay a lake, a hill, a stone house he'd passed any number of times, but which had recently become oddly imbued—but with what? The house could use some attention. NO JOB TOO LARGE OR SMALL had been the motto on the side of Bill's panel truck. Odd that the old man and his sons had never put their carpentry skills to good use close to home. Perhaps some jobs were too large after all.

Cars lined both sides of the road, and for a moment Cameron imagined the Vanderhofs were having some kind of party. Then he saw the sign, a spray-painted half sheet of plywood set against a tree trunk. YARD SALE/SAT.-SUN., it announced.

Several tables were heaped high with items. Dozens of rusted farm implements lay displayed about the lawn. A sign on a large window frame, most of its panes missing, read, "Pitcher Window $20."

"Looks like the Vanderhofs are downsizing," Max said, easing his Volvo in behind an Audi with New Jersey plates. "I think this is something we definitely want to investigate."

Let's not, Cameron wanted to tell him—but how to voice that groundless qualm? It was just a yard sale, after all. Nevertheless, he felt suddenly nervous, as if he were about to embark on some kind of trespass. He looked around for evidence of either of the brothers, but they were nowhere in sight—though he thought that might be poor Jesse's truck parked under the spreading catalpa. Creamy petals from the tree's blooming candles had fallen onto the hood, a litter of bright beauty.

Chained to a stake, an unhappy black mongrel barked its heart out at no one in particular. A stern-looking, gray-haired woman he presumed was the brothers' mother sat in a folding chair and smoked a cigarette with impressive concentration. "Hello," he told her as they approached, but she only looked him over impassively, then stared away into the distance and continued to smoke. Could she tell he'd gazed on her sons with lust? But of course she had no idea who he was—just another outsider not worth giving the time of day to. Several couples—weekenders all, he thought—picked through the bounty on the tables: hand drills, wood chisels, saws, a scythe, old bottles in green, clear, and cobalt, glass insulators, several crude duck decoys, a set of thoroughly rusted andirons, suitcases of every size and color and variety. "Our old man's a pack rat" had been practically the first thing Jesse had volunteered.

On another table lay stacks of folded clothes. Fingering a faded flannel shirt, its cream-colored tartan cross-barred with yellows and greens and blues, he realized, with a hollow feeling, that these clothes must have belonged to Bill. It was too sad, really, to see the dead man's belongings dispensed like this. Was the family really that hard up for cash, or was it just too painful to keep these reminders? When Toby had died, he hadn't been able to clear out his closet for nearly a year, and even years later, no doubt to poor Dan's consternation, he continued to hoard any number of useless old rags: an olive green, sleeveless T-shirt, a pair of black spandex bike pants, a very worn, very grungy pair of cutoff jeans.

At a nearby table, looking plump and rosy-cheeked—or was that a bit of sunburn?—stood Andrew Hackett. He held a large tote bag that said SAVE THE EARTH, into which he was mechanically dropping items without much more than glancing at them. "Can you believe it?" he said, keeping his voice low. "They might as well be giving some of this stuff away. I mean, a lot of it's junk, but some of it—well, I've already filled up the trunk of my car. I should've brought my van."

Cameron watched as Andrew picked up a time-blackened duck decoy and inspected it. "Five dollars," he read aloud from the tag. "I can sell it for three hundred at least."

Cameron tried to quell a momentary flash of revulsion, remembering the many times he'd enjoyed browsing in Andrew's shop, The Pale Horse, in Weed's Mill Falls; he'd even bought a thing or two over the years—culled, no doubt, from yard sales depressingly like this one.

He saw it clearly: how his own house, so lovingly restored, full of sought-out period pieces, would eventually be dispersed into the hands of Andrew or someone even less tenderly disposed. Only last week he'd driven past a garden he'd laid out for a couple from Manhattan—one of the first he'd done in the country. He knew the place had changed hands recently; what he hadn't expected was to see his great curving perennial beds replaced with a new swath of lawn, his billowing privacy screen of groundsel bush ripped out in favor of a stark wooden fence.

Its engine gunning violently, a gray pickup truck rushed the slope of the hill and came to an abrupt stop under the tree next to Jesse's. Almost before the motor was turned off, both doors of the cab swung open and the two brothers carelessly flung themselves out. Cameron stifled the ludicrous impulse to hide. Failing that, he took a few steps away from Andrew, as if it were possible at this late, too late, moment to distance himself from his scavenging acquaintance. But if the brothers saw him, they gave no indication. Kyle dropped to one knee in front of the black dog, which immediately ceased its ferocious barking and nuzzled him greedily. Jesse looked around as if confused by the spectacle of so many strangers milling about his front yard. He hooked his fingers in the belt loops of his jeans (he never seemed to wear a belt) and surveyed the scene.

Thinking their eyes had met, Cameron nodded his way in greeting—foolishly, he thought, catching himself instantly. But Andrew had seen the gesture.

"Friend of yours?" he wondered, pausing to adjust his glasses in a way that struck Cameron, for the first time, as insufferably affected.

"Hardly. He's doing some renovation work for me. He lives here."

"I see. Hunky little number."

With some alarm, Cameron saw that Jesse was sauntering their way.

"Did you see Max?" Cameron said, anxious to extricate himself. "He's around here somewhere. He'd like to say hi, I'm sure."

"Oh, Max I see all the time." Andrew wagged a finger Cameron's way. "It's you I never see. How've you been doing, sister?"

"Fine," Cameron told him hastily, just as Jesse came within earshot. "I'm doing great."

"I'm really glad to hear that. We were all so worried about you this spring. That nasty—"

"Hey," interrupted Jesse, that soul of eloquence and genius of timing.

Cameron realized he was still holding that sad flannel shirt.

"Great stuff you've got here," Andrew told Jesse with something like a smirk, but the young man just stared at him, whether with hostility or just blankness, Cameron couldn't tell. Andrew, however, seemed a little nonplussed.

"Well, nice to see you, Cameron," he said, putting his hand affectionately on Cameron's arm. "I'll be seeing you around."

"Come to my party," Cameron heard himself say, in spite of himself. "You'll be getting an invitation in the mail."

"Love to," Andrew said, his attention attracted by a large porcelain chamber pot on the next table. "I presume Daryl's invited as well?"

"Of course," Cameron told him, sharply conscious of having entirely given himself away—if he hadn't long before. "An old acquaintance, I haven't seen him in years," he explained to Jesse, who stood there looking at nothing in particular, it seemed, and who said nothing for the longest time.

Cameron hesitated, wanting somehow to apologize. But for what? He could see Kyle moving off toward the house, the black dog following avidly, both unaware how the treasury was being looted right under their noses.

"You like that shirt?" Jesse asked.

"This was all your dad's stuff?"

"We got no use for it. Just taking up space. My mom was worried the attic was about to cave in. She was always on Pop about that, but he never did anything."

Cameron wondered if he should mention to Jesse what Andrew had said about the prices, but Jesse kept talking.

"My uncle Roy and her had a disagreement about selling, but it's her stuff now. She just wants to get rid of it. My brother took Pop's watch and his guns, so he's happy. I got his pocketknife, which is a really good pocketknife. Swiss Army." Fumbling in his pocket, he produced his inheritance, then proceeded to fan out the various useful or absurd blades and gadgets.

"Nice," Cameron said, thinking, You dumb fuck, you sort of break my heart.

It was just a thought.

As if afraid somebody might scold him for displaying it, Jesse collapsed the blades and slid the sleek contraption back in his pocket. Up by the house, the black dog had somehow caught on to Andrew. It crouched in attack position, barking wildly while Andrew bravely brandished his tote bag full of loot to fend off the impending lunge.

"Poke," Kyle yelled harshly. "Get your ass over here now, you fucking moron."

But Poke wasn't budging.

The mother—the Vic of *Bilvic*—had risen from her chair and was bearing down on the standoff. "I told you not to let that dog loose," she said. "Why don't you listen to me?"

"The dog don't like the fucking chain," Kyle said, seizing Poke by his collar and hauling him violently away. "There," he said. "No harm done."

As if not quite believing him, she stood at a distance and took a drag on her cigarette. "And you, mister," she said to Andrew. "No harm done?"

"Oh, no. No harm at all." Andrew held up his tote bag crammed with valuables. "I think I'll pay you for these now."

"That damn dog," Jesse told Cameron, who watched as Andrew backed warily away. "Nobody can touch him hardly except Kyle. He'd of taken your friend out if he'd seen half the chance."

"My friend there," Cameron said, "is wilier than you might think. He probably deserves to get bitten now and then."

Jesse cast a sideways glance his direction. "I'm glad we was both rooting for the dog," he said dryly. "Now—you gonna take that shirt? It's yours. My gift to you."

"Really—I couldn't. I've got too many shirts in my closet as it is."

"I owe you. I can't pay back a penny yet. My damn truck ate every last bit of it."

Cameron waved his hand dismissively. "Don't worry about the money. We can always work something out."

"It's a deal, then." Unexpectedly, Jesse extended his hand. His palm was dry, his grip steady. For no longer than was absolutely necessary, the two of them shook on their deal—whatever, exactly, it was.

"Well," Max observed once they were back on the road, "that looks like a fine shirt."

"I feel bad," Cameron confessed, "but he seemed intent on my having it. Why do I have the sense the Vanderhofs are getting robbed blind back there?"

Max had bought an old toolbox, its wood polished almost to velvet by time and the oils of human hands; a tin coal scuttle with elegantly fluted sides; what looked like an old Shaker basket, though it was hard to tell. Andrew would undoubtedly know.

"Things are only worth the price you can get for them," Max said. "Business rule number one. Anyways, folks like those probably need the cash a lot more than they need a bunch of useless old stuff lying around. I take no satisfaction in seeing the ruin of the local folk, not even the Vanderhofs, but I'm also realistic. They're dinosaurs. Their time has come and gone."

They'd begun their steep ascent into the Shawangunks. Heart-stopping views opened up of the Hudson Valley placidly sunning itself down below. A sense of futility seized Cameron. Somewhere down there that yard sale continued to accuse him. His whole life had been mired in possessions, yet the happiest he'd ever been, it seemed to him now, was when he and Toby had spent three months backpacking through Greece and Turkey with nothing but two days' change of clothes and the nearly infinite hopefulness of youth. How had he lost something so precious as that? But he had. Time had taken all that in its fist and crumpled it to nothing.

Then they were on the crest of the ridge. Beneath the canopy of pines and oak, ghostly fire in the shade, the mountain laurel was blooming just as it used to bloom in the Smoky Mountains, years ago, when he was a boy and his family would vacation in Gatlinburg for a week in June.

"It makes me wonder about the old man," he told Max, "collecting all that junk over the years. And for what? Do you think he imagined he'd make a fortune off it one day?"

Max shrugged. "Who knows why anybody does what they do? Bill Vanderhof was a crank and a drunk and probably a little mad to boot. I always liked him. He was sort of the black sheep of that family. It's too bad he's gone. His boys must be pretty broken up."

"I guess. It's a little hard to tell. They're not very emotive. It's strange, though. I sort of wish I'd met Bill."

"The younger son there seemed pretty emotive. Quite eager to chat you up, in fact," Max teased.

"He's a nice enough kid," Cameron allowed, conscious of withholding, for some time now, anything of his dealings with the brothers. With some consternation, he realized that he had no intention whatsoever of telling Max a thing about the money he'd lent—or bestowed, rather, since that was what, on the spur of the moment back there, he seemed rather grandly to have done. Max wouldn't understand, or would understand too well, and Cameron was all at once intent on having his little secret. It would just be between the two of them—or the three of them, he supposed, if Jesse had told his brother about it. But why did he get the feeling Jesse had been silent on the subject as well? He couldn't know for sure, of course, but the thought stirred him.

They had arrived at Minnewaska, the mountaintop lake. From the parking lot, to the northwest, beyond miles of patchwork fields, the Catskills appeared a purplish rampart against the cloudless sky. He took in the view gratefully, though at the same time he was aware of brown spots floating before his eyes. He tried to make them go away, to see through them or past them, but the more he tried, the more maddeningly aware of them he became. And this would never go away. Never again would he see a range of mountains in the distance with the undistracted clarity he used to.

The doctor really had diagnosed the problem correctly, hadn't he? The spots seemed to be getting worse—or was it just that he'd become fixated on them? Stay calm, he told himself. This isn't CMV, you're not going to go blind.

Out in the middle of the air, several turkey vultures hung nearly motionless, borne effortlessly upward on thermals. He had the momentary, disconcerting notion they'd all come directly from the Vanderhof yard sale, their bellies full from feasting on the carcass.

For a Saturday, the picnic area was strangely deserted. Several Indian families, the women beautifully garbed from head to foot in colorful saris, the men pudgy and anxious-looking, occupied several tables. In violation of park rules, a boom box pulsated with a raga full of passionate yearning. Beyond, artfully framed by wind-tortured pines, lay the sparkling lake. Vertical limestone cliffs, slumped catastrophically here and there, ringed the azure water. They used to come here all the time, he and Dan and Max and Perry, to drink wine, even though it wasn't allowed, and watch shirtless boys from New Jersey throw Frisbees or make out with their girlfriends. That hadn't been allowed either, no doubt, but they'd done it anyway. A couple of miles up the trail had been that secluded spot where the Peterskill sluiced over a broad sheet of rock, and on weekends in summer as many as twenty or thirty gay men could be seen sunbathing in the raw, or cruising, or giving handsome strangers blow jobs amidst the stunted pines and blueberry bushes that grew out of meager soil pockets in the stone.

These days, if Max was to be believed, handsome strangers sat on the rocks and read *Ivanhoe*. Cameron had a blind date scheduled, in fact, with that very stranger. Not at Broken Rock—no, it was too far, and too steeply uphill, for him even to consider hiking there anymore—though perhaps, he thought, there was an idea. If things turned bad again—which, sooner or later (how could he kid himself?) they would—he might just drive up here one afternoon, walk the trail as far as he could, then wander off into the underbrush, perhaps find a perch on a rock spectacularly overlooking the Rondout Valley and, in the distance, the sun-dappled Catskills. Some pills, a little Stoli . . .

"Hey, Max," he said as they strolled along the top of the cliff. From the little swimming area below came the ecstatic shouts of boys splashing each other. "Will you promise me something?"

"Anything, sweetie."

"When I die, and you have me cremated, bring a few of the ashes up here for me. Will you do that?"

Max looked at him with a tenderness that made him want to cry, though he'd hardly intended the moment to be so serious—it was just a notion that had occurred to him, more a lark than anything else.

"Oh, honey, of course I'll do that."

"Most of me goes under the lilacs, next to the cats," he reminded his old friend. "But a little of me, I think, I'd like to be up here."

ELEVEN

Wearing a wide-brimmed straw hat that made him look ridiculous, their employer stood before the test patches of paint he'd dabbed on the walls of the shed. "I think this one," he said. "What do you think?"

Kyle looked away like he was bored. Jesse felt somebody had to speak. "Go for it," he said.

Painting was pretty much all there was left to do; then they'd get the rest of their money and be done with it. Not that they had anything else lined up, and no lawns to mow either. It was looking to be a pretty parched summer on all accounts.

"Twilight gray," Cameron read aloud from the label on the paint can. "My shed will be twilight gray. I like that. And for the trim, we should definitely go with forest mist. From the garden, you'll hardly even notice this little structure. Not that it needs to be embarrassed, now that it's got a second lease on life."

Jesse felt embarrassed for him, a little—the way he carried on. He wouldn't be too sorry to see the last of Cameron Barnes.

"We can pick up the paint tomorrow on the way in," Kyle said. "We got plenty to keep us busy today. I still need to hang the door and reglaze the windows. Jesse can start moving your stuff back inside. We're pretty much through in there."

"My *stuff.*" Cameron went over and lifted the edge of the blue tarp. "I've got way too much stuff. Whatever would the Buddha say? I should have a yard sale like you guys did." He sighed, standing with his hands on his hips and looking vaguely perplexed. "Oh, go ahead, put it all back in the shed. I'll deal with it later. Which means I'll never deal with it." Turning abruptly on his heel, he stalked off toward the house, and Jesse watched him for a moment, suddenly struck by how strange everything was. But that passed as quickly as it came, and when Cameron, midway through the garden, called back to the two of them to say, "I'm going out for a while, I'll be back in a couple of hours," everything had returned completely to normal.

Pulling the tarp aside, Jesse gazed down at the assembly of old chairs, side tables, lamps minus their shades, stuff not exactly like Pop's, but similar enough. Their mom was already talking about selling the house, moving someplace new—she was tired of living with broken-down things, and in a house as old as theirs, for every one thing you fixed, two more broke down. "I've been thinking of one of those modular homes, like your uncle Roy has," she'd told him and Kyle.

Jesse wondered how things would change, living somewhere new. He'd miss the pond, the woods—stuff Pop had cared for. Their mom was an indoors person, mostly; she liked her TV, her phone, her cigarettes. With those, she'd be just fine wherever she was living. Kyle never said a word about her plans—he just listened. Once, when they lay in bed, Kyle on the top bunk, himself on the lower, he'd asked his brother what he thought, but Kyle only said, "She'll do what she wants to do. And I sure don't got the money right now to do different."

Jesse picked up a wooden chest and carried it into the shed. They'd done a good job, he thought with satisfaction; the result was nice and sturdy, the roof watertight. He could see Kyle's face framed in the window as he carefully squeezed out a line of caulk along the mullions. The day before, he'd replaced three panes that had broken out. Jesse had the sudden image in his head of that whiskey bottle tossed against the limestone, how it had shattered in splinters of light. Unaware he was being observed, Kyle worked with lip-biting concentration. These past several weeks, Jesse had sensed him winding tighter and tighter; he knew it was a lot of things on his brother's mind, things Kyle had no interest in talking to anybody about, and though he knew what some of them were, he also knew that with Kyle there was always more than you thought.

He brought in another piece of furniture, and another, stacking them neatly against the back wall. Stepping back to study the arrangement, he decided to turn one chair upside down and fit it, jigsaw-wise, on top of another. The chest, he saw, could go underneath the chairs. There'd be plenty of space left over if he paid attention to how things went together.

A rap on the window drew him from his calculations. Kyle was gesturing him to come outside.

"Let's go up to the house," his brother told him.

"What for?"

"Come on. Barnes is long gone. The coast is clear."

Jesse felt a queasy pang, but he followed his brother through the busily blooming garden and up the steps of the back stoop.

"See?" Kyle turned the doorknob. "I didn't figure he'd lock his door."

They'd been in the house before, of course. They'd waited in the kitchen while Cameron advanced them some cash. At the time, Jesse had mostly been struck by the absence of new appliances: the refrigerator had the kind of rounded edges old cars used to; the sink was this massive thing that stood on thick legs; the stove looked to be cast iron, a little like one stored in their barn, though not rusted like that. On the old green hutch in the corner, the paint was peeling. How strange and pointless for somebody with money to be living with all those out-of-date contraptions.

"Um, what are we doing here?" he asked. It felt like the time they'd found a mine opening and eased themselves in. It seemed wrong, even dangerous, to be standing in Cameron's kitchen with him not there. From the refrigerator Kyle took a plastic jug of water—the good water, as Cameron had told them—which he uncapped and lifted to his lips. Their mom was always getting on Kyle for drinking milk straight from the carton, but since no one else was around, Jesse followed his brother's lead. He'd somehow expected bottled water to taste so much better than ordinary water from the tap, but disappointingly the only difference was a kind of plastic aftertaste. Kyle, meanwhile, was nosing around like a raccoon, opening cabinets, pulling out drawers, taking a look in the freezer, sniffing out whatever he might be able to find.

"I always wanted to do this," he explained.

Jesse had to admit to being intrigued. The trespass felt oddly exciting. He'd wondered what the rest of the house looked like, how somebody like Cameron lived. They'd entered the living room, its walls painted a deep blue, the moldings and doors and fireplace mantel a dazzling white—a weird color to paint the walls, but Jesse could just see Cameron with his test patches, patiently searching for exactly the right shade. What a faggot, he couldn't help but think. And now here he was in his house.

Along the mantel marched a series of little white busts, and Jesse was disturbed by a crazy urge to send them flying with the back of his hand. But why did he take against them so, innocuous things that they were? He turned away to cast his gaze on the rest of the room, the old-fashioned, uncomfortable-looking sofa with dark wood framing the velvety upholstery, a pair of rickety, black-and-gold, cane-bottomed chairs. A large painting in a gold frame showed a whitish gray horse, and at its feet a surprised-looking little beagle.

Underfoot, the wide boards of the floor creaked.

On a low table lay stacks of books, and he picked one up gingerly, a picture book, black-and-white photos. In one, an Arab-type kid squatted and smoked a cigarette. In another, two shirtless boys stood, one with his arm around the other, against a mud wall. They wore tiny bathing suits, almost nonexistent. As if he'd been stung, he quickly replaced the heavy volume where he'd found it.

The white busts on the mantel again caught his eye, and he thought of all the stuffed animals lined up on Donna's dresser.

Sterile and pointless—that's what gays were. A dead end. Maybe that was what gave them time to worry over what exact fucking shade of gray to paint a shed.

Kyle had already moved to the next room, and Jesse followed. Here the walls were a dark, sumptuous red, and it was like moving from one mood to another—it could catch you off guard if you weren't prepared. Another hutch, this one fine as opposed to battered, displayed dozens of blue-and-white platters with pagodas and fishing boats and little men with fishing poles. On the big dining room table, a green bowl filled with purplish plums rested above its reflection in the polished wood. Jesse knew expensive when he saw it. The antiques in this unlocked house were worth a quiet little fortune.

The thought occurred to him that maybe all this was a trap; their employer was testing them, watching through binoculars from a distance.

"I don't like this," he told his brother.

Kyle, though, was mounting the stairs. He looked back and said, "Relax, will you? Jeez."

"What if he's setting us up?"

"Will you give me a fucking break?"

Resisting an urge to glance out the window just to be sure, Jesse reluctantly followed his brother up the narrow stairs.

It was hard to tell, at a glance, which bedroom was Cameron's—none of them looked particularly slept-in. Still, the TV and VCR were a giveaway, Jesse thought, and Kyle must have thought so too. "I wouldn't want to know what goes on in *that* bed." He pointed dismissively at the big four-poster affair—though Jesse felt at once pretty certain that nothing much went on there except for sleep and maybe dreaming. Not that he cared. Still, wasn't it awfully lonely living alone in a big place like this, more a museum than a house, everything neatly in place, no stray nothing anywhere (a Mexican cleaning lady came once a week; he'd seen her arrive and depart in her rusted-out Buick). Through the wavy glass of the curtainless window he could see the colorful garden spread out below, its design clear from this height, its radiating flagstone paths, its patios and benches and birdbaths—and down at the far end, a bright yellow splash soon to be gray and invisible, the little shed.

In the absence of anybody to care for, Cameron had made all that. He spent hours tending it. And for what?

Kyle had opened the closet to reveal clothes hanging neatly, shoes lined up on the floor. "If there ain't at least one dress and high heels in here, I'm gonna be disappointed," he said.

Cameron hadn't lied when he said he had a lot of clothes. Kyle thumbed through them purposefully. With alarm, Jesse saw Pop's shirt hanging in there among the rest, but Kyle flipped on by it without seeming to notice.

"You think he dresses up by himself at night and prances around the house?" Jesse felt impelled to say, if for no other reason than to draw attention away from what could look, to some eyes, like incriminating evidence. But incriminating who? What had he been thinking when he gave that old shirt away?

"I have no doubt," Kyle told him. "I think I even seen him one night when I drove by. He looked so fetching I told Leanne she'd better worry."

Jesse echoed his brother's snicker. He knew Kyle and Leanne were going great guns once again: the way they were with each other was like a flock of birds in air, expanding and contracting, defying logic with a logic all its own. Secretly he was glad. It made him nervous when his brother was unattached for too long.

"And what do we have here?" Kyle wondered. It made Jesse's heart jump, but then he saw his brother was finished with the clothes and on to other quarry. He'd pulled out a shiny metal pole. It took Jesse a moment to figure out what he was looking at. The last time he'd seen one of those was by Pop's bedside; the morphine drip had been hanging from it.

"That's strange," Kyle said, returning the stand to the back of the closet. "I wonder what kind of kinky stuff happens with that." He rummaged for a second, then held out another find. He shook the big plastic container; you could hear the rattle of pills. "This guy's really into his vitamins. He's got like a ton of stuff stashed back here. Look—needles. You think he's some kind of drug addict? Wouldn't that take the fucking cake?"

Jesse tried to fight back the sense they'd stumbled on something unfathomable, the kind of thing you were sure to find when you went looking where you had no business.

Kyle's laugh was like a gunshot. "Oh, now. Bingo. The treasure trove."

From the shelf above the clothes rod, he'd plucked a videocassette. "Check it out," he said, handing it to Jesse. *Cuming of Age* read the label on the spine.

"Well, I'll be," Kyle went on merrily.

"Gross," Jesse said in alarm. "Take this thing away from me."

"He's sure got lots of them. Magazines too." Pulling one from the pile, Kyle opened it up, then turned to show the spread to Jesse. A naked young fellow squatted over another guy's huge woodie, impaling himself on it with a surprised, pained look.

Jesse felt himself flush with shame and anger.

"Like what you see, little brother?" Kyle teased.

"You're the pervert," Jesse told him, "not me. I never wanted to set foot in here."

"Admit it. It's making you hard." With an abrupt lunge, Kyle groped him roughly with one hand—but Jesse wasn't hard. Why on earth should he be? Maybe earlier, a little, when they'd first started their expedition, but not now.

"Keep your motherfucking hands off me," he warned his brother. "You need to get serious help."

Kyle laughed wildly. "Okay," he said, "so I was wrong about you. But this is some shit." He stooped to retrieve the magazine. Leafing through its pages, he shook his head. "Amazing. Our dude is some sick cookie to be liking this shit."

"This is really starting to bore me," Jesse said with some urgency. "Let's get out of here." He'd seen enough to make him feel thoroughly ill; he couldn't wait for sunlight and fresh air.

"Sure," Kyle said, returning the magazine to its shelf. "I'm going to take a piss. Then I'll be right down."

Jesse started down the stairs, but he wasn't halfway to the landing before he heard his brother call, in a strained voice, "Hey, Jesse. Come back here for a sec."

In the narrow bathroom, Kyle was standing in front of a little wicker table wedged between toilet and sink. He studied a brown, plastic pill bottle he cradled in his palm.

"What?" Jesse said, but Kyle didn't answer. He set the bottle back in its place and picked up another, then another from the cluster on the table.

"You know," he said in a serious voice, "I'm thinking maybe we shouldn't of drunk outta that water jug in the fridge."

"What're you talking about?"

"I think this guy has bad news, Jesse. I think he's got AIDS or something."

"I don't think you can get it from drinking from the same glass," Jesse said automatically, trying to remember that presentation from school (they'd all spent too much time cracking nervous jokes to pay any real attention).

"I'm not too worried about that," Kyle said. And neither was Jesse. A different kind of dread burrowed its cold way into him. For the second time this summer, here it was—the thing you couldn't argue your way out of, couldn't beg or barter or pretend once it caught you in its grip. It was worse than the truth that way. He felt his face go hot; clammy droplets of sweat seeped from his armpits to trickle down his rib cage. He should've known, he thought. A gay guy—of course he'd have AIDS. Anybody'd be mentally insane to want to be gay in this day and age.

The startling picture stayed in his head: that young guy no older than himself letting some dude shove that big thing up his butt. Why would a fellow let something like that happen to him? Even if it didn't give you a fatal disease, it must hurt like hell. Had Cameron done that kind of thing? He must have, if he was sick. And not just sick, Jesse told himself, but dying.

He wondered at all those medicines left out like that, for anybody to see. Wasn't the guy ashamed? Or—the thought occurred to him again, he didn't know why—had Cameron maybe wanted him and Kyle to find out? Had he known the temptation to come in the house when he wasn't there would be just too much to resist?

But that was crazy, he told himself.

He didn't know why he felt sorry for the guy all of a sudden. Cameron had gone and brought it on himself; nobody'd ever made him do whatever the things were he'd done. All the same, it was so fucking lonely in this big, empty house. The thought of the guy living here all alone, facing the fact that he was going to die and all the pills in the world couldn't save him—it seemed to Jesse, strangely enough, that he of all people knew exactly how Cameron Barnes must feel.

"Hey, buddy," Kyle said softly. "You still awake?" Above his head, Jesse could hear Kyle's mattress creak as he shifted position. The sound always comforted him. Those nights Kyle wasn't there, for one reason or another, he'd lie awake till all hours at the mercy of thoughts his brother's presence somehow managed to keep at bay. He worried, sometimes, what would happen if Kyle ever got serious about somebody and moved out on his own. He worried what was going to happen when their mom sold the house like she said she was going to do.

"Yeah," he told his brother. "I'm still awake."

"I've been thinking . . ." But then Kyle didn't say anything more. Jesse had been thinking too, his brain in tumult all day long, in fact. They hadn't either of them said a word on leaving Cameron's house. They'd walked back to the shed, silent like something had spooked or embarrassed them, and Kyle had turned the radio on loud, to keep away from them whatever it was, and they'd worked straight through till they were done for the day. They'd left before Cameron came back.

Jesse broke the long silence: "We shouldn't never of gone in there."

"I had to find out. I had to make sure." Again, Kyle shifted his weight.

He was lying on his side, Jesse imagined, propped on his elbow, just like that day he'd found him with Brenda LaVoto.

"It was something you were thinking?" The thought, honestly, had never occurred to Jesse. For somebody who was so sick, Cameron didn't look it—not like Pop, certainly.

"Maybe," Kyle admitted. "The thought had definitely occurred to me."

"It wasn't fair."

"You know I was just fucking around when I said he liked you."

Jesse tensed. He lay motionless on his back, staring at the bottom of his brother's mattress above him. As a kid he'd been afraid, sometimes, the bunk bed would collapse and he'd be crushed beneath its weight. That was the kind of laughable thing he used to worry about—before he grew up to the real worries.

"Did I piss you off?" Kyle wondered.

"You go on sometimes. I'm used to it."

"Like I said, I was just fucking around. Me and Brandon, we get that way. Don't think nothing of it."

"I don't," Jesse lied.

"But I been thinking. We got a situation here that's changing all the time. What do you say to that?"

"Okay," Jesse said cautiously.

"Well . . ." Kyle paused, and Jesse waited. Downstairs, the toilet flushed. He listened to the storm of water fill the pipes. Kyle held off till it finished and the house was once again dead quiet. "I think he does like you," he said quietly. "Whatever his reasons. Like I said: no reflection on you. I'm just thinking out loud here. Understand what I'm saying?"

"Okay." Jesse waited for his brother to spring whatever he was going to.

"Now what if . . ." Kyle's voice trailed off into silence.

"What if what?"

"You never told me he gave you money for your truck."

So Brandon must have witnessed that after all. A quiet dread moved through Jesse. "He didn't give it to me," he explained to Kyle. "It was a loan. I'll pay him back." His voice betrayed him, of course; he could hear it plainly, and he knew Kyle could too.

But the lie didn't seem to worry Kyle, exactly. "He's awfully free with his money, don't you think?"

"I guess. He offered, I took him up on it."

"Exactly," Kyle told him. Jesse felt a sudden shift of weight; saw his brother's legs swing down from the bunk. Before he knew it, Kyle was squatting on the floor beside his mattress. "Are you thinking what I'm thinking?" he said. His face might be in the shadows, but Jesse could sense his brother peering at him intently, studying him for all he was worth. And how much was that? For the moment, Kyle seemed to think it might be a lot.

"If you think I'm going after some homo, you're fucking crazy."

"Not going after," Kyle said. "I'm just thinking this is maybe worth, I don't know, worth pursuing, you might say. I mean, just to see what happens."

"There's nothing that's going to happen. Period. That's final."

"I don't mean anything's got to happen. But look. The guy's loaded. We know that. Far as I can tell, he ain't got family, he ain't got much of nobody. And it looks like he's facing some pretty deep shit. Maybe he could use somebody being friendly toward him. Maybe he'd be grateful of that person."

"Then why don't you go and be his friend?"

"Like I said, Jesse, you're the one I think he likes. I can tell. Brandon could tell. And I get the feeling you don't half hate him. I mean, you could stand to be around him some, couldn't you?"

Brandon's as full of shit as they come, Jesse wanted to tell Kyle, only he didn't dare.

Kyle's voice was warm and sympathetic, the kind of tone that drew you into his circle of light. "Think about it." He touched Jesse's bare shoulder in the dark, a contact that made Jesse jump. "What is it they say? Grab the moment and shake it up? Think family, Jesse. We need you right now. And you don't need to go anywhere you don't want to go. Up ahead, you see the road looking iffy, then you just stop and pull back. Easy enough. I trust you in this, Jesse. You're my brother. I love you, man. Who else can I trust?"

Jesse didn't think he believed in heaven, but he had the weird sense, just then, of their old man peering down. What the look on his face might be, what was in his head, Jesse couldn't tell. But he definitely felt that more than just him and Kyle was in the room right then, and it spooked him a little. Tomorrow was their last day on the job. Maybe there was other work. Maybe Cameron needed somebody to help out in that garden of his. He'd mentioned he was giving a party, hadn't he?

He wondered if Pop knew the secret things Cameron Barnes was soon to find out all by himself.

"I don't like this," he told Kyle, whose hand still rested on his shoulder, a comfort and a burden both. "But I'll go with it if it's what you want. I'll see what happens. Just remember—it's your idea, not mine. So if you ever call me a faggot, I'll kill you. I'll slit your throat in the middle of the night while you're sound asleep and you won't ever be the wiser."

"I have no doubt of that," Kyle told him, taking away his hand. He stood up, and Jesse could see the ghostly stripes of his boxers in the dark. "In fact, little brother, I'll deserve it."

PART TWO

The Chaos Garden

TWELVE

He'd showered and shaved. After far too much consideration, he'd put on a white shirt and light-colored slacks. He'd even dabbed on a bit of cologne. How long since he'd done that?

Cameron's heart fell the instant he walked into Zanzibar. There in the corner, alone at a table for two, sat a middle-aged man in a lemon-yellow polo shirt, its collar turned up, an affectation he'd always detested. The man wore plaid shorts, loafers with no socks. Horn-rimmed glasses perched fussily on his nose. What on earth had Max been thinking? Surely after a quarter of a century he knew Cameron better than that. Or did Max now think his case so dire he'd settle for anything?

If this is a joke . . . , he told himself as the man looked up, looked past him, smiled at someone who had just come in. A slim, chic, well-tanned woman moved past Cameron as the man rose to greet her with a kiss.

She turned, and Cameron recognized her. "Barbara," he said. "Nice to see you."

"Oh, Cameron. How lovely. This is my husband, Bernard."

"Pleased to meet you," said Bernard.

"Cameron's doing our garden," Barbara reminded him.

"Ah, yes."

"Bernard couldn't care less," Barbara said. "Don't take it personally. *I* think it's looking fabulous, and that's what counts."

"Thank you," Cameron told her, wondering how she could tell anything at this early stage. His crew had barely commenced with the blue-stone paths and patio. They hadn't even begun to build the retaining walls that would give a pleasing shape to the whole. And the plantings were a full month away.

"Keep up the good work," said Bernard.

Cameron wished, sometimes, he were the kind of person who said things he'd later have to regret. But he was far too well trained for that, bestowing instead his most ingratiating smile on his employers.

His own date was sitting at the bar talking to Max, who waved him over.

"Meet Elliot." In an instant Cameron forgave Max, though he still didn't know why he'd allowed his friend to talk him into such folly. Elliot Shore was, at first glance, entirely plausible, even mildly thrilling—dressed all in black (T-shirt, jeans, sneakers), a trim man of thirty-five or forty, with long salt-and-pepper hair pulled back in a ponytail. Cameron had always liked long hair, though Toby had never worn his in a ponytail.

"Hey, good-looking." Elliot thrust out his hand. "I've heard so much about you."

"If it's from Max, it's all lies," Cameron said, more for Max's benefit than for Elliot's. He didn't want his friend to think he was taking any of this too seriously, though he did, at the moment, feel oddly grateful that this handsome man had wanted to meet him.

"You two," Max said. "Go on over and sit down. Get to know each other. It's a date, after all."

"Yes, Mother," Elliot told him as they moved off to a table by the window. "He's so quaint, don't you think?"

"Starry-eyed romantic. It's amazing, after all these years."

"And you?"

"I'm hardly starry-eyed about anything anymore," Cameron said.

Elliot leaned close. "CMV?" he asked confidentially.

"No, no," Cameron said, slightly taken aback. "My eyesight's fine."

"That's good to hear. So's mine. And my appetite. So what's good here? I've only had the spinach salad for lunch."

Cameron scanned the all-too-familiar menu, regretting they hadn't arranged to meet elsewhere, perhaps in Kingston or New Paltz. He could see their matchmaker at the bar, ostentatiously pretending to ignore them. "Mostly it's tofu tarted up to look like meat," he told Elliot. "Something I'll never understand about vegetarian restaurants in this country. There're all these fabulous meatless cuisines out there in the world, but all American restaurants can come up with is ersatz stuff like soy burgers and unchicken salad and meatless meat loaf."

"I see your point," Elliot said. "Obviously you've thought about this. Still, maybe I'll try the meat loaf."

"Actually, it's probably the best thing on the menu. And I didn't mean to rant there. I guess I'm a little nervous."

"Oh." Elliot put his menu down and looked at him. *"I'm* not making you nervous, I hope?"

"You wouldn't think you'd forget how to do all this, but you do forget. At least, I have," Cameron said, silently thanking Max for sending over a waiter rather than hovering at their table himself. The handsome boy (where did Max find such specimens?) looked from one to the other expectantly.

Elliot took charge. "Two meatless meat loafs," he said briskly. "And a bottle of the pinot noir. How does that sound?" he asked Cameron. "Max told me you still drank wine."

"Gee. What else did he tell you?"

Elliot took the question seriously. "Let's see. That you're coming out of a long-term relationship. That your new meds are doing the trick. That you're having a bit of trouble finding your way back into the world."

"He said that?"

"He cares about you very much."

"Well, I can see you've got all the advantage. I know practically nothing about you. So you should probably start at the beginning."

"Sure. Glad to. Of course, I'm positive like yourself. Was in a long-term relationship but my partner and I split about six months ago. He was positive too, but he had issues. Or maybe I should say, we had different issues. He was extremely sex-negative. It imbued him with all this bad energy, which he wouldn't even admit to. I'd be horny as hell and he'd just sit there on the sofa watching TV and emanating this truly evil karma. So I said to myself, 'You've got to change the energy equation here, for your own health.' So I got out. Best thing I ever did. Now I'm single, looking for a man I can truly be happy with. Share both a soul communion and a body commitment. I'm working again—graphic design. Just bought a house up here, though my work's still mostly in the city. But I'm up here for weekends, and hoping to find a way to spend more time. I always dreamed of having a house in the country, but my partner would say, 'No, Elliot, we've got to watch our expenditures.' My attitude was, like, fuck it. Maybe that's fatalistic, but I say, you only live once, no matter what your health is like. The worst that can happen is, you die. And that's going to happen to all of us.

"The Buddha tells us that we have to walk away from our illness. That's the only way. See, I think there's this radiance in all of us, but we're mostly blind to it. And that's what sickens us. It's not so much disease. Viruses are just opportunistic. They're waiting there to take advantage of our blindness. When we're blind to our radiance, that's when they step in and overcome us. *Trust the radiance* is my motto."

The waiter served them their meatless meat loaf. "The plates are hot," he told them. "Enjoy."

Now *that's* radiance, Cameron thought, watching those tight-clad buttocks retreat from their table. Nothing disheartened him more than all the New Age claptrap otherwise perfectly intelligent people seemed to go in for these days. The *Stone Hollow Reporter* was full of ads for psychics, aroma therapists, feng shui consultants, tantric healers.

Meatless meat loaf, he supposed, forking a bite into his mouth and chewing, was only another form of the silliness, though he entirely approved, at least on principle, of a vegetarian diet. Still, one of the things he'd admired, perversely, about Dan had been his robust predeliction for pork chops, veal scallopini, sausages of all kinds. He'd made a powerfully memorable cassoulet.

But he was not about to start feeling nostalgic for Dan. Their whole time together now seemed false, a sad pas de deux of needs and obligations they'd danced far too long for either's good.

Elliot was a fastidious eater, obviously well trained as a child; he cut his food silently, his knife never touching the plate. What would he be like as a lover? Perhaps if one could convince him to keep his mouth shut . . .

Elliot saw he was being observed. "It's quite good," he said, holding up a brown chunk he'd speared on his fork. "So now let me get a fix on you. For starters, tell me how you know Max. Not, I understand, like the rest of us—through either Zanzibar, town politics, or both."

"No. Max and I were roommates at Oberlin."

"Long-term friendships fascinate me. I don't know why I'm so curious. I guess because I've never had any. Don't get me wrong. I'm certainly not a weirdo or anything. It just seems like, with me, I keep challenging myself to grow and change, while most people I know seem to want to stay in the same place. It's depressing."

Cameron could see Max sending covert glances their way. "You know," he said, speaking perhaps a notch more loudly, though there was little chance his voice would carry across the room, "I hated Max when I first knew him. I'd never met a New York Jew before, let alone tried to live in the same room with one. Memphis hadn't exactly prepared me for Max, he was so totally unlike anybody I'd ever known back then. I remember he had this sort of fetish for Kurt Weill and Bertolt Brecht. He'd dance around the dorm room singing 'Mack the Knife' in this hoarse, thoroughly unpleasant voice. *Auf deutsch,* no less. *'Und der Haifisch, der hat Zähne, und der trägt sie ins Gesicht.'* God, I can still hear it. I thought he was completely insane. He and his friends, who'd all gone to Horace Mann with him. They used to sit around the room and talk politics and philosophy in this really irritating way—irritating because I thought I was pretty sophisticated, but they intimidated the hell out of me. Plus, they smoked a lot of dope, which sheltered me wasn't exactly ready for either."

"And then you fell in love," Elliot said.

Cameron had to laugh. "Yeah, well, that was later. That first year we were both pretty deeply in the closet. Max was actually in deeper than I was, if you can imagine that. God, I remember going to my first Gay Union dance that spring—sneaking there, really, because I was terrified Max my straight roommate would somehow find out. It was in a dorm lounge on the south campus. I'd never imagined so many homosexuals actually existed. I mean, there were probably thirty of us jammed into that little space. The record player kept skipping because guys dancing were bumping up against the table, and the DJ, this total queen from the conservatory, kept hissing, "Stay away from the table, girls!" I started dancing with this boy from Minnesota. Jay. Eventually we ended up back in his room, where he proceeded to get very drunk on a pint of bourbon. I, on the other hand, wanted to keep a clear head for the great sex I was just sure was going to happen."

"So was that your first time?"

"Well, nothing happened. Practically nothing. Once Jay got himself sufficiently fueled, all we did was kiss and grope. Kept our clothes on the whole time. Jay was afraid his roommate would show up. I think he was just freaked-out. Anyway, we saw each other the next day in the cafeteria. Or I saw him. He wouldn't even look in my direction. It was like I didn't even exist. I can't tell you how unnerving that was. It sort of sent me right back into the closet."

Still, Cameron remembered that kiss so well. Tommy McCalla would never have allowed such a thing; their script had been strictly limited to the one unreciprocated act. That kiss had meant the world to Cameron at the time.

"If it makes you feel any better," Elliot said, "the first guy I slept with at Princeton told me, just as he was pulling me into his bed, 'If we're going to do what I think we're going to do, I'm going to have to hate you for it in the morning.' Of course, I was so desperate I wasn't going to let a little thing like being hated the next morning deter me one bit. In fact, it let me focus on the moment and forget all about the future. For what I see now was pretty bad sex, it was pretty damn terrific, let me tell you."

"And did he hate you?"

"I'm sure he did. That didn't stop him from coming back. We were off and on for nearly the whole year, till he graduated. Whether he ever came out, I have no idea. Probably he's married with kids somewhere, and saying the same tired old line to the guys he picks up on the side. But you still haven't told me about how you changed your mind about Max."

"I can't even say, really. I remember this day in winter, I remember the way the light was coming in through the windows, late-afternoon light. I was sitting at my desk. Max was lying on his stomach on the floor, his arms propped on a pillow. That was his favorite way to read. It used to drive me crazy. But I remember looking at him and thinking, 'I can't believe this. I'm actually falling in love with this irritating Jewish guy from the Bronx.' Only he wasn't this strange, irritating—intimidating— person anymore. He was just Max Greenblatt. And I had to admire how smart he was, all that intensity that put me off at first. The pushiness and the opinions and the self-righteousness and sheer brilliance—everything we love and hate Max for."

"So you blurted out, 'Will you sleep with me?' "

"Hardly. I was much too scared and ashamed to tell anybody I loved them. So after freshman year, we more or less went our separate ways. Then, the beginning of my senior year, guess who I saw at a Gay Union dance. I couldn't believe my eyes. He walked right up to me and said, 'Hey there, roommate,' and it was like something just fell into place for both of us."

"That's really cool."

"After that we were together our whole senior year, then we lived together for three years after that in New York, and you know how it is. Things changed, we both evolved. And here we are. Stone Hollow, New York. About as far from where we both thought we'd be as is humanly possible."

They'd finished their meal. Elliot poured the last of the wine into their glasses. Cameron wondered whether he should talk about Toby. To leave him out of any reckoning was to render the story drastically incomplete.

But Elliot had other plans. "So what do we now? Want to come see my place? Proud-new-homeowner syndrome, I know."

"Why not?" Cameron heard himself say. Their conversation had not been unenjoyable, even though part of him wished nothing more than to go home, feed his cats, take his pills, crawl into bed.

From behind the register, Max beamed at them. Could he tell things hadn't gone completely badly?

"What an excellent meal," Elliot reported. "And even better conservation. Of course, we talked about nothing but you."

"Oh, go fish," Max said. "So what are you guys doing now?"

"We're just going to hang out at my place. I thought I'd give him the tour."

"You'll like what he's doing with it," Max told Cameron. Max's eyes glittered—with encouragement, gratification, perhaps even a little envy? They'd of course have to have a long talk about all this tomorrow.

Cameron followed Elliot's VW—one of those cute, too cute, new Beetles he was amazed anyone actually bought for himself—out toward Weed's Mill Falls, then up a private road for a quarter of a mile. The house was little more than a tidy shack in the woods. Even at night he could tell the place got almost no sun. No garden would grow there. But inside (Elliot flicked on the lights) was cheery enough. Various Buddhist accoutrements decorated the spare space: a shelf of meditating bronze Buddhas, intricately stamped wall hangings, a prayer wheel, an obsessively carved and brightly painted wooden altar.

As Cameron scrutinized these, his metaphysical skepticism leavened by a certain aesthetic appreciation, Elliot moved swiftly to the kitchen, separated from the living room only by a breakfast bar on which sat, in surprisingly playful opposition to the spiritual decor, half a dozen cookie jars in shapes ranging from a rooster to a cat to a rotund and beaming black mammy. He took bottles from a cabinet and shook an assortment of pills and capsules into his palm. "I have such a hard time with pills," he said, "I'm on this new regime. I used to be on that awful, three-times-a-day Crixivan combo. I just couldn't do it. I missed too many doses, even though it did bring my viral load down to like ten thousand. I went cold turkey for a year, cleared my system out, got rid of the poison. I felt so much better, but my viral load had shot up to something horrifying like three hundred seventy-five thousand and my T cells were seventy. So I had to get back on." Elliot paused to swallow his pills. "Abacavir-nevirapine-ddI combo. What're you taking?"

Talking meds was about the last thing Cameron was interested in (he should be at home, taking his right now); still, it was a strange kind of intimacy, generously offered, and it seemed churlish not to reply in kind. "I've been on nearly everything. AZT early on, which nearly killed me. I developed a resistance anyway, so they had to take me off. I was on nevirapine for a while too. Saquinavir. Who can remember them all? At its worst my load was in the seven hundred thousand range. Now I'm taking a bunch of stuff, but it really seems to be doing the trick. My load's undetectable. My CD4s are in the five hundreds. My health is actually pretty good these days except for some neuropathy in my feet. And of course I'm constantly on antinausea and diarrhea meds."

"Aren't we all? You've got a good doctor down in the city?"

"He's up here, actually."

"You feel comfortable with a doctor up here?"

"Well, sure. I've done quite well by him, I think. I mean, I'm still alive, aren't I?"

"I don't know," Elliot said. "I'm not sure I'd trust my life to the kind of treatment that's available up here. Would you like anything to drink?"

"Being in the city didn't exactly help all my friends who died. And, no, nothing to drink. I'm fine."

"Shall we sit on the sofa? I went on this fabulous shopping spree at IKEA. Had all this stuff shipped up. It was so much fun."

Cameron tried to imagine Elliot's shopping spree in the abundant city. He wished he could somehow tell his date about Toby.

Elliot stretched luxuriously—almost obscenely, it seemed to Cameron, for whom the human body, its gross physical presence in the world, its ripe, seething mortality, had suddenly become distasteful.

"I don't know about you," Elliot said, "but I had a really fine time this evening. I'd say we've got quite a lot in common."

"That's probably true," Cameron said, hearing the faint chill that entered his voice. But what, exactly, was he backing away from? Elliot was perfectly nice, and Cameron tried to imagine the two of them together. But nothing came. It was as if something inside him was broken now, perhaps irreparably.

"Max was right about you," Elliot said, oblivious to this secret ruin. "You're kind of reserved, but then when you open up, you're pretty wonderful. I think the two of us could have a bit of fun. What do you say? Are you feeling a little romantic tonight?"

In the bazaars of Istanbul, Cameron and Toby had learned the hard way that you reached a point, when bargaining for a carpet, beyond which it was rude to break off the negotiations, beyond which you were committed to going through with it. But when, in real life, did one reach that point? Max had set them up, they'd had dinner. He thought he probably shouldn't have accepted Elliot's invitation to come admire his house.

"You should understand," he confessed, "I haven't had sex with anyone in a very long time. Dan and I stopped soon after I got my diagnosis. It was me as much as it was him. No, that's not true. It really was entirely me. He wanted to go on. I wouldn't risk it, even though he was willing to take that risk. I guess, in a way, I was the one who engineered the death of that relationship. Or maybe the illness engineered it."

"I hate talk like that." Elliot gently rubbed Cameron's knee. "The illness doesn't engineer a single damn thing. It's all up to us."

"Our radiance."

"I can see you're not so crazy about that term."

Cameron placed his hand over Elliot's, stilling the tender though slightly annoying motion. "Elliot," he said. "I'm suddenly feeling very exhausted. You've given me a lot to think about tonight."

"Do I bore you?"

"No," Cameron said, surprised by Elliot's querulous tone; he hadn't pegged Elliot as particularly insecure. "You're attractive. You're engaging. I'm afraid it's just me. I've got too many things I haven't sorted through."

"There're some things you can't sort through by yourself."

"True enough. And some other things you have to sort through without any help from anybody. It's figuring out which is which that's hard."

"Max warned you'd be a long shot."

"Please don't take it personally."

"I worry about guys like you."

That's not going to work, Cameron wanted to tell him. It's far too late for that stratagem. Instead he said, getting up from the sofa, "I'm going to go now." Elliot stood as well. "Your house is great. It's nice you're in the neighborhood. Thanks for a lovely evening."

"At least a hug?"

"Of course." He allowed Elliot to enfold him in his arms, a surprisingly affectionate embrace, he thought, given the way the evening was ending. For a moment he gave in to the sheer animal consolation of touch. For a moment, as Elliot's lips grazed his neck, he nearly considered giving in entirely. But then the old broken thing in him whispered it was no good, it couldn't be fixed ever again.

One used to see him on Seventh Avenue nearly every day—a sleek figure gliding by on a bicycle, weaving recklessly but effortlessly in and out of traffic. He wore sneakers with no socks, black spandex, colorful T-shirts. His shoulder-length hair trailed in the breeze, not unlike that of those exuberant figures that adorned Rockefeller Center. His face too was sculpted, his limbs smooth and bronzed. Glimpsed every couple of days, he became a stirring punctuation in an otherwise routine morning or afternoon of errands, someone never to be known, but whom one registered, someone who accrued, over time, a psychic significance all the more substantial for being so entirely private. So that it was uncanny when that beautiful young man pulled up alongside one at the curb one morning and said, as if nothing were more ordinary, "Hey there, how's it going?"

In that singular moment life seemed grandly inevitable, as if reality began in desire, as if secretly everything had been arranged from the very beginning, and all one had to do was trust its unfolding.

"Hi," he had answered in disbelief as Toby Vail dismounted his bike and walked it beside him.

Leaning toward the bathroom mirror, Cameron examined the hollow-cheeked face that peered back warily. How many years since that morning? From its little brown bottle, he shook out the blue pill into his palm. Then, from another bottle, a second pill, and from another, a third, a fourth, a fifth. Then several capsules of different sizes and colors.

It would be eighteen, wouldn't it? Eighteen years since they'd met, nine since Toby had died alone, in the middle of the night, tied down to a bed in a room at St. Vincent's. Those years had made Cameron old. His face, he concluded as he padded barefoot downstairs to the kitchen, was that of a man who'd lost heart. Hadn't Elliot been able to see that clearly?

Past some point—but when, exactly?—the night had turned into a Stoli night. Pouring himself a generous inch from the bottle he kept in the freezer, he filled the glass the rest of the way with orange juice, then began the onerous task of swallowing.

"I see you all the time," Toby had said, "and I thought, I like the look of this guy, I'm going to introduce myself to him. I hope you don't mind my being so forward."

He'd grown up in Tulsa; he was one-quarter Cherokee from his grandmother, Verena Blackhawk. He was working as a bike messenger while attending the Tisch School of Performing Arts. "Like every other mildly good-looking fellow in New York, I want to be an actor," he explained.

If Cameron had labored mightily to befriend Mitchell Johnson, a campaign that had lasted a full year before the first faint glimmers of success, with Toby all that—and more—seemed to happen virtually overnight. Later, when Toby fell ill and he himself was diagnosed, there seemed the same inevitability at work as in his initial meeting with the talented, doomed actor—as if the world once again made sense, only of a more nightmarish kind.

He'd swallowed the last of his pills—his throat always constricted in protest for the final couple. It was early still, only eleven, but he felt exhausted. Or no—a weariness beyond exhaustion.

Nine years they'd had together. A brilliance gradually dimming. But how very brilliant the beginning had been. They'd taken off for Greece and Turkey, hitchhiking or riding filthy, exhilarating buses north from Athens through wild Thessaly and lonely Thrace. They hit Thessaloníki in the middle of a terrific heat wave. A thunderstorm surprised them in the deserted ruins of Abdera, lightning sparking amid the scrambled stones and panicking goats. They crossed into Turkey at Edirne, made their way to Istanbul, then south into Anatolia proper. In the ancient theater at Termessos, Cameron had felt the bright blue sky open wide and a golden contentment descend on him like light. In that astonishing moment he and his love were immortal. Time would not change them.

On the rooftop of the Dogan Pansiyon in Anamur, beneath a canopy of grapevines, they had made love. They had a three-way with a dark-eyed, seventeen-year-old waiter from their hotel in Antalya, and another with a homesick young soldier from Van, whom they'd met strolling at dusk on the beach at Side, where ancient buildings lay half-buried in sand and sea. Early on he'd discovered Toby's deeply essential promiscuity, the fearless joy with which he flung himself at every opportunity life presented to him. It went against everything in Cameron's nature, but he'd made the decision to embrace Toby fully—his enchanting, challenging totality. Looking back now, he saw it all as magnificent intoxication, the reeling wisdom of too much ouzo or raki consumed among strangers in tavernas on sultry summer nights.

Gulping the last of his Stoli and orange juice, he rinsed the glass and set it in the sink. He turned to go upstairs, but something gave him pause. He stopped, listened, then moved to the door and switched on the porch light.

Why, Dan used to ask, do you insist on feeding the cats on the back porch? You know it just attracts pests.

How to explain that he *liked* to attract pests; that he remembered, so acutely it still hurt, how at restaurants all across Greece and Turkey, the sound of mewling cats would expose him and Toby to disapproving stares as they surreptitiously dropped bits of fish or lamb from their plates for one, two, then before you knew it, half a dozen skinny, matted, desperate creatures.

Tonight a possum had ambled up the steps and was nuzzling the remains of Casper and Diva's dinner. Of all his nocturnal visitors, possums were perhaps Cameron's favorite—with their coarse fur and rat tails and eerily human feet, they were such crudely designed little creatures, their survival a testimony to sheer evolutionary dumb luck. The first time he'd seen one on their porch, Dan had called out to Cameron in alarm, "There's a huge rat out there!"

Oblivious to its observer, the possum ate ravenously.

THIRTEEN

Uncle Roy had built himself a pretty nice house in the new development behind the Family Market, a two-story modular with everything modern—electric stove, built-in microwave, dishwasher, disposal. His mom looked it all over, not for the first time, with keenest envy.

"Now something like this is exactly what I'd like," she said to all of them who'd listen—his aunt Doty, his cousins Selena and Fawn from the Rosendale Vanderhofs, Donna. Somehow he'd found himself in the kitchen with the women. "Not that I could afford anything this big, but something small would suit me fine. I've been reading the brochures. These come in all sizes, and some are very reasonable." She paused to lift two platters of deviled eggs from the kitchen table, one in each hand, then decided against it. "I'm going to tip these things right out on the floor," she said. "Jesse, help me carry these out."

"Let me get both," he told her.

"Be careful. I spent all morning on those."

"I got 'em," he assured her, escaping that brand-new kitchen for the bright outdoors where Uncle Roy had sat his big bulk down in a lawn chair, one of a circle deployed around the barbecue grill. Uncle Jimmy and his boy Mike had joined him; Uncle Otto was minding the grill. He wore an apron that said DON'T SHOOT THE CHEF.

"Here, son," Uncle Roy called out as Jesse set the platters on the picnic table. "Don't mess with that." He motioned toward the house. "Let them take care of it. Want one of these?" Reaching into the ice bucket by his side, he drew out a can of Bud and pointed it Jesse's way. "And relax. Why you seem so jumpy?"

"I ain't jumpy."

"You sure look that way. Get on out there and enjoy yourself." He gestured toward the empty lot next door, where Kyle and Brandon and a couple of other cousins were dueling back and forth on their quads and three-wheelers; fretful spurts of acceleration filled the air like bees around a disturbed hive.

Not knowing what else to do, Jesse took the cold can from his uncle. He wished Brandon wasn't out there—it was supposed to be just family—but Kyle had brought him along, so what could you do? He guessed he should go on over and join them. He sort of liked his cousins, Kenny the cop and Little Will, who he saw about once a month on average; certainly they'd never done the least thing to piss him off. And anyway, he always figured it was smart to stay on Kenny's good side, which meant staying on Little Will's good side as well.

"Hey, you kids!" Uncle Roy's voice boomed across the lawn. Instantly, the little ones in the wading pool froze. His voice had that effect on people. "Stop so much splashing. You hear me?"

The whiskey shot Kyle had offered before they set out having long since worn off, Jesse swigged the cold beer gratefully. Uncle Roy picked up talking where he'd left off, some story about the highway department Jesse was pretty sure he'd heard before. There'd be plenty of time to listen to Uncle Roy later. Pop had always said his older brother could outtalk a mockingbird, but he'd respected him all the same—his success, his ease in the world. The way men and women flocked to him. For fifteen years Uncle Roy had been Stone Hollow's mayor, always trouncing any opponent who dared throw his hat in the ring. He never let you forget that, and the truth was, half of them here today owed their jobs to Uncle Roy. He enjoyed being generous that way; he was born bighearted to a fault, people said. He'd offered Pop this job and that down the line, though Pop preferred to go his own way. Fixing things up had been Pop's passion. Half the houses of Stone Hollow, it sometimes seemed, he'd improved with aluminum siding, and it always pissed him off to see some outsider move into town and strip his handiwork off an old house that had looked like shit before he came around. It puzzled Pop no end—there was no figuring certain people.

Having finished his beer, Jesse looked around for a place to unload the empty. Uncle Roy must've been keeping his eye on him. "Over there," he said. "Trash." His uncle gestured to a can labeled TRASH. His uncle thought of every little thing when throwing a picnic or doing anything else. *Your Pop never picked up that useful trait,* he could hear his mom say bitterly. Oh, well. At least he and Kyle had had the forethought to bring their machines, lashing them in their truck beds for the drive over. His brother had been worried there wouldn't be nothing to do. Leaving the grown-ups, he made his way over to his three-wheeler and started her up, gunned the engine to alert the others, and propelled himself into the fray.

It was some kind of freewheeling war between Kyle and Brandon, on the one side, and his cousins on the other. They all looked at him like—whose side are you on? And, to tell the truth, he didn't know. But then Kyle grinned at him in such a way there wasn't any doubt. He wheeled his machine around and bore down on Kenny, who looked taken off guard by the attack, swerving sharply and tilting way over before righting himself. With three to two, it was a serious case of harassment—they drove the cousins all over the place, herding them like they were a bunch of Red Indians on the run. Kyle seemed to like getting the best of a cop, even an off-duty one.

Riding always cleared Jesse's head, made him feel both excited and calm, like nobody could touch him. He didn't have to talk to nobody, or listen to nobody, no figuring out what you were supposed to do or say—just ride. But he'd joined the game too late, it seemed. Kyle and Brandon were getting tired of the sport they were making with Kenny and Little Will, and Kyle signaled for them all to take a break. Jesse could see Aunt Doty standing on the back deck, waving them over to eat.

He felt disappointed—he'd just been starting to relax into things a little—so as the others pulled their machines off to the side, he continued to do a few spins and turns. But then he was conscious of being watched by the others. What was he up to? Why wasn't he heeding the call like everybody else? Reluctantly, he pulled in beside the others and shut his engine down. The sudden stillness was a little disconcerting. Too much quiet spooked him—out in the woods, sometimes, when everything was completely still, you could almost imagine a voice was going to speak to you. He wished, suddenly, there was a radio playing. As he walked toward the house, though, the squeals of the little kids in the aboveground pool, the voices of his mom and sister and aunts and uncles and cousins, the voices of his girlfriend and his brother and his brother's girlfriend—they all seemed to wrap themselves around him like a big comforting embrace. He made his way over to the picnic table that was crammed with food— hamburgers and hot dogs and kielbasa from the grill, potato salad and macaroni salad, his aunt Doty's famous baked beans, his mom's deviled eggs. After loading his plate up, he found a place on the grass next to Donna and Leanne and a little girl he wasn't sure he knew. Maybe three years old, she wore a white dress like she was going to a wedding. She just stood there, thumb in her mouth, not saying a word, not eating, completely ignored by both Donna and Leanne. She seemed like she was content, though. He looked at her and she looked at him with a serious expression, and then he looked away.

As he ate hungrily, he pondered the undeniable fact of Donna's weight versus Leanne's trim, attractive body. It wasn't like Donna was fat, exactly; but when he looked at her, he was starting to see her mother, who wasn't what you'd call thin. Kyle had told him, not too long back, as they lay in their beds at night, that what had brought him and Leanne back together was, they both loved to fuck. Who doesn't? he'd told Kyle; but the truth was, he and Donna never fucked, really. They put their hands on each other from time to time; they kissed and hugged and cuddled, but never did they fuck the way he was sure Kyle meant he and Leanne fucked. In his mind's cold, hungry eye he could see his brother's taut back as he thrust himself methodically into Leanne, a rhythm like the rhythm he used to hear from the top bunk when he was too young to figure certain things out.

He hadn't thought of that noise in a while, he considered as he half-listened to Leanne tell Donna she was thinking of trading in her Trans Am. "Kyle loves that car," she was saying, "sometimes I think more than he loves me. Maybe that's why I want to move on to something else. Maybe I'm the jealous type." She laughed that strange, horsey laugh of hers, but Donna didn't join in. Donna was a very serious type—kidding around wasn't something she indulged in much. He couldn't imagine her making jokes about him like that, which he guessed was a comforting thought, especially set next to the thought of Kyle's sweaty, pumping back.

All over the lawn his relatives had settled in small groups, some in chairs, some cross-legged on the browned-over grass, everybody trying to find some little piece of shade. The sky was drought-blue, impervious to any hope of rain. An ant ran along his arm, and he brushed it off. He tried to think of how to join the conversation, but nothing came to him, so he asked, "Anybody want seconds?"

"Not for me." Leanne patted her flat stomach beneath the turquoise spandex she wore to show it off. "I've eaten way too much already. Gonna have to starve myself for a week."

"I could go for another of those hamburgers," Donna said.

It made him happy to be useful. Taking their plates over to the picnic table, he noticed once again he'd managed to end up with the women. Kyle and Brandon sat with Kenny and Little Will. His sister and his mom sat with his aunts and girl cousins. The older men were clumped around the grill, where Uncle Roy commanded their attention. As he filled his plate, then Donna's, he idly listened in. As usual with Uncle Roy, the subject was politics. It wasn't something Jesse ever paid much heed to—but then neither had Pop. About the only thing political Pop ever did was to let Uncle Roy put up campaign signs in the front lawn, where the curve in the road made them especially visible, big sheets of plywood stenciled:

RE-ELECT ROY VANDERHOF MAYOR
JUSTICE—DECENCEY—THE AMERICAN WAY

Not that Uncle Roy needed any help from Pop in winning elections.

"It's certain people around here's got big mouths and bigger wallets," Uncle Roy was saying. "But I don't have to tell you that. Look at the speedway up there where you are, Jimmy. How much have them noise lawsuits cost the town?"

"Plenty," Jimmy said. "And for what?"

"It's the principle of the thing," Roy said. "That's the trouble: people with no principles moving in. People who never heard of live and let live except where it comes to them. Man can't make a decent living without folks interfering. It's the country—it's *noisy*. What'd they expect? You ever hear a cow in heat? I been saying for years it could come to this, and nobody was listening, but you look around and you got to admit, it *has* come to this. Hell, we got three lawsuits in Stone Hollow at this minute. That any way for a town to try to run itself? But how do you keep these folks out? You can't. Look at Main Street. I know Main Street's had a mighty hard time. Now these new fellows aim to change all that. Fine. But you just can't wave some fairy wand. There ain't enough parking, for one thing. Most of them old buildings are breaking half the fire and safety codes. If I was building inspector, I'd tear down the lot of them—but I'm not. Tommy does his job as he sees fit. But mark my word: these new fellows are interested in one thing, and that's making a profit. They may yammer on about preserving the town's character, but they don't know the first thing about this town's character. They didn't grow up here, and the minute things get tough, they're gonna be out of here to someplace else. They seem to have the idea this is going to be another Woodstock. You been down Main Street recently? Hell, it's halfway there. This fellow Greenblatt—Max—he's starting to act like somebody already elected him goddamned mayor. My memory ain't what it used to be, but I don't seem to remember him winning any election around here. Comes to Town Council meetings raising a ruckus about this and that. Zoning violations, master plan, the whatnot. It's the fact ordinary people can't afford to live here anymore I'm worried about."

"Fag Hollow," Kyle said. Everybody looked at him. Jesse hadn't noticed his brother wander up. Kyle stood with a beer in his hand and repeated, "Fag Hollow. What I call Main Street anymore. You can't stir 'em with a stick down there—but who'd want to?"

Some of the men snorted or snickered. Roy turned his bulk in his seat and seemed to study Kyle for half a minute. "Queer don't matter one way or the other to me," he said. "Some are, some aren't."

"I was making an observation, is all," Kyle explained. "Me and Jesse was just working for one. You couldn't help but notice."

Jesse felt himself go tense. Kyle might be safely done with Cameron, but he couldn't afford that same ease. He still was working for the guy. His last day on the job, he'd offered to help out around the garden once in a while as a way of paying back some of what he owed. But Cameron wasn't taking any free labor; he insisted on paying a regular wage. So now he saw him three days a week. With Kyle no longer around, Cameron treated him different, it seemed like—friendlier, often offering a beer at the end of the day, which, against his better judgment, he'd accept. He didn't want to be beholden, as Pop used to say, but already he was beholden. Cameron made him nervous, though, striking up conversation the way he did—at first Jesse had just wanted to say, Let me drink my beer and go. But then he remembered how this was the whole point—to get to know his employer. Of course, there wasn't much to talk about. He didn't have anything in common with a guy like that. So he let Cameron talk about the gardens he'd built, even bring out a photo album with pictures showing lavish spreads for folks who had more money than they knew what to do with, but he had to admit they looked pretty great, beautiful flowers everywhere, stone walks and pools, plenty of benches to sit on and admire the view. He'd always had a secret fondness for green things—his grandmother used to grow flowers and some vegetables in a little fenced plot by the side of the house, but after she died nobody tended them anymore, and now even the fence was fallen down.

"Live and let live," Uncle Roy was saying. "That and the golden rule's how I live my life. You find a better way, you let me know."

Jesse was surprised to see Kyle looking like a puppy that had just got swatted down. It was true they were both a little afraid of Uncle Roy—everybody was. Larger-than-life in more ways than one, his mom had once said—and she was a little afraid of Pop's older brother too. Still, Jesse knew Kyle wasn't someone who much liked getting swatted down, no matter who was doing the swatting.

With a certain relief, Jesse remembered why he'd come over here to where Uncle Roy was holding court in the first place. He'd sort of lost his own appetite, but he fixed Donna's hamburger with extra care, fancying it up with lettuce and tomato slices and mustard and mayonnaise the way he knew she liked it. For good measure he added a dollop of baked beans and a handful of potato chips.

His girlfriend and Leanne were where he'd left them, only the toddler had wandered off, or her mother had come gotten her, or crows had carried her away. Donna, her back to him, spoke softly. "Oh, a good eight inches," she said. At least that was what he thought he heard, and he had the weirdest sense she was talking about him. Leanne was nodding, a vague smile on her face, her eyelids half-shut in a sort of drowse. Seeing him seemed to snap her abruptly awake.

"We thought you'd got lost or something," she told him while Donna turned around and looked at him—he could swear—with guilty surprise.

"Sorry," he said, handing down her plate. "I got busy listening to Uncle Roy."

Of course, if she really had been talking about him she'd been lying—

but it wouldn't have been the first time, he thought with uneasy pride.

"Your uncle sure does love to talk," Leanne said. "And when he does, seems like everybody listens."

"Uncle Roy's a politician," Donna said. "Of course he likes to talk."

"All the Vanderhofs love to talk, far as I can tell," said Leanne. " 'Cept for Jesse here. You always was the silent one of the bunch. So what kind of thoughts you keeping to yourself? I wonder. Hello—who's really in there? The secret, Jesse; the one you keep all hid."

Leanne's teasing made him uncomfortable. "Knock it off," he told her.

She just smiled at him, that pretty smile she had, the kind Kyle said one night, way back before she was his, he'd downright die for.

"You hear about the bear?" she asked.

He looked at her with confusion. "What bear?"

"The one we was just talking about."

"People been seeing it all over," Donna added. "Out by the Rural Cemetery. Hasbrouck Estates. Getting in the trash, pulling down bird feeders. C.J. told me it left eight-inch claw marks on the hood of his daddy's car."

"I'd hate to have a bear wandering around my backyard," Leanne said.

"They'll have to shoot it," said Donna. "It'll go back up in the mountains if it knows what's good for it."

"Wild animals never know what's good for them," Leanne told them—like she knew.

Jesse'd always hated her, from the very first Kyle ever laid eyes on her. It was just another traitorous secret he held close to his chest.

FOURTEEN

There were no seats left, so Cameron stood at the back of the crowded room. Max had pressed him to come. "Numbers count," he'd said. "We've got to show them they can't pull anything on us."

Cameron believed in being a loyal friend, though the close, sweltering air of the Rec Center made him feel less than well.

At a table in front, sharing a single microphone, sat the mayor, the highway supervisor, the four town councilmen—only one of whom was even remotely "sympathetic," as Max put it, though come November that was bound to change.

Otto Vanderhof was explaining in a voice of weary impatience that the town had important liability issues to consider.

"What happens," he said, holding the microphone close, too close, so that *happens* exploded midword, "what happens when a school bus driver doesn't have a clear line of sight? What happens to those kids when there's a rollover, when the bus plows into that big old maple tree that's gotten too big to be where it is? When it's raining out, and the road's flooded for improper drainage—what happens? Or an ambulance has to slow down on some of these curvy old roads and somebody you love is in back with a heart attack? I love nature just as much as the next person, but I love people more, I say let's put people first. That's what the law says too, and when you elected me, I swore on the Bible, 'so help me God,' to uphold the law. You can replace an old broken-down stone wall, you can

plant a new tree, you can plant fifty of them. But one single human life—
you can't go replacing that once it's gone."

Stout as an old maple himself, he paused to catch his breath. Over his
denim shirt he wore rainbow-colored suspenders, presumably unaware
they might, in other circumstances, be construed as having some political
significance. Cameron rather enjoyed listening to Otto's rant. The highway supervisor reminded him, a little, of those preachers he had grown up
on, and hated, and now, whenever he saw them on TV, had a sneaking
nostalgia for (in part because it drove Dan crazy whenever he paused for a
few moments on the Christian Channel). *Don't make me confiscate the
remote,* Dan would warn.

But that was over now. Cameron didn't miss it one bit. Really he didn't.

A mousy, dark-haired woman Max had introduced him to any number
of times, and whose name he could never remember, took Otto to task.

"Has the town ever, in the last fifty years, been sued for any of those
ridiculous scenarios you've just spun?" she asked to applause from much
of the audience (Max had certainly done a good job of bringing out his
people).

Smothering the microphone with his palm, Otto leaned over to confer
with his brother. Roy frowned, shook his head, then whispered something
to Otto, who uncovered the microphone noisily and declared, "It's good
management that assures things like that don't happen. That's my job.
Good management."

"Where's the good management in destroying Stone Hollow's heritage?" the woman asked, and now Cameron remembered: she was one of
several residents who'd filed a lawsuit against the town charging the highway department with trespassing and destruction of private property. Or
had threatened to. He wasn't sure which. "Those of us who treasure this
town's—"

Pointing a thick finger her way, Otto interrupted. "Listen, little lady.
Don't go lecturing this council about heritage. Some of us in this room
grew up here. We *are* this town's heritage. If it wasn't for us—"

Roy intervened, "Now, now. This is everybody's town. We have a disagreement of opinions. But that's what we're all here to work out."

"Otto," Max called out from the front row. "Isn't it true a state highway
study concluded that widening rural roads simply increases speeding?
That the rate of accidents actually goes up rather than down?"

"I haven't seen that study," Otto said.

"I sent it to your office, Otto," Max reminded him.

"It has not come to my attention."

"I sent it certified mail. You signed for it." He waved a green slip in the air. A murmur rippled through the crowd.

Again Otto conferred with his brother.

"We need some order here," Roy said. "Too many people are speaking out of turn. If we don't have order, I'm going to have to close this meeting down."

"You can't do that," shouted bald-shaven, pierced Daryl Dahlheim from the middle of the room. His black, sleeveless T-shirt read OH MY GOD I'M SO QUEER. "You can't silence a whole town."

"You don't speak for the town," a burly man standing near Cameron called out. "You and your little group of special interests—"

Daryl turned to face him. "What does that mean?"

"—your special-interest agenda," the man went on. "Maybe you should go get an AIDS test instead of wasting your time and ours."

The uproar became general as Roy hammered his gavel and bellowed through the microphone, "I'm sorry, folks. I gave you fair warning. I hereby declare this meeting adjourned." He banged twice and, leaning back in his chair, folded his beefy arms across his chest.

Cameron breathed more freely once he was outside in the parking lot. The air was warm but at least not stifling. As if at a loss, riled-up partisans from both sides milled about in the gorgeous twilight. Some drifted away to their pickup trucks or Hondas. The meeting had made Cameron nervous and sad. He tried to imagine what Daryl must have looked like to the fellow who'd shouted him down.

A crafty smile on his face, Max strode toward him and said, "That was certainly a fruitful meeting."

Cameron looked at his old friend. "Are you kidding?"

Max gripped his arm and led him away from the parking lot toward the little picnic area—DuBois Park—that sloped down to the Schneidekill. "Look at it this way. Can anybody who was in that room now have any illusion about what's going on? It's a complete disgrace, the collusion between those two. And the rest of the council sits there without a word like the shameless lackeys they are."

"I'm not going to any more of these meetings," Cameron told him.

"What?"

"This stuff all makes me very uncomfortable."

"Revolution is never comfortable. Haven't you known me long enough by now?"

"Do we need this particular revolution?"

"Cameron, you have exactly the same position on this road-widening issue as I have. You've seen the barbaric things they've been doing."

"I know. It's just . . . Never mind."

They wandered past deserted picnic tables, brick barbecue grills that must date back to the forties or fifties. Neither he nor anyone he knew had ever had a picnic here, though on sunny summer weekends the park would be full. "Look," Max told him, "you have too many qualms about things. I don't like to see you retreat from everything like this."

"I'm not retreating."

"Are you sure? First you blame gay men for spreading AIDS. Now this."

Max's words stunned him. "I don't blame gay men for spreading AIDS," he protested. "Where on earth did that come from?"

"Then what's all this about never having sex ever again?"

"When did I ever say anything like that?"

Max ignored him. "It infuriates me to see you just give up. You act like you're in prison or something. You don't owe the world a thing, sweetie. You never have. The world fucks us queers, treats us like animals. But we don't have to buy into it. When I first knew you, you were so scared, so shy. Remember? I like to think I helped you out of that. Remember how long it took me to seduce you? What I really hate is to see you go back in that prison. And of your own free will."

"You never said this to me before."

"You were too sick to hear it. I thought it didn't matter then."

"And now it does?"

"Absolutely. You know I never liked Dan."

"But you liked Toby."

"Everybody liked Toby. Everybody liked Toby too much."

"What does that mean?"

"I don't know. I take that back."

"Are you saying he got fucked to death?"

"Forget I said that."

"But that's my point. I don't want any more Tobys to die. And you have to face facts. I have no business having sex with anybody, positive or negative."

"I don't want you to have sex, necessarily," Max said.

"Then what?"

"I want you to have love."

"But I have love. From you, from Perry."

"That's not what I mean. I want there to be that one person in your life again. You need that absolutely. And it drives me crazy that you've given up on looking for it. I did what I could. I set you up with Elliot, but no . . ."

"You've talked to Elliot."

"Of course I've talked to Elliot. And now I'm talking to you. Admit it—you pushed him away the other night."

"He wasn't right for me."

"Who's right for you, then?"

"For me? Nobody. I'm afraid I'm through with all that." But did he really mean that? He had no idea—but they'd both stopped saying anything they had any idea about some time ago. It was the kind of free-for-all he and Max used to have all the time, before he got sick and suddenly everyone, Max included, started treating him gently. He wasn't sure he was ready for Max's brutal honesty anymore.

"See? That's just what I'm talking about. It makes me so fucking crazy."

"I'm sorry," Cameron said.

"You know I love you. Like I love nobody else. You know I only have your best interests at heart."

"I know that," Cameron told him. "I love you too. I always will."

Drought had lowered the Schneidekill considerably; it flowed sluggishly among boulders usually invisible. A mixed group of mallards and Canada geese floated peacefully, just this side of the old cantilever bridge whose rust-flecked gray the state highway crew had recently repainted bright red. In colonial times there'd been a ford where the bridge now crossed. He might have made a stink about the garish new color, had he been so inclined. He might have started a campaign. Max, on the other hand, seemed not to care.

Still nervy after the noise and excitement of the speedway, they sat in a booth in air-conditioned Stewart's and sucked down sodas. Every other Friday night the four of them—him and Kyle, Donna and Leanne—would drive out to Accord to watch Brandon race his Chevy Nova. Usually Pop had come along, sitting high in the stands and trading sips of whiskey with Kyle while they followed the yellow Chevy with BIG AL'S written in red across the hood and doors. Two hundred bucks was what Big Al had paid to sponsor Brandon Schneidewind, who, in his second year at the track, had managed to turn himself into a crowd favorite.

Tonight he'd placed fourth in a field of twenty. It was the first race they'd been to since Pop had passed on, and the loudspeaker had announced that the driver of car #7 wanted to dedicate the race to the late great Mr. William Vanderhof. Kyle had bellowed his approval. Leanne had wiped a tear from her eye. Donna had just sat there resting her chin on her fists. Jesse had wondered, not for the first time, if one of the reasons Pop had always held Brandon in such high esteem was that he risked his neck at the speedway on Friday nights.

Any minute, Jesse expected, the guy would walk into Stewart's for a bit of well-deserved boasting and swagger. And they'd all give it to him. Even Jesse wouldn't begrudge him his due.

"What're you looking at?" Kyle asked Leanne. He was rifling through the Lotto tickets he'd shelled out twenty bucks for. "You gotta be in it to win it."

Those pink tickets, thick with magic numbers hid somewhere in among all the ordinary ones, recalled Jesse unpleasantly to Kyle's wild talk from last week. The plan, insofar as you could call it a plan, seemed to be in progress. It wasn't much, nothing he could make himself feel too sneaky about. Still, he wished he didn't have in his head what Kyle had put there.

"You don't think I'm gonna turn you loose at my first million?" Kyle asked Leanne. "If the dough's what you're hanging around for, forget it. I'm gonna supersize all around."

"Dream on," she told him.

"You should see what I dream," he bragged. "You'd blush right down to your belly button."

"Oh, please."

Jesse watched Donna watch the two of them. She had no expression on her face. He'd been noticing recently how she went blank like that, like she was bored out of her mind. Like she'd gone someplace else altogether.

Kyle cocked his head sideways to look at Leanne. "Hey, tell me," he said. "I'm curious. Do chicks have wet dreams?"

Donna's expression went from blank to something more like plain annoyance.

Leanne rolled her eyes. "Not about morons like you."

"Think of it," Kyle said. "Going through life without no wet dreams. Jesse and me have wet dreams nearly every night. Don't we?"

"You don't have to talk so loud," Donna mumbled, but Kyle, thankfully, wasn't listening.

"Well?" Kyle prompted.

Jesse realized he was being talked to.

"Oh, look," Leanne pointed out. "Jesse's blushing. Your boyfriend's cute when he blushes. Don't you think, Donna? The tips of his ears get all red."

Jesse knew Leanne could walk all over the likes of Donna. His girlfriend wasn't a match for her at all. But that was fine with him. Kyle and Leanne were back and forth all the time, worrying at each other like two bluejays dueling in air. He didn't know how they stood it. Lots of the time he and Donna just hung out without saying much of anything.

"Lay off," Kyle warned his girlfriend. "The quiet ones are the deep ones. And you're a deep one, ain't you, little brother?"

"Now you're the one's making him blush," said Leanne.

Donna was folding her straw into shorter and shorter segments. She stared at the tabletop. Jesse wondered where she went when she went away. He tried to convince himself it hadn't a thing to do with him. With a brother like Sean, he told himself, there'd have to be a cold, dead lump inside you that never dissolved. But he and Donna never talked much about that.

He wondered if there were unicorns where she went to.

The bell above the door jingled. He looked up, but it wasn't Brandon. Gary Dunkel had walked in. It was like a hand had dragged across the bottom of a clear stream, muddying it for a second before things settled back. He half prayed Gary wouldn't notice him or would maybe pretend he didn't notice. He wore khaki trousers, a dark blue tennis shirt. We're looking quite the college dude, Jesse thought scornfully. Through the window, he could see Gary's Toyota at the gas pump. Friday night, and the college dude was out by himself. He didn't seem lonely, but then there'd always been this kind of solitude around him, like no matter who he was with, he stayed unentangled. Maybe that was why it had meant what it did when Gary had sat with him at lunch, back when they were pals.

Gary paid for the gas, then sauntered over to their booth.

"Hey, how's it going?" he said, holding out his hand to be shaken. Gary was always a great one for shaking hands, his grip firm and steady, and even when you felt like you should let go, he still held you clasped to him. Jesse remembered how that used to feel, that extra moment you didn't know what to do with.

"What's up?" Jesse said, but this time Gary's handshake was quick and matter-of-fact; this time Jesse was the one left holding on too long. Sheepishly he released his grip.

"Just saw the strangest thing," Gary said. "Up by the cemetery. A bear. Can you believe it? Walking right across the road in front of me—like he owned the place." Jesse could see Gary give Kyle and Leanne and Donna the once-over as he spoke, but they didn't interest him. Jesse was the one he was talking to.

There was a time when he'd have carried that in his chest for days.

"Sure it wasn't a dog?" Kyle asked.

"I saw what I saw. That was a bear if it was anything."

"I guess you would know," Kyle said.

"I guess." Gary shoved his hands in his pockets, looked around like he'd suddenly remembered something. Maybe that he wasn't wanted. "Well," he said—and again, it was directed at Jesse, not the rest of them— "I'll be seeing you around."

But Jesse didn't want to see him around. He was sorry Gary had come over. He felt like he'd been caught at something—though what went on inside his chest, he reminded himself, nobody else could know.

"Skeezy guy," Kyle said, making a point of watching through the window as Gary walked to his car. "Besides, there wasn't no fucking bear up by the cemetery."

"They're gonna end up shooting it," Donna said. "They'll have to."

Why, Jesse wondered, did she always have to say that same damn thing whenever the subject came up? What was she thinking?

Kyle glanced her way only for a second—an "Are you nuts?" look—then returned his gaze to the window. Gary had no clue he was being studied so closely. He went about sponging his windshield, then wiped it clean with the squeegee.

"That bear's been all over," Donna continued. "It's wrecking havoc. People won't stand for that. I wish it'd go back where it came from. Be safe that way."

Kyle continued to stare out the window. Gary got in his car and pulled his seat belt across his chest.

"You ain't heard about the bear?" Leanne nudged Kyle with her elbow.

It brought Kyle back to them. He spoke like he was reminiscing about something he'd nearly forgotten about. "Gary there took a sort of shine to Jesse once upon a time," he said. "You nipped that one in the bud pretty quick, didn't you, buddy?"

Jesse felt the tips of his ears burn brightly. "I don't know what you're talking about," he started to say—but just then Brandon, still flushed with excitement, his hair wet from a victory shower, bounded through the door, and it was to the hero of the moment, mercifully, that they turned all their attention.

FIFTEEN

For the past few weeks he'd taken to turning the sprinkler on—rather guiltily, and only after dusk began to fall. Reservoir levels were at sixty percent of normal—out for a drive just the other day, he'd seen the great swath of exposed shoreline at the Ashokan—and in New Jersey, rationing was already mandatory. This July evening, even though a promising front of clouds had started to roll in and the forecast called for a possibility of thunderstorms, he dragged the unwieldy length of hose around to a patch of thirsty garden ("You should really get a sprinkler system put in," Dan had always urged, but then Cameron had gotten sick, and an expensive sprinkler system hadn't seemed that much of a priority anymore). The movement toward native gardens and Xeriscapes and the like had always stirred in Cameron a certain skepticism—what was a garden, after all, if not a place for pampered beauties to bloom? But as time went by, as the globe warmed and the ozone thinned and the Sahara spread, he came more and more to appreciate those tough, indigenous plants like sedums and prairie grasses and thistles and black-eyed Susans that endured all extremes of local weather. In particular, he'd grown to love the old cluster of yuccas that had come with the house, leathery survivors he'd nearly torn out when he first moved in. Now their spiky leaves and those great exotic pillars of blossoms they thrust up in midsummer seemed quite inspiring. Let the drought worsen as it might, those stately denizens of the garden would sail through just fine.

And, of course, the deer, lately desperate for succulent greens, wouldn't touch them.

To the west, lightning flickered. He hesitated at the faucet, trying to decide which superstitious course to take—would turning the sprinkler on now avert or guarantee the approaching storm? *Don't be ridiculous,* he heard Dan say with brutal logic, even as he turned on the tap and heard the sprinkler seethe, cough, then settle into its monotonous work.

A low rumble of thunder fanned out across the landscape. Storms had always unnerved Cameron a bit; he remembered long evenings of alarm in Memphis—the bruised sky, the heavy stillness in the air. Even now he dreamed, from time to time, he was back there, standing on the front steps, and watching, against a crimson sunset, five, six, seven green tornadoes move leisurely across the flat land, pulling up everything in their slow-motion path. He might suffer, still, the cold and snows of New York winters, the sharp lightning strikes of its summer thunderstorms—but the South's tornado weather was something he was very relieved to have left behind him.

Across the patio, as if urged along by a burst of wind, Casper flittered toward him. Cameron spoke aloud, as he often did when no other humans were around: "Hey, little fellow, let's you and me go inside."

Casper seemed to agree, dashing ahead and scampering up the steps of the back stoop. "Diva," Cameron called as the rising wind set off a series of urgent gestures among the tree branches. But Diva had a mind of her own. Casper was the homebody, never venturing far, preferring a life of ease to that of adventure. Diva was the smarter of the two, the willful one. She'd disappear one day; Cameron was sure of that.

A pop of lightning, then an earsplitting eruption of thunder, swept human and cat indoors. Exhilarated and anxious, Cameron went about shutting windows upstairs and down. It had gotten so dark all of a sudden that he turned on a light; then, wondering what the weather channel might have to say, he switched on the television as well. An urgent buzzer reinforced the words scrolling across the bottom of the screen: SEVERE THUNDERSTORM WARNING. Radar showed a heart of angry red in the broad line of green and yellow that snaked across the map of the region. "Uh-oh," he told Casper. "Batten down the hatches. It's a comin' our way." Outside, the real storm began to shake and rattle. Wind gusts shook the house. Lightning plied the sky. The power in the house faltered for a moment, then came back on, and Cameron clicked off the TV, even went so far as to unplug it, the way his mother used to do when storms approached. She'd known, hadn't she, how quickly dangerous situations could develop out of nowhere. Only minutes ago he'd been hauling his hose through the garden, careful not to drag it across a bed of bee balm—and now the house shuddered with strokes of thunder and bursts of wind, and a person stranded out in this tempest stood in even more danger than a fragile flower stalk.

From the woods across the street came a loud crack, followed by a concussive thud. It didn't take much to bring down the mostly second-growth locusts and swamp maples that flourished over there, tall and spindly from the ruthless competition for sunlight. He heard another tree splinter, felt another thump that shook the house. Then another, even more alarming crash. All around, trees were falling in the strange dark that had blown in with the storm. But no rain fell. That was the strangest thing. All this fury, and not a drop of rain. Suddenly spooked, he grabbed a flashlight from the kitchen, gathered Casper up in his arms, and scurried down the stairs to the basement.

He'd never have done something like this were Dan around; he'd have been too embarrassed. But he was on his own now, and he found himself enjoying his fear as much as suffering from it. He moved amid the half-forgotten junk they'd stored over their eight years in the house—an old pair of quite hideous stained-glass French doors, an oriental-style cabinet (why had they ever bought that, even if it *had* been a virtual steal?). Through the little ground-level windows, he could tell the rain had finally been unleashed. Now that he and Casper were stowed underground and perfectly safe, his fear began to feel faintly absurd. What was there to be afraid of, after all? He'd faced worse than a simple thunderstorm—he'd undoubtedly face far worse in the future. Blown away by the fierce winds of a summer storm—how would that be for an epitaph? The absurdity of it all at once struck him fully. In Turkey, among the ruins of ancient Perge, he and Toby had been caught in a sudden thunderstorm. As lightning delved into the plain all around them, they'd sheltered among a line of stone arches, sharing their refuge with a dozen goats dully huddled together, and after several minutes, as quickly as it had sprung up, the storm had faded, and in the distance, past the colonnaded avenue, a rainbow shimmered.

Toby was long gone; the goats too, no doubt. Only he was still alive in this world, only he could feel the sting of wind and pelting rain. Had he ever, in his life, stood out in a downpour just for the thrill and terror of it? "Okay," he ordered Casper, "you stay down here." Remounting the stairs, he went out onto the gale-swept front porch. Wind tore at the wisteria, which clung to the house for dear life. Rain lashed the garden, beating down the tall liatris and rose campion. Without a moment's hesitation Cameron marched down the front steps. It was like a movie, only it wasn't a movie. The big bullets of rain, surprisingly cold, made him shiver; they ran down his neck and stuck his shirt to his back. A little experimentally, he thrust both his arms into the air, opening his palms heavenward (he was glad no one was around to see) and shouting into the wind and rain. Not in anger, nor in joy—just a purely animal shout.

With an incandescent snap, lightning hit the telephone pole not fifty yards down the road. The nearly instantaneous wallop of thunder made the ground shudder. One good bit of theater deserves another. Reflexively shielding his head, Cameron scampered back up the porch steps. "Coward," he accused himself, laughing out loud at his ignoble rout. "You're going to die anyway. What the hell are you afraid of?"

But he was not going to die quite yet, and that, somehow, made all the difference.

Indoors, the power was out. The rain had soaked him through; stripping off his leaden clothes, he toweled himself dry. Having won that particular skirmish—or had they fought to a draw?—the lightning moved off to another part of the sky; thunder, pacified, almost soothing, murmured in the distance. Already the rain was petering out. For all its saber rattling, the storm had scarcely even touched the drought.

Exhausted, refreshed, Cameron went upstairs to his bedroom and pulled on a dry pair of pants. Reaching into the closet, his fingers fell randomly on a shirt. He'd halfway pulled it from the hanger before he realized whose it was. What was it like to be lying under the earth as a summer storm passed over? But of course, the dead knew nothing of that. Nothing at all. He'd never even tried the shirt on. It fit him perfectly. He was surprised, a little, to find he didn't feel reluctant to wear it. Jesse had given it to him, after all. He must have meant him to wear it. The well-worn cotton was smooth against his skin.

As he descended the stairs, he heard an urgent rustle at the back door.

He opened the screen and in dashed Diva, half-drowned, her fur slicked back like an otter's. She was not pleased. Circling about the kitchen, she meowed furiously. He gathered a wad of paper towels and began to rub her dry. "You and me," he said. "Two divas without a lick of sense."

From behind the basement door Casper too implored release and, when sprung, gave Diva's pink little anus a good thorough sniff. "Very nice," Cameron told them both, opening a can of their favorite food and dividing it into two portions so they wouldn't squabble. Then he went out onto the back stoop to take in the cooling, shattered air. Out in the dark of his garden he could hear the sprinkler going about its monotonous work as if nothing at all had happened.

Had someone been pounding on the back door? Something, at any rate, had woken him. The lamp beside his bed was on, he must have fallen asleep reading, but then he remembered the electricity had been out. Had he turned the lamp on anyway? He lay motionless, listening to the quiet around him. The clock beside his bed flashed 12:24, which hardly gave him a clue as to the actual time; all it meant was that the electricity's coming back on hadn't been what had woken him.

Ever since Dan had left, he'd kept a baseball bat under his bed, just in case—though he felt, in general, very safe in his house on a lonely country road.

He realized he'd been dreaming. He'd been making love to Dan, and though the exact details eluded him, a quietly rapturous blur filled him.

It had been years since they had made love like that. The sense of loss was so complete it left him gasping for air. For a moment he thought it might be possible his heart had failed him, he was dying as he'd always feared—alone, in the middle of the night.

But he wasn't dying. He lay on his back and gazed at the ceiling and took a series of even, calming breaths. Already the dream's embers had faded. He wasn't even completely sure, now, whether he'd been dreaming of Dan at all. When he was fifteen, he'd dreamed he stood in a vast empty field waiting for Mitchell Johnson. But in the dream, Mitchell never came. He'd gone away, no one knew where, and when Cameron woke, the dream-grief at Mitchell's disappearance stayed with him, he felt inexplicably shattered, and when he saw Mitchell again—the handsome fellow came loping into the bandroom the next afternoon, trumpet case in hand, smiling agreeably to everyone, Cameron included—he nearly burst into tears.

Poor Mitchell. He never had a clue what he'd meant to Cameron, and no doubt he'd be horrified to realize it was he and he alone who'd sparked the wrong kind of love in a boy he'd been casual friends with so long ago. My life began with you, Cameron silently addressed this absent figure his dream of Dan had unexpectedly conjured. And if you only knew where that life ended up taking me . . .

Ridiculous, he told himself. You don't know where my life took me, just as I don't know where yours took you. He had no illusions. Mitchell could have been anyone, the random stuff of a random dream seized upon by a fifteen-year-old ripe for sexual longing. For three years he'd worshiped at that barren shrine, and when he went away to Oberlin, he'd been right to put Mitchell Johnson completely behind him. Mitchell, Tommy McCalla, everything, in fact, that had seemed to offer itself as life but had instead been only a poor substitute for the real life he'd gone on to find— with Max, with Jamie and Roger, with Toby. With Dan Futrell.

He wondered if he should go downstairs just to check on things, but five minutes had passed since he'd bolted awake and nothing indicated that anything at all was amiss. From the eaves, from the limbs of trees, came the random footfall of water droplets. Moisture had clarified the residual sheen of the tree frogs. Around the lamp by his bed, the usual fascinating collection of bugs buzzed and circled, each crazy for whatever promise the light must hold for them. For a minute or two he watched a lacy green thing, incredibly delicate, fling itself at the irresistible lure of the lightbulb. Then he reached over and switched off the lamp. Was that merciful, he wondered, or cruel?

"Till this morning, I had no idea of the extent of the damage," Cameron told Jesse. "Then I looked out my window and—well, you can see."

The huge old oak at the back of the garden had split in half. Its massive trunk, still upright, ended in a jagged *V*. The two great divided branches, in whose crotch some long-ago boy had once built his tree house, had both crashed to the ground, where they lay like slain giants. A couple of locusts, unlucky in their choice of a neighbor, had been brought down as well.

His first impulse had been to mourn—not only the tree, but something larger. Surveying the wreckage he'd thought, Forget caring for things whose rout is inevitable. Forget the past few months' renewal. Forget any ideas about giving a garden party. I retreat. I surrender.

But then a surge of defiance had come over him. For a week Jesse had come every other day to weed, to deadhead and prune back and mulch, and before Cameron's eyes the garden had become his again, no longer a reminder of some other life he'd once lived, but an ongoing promise. And a strange thing: this strapping, untalkative lad was now implicated in his garden, not so much a fixture as—this was strangest of all—some animating spirit.

Surely that had to be celebrated, one way or another.

"Me and Kyle were out to two A.M. helping clear the roads," Jesse said, seemingly oblivious to the heartbreak of one particular tree, no matter how freighted with sentiment. "Fire department needed all the help it could get. Route 32 totally blocked off. Springtown Road. There was this big transformer fire in Weed's Mill Falls, live wire down, all kinds of shit. Hell of a night for folks."

"My electricity was out for about five hours," Cameron reported.

"Well, you were lucky, considering. Some people's is still out."

Cameron took the implicit reprimand as his due. "It was certainly good of you to come over like this. You must be exhausted."

"I'm fine. I don't sleep too much anyways. Mostly I just lie awake."

And I wish you could tell me why, Cameron thought. I wish we could share, you and I, all the various reasons a man might lie sleepless through a long, lonely night. But knowing Jesse Vanderhof was a dead-end street if ever there was such a thing, he reminded himself sternly. He was not in love. He was, rather, back in the tumultuous, mortal predicament that was ordinary life.

"I can get all this downed stuff cleared for you, no problem," Jesse said. "But I'm gonna need Kyle to help with that trunk. Don't you worry. We'll get you looking good as new."

"Excellent. I'll leave you to your work, then."

As he walked away, though, it was precisely that necessity—of leaving Jesse to his work—that keenly bore in on him. He hated being out of the world the way he was, this frailty that would be with him till he died, and by the time he entered his house the impossibility of the two of them ever sweating together in the sun as comrades had worked him into a fit of unparalleled bleakness.

Mounting the narrow stairs to his bedroom, he sat at his desk and pulled out a stack of bills. From the window, he had a good view of the wrecked tree. He watched as Jesse pulled his failing pickup around and backed it up to the work site. Normally the sound of a chain saw was something Cameron hated. Whenever he heard one in the distance, he went into a sort of righteous alarm—somebody, undoubtedly, was up to no good, destroying this or that perfectly healthy tree—but this morning the buzz of Jesse's saw came through the open window as pure, ebullient noise.

He wrote out half a dozen checks, pausing to notice, not for the first time, how, in the last couple of years, his once bold handwriting had become as spidery and diffident as an old man's. Then he peered once more out the window. Jesse had removed his T-shirt and hung it from a snag on the shattered tree trunk.

On a sudden impulse, Cameron pushed his checkbook aside and rose from his desk. He put on his straw hat and went back out into his wounded garden. Twigs and small branches littered the flowerbeds, and he went about gathering them up as Jesse's chain saw sang away among the limbs of the fallen oak. After a while, all that stooping and rising made him feel a little dizzy. Depositing his load of sticks near the compost heap, he sat down on a bench in the shade, a vantage from which he could observe his young redneck at work. Jesse had his back to him, and Cameron indulged in several moments' thoughtful contemplation of that thoughtlessly perfect body. All things come to an end, of course, and soon enough he noticed he was being observed in return. With surprising friendliness Jesse smiled—hadn't Mitchell Johnson smiled like that long ago, in the corridors of high school? Holding the chain saw easily in one hand, Jesse waved with the other, a wave that metamorphosed, as Cameron realized, into a summons.

Was he to be rebuked for staring? He stood up from the bench and sauntered, as casually as possible, toward Jesse and his chain saw.

Jesse spoke over the saw's idling drone, "Wanna give me a hand with this? You could drag them limbs over to the truck and free me up some work space. That is, if you feel like helping."

"Sure," Cameron told him.

"You might want some gloves. I think there's a pair laying in the back of the truck."

With a kind of reverence Cameron slid his hands into the soft, well-worn leather. Use had molded them to Jesse's contours—or at least that was what he pretended. Still, some boundary had been crossed. Of that he was certain. Feeling oddly buoyant, he hauled a largish branch from the tangle and dragged it over to the truck, whose recovery, he reminded himself, he had helped finance. Surely Jesse remained aware of that too. He worked ahead of Cameron, farther up the fallen trunk. Cameron heaved limb after limb into the truck bed. In the hot morning sun, where only yesterday there'd been shade, they worked together.

A kind of ache never left Cameron these days, not even so much an ache as the ghost of an ache, but now it surfaced all through him. How quickly dull fatigue set in. And yet he hesitated to give up; he hated the thought of revealing himself to Jesse, just at this moment when they'd been brought so pleasantly together. Besides, what exactly would he say? I'm not well? I have AIDS?

He threw another large branch into the back of the truck and trudged over to where Jesse, like the sorcerer's apprentice, continued to produce more and more for him to haul away. Grasping another, he tugged, and it pulled free of the thicket of limbs and leaves. All at once he felt the strangest shock go through him. A wave charged with light—that was how it felt—lifted him up and then plunged him under. As a boy at Myrtle Beach he'd gone down in the surf like that, only to come up struggling. This time he did not struggle. He felt he was falling, but at the same time felt a suspension, a delicious ease, as if certain something, he didn't know what, would catch him.

The next he knew, Jesse was squatting by his side, peering down at him with a look of concern—or would that be a frown of perplexity?

"Easy," Jesse told him, though Cameron had no intention of taking his predicament anything but easily. He was lying on his back, his limbs leaden, his tongue dry. He tried to speak, but no words came.

"Ambulance'll be here any minute," Jesse comforted him, though the news was, in its way, the opposite of comforting. Clearly he'd passed out, but for how long?

"I fell down," he managed to say, but the words sounded ludicrous.

"I couldn't get you to respond or nothing, so I went up to the house to call 911. Maybe I should go around front to wait. Don't move or nothing. Just lay there and I'll be right back, I promise." And reaching out, Jesse touched his shoulder, a reassuring pat, nothing more. But also nothing less.

"I'm fine, I'll just rest here," Cameron assured his benefactor as Jesse rose from his squat and retrieved his shirt from the trunk of the oak. The young man's words and gesture struck Cameron, in his sweet lethargy, as unmistakably tender, and he had a wry thought—had Jesse been scared enough to try mouth-to-mouth resuscitation on him? But that, of course, was just a thought—though the kind of thought that meant he was already coming around from his mysterious little episode.

When was the last time he'd lain on his back on the ground and looked up at the sky? Somewhere nearby a mockingbird was singing its mad little heart out. Farther away, a siren. The sky had never seemed quite so marvelous—storm-cleansed, clear as crystal, a gorgeous, flawless blue. Azure. Cerulean. Lapis lazuli. Though only for a moment. Then the little brown spots that had plagued him all summer came swarming before his eyes. He could go for hours without noticing them, but once he did, he couldn't unsee those maddening, persistent flaws no matter how he tried.

SIXTEEN

He paused briefly at the half-closed door before knocking. Why he'd
come, exactly, he wasn't sure; but Kyle had said, *You bet you should go
visit him. Just be careful you don't pick up no germs.*

So here he was.

He felt bad for Cameron in a way that surprised him, because he
assured himself he wasn't really that caring a person. But part of him had
just not believed, despite the evidence of all those pills, despite the fact the
guy was gay as a goose, that here was somebody who had IT. The very
word made him shiver: there was cancer and heart disease and leukemia,
all the terrible diseases, and then there was AIDS, the one disease, if he
ever found out he had it, there was no doubt what he'd do. Drink a bottle
of whiskey and blow his sorry head off and wish he'd never been born.
Though he wished that last one from time to time anyway, not that anybody cared or ever need know.

He wondered, for a moment, what Brandon would say when he heard
Jesse Vanderhof had gone and killed himself; then he rapped his knuckles
against the reassuringly solid door.

Inside he could hear voices, and instantly he wished he hadn't knocked,
but already somebody was saying "Come in," already he'd cautiously
pushed the door open. Cameron sat up in the hospital bed. Two other men
were in the room, visitors, because the other bed was all neatly made up,
obviously unoccupied. The older of the two sat in a chair; hair and mus-

tache were grizzled, his lime green polo shirt revealed surprisingly muscular upper arms. Jesse had seen him before, he was some kind of friend of Cameron's, which made sense, after all. The other one stood with his back to the window, leaning on the sill. His dark hair fell into his eyes. He was what you'd call a handsome guy.

"Jesse," Cameron said, sounding surprised, sounding happy, and Jesse wished desperately he'd never listened to Kyle and come. He held out the flowers he'd brought.

"From your garden," he said in a rush. "Hope you don't mind."

"How kind. They're beautiful, if I do say so myself. Look," Cameron told his visitors. "Oh, by the way, Jesse, these are my friends Max and Perry."

They ate him up with their eyes, all the while smiling, saying, "Nice to meet you."

"Jesse's the one who saved my life."

"You'd of been okay," he assured the sick man nervously. "You just had a fainting spell."

"The doctor's calling it a seizure. Though he's not sure exactly what caused it. He's put me on antiseizure medication."

"Wasn't much of a seizure," Jesse felt he should say. "One thing I knew, you was upright and hauling branches, the next you was just laying there. You didn't seize or nothing."

"I suppose you're the only one who would know. I'll relay that to Dr. Vishnaraman."

The name made Jesse go cold. Parking in the lot, he'd been nearly overcome by panic or nausea, it was hard to say which, exactly, but for a full ten minutes he'd sat in the truck before working up the nerve to venture inside.

"I knew your dad," the one named Max was saying. "I was very sorry to hear he passed away."

It suddenly came to Jesse that Max was the one his uncle Roy had been speaking of some days ago. He couldn't recall Pop ever mentioning him one way or another. With a spasm of the old panic or nausea he thought he'd left in the parking lot, he realized that he was standing in a room with three homosexuals, and what was he supposed to say?

"What can you do?" he told Max, somehow taking against him for having brought Pop into this. "That's life."

"True," Max said, "but that never makes it any easier."

Jesse shrugged. "Where should I put these?" He held out the flowers, realizing he should have stuck them in a jar before coming down. Where they'd lain on the seat beside him, they were starting to wilt a little.

"I'll take them," the one named Perry told him. "Surely they'll have a vase down at the nurses' station to put them in."

On the windowsill behind him, hidden till he stepped forward, sat a big, expensive bundle of pink roses in a blue glass vase. Cameron must have seen Jesse staring, because he said, "Max and Perry brought those."

"He likes yours more, I can tell," Max teased as Perry, taking from Jesse his ragged bouquet, moved past, touching Jesse lightly on the shoulder in the narrow passage between the foot of the bed and the wall. The touch of his fingers, just a light brush to say "Excuse me," made Jesse jump, he couldn't help it, a reflex so noticeable Perry said, "Sorry, didn't mean to startle you."

Mortified, Jesse flattened himself against the wall and let Perry pass without saying a word. He wondered how long he was supposed to stay, if he could leave now, though Kyle had made it clear he thought a nice long visit was in order. "You're his friend now," he'd told Jesse as they lay in their beds and talked things through. "He owes you."

Easy enough for you to say, Jesse thought, but he hadn't said anything; he'd lain in a sort of drowse listening to Kyle scheme and plan. "He's a lonesome fag who's got more money than he knows what to do with. Look what he gave you for the truck. It makes him happy to give it away. It makes us happy to take some of it. Everybody's happy. Nobody gets hurt."

How much of that was true, Jesse didn't even dare think about. What was hurt, after all?

He thinks you're his friend, he told himself reluctantly, looking at Cameron—who seemed perfectly healthy, truth be told—sitting up in the bed and talking with Max, who was saying he'd call later, and if they let Cameron go home tomorrow, he'd be there to pick him up. Cameron held out his hand, and Max took it in both his, stroking the back of it with his thumb. Jesse put his hands in his pockets and tried not to stare—it was like, for a minute, they'd forgotten he was even there. He looked up to the TV set mounted on the wall for some kind of rescue, but saw it wasn't on. So he looked again at the expensive roses on the windowsill and felt a flush of shame so bad it made him feel sick. How long could it take Perry to find something to put his stupid flowers in?

He looked up expectantly—not *too* expectantly, he hoped—as the door opened. But it wasn't Perry returning with his flowers. "Good day," the dark little man announced, sizing up the three of them with a cool, professional look. Jesse looked away rather than meet his gaze, but Dr. Vishnaraman showed no sign of having any idea who he was. "How are we feeling this afternoon?" he asked, like everybody in the room was one of his patients—if not now, then later. He wore what looked like a very expensive suit underneath his white lab coat.

"Perfectly fine," Cameron told him. "Except the food is atrocious. But I do love the view."

The doctor smiled a thin, patient smile and glanced down at his clipboard.

Perry had slipped into the room and stood beside Jesse, tapping him lightly on the shoulder. "Did I miss anything exciting?" he said in a low voice—like they were all in on this together, like they were the best of friends.

Irked by Perry's touch, Jesse said nothing, only shook his head. Besides, he didn't know whether you were supposed to talk when the doctor was in the room, and he didn't want to do anything to make himself noticed.

"It's a little kitschy," Perry told him. "It was all they could do."

Jesse wasn't quite sure what *kitschy* meant, but he took the vase and his flowers just to have done with it. "Thanks, man," he mumbled under his breath, holding his gift awkwardly and wishing he was anywhere but here.

"I'm going to keep you here a couple more days," Dr. Vish told Cameron. "Just to make sure the antiseizure drug is working. We don't want another occurrence. You might not be so lucky next time. You might be driving a car, or crossing a busy street. So just to be on the safe side." He reached down and patted Cameron's leg where it lay under the sheet.

"Jesse over there's the one who called 911. I have him to thank."

Dr. Vishnaraman looked at him with mild curiosity. "Pardon me," he said. "I believe I know you."

"My dad."

"Of course," the doctor said, nodding gravely. "Please convey my sad condolences to your family."

"Yeah," Jesse told him, imagining, as in a nightmare, the doctor continuing, But what is a young man like you doing here with people like this? Your poor dad must be turning over in his grave.

I can explain, Jesse rehearsed silently, but the explanation suddenly looked flat and unconvincing, and besides, Dr. Vishnaraman did not seem to find it at all strange for Jesse to be at the hospital visiting a man who had AIDS.

"I trust him," Cameron said when the doctor had left.

"I still wish you'd get a real doctor down in New York," Max told him. "Somebody who specializes."

"It's a strange thing." Cameron sighed. "I have absolutely no desire to go to New York these days for anything. Not even for my health."

"I've told you, I'll drive you down there anytime you want." Max looked at Jesse and winked. "We have this ongoing argument. As you can see."

Mutely, to keep Max at bay, Jesse held out the flowers in the vase.

"Perfect," Cameron judged. "They're perking right back up. Set them over here on the windowsill where I can see them. It was so thoughtful of you to bring them."

Way too much was being made of those dumb-ass flowers, Jesse thought as he set his meager gift next to the pink roses in their blue vase. He had half a mind to mention they were Kyle's idea, not his. But things had moved past that before he'd even begun to decide what to say and what not to say.

"Well, sweetie," Max was telling Cameron, "you be good now, and I'll see you first thing tomorrow." Then, like it was the most natural thing, he bent over and kissed Cameron on the lips. Disconcerted, Jesse looked away—only to find himself meeting Perry's gaze, which he looked away from as well, to the safety of the linoleum-tiled floor. But he was conscious that Perry had been watching him.

"Bye, honey," Perry said, moving forward to engage the sick man as well. Jesse wouldn't look. He continued to study the floor while a profound sense of emptiness opened up somewhere in his gut.

"You're not leaving too, I hope?"

It took Jesse a moment to realize that Cameron was speaking to him. He looked up to see Max and Perry moving toward the door. "Nice to meet you, Jesse," Max said, and Perry, looking him directly in the eye—Jesse hesitated, this time, before glancing warily away—echoed the sentiment.

165

"Yeah," Jesse told them both; then, in answer to Cameron's question, he hazarded reluctantly, "I don't guess I'll leave right yet," wondering if it was too late to call everything off, to lie to his brother, say, He don't like me after all, it's not going to work, whatever you were thinking. But the funny, awful thing was—Cameron did like him, and Jesse felt himself hard put to account for the peculiar sensation that provoked in him.

Beyond the window, past the flowers, past the clutter of Kingston, the Catskills slept peacefully on the horizon. It was the same view as from Pop's old room, except Pop's room had been the next floor up.

"I love those mountains," Cameron said, almost like he could read Jesse's thoughts. "When I was in here last time—and that time I was *really* sick—I used to just sit in bed and look at them for hours. It was so comforting. I kept thinking to myself, if I die, all it means is, I'm going to join those mountains." He laughed. "The things you'll do to cheer yourself up. But it did cheer me up. Or at least make me feel peaceful. I've got AIDS, if you haven't figured that out already. Which probably you have. I just thought I should say it. You know, full disclosure."

Jesse hesitated, because what was he supposed to say? I saw your pill bottles? I know all about you? Though of course he hardly knew a thing. That was what he found so strange and disconcerting.

"I'm really sorry to hear that," he told Cameron politely, wishing he could somehow beam himself beyond the window pane to the mountains' tranquil solitude.

Once again, Cameron was reading his thoughts. "It's strange," he said. "I moved here because of the mountains. When I was a kid, growing up in the South, Memphis, flat as a pancake, the mountains were someplace you had to drive hours and hours to get to. It was a great treat. We used to spend a week in the Smoky Mountains every summer—camping, hiking. And then I came here, and it's like being on vacation all the time. If you'd told me, when I was growing up, that one day I'd live within a stone's throw of beautiful mountains, I'd never have believed it. That's what's so strange—the places you end up, you never, ever thought you'd be."

So he was still talking about AIDS, Jesse thought. He figured he should probably stop staring out the window now and look at Cameron, so he turned around, but Cameron wasn't looking at him. He was studying his hospital bracelet, turning it around and around on his wrist, and Jesse had to wonder if maybe he was less interesting to Cameron than he thought.

"The mountains were just something I always grew up with," he said.

"Oh, but you're young," Cameron told him.

But what did that mean? Jesse wanted to ask. Watching Pop die hadn't taught him a thing. He still didn't have a clue what you were supposed to say to somebody lying in a hospital bed with a death sentence on them; he only knew you were supposed to say something. What would Kyle do? But Kyle had only been able to say that what was so wasn't so, and that hadn't been any help at all; it hadn't stopped Pop from dying one bit.

"You're young," Cameron went on, "and you have a whole world in front of you." He was still looking at his wrist like that green plastic bracelet fascinated him, like he had no clue how it came to be fastened to him like a handcuff. And maybe that was what you felt—a kind of fascination to find yourself where you were, fastened to this disease that wouldn't let you go.

How'd you get it? Jesse longed to ask, the way you might long to look over the sheer drop of a cliff if you were somebody terrified of heights. And then, hardly knowing he was speaking the words, he found himself asking exactly that, aware how strange it must sound, how rude. He's a fag who's dying, he told himself with a spasm of meanness. What do I care what kind of questions I ask him if there're answers I really need to know?

To look at it that way made everything suddenly easier. Kyle, he felt, would be impressed.

"How'd I get it?" Cameron repeated the question. "Well, aren't you the surprising one. I mean, we hardly know each other—and *nobody* ever asks me that, though I'm sure everybody must be dying to. Why do you want to know, exactly?"

"You're right. I got no business asking," Jesse said. "I wasn't using my head there." Why did anybody die? You take a drink of something you shouldn't, and then another and another, you put your dick somewhere you're not supposed to, you drive too fast with your buddies along a country road at night after winning a basketball game.

But Cameron didn't seem like he was offended. In fact, he seemed eager to talk. "Sit down," he invited. "You don't have to be so nervous around me. It's not like I'm going to bite or anything. And I'm bored to death of being here. If it'll make the time pass, I'll answer any question you want to ask me. So please." He gestured toward the chair by the window.

Jesse, however, remained standing. "I never knew anybody with AIDS before," he confessed. "I mean, to be honest, it freaks me out a little."

"Well, you're definitely not going to get it from sitting here and keeping me company for a little while."

"I guess not," Jesse agreed, settling into the chair and trying to reassure himself there really was no harm in talking to somebody like Cameron so long as he watched what he said. Besides, Cameron seemed happy to do all the talking.

"How'd I get to these mountains, you want to know? Well, believe it or not, I probably didn't start out too different from you. Just your average, ordinary kid. Then one day I had the really wonderful misfortune to fall in love with this boy from my school." Cameron smiled to himself, still gazing out the window. "One day he was just a guy who played trumpet in the band; the next day, it was like he had this magic glow around him. Boy, do I remember that. I started living that very day. I remember walking around in a kind of daze—agony and excitement and just absolute rapture all wrapped into one brand-new emotion I never knew existed before. But why am I telling you all that? You know perfectly well what's it's like to fall in love. Of course, it didn't change anything, really. That was the most painful part. Inside, everything was different, it was like I was on fire, this flame burning inside me, but the days went along just like nothing had happened. Mitchell Johnson was still just this guy I barely knew. So I set out on a campaign to be his best friend. I was ruthless. I ditched my old friends. I made friends with his crowd. And you know, it sort of worked. We started eating lunch together, hanging out at the mall after school, going to see a movie now and then.

"But here's the sad part, the ironic part. The more I succeeded, the better I got to know him, the more I could see it was all hopeless. I mean, I thought he was perfect, but at the same time . . . well, I remember one day in the cafeteria he was complaining about his French teacher, Mr. La-Mont, who everybody thought was quite a character, and Mitchell said in this knowing voice, like he was sharing a disgusting secret with me, 'He's, you know, *that way.*' His eyebrows arched up, his mouth turned down. He made a limp wrist. It just came to me so clearly—that I was, you know, *that way* too, which had never really occurred to me before. It was kind of devastating. Because I just thought I was this normal guy who was in love with Mitchell Johnson; it had never occurred to me that that meant

168

I too was *that way*. And then it occurred to me that the only reason Mitchell was friends with me was because he had no idea I was *that way,* and if he ever found out, he wouldn't have anything to do with me anymore. But of course, if anything that I wanted to happen between us was ever going to happen, then he'd have to find out, and so, whichever way you looked at it, what I wanted was impossible."

It wasn't the kind of talk Jesse was used to. He didn't know anybody who talked like that, about things you'd normally be ashamed of.

"Did you keep on being friends with him?"

"With Mitchell? Oh, till the bitter end. Through girlfriends, and breakups with girlfriends, and him confiding in me every single lust that blew through him. Then we graduated, and I went away to college and he stayed in Memphis and that was that. I lost all touch with him. I don't think he ever had a clue."

"Huh," Jesse said. Had anybody ever made him walk around in a daze like that, like everything in the world was changed? If so, he sure couldn't remember it, though he did remember Donna asking him one day, did he want to go out with her? They'd been standing in the school parking lot; her bus was late, so he was waiting there with her. He'd been hanging around with her more and more that spring of junior year, and it just seemed a logical progression from one thing to the next. But he never walked around in a daze. All he'd felt was a kind of relief, like something that needed to happen had finally happened.

"So you're probably thinking that's it," Cameron said. "Loyal, unrequited love till finally I broke free. But no. It was messier. I ended up with this other kid I didn't even like, this handsome thug on the wrestling team. Spent my high school years sucking him off in his parents' garage after school. Pretty sordid, if you ask me. He wasn't even gay, I don't think, just a bully who had my number and needed to get his rocks off on a regular basis. I'm not shocking you too much, am I? I don't see any point in talking if I'm not going to tell the truth. It's the one thing I like about hospital rooms. You get to say whatever's on your mind."

"I ain't too shocked," Jesse said, though he was, in fact, a little. Was that what it all came down to? Sucking some guy off? Cameron's tale made him shudder. What he felt mostly was a sense of doom—like when their dog Apache had run in front of a car, and he'd watched it from the front porch, helpless to stop it from happening. He wanted to tell that kid on his knees in the garage, Stop before it's too late, but it was already too late, it was years too late.

"The last thing I want is to scare you off," Cameron said.

"I don't scare too easy."

"Good. I'm enjoying talking to you. But I think maybe you should go now. All this talking, suddenly, it's worn me out. I think I might need to take a nap."

"That's okay. Sure." Jesse was surprised at how disappointed he felt. But why? None of this had all that much to do with him. Still, Cameron wasn't a bad talker, and a hospital room wasn't the worst place to listen.

"I probably told you way more than you wanted to know."

"No," Jesse assured him. "It was all pretty interesting."

"If you feel like it, stop by again. You know where I am. I'd enjoy the company."

"Well, maybe," Jesse said. "I'll see how it goes."

"Oh, one last thing. I was going to ask Max, but I forgot. Would you mind stopping by the house and making sure the cats have food and water? In all the commotion it probably never even got locked."

"I locked it for you."

"There's a key under the back stoop. Just reach your hand around there; you'll find it."

"No problem," Jesse said, suddenly guilty at the liberties he and Kyle had taken that day. But Cameron didn't have a clue, did he?

Cameron held out his hand. "Thanks. For the flowers. For everything."

"No problem," Jesse repeated, reaching out to take the sick man's hand.

It clasped his own with surprising strength, for a guy who was dying. In that instant, the strangest memory came to him. Gary Dunkel. He'd walked around in a daze once for Gary Dunkel.

But that was years ago. He didn't even like Gary Dunkel anymore.

Most of all, as he charged into the healing warmth of the sun, he wanted to find Kyle. It was Kyle who'd put him up to this. Now he wanted to tell his brother it had gone okay. Everything according to plan. But Kyle was out in Kerhonkson, painting some weekender's barn. With Brandon. And why, as he climbed in his truck, did he feel vaguely wronged—like Cameron had stuck a hand in his pocket, like he'd stolen something from him? But of course that didn't make any sense. He'd been smart enough to keep his own mouth shut. Talk however much he liked, Cameron wasn't getting a thing out of him. That was for sure.

In the wide fields the corn was dying. Maybe he resented, a little, that he'd been stuck visiting the hospital. Not a month ago he'd been free of all this shit, no idea it was even lurking over the horizon. What wouldn't he give to go back to that peaceful time?

But that time hadn't been peaceful either, had it? Pop dying, and before that money troubles, the time Donna missed her period, Pop at midnight arguing with the walls—when had there ever been a peaceful time of it?

On his way out, he'd made sure to stop in the rest room and scrub his hands. He wondered at anybody kissing Cameron on the lips, but those two guys hadn't seemed to mind. He remembered the way Perry had looked at him. Well, Perry was a handsome guy, anybody could see that.

Inexplicably miserable, Jesse pulled into the potholed parking lot of the Family Market, trying to skid his truck to a satisfying halt with the kind of finesse that came so easily to his brother, but all it got him was some woman behind her shopping cart shooting him a dirty look. In response, he turned up the radio full blast, just for a few seconds, then cut the engine and climbed down from the cab.

C.J. and some girl Jesse used to go to high school with were minding the empty registers. Brandy? Brittany? From a distance he couldn't make out her name tag, but he told himself she was pretty cute.

"Hey." He approached C.J. "Donna here?"

C.J. smiled that annoying smile of his, and Jesse had a sudden, involuntary picture of taking hold of the kid's spiky hairdo and pushing him facedown onto the dirty tile floor. The keen pleasure of that thought took him by surprise, especially since the kid had never done him a bit of wrong.

C.J. shook his head. "She done left, oh, about"—looking down at his plastic wristwatch—"I don't know, half a hour ago."

I bet you'd just love for somebody to fuck you in the butt, Jesse caught himself thinking. I bet that's what that smile of yours is all about.

He shook himself from the evil stupor of that thought. "Okay, man. Catch you later."

But C.J. wasn't paying him any more attention. Some old man had dumped out practically a shopping-basket-ful of Ramen noodles on the conveyer belt.

With a sudden throb, Jesse thought of Kyle and Brandon painting that barn, long brushstrokes, radio playing, sun shining overhead. Best buddies with nothing in the world to shade that peaceful situation.

The house stood open and defenseless. It felt strange to venture in there alone, un-watched-over. It was like someone had died. But Cameron hadn't died. He'd be coming back to this house in a day or two; everything would go on in the same old way. Jesse supposed he was glad for the guy, glad he was getting out of the hospital instead of going straight into the ground, glad he was getting another chance. Still, the prospect of the two of them returning to the same routine with each other depressed him.

When he poured some pellets of food into the empty bowl, two cats, one black, the other white, appeared out of nowhere. He didn't think he knew their names. They ate greedily, without so much as a sign they even registered his presence. He didn't much care for cats.

He wondered what Kyle would want him to do right now. The house was his for the taking, though he knew Kyle had bigger plans than snagging some fellow's credit card (their knuckle-brained cousin over in Kerhonkson had tried that game once). So what, exactly, did Kyle figure was going to happen? He was a great one for making plans—join the army, sign up for the police academy, win the lottery—but when did he ever carry through on any of that shit? It felt traitorous to think such a thing, but there it was.

Taking one of Cameron's beers from the fridge, he went out into the garden. The oak tree pointed its shattered V of a trunk skyward. The two big limbs, each as thick as a man, lay where they'd fallen. If he'd been thinking, he could've brought over the twenty-four-inch chain saw and finished the job, but as usual he wasn't thinking. On a shaded bench he sat and sipped at his beer. The sultry air was completely still. Somewhere an invisible bird went on and on, sounding like a rusty hinge. Everywhere among the confusion of flowers, little white butterflies were dancing. He'd never sat out here in the garden by himself. You could feel very calm in this place.

He tried to imagine what you'd have to do to hit the jackpot his brother saw when he looked at Cameron Barnes. There was no way. The guy had AIDS. You'd have to be crazy to even think of trying any of that shit with him. Even if you bagged a million bucks out of it, you'd still be fucked, and fucked royally.

Up the path the black cat came stalking; it paused, alert to something he couldn't see, then resumed its cautious progress. Up to no good, Jesse thought as the sleek little animal made a neat pounce into the bushes and disappeared.

The summer had turned out so different than he could have imagined. Sometimes he went to Pop's death, touching it gingerly, the way you might a bruise. He wondered what Pop would think of this shit with Cameron Barnes. But the thing was, if Pop was still around to know about it, then it'd never be happening in the first place.

All that was too hard to think about. He could stop by the cemetery, he realized. It was right up the road. But he knew he wouldn't. He hadn't been there once since the funeral, when they'd buried Pop in style.

In the breezeless air, a single flower stalk in the bed in front of him started to shake back and forth. He watched, curious, as it trembled violently, like some invisible wind had caught it up but left all the others alone. Then it seemed to heave itself right out of the ground and lean into the stalk next to it, which itself began mysteriously to stir.

A mole was moving underground. Jesse could see the little hump of dirt as it inched forward in fits and starts, taking down the second stalk in its progress. They were the bane of Cameron's garden, though the guy was reluctant to do anything to stop them. Same with the deer that wandered through every night and nipped the buds off roses and daylilies, chomped the big hosta leaves right down to the ground. How could he stand to see all his hard work undone like that? And Jesse's hard work too: on his hands and knees, he'd weeded that bed only last week.

What Cameron didn't know wouldn't hurt him. In a sudden fit of irritation, Jesse strode out to the shed and returned with a shovel. The mole had taken down another stalk. He could tell where it was; it lay throbbing just below the soil it had pushed up. Without hesitating, Jesse plunged the blade of the shovel into the soft earth. Several times he repeated the thrust, just to be sure. Normally he didn't go in for killing things, but he felt a strange satisfaction flood through him. There were times when you just couldn't afford to think too much. You just had to do something.

The black cat had disappeared. The white one lay sunning itself on a flagstone of the path. It didn't even move when he stepped over it.

Don't think, he thought, bounding up the narrow stairs three at a time to Cameron's bedroom. Cameron's checkbook lay open on his desk. But Jesse didn't touch it. Instead, he went to Cameron's clothes closet and pulled open the door. Pop's old flannel shirt hung there like a beacon, but that wasn't what he was after.

SEVENTEEN

There'd been so little to break the transcendental tedium of gazing out the window that he welcomed every intrusion. A nurse came by to take his temperature; an affable priest stopped in to ask if he needed any spiritual assistance. ("Alas, no," Cameron had told him. "But thanks anyway.") Lunch arrived—applesauce, cream of chicken soup, an unidentifiable portion of meat smothered in gravy. A carton of milk. If he'd really checked off those choices on the menu the night before, he was in far worse shape than he feared.

He poked a bit at the meat, which, even when chewed, remained a mystery, though its taste and consistency were not all that unpleasant. He remembered how, at her home in Bromley, Mrs. Waddeston had served him a tongue sandwich once, which he'd avidly consumed before thinking to ask what it was. Odd what you remembered of someone long gone. And yet it was a kind of intermittent life they continued to lead, wasn't it? Posthumous flickers, better than nothing. Oh, Mrs. Waddeston, he thought, looking out at the consolingly matter-of-fact Catskills in the distance. In the middle of dinner, at a friend's house, she'd announced, "I don't feel well at all." Those had been her last words.

Widely spaced cloud shadows mottled the sunny mountains with their darker accents. He realized he couldn't remember the last words Toby had spoken. They'd been blurred, garbled, a long descent into incoherence. There was nothing, really, to remember.

There was everything to remember. There was Toby drinking vodka and lemonade on a summery afternoon, windows flung open, a breeze wafting in from the fire escape with its pots of scented geraniums and lavender and rosemary (even in the city there'd been a garden to cobble together in the least promising of spaces); the stereo was blasting *Petrushka,* one of Toby's favorites—he loved brash, athletic orchestral music, *The Rite of Spring* and Janáceck's *Sinfonietta* and Carl Ruggles's *Sun-treader,* none of it music Cameron could bear to listen to without Toby's embodiment of those exuberant sounds any longer in the world.

There was the first time he ever went to see Toby onstage, not in one of the desperately off-off-Broadway plays Toby valiantly shone in back in those days, but in a concert of gamelan, that Balinese ensemble of gongs and drums and lustrously tuned metal instruments. Toby had played in one at Wesleyan as an undergraduate; he saw it as spiritual training of the highest order, and when he'd moved to New York, he'd sought one out, The Venerable Shining Cloud, a collection of professional and amateur musicians who rehearsed weekly under the tutelage of a charismatic woman from Jakarta and gave a public concert twice a year.

Cameron had never seen or heard such music performed before. The dozen or so barefoot players wore black sarongs and dazzling white shirts; all had red bandannas tied about their foreheads. Hands pressed together as in prayer, they bowed in unison, then seated themselves behind their instruments. Toby was one of the drummers. A low gong sounded, solemn and mysterious, and each of the players reached simultaneously, ceremoniously, for a mallet. Almost casually, more suggestion than statement, a single instrument rang out four or five mellow notes, then suddenly the entire clanging ensemble entered, hammers on metal, strident, melodious, bracing. Urging it all on, Toby drummed powerfully, elaborating the straightforward beat of a second drummer with triplets and counter-rhythms. Riding the crest of all that sound, Toby looked from side to side—at his fellow drummer, the other players—and suddenly broke into a great smile, as if in sheer, disbelieving delight at the pleasure his drumming called forth. For the other players, as he could surely see, were as delighted as he at the sound they were making. And the audience was delighted too. On and on he led them, through cascades, then limpid pools, then back into surges of galvanic energy. Finally he struck a series of rapid signals; the whole moved swiftly to a close. With the last resonating stroke of the low gong he raised his right hand, fluttering it in midair—the way a leaf trembles in a breeze—as the shimmer of sound slowly died away into silence.

Who were you? Cameron wondered, lying in his bed in the Benedictine Hospital. Who were you that you could betray me a thousand times and I'd forgive you everything? Forgive you even your own death. Forgive you even mine.

But he would not die today, he reminded himself, holding on to the memory of Toby beaming and rising, making once again that little prayerful bow as if to say thank you—to everyone, for everything (not everyone had thought him as drop-dead beautiful as Cameron did). No, Dr. Vishnaraman had assured him this was a minor setback, nothing more. He'd share this planet with mountains and memories for at least a little while longer.

Perhaps, he thought, his gaze lingering on the cold comfort of the Catskills, he shouldn't have sent that priest away so hastily—but it was only a thought. He'd been allergic to religion of any kind ever since he turned fifteen, found himself in love with another boy, and, anticipating even greater betrayals to come, refused any longer to accompany his decent, God-fearing parents to the Scenic Highway Baptist Church. None of that for him: not Jesus, nor the Buddha, nor Allah as hauntingly sung from the minarets of Istanbul. Especially not Elliot's radiance, whatever that was, or any other feebleminded New Age concoction. It was hard enough believing, sometimes, even in the palpability of a hazy range of mountains in the distance.

A hesitant knock at his hospital room door redirected his gaze from the window.

"Come in," he said, then repeated the command.

Warily, Jesse slid into the room. "Oh," said the young man, as if startled, "you're eating your lunch."

"Caught in the act," Cameron admitted, though the barely touched lunch before him was the last thing on his mind. The delight he felt at seeing the young man surprised him. He hadn't expected him at all. He'd been mischievous the day before. Perhaps he'd felt he had nothing much to lose. Or perhaps he'd been curious to see just where a conversation might take the two of them. They'd gotten much farther than he'd imagined, though he'd done most of the talking. But sometimes, he knew, listening said just as much as speech.

"You got more flowers." Jesse nodded toward the windowsill, where his own assortment of garden flowers and Max and Perry's roses had been joined by chrysanthemums from Abe and Lillian, a dazzling gather of cerulean delphiniums from Jorge, a peace lily from Chuck and Peter.

"More friends stopped by right after you left yesterday. It's almost too showy, don't you think?"

Questions like that appeared to embarrass Jesse. His tactic was to ignore them and move on. "I was just passing by," he said. "If you're busy, I don't have to stay." He stood at the front of the bed, hands crossed in front of him—a solemn stance, the way you might stand at a funeral.

"No, no. Please. Anything to distract me from hospital food."

"What you got there?" Jesse ventured a look. "When Pop was in here, he said the food wasn't too bad. I actually ate some of it, since he wasn't too hungry. Mostly he favored the Jell-O and Popsicles."

"Wise choices, I'm sure."

"He couldn't keep too much down."

"Sit. You're making me nervous standing there."

"Sorry." Jesse sank obediently into the chair, his legs sprawled loosely before him. "You're sure you want me to stay?"

"Of course, I quite enjoyed talking to you yesterday, though I'm afraid I hardly let you get a word in edgewise."

"I talk too much as it is," Jesse said. "It's better when I'm listening."

Despite the impervious demeanor the young man worked so hard to maintain, he could sometimes seem like a dog that had been smacked around a few too many times. What would it take, Cameron wondered, to get him to open up? Mitchell Johnson had been much the same—that straight, earnest, masculine reticence. It was maddening, though at the same time engaging, a challenge to be overcome.

"You owe me some talk," Cameron said. "It's only fair. Here you know all sorts of things about me; I don't know the first thing about you, really. You've got a brother, you've got a lemon of a truck; your dad died last month. So what else should I know about Jesse Vanderhof? Do you have plans for yourself? Dreams, goals? What's your bliss, as they say?"

Jesse screwed up his face (had that last bit gone too far?).

"I got no plans, at least for the time being. Just trying to stay on my feet, you know. Keep some money coming in."

"Do you have a girlfriend?"

For a moment Jesse had that frozen look possums got when you flicked on the porch light and surprised them raiding the cats' food. "Uh, Donna," he said. "Yeah. We been going out, oh, two years now. We go way back. Went to school together."

"Tell me about her."

"What's to tell? She's good for me to be with. Keeps me out of trouble, you know."

"Like what trouble?"

Jesse only shrugged. "I don't know. The kind a guy like me gets in when he's on his own."

"You thinking of getting married?"

"We talk about it. Probably it'll happen. Yeah. Marry, have a couple kids. The whole nine yards. It's what you do, I guess."

So Jesse was as thoroughly conventional as they came. What else had he expected?

"It's not what *I* did," Cameron said.

"Well, but you're . . . well, you do your own thing."

"Which is what?"

"I don't know about you guys. Really I don't. But it sounds like a hell of a lonesome kind of life, if you ask me. I mean, don't you miss not having your own family?"

"My friends are my family," Cameron said curtly. He'd refrain from adding how many of those friends were now dead.

Jesse was buying none of it. "It ain't the same. I mean, you got a real family somewhere, don't you? Blood family."

"I haven't seen them in years."

"No!" Jesse's tone was one of wonderment. "Is that really true? Don't that make you so sad?"

"Well, you know, life's sad. The way I look at it, I was pretty much a disappointment to my family, and, frankly, they were a disappointment to me too. When I came out to them—this was after I graduated college and was living in New York—they didn't exactly take it very well. Neither my parents nor my brother. I'd thought Galen might at least be, well, you know, enlightened. But he was probably even less thrilled than they were. I think he felt like I'd let him down in some way. Like he was tainted now because of me. Maybe I didn't handle it well. I sort of said, 'I don't need this shit,' and then I just never looked back. I've been back to the South

179

exactly once since then, when my grandmother died and I went to her funeral. Let's just say, I got a pretty chilly reception down there. Even though I hadn't seen my family in nearly ten years. Oh, well." He pushed his food tray, barely touched, to the side. "What're you going to do?"

Jesse sat hunched over, his chin resting on his fists.

"Did I say something wrong?"

Jesse shook his head and stared at the mismatched linoleum tiles of the floor, as if reading some doom inscribed in their disorder. One workboot-clad foot tapped nervously. Curious, Cameron watched him. Why had he come back for a second visit? Was it pity? Fascination? Or just some redneck desire to ingratiate himself with the boss?

"Man, I hate that story."

Cameron waited for a moment. "What part?"

"How does it feel to have to live so far from home?"

"Tell me," Cameron said. "Just out of curiosity. How much time have you ever spent away from Stone Hollow? Do you ever get down to New York, for example?"

Jesse snorted. "Mrs. Wynkoop's eleventh-grade science class took a bus down to the Natural History Museum."

"And?"

Jesse shrugged. "Why would I want to go anywhere? Though once we almost went to Six Flags, New Jersey. You ever been there? Who knows why Pop got it into his head. Me and Kyle were just kids. I remember we were so excited. We used to lie in bed with the lights out and whisper back and forth, you know, how great it was gonna be. I mean, we didn't hardly know what to expect, but that didn't stop us. We just kept making things up, all these great rides we were gonna ride. Kyle was really good at that. He could describe them like he'd already been on them before. The pirate ride, the astronaut ride. There was one—it sounded so great—the danger ride. I mean, you'd practically die from fright on that one.

"But we never got there. We started out just fine, we were probably halfway there. Then Pop decided there was something wrong with the car and we better turn back. Kyle kept saying there wasn't nothing wrong with the car, but Pop, I remember, turned around and glared at us three kids in the backseat and said, 'What the fuck do you little squirts know about anything?' So we turned around and came home. Didn't say a word the whole way. None of us, not even our mom. Maybe there really was something wrong with the car. I don't know. I just remember feeling this kind of relief, even though I'd been looking forward to it like it was gonna be Christmas or something. But see? Now you got me jabbering. That's a pretty stupid-ass story, right?"

"Hardly. It's fascinating."

"I shouldn't go off talking like that."

"It gets no farther than this room. Anything you tell me is in strictest confidence."

How to account, though, for the secret thrill of confession? For weeks Cameron had gazed at the brothers' impervious surface; now, to see this glimpse, however inconsequential, gave him, to his embarrassment—consternation, really—the stirrings of a hard-on. To conceal any trace that might betray him beneath the thin sheets, he raised his knees, rather wishing he hadn't pushed his meal tray aside. He'd not realized he'd been so starved for so long that such a meager morsel would suffice.

"I got no secrets," Jesse said.

"Well, then, we're alike that way."

Jesse grinned. "Don't get your hopes up, mister."

"Oh, I no longer have hopes," Cameron told him, nonetheless struck by an odd hint of flirtation in his visitor's banter—no doubt illusory. "That's my one big problem," he continued, his fledgling hard-on seeming intent on contradicting his every word. "It's not dying that scares me, Jesse. I've been at death's door. I actually felt pretty much at peace there. It's this other thing I'm finding difficult. This pretense of getting on with things. It's funny. I haven't told anyone this. My friends would be shocked to hear it. And now I'm telling you."

It didn't seem to please Jesse; he was back to looking despondent. "So, then maybe we both got our secrets after all," he said.

Cameron felt on the threshold of something lovely and aching and fearful—but then through another threshold, with a quick rap on the door to announce himself, Max sailed into the room. He paused, hands on hips, to survey the scene. "Oh my God. Are you still here?"

"Which of us are you referring to?" Cameron asked. That flicker of annoyance was uncalled for, of course. Still, he watched the moment recede like a wave from its high-water mark on the beach. How was Max to know what odd thing he'd interrupted? Not that Cameron had any clear idea himself.

He noted, though, how Jesse visibly recoiled from Max's presence in the small room. And Max, while not recoiling, nonetheless seemed wary.

Jesse rose to his feet, "I got to be going," he said, edging toward the door.

"I should be going home tomorrow," Cameron told him. "Will I see you?"

"I'll stop by. Sure."

Max stood aside to let Jesse pass, and in three quick strides, as if running for his life, he was out of the room.

"Well," Max said, "what was that all about?"

"Nothing. Absolutely nothing. Though he *is* fond of me, I think. In his way."

"Ach." Max seated himself in the chair Jesse had just vacated. "He's probably just after your money."

"Well, thanks a lot," Cameron said, not at all pleased to be in so many respects so suddenly deflated.

Opening the front door just a crack, Donna seemed surprised to see him. It irked him a little. He was her boyfriend, wasn't he? Shouldn't she be happy he'd dropped by?

"Come on in," she told him, leading him through the darkened living room where Sean roused himself from his television watching only long enough to answer the usual "How's it going?" Jesse was grateful not to have to say anything more.

He'd always thought of Donna's bedroom as some kind of refuge—but from what? All her animals watched him with vacant stares. He'd had a dream once: he opened his own bedroom window in the middle of the night, and down on the lawn, in bright moonlight, stood all Donna's animals, and they were talking amongst themselves, all excited about something, only he couldn't make out a word they were saying. It wasn't much of a dream, not like other dreams he'd had, long war sagas where he and Kyle fought against some horrifying enemy, or other senseless, annoying episodes involving guys he'd never in his life met before, but it was the one dream that remained most vivid to him, almost like it wasn't a dream, but something that really happened one night. Though of course that was impossible.

He wished he could tell her about Cameron, he wished they could have a laugh together about it, like they did when strange things happened to them, like the time he sideswiped a deer and got left with a reek of piss along the side of his truck it took him days to get rid of, or the time Joey locked C.J. in the meat locker at the Family Market.

Jesse wasn't much good at lying, though he'd always been pretty good at saying nothing. Still, as he lay back on her bed, among her unicorns and other creatures, he was assailed without warning by the feeling he was no more than those seed pods in autumn you can crush in your fist and there's nothing inside except a little airy remnant.

"Lay with me," he told Donna. "Let's take a nap."

"Really?" she asked, like she didn't believe him. But he patted the bedspread next to him, so she closed the door behind her and locked it. They'd didn't take naps too often, but she knew what they were for, how one thing led to another. She sat down beside him on the bed, and with the palm of her hand stroked his belly through the fabric of his T-shirt. She seemed pretty happy for the opportunity. Soon enough her hand was up under his T-shirt, rubbing circles on his bare skin, her wrist and forearm pressing his jeans where a woodie'd sprung up down there. He put his hands behind his head and lay there while she massaged him. How long had it been? It concerned him that he couldn't quite remember. Maybe Donna was a secret dyke, he considered, maybe that explained why the burner was on so low.

"Hey there," he said in pretend surprise as she unbuttoned his jeans and slid her hands in. Her fingers felt icy on him, and he thought sadly, No, Donna wasn't the reason; if anybody's flame burned low, it was his. "Come here," he said, reaching up and pulling her down on top of him so their mouths met and her hair fell down into his eyes. He felt smothered by her, but he could live with that, at least for the time being. He concentrated on kissing her up for a while, then pulled back to suggest, "Let's turn the radio on."

He didn't watch her as she undressed, but her animals did. He watched them watching her with their eyes that never blinked. She came over to the bed and pulled off his workboots, then his pants, while he slipped his T-shirt over his head. His woodie stood ready for mischief or grief. Any girl should be proud of giving a guy a woodie like that, he thought. For better or worse, as Kyle was fond of saying, a guy's woodie don't lie.

At the moment, he took a measure of comfort in that.

"Jesse, sweet, you bring a rubber?" she asked in a faraway kind of voice. Of course he hadn't been thinking. "Nope," he told her reluctantly.

"Well, you're in luck, 'cause I do."

"What're you doing with a rubber?"

But she just smirked at him and went over to her dresser as dread descended.

They settled on the bed, and she unrolled the rubber down his soldier. The radio was playing one of those boy bands that was all the rage, pretty little faggots lisping about girls they'd never gotten a woodie from in their life. He'd never noticed how all the animals had these frozen grins, like they were in on some insane joke, and Jesse remembered, suddenly, that row of white busts on the mantel at Cameron's house he'd had the urge to knock to smithereens. But he wouldn't think about that. Just as he wouldn't think about how that virus had somehow found its way inside the poor guy's body, either up his butt or down his throat.

He wondered, as Donna settled her weight down onto him, as he felt himself push up into her and she groaned a little, what exactly she was feeling just then. Was it discomfort or pleasure, or both together? And her brother: could he hear past the music from the radio, and if he did, what did he think about? Or did he ever think about anything?

Getting down to the work at hand, Jesse kind of hoped not. It was pretty nice not to think of anything for a change, he decided.

Afterward, they lay in a drowse and she smoked her cigarette. Why didn't they do this more often? he wondered. It had been, all in all, pretty satisfactory. A question occurred to him.

"Did you really tell Leanne my dick was eight inches?"

Donna seemed surprised. "Why would I do a thing like that?"

"I don't know." He propped his head on his elbow to watch her as she lay on her back. She took a long, satisfied drag on her cigarette. She was getting a double chin like her mom.

"You're silly," she told him.

"Why do you stick around with me?"

"Silly, because you're sweet." Donna blew out a pale blue smoke he watched disappear into thin air.

"I'm not sweet," he told her. "You don't know the half of it." What he'd done yesterday in the sick man's house was despicable, but Cameron would never miss what was gone. And Jesse himself would probably never even have cause to take it out from where he'd stashed it. So why the fuck had he taken it in the first place? What exactly was it to be a token of?

Donna had rolled over on her side so she was looking straight at him. "Oh," she said with a smile that made him a little sick to his stomach, "I think I know you pretty well, Jesse. Probably better than anybody."

EIGHTEEN

Cameron paused at the door to scoop Casper into his arms. "Well, I see somebody missed me," he told the purring cat. "Oh, look, you're drooling."

And indeed, a big viscous tear of saliva depended from the side of Casper's mouth.

"I feel I should avert my eyes," Max said. "Nobody ever drools like that for me anymore. You've got messages. Shall I play them?"

"Please," Cameron said, gently lowering Casper's bulk to the floor. "While I wash off the love drool."

Max hit the button, and after the electronic beep a young-sounding voice announced, "Hey, my friend, it's Crazy Jamey. Why don't you suck my cock? You know you want to."

Max raised an eyebrow as a second beep sounded.

"Cameron, hi, it's me, just calling to see how you're doing. Um, we need to touch base about the party, okay? So call me."

Now what were the chances of those two colliding once again? Cameron wondered. He'd considered phoning Dan to let him know about his episode, but then had decided against alarming his ex unnecessarily. The last thing he wanted was to seem manipulative—though he knew a stoic silence could be as manipulative as anything else.

"I'm not even going to ask about that first call," Max said.

"See how exciting my life is? He treats me to his fantasies about once every couple of weeks. It's got to be some neighborhood kid."

"You should really get caller ID. Doesn't that sort of thing bother you?"

Cameron shrugged. "I think I'm used to it by now. But let me guess—when you're mayor, you'll put a stop to nonsense like that."

"Or at least make sure it gets spread around more equitably. A Crazy Jamey to light up every phone line." Max clapped his hand over his mouth. "Will you listen to me? I've really got to watch what I say if I'm going to make a credible candidate."

"I think maybe you're right. But you know what? I always liked your scurrilous mouth."

"That's why you'll never be my campaign manager."

"Anyway, it's not the calls from some kid who's horny and confused that threaten my peace of mind."

"Ouch," Max said. "So you're not as okay about this as you've been telling me?"

"It's just a little hard sometimes," Cameron confessed. "Every once in a while, right out of the blue, I feel punched in the heart."

It had been Max who'd brought them together in the first place, at a dinner party nearly canceled by a mid-March blizzard that had blindsided Manhattan and postponed, for a full day, Perry's scheduled return from a photo jaunt in sunny Morocco. Thus it ended up a cozy foursome, Cameron, Max, a jaw-droppingly pretentious playwright named Rick Something-or-other whose predicted ascent to the Broadway firmament never materialized, and a friend of Rick's from college, a handsome young man with a dimpled smile and striking emerald eyes. Cameron had taken against this new face immediately, but as the evening progressed, Dan Futrell turned out to be funny, quick-witted, self-deprecating, and when, a few days later, Cameron received a note in the mail—"What a pleasure it was to meet you"—he found himself thoroughly charmed by the gallant gesture.

"All the more reason," Max was saying, "to find someone new."

"Yeah, yeah, I shouldn't have brought it up. I'll be fine. It's just nice to be home. I'm not going to sit and brood, believe me. Anyway, Jesse's coming by later. There's tons to do if this garden party's still going to happen."

"Maybe you should cancel. Your health is way more important."

"Jesse's a great help." Cameron said. "We'll manage nicely."

Max looked at him with a twinkle in his eye. "When I say move on, I'm not thinking some twenty-year-old redneck who's going to steal the china and end up murdering you in your sleep."

"Please. Don't be ridiculous."

"As long as you agree not to be ridiculous as well."

To distract them both from being ridiculous, Cameron fed Casper a cat treat, then two or three.

"Okay, I'm off," Max said. "Stay out of the sun. And remember to take your new medicine."

"I would hate to disappoint Dr. Vishnaraman, but more pills. Just what I need."

Without saying a word, Max stepped forward and embraced him, gripping him so tightly he nearly forced tears from Cameron's eyes. For most of a minute they clung to each other, till Casper made it known, with a peremptory meow, that more cat treats were in order.

"Don't worry about me," Cameron told his friend.

Max nodded, apparently not trusting himself to speak.

He loved Max thoroughly, but there was a great, inexplicable relief to being all alone in his house after two days in a hospital bed. Pouring himself a glass of water from the fridge, he played his messages again. Who was Crazy Jamey anyway? Listening to Dan's voice that followed, he found himself conjuring an ATV roaring through the woods, a strapping lad, helmet in hand, banging at the front door. Kneeling before the contemptuously silent kid, he'd reach his hand into Crazy Jamey's jeans to pull out a nice cock he'd loll about lovingly in his mouth, drawing from Crazy Jamey low animal murmurs, then a warm, sweet-salty release.

Even a minor firing of the libido was enough, these days, to get him aroused. He wondered if he should tell Dr. Vishnaraman—though he could imagine what the good doctor would say: Life is precious. Treasure your sensations.

Still puzzling a bit over the tone of Dan's message, he mounted the stairs to the bedroom. The closet door stood ajar, and as he went to close it, something made him pause.

In his later, bedridden days, Toby had turned at least part of his failing attention to porn videos. He and Cameron had been the first on their block to own a VCR, and Toby would lie in the darkened bedroom and watch for hours. "Most of the time they don't even make me hard," he said. "But they don't make me sad, either. At least I can still follow the plots." They

188

were another of Toby's possessions Cameron hadn't been able to part with. Now they gathered dust on a shelf in the same closet that still held so many of Toby's clothes. No doubt he should have been more attentive to Dan's complaint that he sometimes felt he was in a three-way with a ghost. Maybe it *was* a little creepy to have preserved those mementos, to have refused to let go, moving them upstate along with Toby's ailing Cleopatra, who outlived the move by scarcely a month. Well, too late for second thoughts, he mused as he found himself pulling one tape after another off the closet shelf, campily evocative titles such as *Cuming of Age, Lockerroom Buddies, Schoolmates.*

He chose at random. Feeling vaguely foolish, he lay on the bed and undid his trousers and watched as the tape, unrewound, took up where it had left off years ago, stopped midscene. Had Toby gotten bored, or had he managed to wring a difficult orgasm from the action on-screen? He was half-tempted to put the tape in reverse for a couple of minutes and then replay the sequence that had brought poor Toby off, but inertia overcame that momentary fantasy, and he allowed the scene to run its course.

On a bed three figures went at it with admirable verve. One had a nicely athletic body but was unpleasantly brutish in the face; the other two, scrawnier, were cute in that hectic late-seventies way, and Cameron remembered that they had been brothers: the Noll brothers, Kip and— what had been the younger one's name? He seriously doubted they were really brothers—they looked hardly anything alike—but it was enjoyable to play along with the fiction.

Scott. That was the little brother's name. Kip and his friend Steve had come home from tossing a Frisbee in the park to find him jerking off. What else to do but punish the little twerp? Accompanied by music that must once have seemed funky, Steve energetically plugged the younger brother's butt while Kip, or at least the clumsily dubbed voice that was supposed to be Kip's, poured out a monologue downright touching in its enthusiasm: "Damn, he's taking it all. I can't believe it. It's not too big for you, Scott, is it? He's tearing your goddamn ass up, isn't he, Scott? You like it, don't you, little brother? Yes, you like it. He's doing a number on your ass. Make him scream, man. Make him feel it. This'll teach him. He's learning good now."

Scott's face registered alarm, pain, an earnest desire to do well. Were they all dead now, these eager young men? Probably they had been junkies, hustlers, probably it was shameful to be watching ghosts enact their own doom. At the same time, Cameron basked in their light that was still traveling, after all these years, from that vanished world that was the past (were any of those three boys by some miracle still alive, they'd be not much younger than he).

Kip and Steve had begun taking turns doing a number, as Kip put it, on little brother's ass. Not a condom in sight, but who had used condoms in those days? Coming late into Cameron's life, Dan was the only one he'd been consistently safe with, and it was a good thing, given his ex's penchant for being used roughly. Who could have known that Dan of the dimpled smile and urbane charm would crave abasement? "God this is humiliating," he liked to say.

After everything that had happened, was there any longer the faintest possibility of patching things up between them? Soul mates, they'd called themselves, after it became clear that they were no longer, technically speaking, lovers. But he could hardly even remember, anymore, what it had been like to be soul mates with Dan Futrell, let alone lovers, everything having devolved so long ago into a sort of low-grade irritability, two prisoners sharing month after month the same narrow cell that was their relationship, all that initial heroism dimmed to bitterness and mutual recrimination.

He'd drifted off, lost his hard-on. On the TV screen, cute, voluble Kip continued to cheerlead. "I don't know if he can take it again, man," he rhapsodized as Steve switched positions with him and resumed his avid sodomy of young Scott. "It's too fucking big for him. I can't believe it. My brother's got such a beautiful ass."

Like a bird suddenly sprung from its cage, Cameron's mind flew free. His cock revved back up in an instant. "My little brother's got such a beautiful ass," moaned Kyle even as Steve's ejaculation spurted onto Jesse's smooth back and Cameron gave it up too with a groan of animal pleasure, the only kind that mattered, really, desperate and sorrowful and deaf to any responsibility at all but its own heartache.

Where had that come from? Those two didn't look anything like the Vanderhof brothers. Bemused, embarrassed, Cameron shook loose the unexpected knot of fantasies gathered in his head. But as he daubed himself with a Kleenex—my poisonous semen, he thought to himself—he became aware that Steve, pushing his own creamy dollop around the hollow of Scott's back with his big tool, was crooning, "My fantasy came true. Finally I did it. I finally fucked your brother's ass."

"My brother's got a nice fucking ass," Kip agreed, blithely unaware of the viewer's strange complicity in all this. "I'm going to have to start passing him around. Good thing you came over. My brother needed that. He needed it so bad."

"Man, that was a scene and a half," Steve affirmed.

Kip laughed. "God, I think you killed him. I don't think he's moving. Fucking impaled him." And indeed, Scott lay still, facedown on the bed. Then, as if utterly bored with everything that had happened, he reached up and scratched the tip of his nose.

With a melancholy sigh, Cameron clicked off the VCR.

He felt, then, not so much ashamed as simply self-conscious when, an hour later, Jesse arrived in his hiccuping truck. Even Cameron, who knew nothing about motors, could tell things were not well beneath that hood. In fits and starts it negotiated the short length of the drive, finally stalling itself to a halt.

What would the poor kid think if he knew? As a boy, Cameron had suspected that adults could tell when he'd been masturbating—that it showed in some subtle way in his features, his stance—and he'd likewise imagined, the impish twin of that paranoia, that he too possessed a detective capability, that he could discern in other boys secret signs they'd been jacking off. He couldn't really tell, of course, but he used to entertain himself in class that way.

There's nothing wrong with indulging a fantasy or two, he reminded himself as Jesse, beaming uncharacteristically and pulling at the brim of his baseball cap, walked toward him across the lawn.

Of his own accord the young man reached out to grasp Cameron's hand. "You don't look like somebody who was just in a hospital bed."

"Well, thank you." Cameron took the rough palm in his own somewhat guilty grip. "I don't *feel* like somebody who was just in the hospital."

"I won't put you to work no more," Jesse joked. "It's what I get. Them tree limbs practically did you in."

Was he mistaken, or could he detect the glimmer of some tentative, newfound intimacy? Jesse had, after all, shared in his peculiar misadventure as no one else. He'd witnessed him out cold on the lawn; he'd taken care of him in those minutes that mattered.

But perhaps he was making way too much of everything. Being ridiculous. Jesse'd only done what any decent person would do.

"Sorry I took a rain check on you there," Cameron told him. "Thanks for finishing up."

"I didn't finish. My chain saw give out. I had to leave them two big limbs laying back there. You didn't notice?"

"Actually, I haven't been back there yet. I didn't want to tempt fate."

"Don't worry. I'll protect you."

If only, Cameron thought as they walked back to where two rough-hided, lichen-spotted leviathans lay fallen amid ferns the oak's shade had nurtured. The ferns had taken quite a beating—would they grow back in the unaccustomed sunlight, or did this herald their end as well? If a tree falls in the forest, where do the reverberations end?

A thought occurred to him. "I'm thinking maybe we should just leave it be."

Jesse regarded him curiously. "It's up to you."

"There's something wonderfully sculptural about it, don't you think? It reminds me of the colossus of the Apennines at Pratolino, in Tuscany— this huge, bristling allegorical fellow who looks like he's emerging right out of the earth itself. Terrifying and powerful and mysterious . . . You're looking skeptical."

Jesse shrugged. "It's a dead tree," he pointed out.

They had nothing whatsoever in common. And why should they? Of course it was just a dead tree. Forget that it had been growing since before the Revolutionary War. Forget that a couple of faggots in the late twentieth century had unsuccessfully tried to make a home under its protective wings.

"We'll leave it," he said decisively. "At least for now. If nothing else, it'll be a conversation piece for my guests. They can bring their cocktails back here and pay their respects. Maybe I'll festoon it. Put votive candles out." He was conscious of a certain defiance in his ravings.

As if to stamp out all that nonsense, Jesse leapt up onto one of the logs and walked along its length. "So you're still having your party?"

"Absolutely. And I hope you're going to be there."

"Me?" Jesse looked more alarmed than pleased.

"Of course. You did all this work. The garden wouldn't be half-presentable if it weren't for you."

"I don't know. What kind of party is it?"

"Just friends. People from all around. They're nice, I promise. They won't bite. Max and Perry will be there."

Frowning, Jesse jumped down off the oak. "What did you say these ferns were called?"

"Cinnamon," Cameron told him, remembering the almost erotic pang he'd felt the first time Jesse had asked him the name of a plant in his garden.

"That's it. Cinnamon fern." Jesse spoke the name emphatically, as if to store it someplace where it wouldn't get lost. "Pop used to call everything forsythia if he didn't know its name."

"Really?" Cameron laughed, as much at the return of their fragile, perhaps illusory camaraderie as anything else. Whatever happens, he thought with a satisfaction that wasn't at all mean, I've made my mark on him. He'll never be quite the same as he was.

"I swear," Jesse told him. "Would I lie to you?"

Actually, I don't know, Cameron thought, but for the moment he decided to trust his improbable savior completely. He felt a generosity that was not entirely irrational well up in him. "I know one thing that doesn't lie," he said. "The sound of your truck. It sounds like shit. I thought Al was going to fix it for you."

His thoughts had run ahead of them both: he regretted having caught Jesse off guard. "More's broke there than can be fixed," he said mournfully.

"Well, look." Cameron was aware he was throwing caution to the winds. He could see it flutter like so much bright confetti. There was something exhilarating about releasing whole handfuls of it into the steady breeze. "Let me give you some money for a truck that runs."

The young man looked embarrassed. "Mine runs," he said with a touch of pride.

"Barely," Cameron pointed out. He didn't know why he loved that stubborn resistance in Jesse. "You need a real truck."

"I owe you way too much already. I can't take your money. It wouldn't be right."

"I don't recall you owing a thing. Didn't we settle all that?"

Jesse looked chagrined. He studied the ground, his scuffed workboots.

"Say, six thousand dollars," Cameron urged boldly. "Clear and simple, no strings attached. Token of my gratitude. I mean it." He couldn't quite believe he was saying what he was saying, but now it was said; it couldn't be taken back.

"I'd have to think about it. I'd give you something in return. I don't know what, exactly."

"You've already given me plenty." Cameron fixed the skeptical young redneck forthrightly in his gaze. "You saved my life."

Late sunlight slanted through the windows. He'd waited till after supper to return Dan's call.

Dan sounded relaxed, perhaps a little buzzed. "Hey, Cameron, how's it going?" It was still early, just after eight, but Dan usually started his pleasures promptly at five.

But that's no longer any of your business, Cameron reminded himself—if, indeed, it ever had been. He wondered, now, about that. Where did concern stop and interference begin? But he wouldn't revisit that old quarrel.

"Fine," he told Dan. "Everything's fine. Though I have a bit of bad news. Our big oak tree came down in a windstorm."

"I'm not surprised. Didn't I always say it needed to come down?"

Had Dan really always said that?

"The garden certainly looks bereft without it. Otherwise, things aren't in that bad a shape. Considering the drought."

"Has it been dry? You really don't notice it too much here in the city."

"It's been extremely dry," he said, wondering if Dan was somehow trying to provoke him. "But I've got good gardening help. I broke down and hired somebody."

"It's about time. I've always thought the garden was a little too much for you. It was definitely getting out of control."

"You called it The Chaos Garden."

"Did I really? I don't remember that."

"I don't think I'd make something like that up."

"And I don't think I'd say something like that."

"It doesn't matter," Cameron said, vaguely miffed at Dan's complete lack of interest in the new gardener. Well, he'd meet him soon enough. "Did you get your invitation?"

"I did. It looks nice. You must've spent forever on them."

"A while." He'd bought blank rice-paper cards and painted a water-color iris on each. "I sent out a hundred this year."

"Yikes. Can you manage that many people?"

"I was thinking you might like to come up the day before."

At the pause on the other end, he told himself he already knew, he'd known ever since he'd heard Dan's message this morning.

"Well, see, unfortunately, that's what I was calling about. It doesn't look like I can make the party."

"Okay," Cameron said as neutrally as he could. "What's come up?"

"Well, I have this invitation to go to Miami. This friend of mine has a house down there, and several of us were going to fly down. Just for the weekend. I've never been to South Beach. I didn't realize it was going to be the same weekend. We always used to have the party at the end of June. How was I to know? I'm really sorry about this, but it just feels like it'd be a shame to miss out on this trip. Plus, I've already bought the ticket."

"I thought we agreed we hated homosexuals who flew off to places like South Beach," Cameron heard himself say, even as he thought, So is this your new lover you haven't told me about?

But hadn't he just been flaunting Jesse?

"Cameron," Dan told him. "Don't be mean. Please."

Hadn't Dan always been the kinder, more reasonable half of their rela-tionship?

"I'm sorry," Cameron said. "It's just—I'm feeling a little fragile. I just got out of the hospital. I had a seizure."

"Oh my God. And you didn't call me?"

"I was only in for two days. I didn't want to bother you. You've got your own life to lead. I didn't want to worry you needlessly." He was being truly despicable, he thought, but he couldn't help himself. It was the old, insoluble problem. He couldn't let go of anything. He clung to it all for dear, desperate life, even what wasn't worth clinging to—even, per-haps, life itself.

"Why are you doing this to me?" Dan asked and for a moment Cameron feared the voice on the other end might actually break into tears.

"I'm not doing anything," he said, pitilessly reminding himself that Dan had been fond of tears, that there'd been occasions, over the years, when he'd put them to stunningly good use. "I'm just telling you what happened."

"You're making me feel guilty, is what you're doing. And I don't like it."

"Well, you're making me feel like *shit,*" Cameron fired back. "And I don't much like it either."

There was a brief pause; then Dan said, "I don't want to talk anymore if we're going to talk like this."

"Fine," Cameron told him. "Good-bye, then."

He surprised himself by hanging up, but barely had he done so before the phone started to ring. A sudden bizarre thought made him laugh out loud. It wasn't Dan calling back to smooth things over, as it had always been Dan, it seemed in retrospect, who had initiated their reconciliations. No, it was Crazy Jamey calling. If there was any logic to the world, it would have to be Crazy Jamey. But of course he knew it was Dan. Even now, heroically, Dan would try to salvage what was no longer salvageable. Pick it up, you asshole, Cameron told himself even as he let the machine take the call for him. His recorded voice sounded brittle, self-important. No wonder Crazy Jamey wanted to harass the person behind that voice.

The prompt sounded, then only a dial tone's cool finality.

NINETEEN

The plump, pink real estate agent scratched his head and screwed up his face and looked pained, like somebody trying to pass a reluctant stool. "You're talking maybe twenty-five thousand dollars instant money some-body's going to have to put in this place," he told them. "And that's just for starters. You'd need another twenty-five at least to get her anything like up to speed. She's really pretty far gone, unfortunately. It's a shame."

It was hard not to take it as a rebuke—and mostly to Pop. How was it he'd fixed everybody else's house for miles around without calculating the dire condition of his own?

Lurking on the edge of the conversation, Kyle wasn't saying a word, though his eyes spelled murder. He held Poke tight by the collar. Their mom sucked down one cigarette after another and tried to look like she wasn't too surprised.

"My husband was ill for quite some time. His bills from the hospital are still coming in. Maintaining this house was the last of our worries," she told the agent, Craig Hallenbeck. Jesse'd gone to school with his younger brother, a smart-alecky little shit who used to drive around in his daddy's cast-off Saturn.

Of course anybody, including Craig Hallenbeck, could see the house's sorry shape wasn't the kind that happens overnight. The mortar needed repointing something desperate. The interior kitchen wall was ruined with water damage; seepage had rotted the ceiling beams as well. And the roof was a disaster: with your fingers you could break off the mossy old shingles with hardly an effort.

"I couldn't list this for more than sixty thousand," Craig told them. In the heat of midday, he had dark circles under the arms of his white shirt. Sweat beaded on his forehead. "And I might think about having that junked vehicle towed." He gestured toward Jesse's pickup. "It wouldn't hurt to give the front yard a once-over. You'd be amazed how the little things can detract from the value of a property."

"You mean, the yard sale?" their mom asked suspiciously.

Craig looked embarrassed. "I didn't realize you were having a yard sale."

"We were a while back. This is the leftovers."

"It was just a suggestion. Now let's go do that septic test and I'll be out of here. If somebody could just show me to the bathroom."

The three of them hesitated—nobody wanted anything more to do with this fellow who'd shot them down with a smile—but then Kyle nodded Jesse's way, so Jesse relented and led the fellow up to the house. Craig seemed to sigh as he gazed into the rust-streaked toilet bowl, and Jesse had a hollow sense of how, exactly, the place where he lived looked to the eyes of a professional.

From a packet, Craig extracted a wafer, dropped it in the toilet, then flushed. "Okay. Let's go see what happens. Hopefully nothing. Keep your fingers crossed."

But already, as they emerged from the dark house into the sunlight, their mom was calling over to them, "What's it mean if it goes purple?"

Jesse could see Kyle, Poke in tow, stalking down to his truck.

"I was afraid of this." For an instant Jesse thought Craig meant his brother's sudden rage—but the agent didn't know his brother. "Any idea when this system was last replaced?" Craig chattered on, seemingly unaware his life might be worth just about nothing.

"I don't think it's ever been replaced," Jesse said. "You'd have to ask my mom. But it ain't been working too well for some time now. I mean, you flush and somebody's showering, it sort of gets backed up."

"I see." Craig nodded grimly. Jesse watched Kyle's truck spurt down the drive, fishtailing in the gravel at the bottom of the hill before grabbing the asphalt and roaring off.

Their mom looked off in that direction too, and Jesse was reminded once again how she worried about Kyle feeling everything so deeply. Oblivious, Craig stood and pondered the spreading patch of bad news in the sparse grass.

"How much is this going to set me back?" their mom finally asked.

Craig had that pained look on his face again. "Three, four thousand. Unfortunately, it's got to be done. I can't legally sell it like it is. If you want, I can give you the name of a man who's worked for me in the past. He'll give you a fair deal."

Their mom squinted at him as she shook a last cigarette from her case. "My new house looks to be getting smaller all the time," she told him. "Maybe I should just stay put."

"Let's be optimistic," Craig said, his eyes darting all around the property. "The market's strong. Lots of seasonal buyers. Folks from New York. It's a great time to be selling. Trust me on that."

Craig wiped the honest sweat from his brow. Jesse imagined how you could pop him with a pin, how he was like one of those raccoon carcasses on the side of the road, all swollen up with putrefaction gas, all full of himself, you could say.

They strolled leisurely among the oldest graves, pausing here and there for Cameron to point out the occasional element of special interest—the fenced-off de Hulter plot, for instance, one Josiah de Hulter having built Cameron's house back in the 1820s. Seven generations of de Hulters had lived there before dwindling to a single aged spinster in the early 1980s.

"I'm impressed," Elliot said, squatting to make out the inscription half-obscured by pale green and yellow lichens. "You've really done your research."

He wore shorts, sandals. Cameron queasily noted that several of Elliot's toenails were likewise obscured by a yellow, crusty fungus. "Dan used to joke I knew more about Stone Hollow than the locals. It's probably true. Most of them seem remarkably uninterested in the town's past, whereas I love collecting old facts about a place. In lieu, I guess, of my own."

He'd not intended to follow up on his abortive date with his new neighbor—what, after all, was the point?—but Elliot had been either annoyingly or sweetly persistent, Cameron wasn't sure which, leaving any number of messages that usually began "Hey, good-looking" and then went on to say how much he'd enjoyed their evening, would Cameron like to get together sometime for a cup of coffee, maybe a walk?

In the end, Cameron had called him back.

"I wish you'd let me know you were in the hospital," Elliot said. He fingered attentively the de Hulter stone's classic, heavily weathered bas-relief—two hands clasped in friendship.

It hadn't occurred to Cameron to let him know. "It was nothing, really. Just a small seizure. They had me in and out of Benedictine before I even knew it."

Still crouched before the de Hulter stone, Elliot turned to look at him. He spoke gently. "I'd like you to think of me as somebody you could call on, you know. And vice versa. If I came on too strong the other evening, I apologize."

"Nonsense. I should be the one to apologize. I'm afraid I was a little, well, distracted."

Elliot rose and looked him straight in the eye. "By what? Can I ask you that?"

Cameron found he had no answer. Just below the surface, however, flickered a truth too ridiculous to speak—that what distracted him amounted to no more than the half-articulate, smart-as-a-box-of-rocks redneck who helped around the garden. Could he be so foolish as to turn aside this perfectly decent man for a prospect as bleak and far-fetched as that? Of all the people on the planet, who was more patently inappropriate—let alone off-limits, utterly unhavable—than Jesse Vanderhof, who for starters wasn't even remotely gay?

So he said to Elliot, "If I told you I was trying to hear something the other night, would that make any sense? All my life I've had to resist what other people thought I should want. Most of the time, the little voice inside me that tells me what I do want is so quiet I have to create this silence around myself in order to hear it at all. Tune out the tyranny of all the other voices. I'm talking straight *and* gay. I mean, so many gay people seem to think that if you're gay, then you should cut your hair a certain way, and go on vacation in certain particular places, and listen to completely predictable kinds of music. For the record: I hate musicals, Key West, quiche. I just think desire's a lot more complicated than all that. People need to be attentive to what makes them tick. And what doesn't.

What am I saying—'people'? I mean, *I* have to be more attentive. See, I told you this wouldn't make any sense."

"I think there's something very passionate in what you just said. But you sound like a very lonely person."

Hadn't Jesse said more or less the same, though for very different reasons?

"I'm not sure how to answer that," Cameron said.

"I don't mean it as a criticism."

"No, of course not. Am I lonely? I guess I don't think in those terms. Certainly there've been times in my life when I *wasn't* lonely."

"Like when?"

"It's been a while. He died. I grieved. Eventually my well-meaning friends suggested it was time to move on. So I did. But not really. And why should I? Why the fuck should I get over Toby?"

Elliot touched his arm. "I didn't know."

"That's okay. Nobody does."

"Not Max?"

Cameron needed to ponder that only briefly. "Some friends," he said, "have been your friends for so long, they have this very definitive idea about who you are, and it's not really possible to change it. So, no, for Max I'm the person Max thinks I am. The person he's sure I am. And that's fine. Those friends are very valuable. But they can drown you out if you're not careful."

"So, you're saying it wasn't so much me as it was the blind-date aspect of the whole thing."

"Something like that," Cameron said, though he was pretty sure that wasn't what he was trying to say at all.

They'd reached the newer part of the cemetery. A bier of flowers, already wilting in the heat, covered a fresh grave. Row after row of low stones marched in regiment across the neatly clipped, sunburnt grass. At the far end of those stones, near where a temporary tag marked Bill Vanderhof's resting place, Cameron glimpsed something that gave him pause. A body—human, supine—lay on the ground. Some superstitious little fear quickened in him. Someone was lying by Bill Vanderhof's grave.

He wondered if Elliot had noticed anything. Suddenly he didn't want to go anywhere near that part of the cemetery. The figure on the ground was either Jesse or Kyle. He was sure of it. Whichever brother it was, he lay motionless in the full sun, arms clasped over his chest, almost ceremonially, in a ritual of grief so strange, so full of surrender, even despair, that it felt shameful to witness it, however accidentally.

"Let's not walk out here in the sun," he told Elliot. "This part of the cemetery is completely uninteresting."

He'd observed in the past several weeks that someone was regularly visiting the grave. A small collection of coins and pebbles had begun to accrue around the base of that forlorn identification tag. From years of walking in the cemetery, he knew the locals were prone to paying that sort of homage, especially to those dead before their time. Certain graves sprouted toys, angel figurines, plastic lambs, windmills in the shape of sunflowers, a favorite baseball or sports jersey. Secretly he admired the practice, its pagan undertones. Hadn't he himself, when Hermione had got hit in the road, buried her beneath the lilacs Egyptian-style—with a mouse toy, sprigs of catnip, several cans of her favorite cat food?

He was relieved when he and Elliot reached the front gate without interruption—as if they'd made a narrow escape, though from what, exactly, he couldn't quite say. Only that it involved another world about which neither Elliot nor anyone else Cameron knew had any clue at all.

He realized, with a bit of surprise, that he preferred it that way.

A dozen danger dives behind them, they took in the sun on the warm, flat rocks by the Schneidekill. Overhead, turkey vultures drifted in patient flight—five, six, seven, he counted. It always felt a little weird when they decided to circle you, like they knew something you didn't.

"You and me can fix this thing," Kyle said. After an hour or so he'd come back to the house, though with more than a whiff on his breath. He'd obviously been thinking. "We dig her out, pop in a new tank. Easy as shit." He laughed quietly at his own joke. Kyle's confidence, his optimism, was hard to resist. Still, Jesse quailed a little at the task his brother had set out for them. At school, years ago, a boy had told him about stepping on a squishy spot in his backyard, and before he knew it he was sinking into mud that wasn't mud but a sort of liquid shit, and afterward he came down with hepatitis and nearly died.

The same hepatitis they diagnosed Pop with at first, before the hammer slammed down on all of them.

"You ever think," Jesse wondered aloud as the turkey vultures spiraled lazily in search of anything lying around dead, "there's something about that old house doesn't want to be sold?"

Kyle sat up, circled his arms around his knees. He looked out at the river for a long time, and Jesse regretted having broached the thought. On Kyle's face there was an expression so forlorn and distant—Jesse thought he'd never seen such a look on his brother. "Pop wouldn't've wanted it sold," Kyle said after a while. "But Pop wouldn't've wanted a lot of things. He's dead, though, so he don't get to want anything. That's the way it works, ain't it?"

Jesse had no answer; the question took him aback.

Kyle went on, "I mean, do you ever consider whether there's a heaven up there, someplace we might all be together someday?"

"What're you saying?" They never talked about stuff like that; the little chapel off the funeral home was the closest he or his brother had come to church in years.

"Who the fuck knows?" Kyle was still looking off across the river where a sheer wall of cliffs rose up. The layers of rock tilted crazily, like somebody had taken the whole land and upheaved it, only Jesse knew it had taken millions of years for something like that to happen. The solid ground beneath them right now was moving too, one long, vast unsettling of everything, only so slow you'd never know it, even as it carried you away.

Down the riverbank, two figures picked their way along the shore, hopping from boulder to boulder. Their occasional laughter drifted over the water's mumbling monotony. One of them paused from time to time to take a picture of something or other with the camera he carried. With a catch in his gut, Jesse recognized them—and Max must have recognized him as well, because he waved and yelled, "Hiya there!" Perry looked Jesse's way too, though he had the sense not to yell or wave or anything.

Jesse wasn't sure which of the two made him more uncomfortable. Go the fuck away, he wished as a swarm of anxiety filled his chest, but that silent message seemed lost on Max; if anything, it drew him toward them where they lay on the flat shelf of rock. Instinctively, Jesse reached for his shirt.

"They *know* you?" Kyle asked.

"They're these friends of Cameron's. They were at the hospital when I was there." Did it seem strange he hadn't mentioned them before? But why should he? They weren't any part of the story he'd had to tell his brother afterward ("It was fine. Yeah, he liked the flowers. Yeah, he likes me okay. So what?").

"Is this guy a faggot or what?" Kyle observed as Max clambered toward them over a jumble of boulders. And Kyle was right—that was exactly what Max looked like, prancing and saying, "Oof, oh my God," as he tried to keep from slipping into the water. He wore socks and sandals, white shorts, a ridiculous Hawaiian shirt. His mustache made him look a little like a walrus, though his body wasn't a walrus body; his body was actually pretty trim and fit.

With a great leap, Max bounded onto the stone where they sat. Jesse buttoned his shirt, conscious of Max's hungry eyes, but Kyle just sat there letting the faggot's gaze take him in. He oozed cool contempt, the exact opposite of sweat.

"Fancy meeting you here," Max said. "How ya doing? I'm Max, remember? Max," he repeated, turning to Kyle. "Pleased to meet you."

Kyle said nothing, only gave him that perfected look Jesse would give anything to master.

"Hello," Jesse told Max curtly, but not too curtly. He was Cameron's friend, after all. Not that that mattered—though he was surprised to find that it did, somehow. Jesse tried to imagine their friendship, or whatever it was between guys like that, but only came up against a blank wall without even a single tag of graffiti to clue him in.

"Come here often?" Max went on. "It's so empty today. Usually we're here on weekends, when you can't stir them with a stick. It's nice having the place to yourself."

Kyle just watched the homo go on, saying nothing, and Jesse realized, with a spike of annoyance, that he would have to do the talking. He'd never have met Max if it wasn't for Kyle pushing him to visit the hospital in the first place.

"We go swimming here," Jesse said, but he couldn't think of anything else to say, and fortunately—or unfortunately—Perry was on his way over. With more agility than Max, he picked his way across the slippery stones to land on the slab where they sat. Then, without saying a word, he raised his camera and snapped three or four times in quick succession.

"Hey," Kyle said. "What's with the fucking camera?"

"Sorry," Perry apologized. "Bad habit of mine."

"Don't it again," Kyle told him.

"Sorry, man." There was definitely something of the kid caught red-handed about the smile Perry flashed them. "No hard feelings?"

Kyle studied Perry for a minute, almost like he was amused. Jesse was surprised to see his brother disarmed like that. Perry was a dangerous one, the kind best kept away from. Jesse could just tell. Before you knew it, Perry could talk you into things you might end up regretting.

"I'm gonna swim some more," Kyle announced. "You coming?" He nudged Jesse, then stood and adjusted the waistband of his trunks. Jesse hesitated a moment—he didn't want to be rude to Cameron's friends, but still less did he want to seem too friendly to them. In the end, he followed his brother's lead. Aware of Perry's and Max's scrutiny—for all that they feigned not to notice—he took his shirt back off and laid it beside his sneakers on the flat rock.

"Cameron tells me he's invited you to his party," Max said. "Will we see you there?"

"I don't know." Jesse watched his brother far out in the Schneidekill, well away from the dangers of the shore. "Maybe."

"I certainly hope so. It should be quite the experience."

As Jesse headed out into deeper water, a thought struck him, and he paused to look back over his shoulder toward shore. But Max and Perry weren't going through the shirts and shoes he and his brother had left unguarded, they weren't snapping any more photos—they hadn't turned into vultures ready to feast on any carcass that came their way. He'd had a sudden fear of all that.

Already they were disappearing along the trail into the brush that grew thick by the water's edge.

"You got a stronger stomach than me, little brother," Kyle said when he reached him.

"Look, we gotta talk about this shit."

"Then talk."

"What'm I supposed to be doing?" Jesse asked as they treaded water together. "Tell me there's some plan here, we're not just punching around in the dark."

"What're you talking about?"

"Cameron. He gave me money to get a new truck."

"What the fuck are you talking about?"

"I'm not shitting you. He promised me six thousand bucks, told me to go find a truck that didn't suck."

"No fucking way. And you kept that from me?"

"I'm telling you now. It was just yesterday, and you were out with Leanne last night."

"Don't fucking remind me."

"Oh."

"Shit." Kyle laughed triumphantly. He splashed water Jesse's way. "Six thousand bucks. That's fucking amazing. You fucking amaze me, little brother. You got a new truck out of that faggot. That is brilliant. That is success, man."

Jesse wished he could be quite so sure. And in the meantime, the vultures hadn't left. They went right on circling, black reminders in the clear blue sky.

TWENTY

The sun was up but not yet visible; the world lay in a shock of humid fog. Jesse walked swiftly across the overgrown field, wading through chest-high weeds and grasses. Spiders had spun their webs overnight, and these clung to him stickily. At the far end of the field he entered the woods where old stone walls crisscrossed, slumping now into ruin. The crackle of his footsteps hung in the mist. The land was rolling, but soon became steeper. Here and there stone outcrops broke the leafy forest floor. Walking became trickier, but a sense of nervous excitement urged him on, and soon he was deep in the woods, negotiating his way among looming blocks of stone stacked up in towers or tumbled down in chaos like the ruins of some forgotten city. He'd been all through these woods in his time, but he didn't think he'd ever been here, and yet he felt none of that little panic that tugged at you when you realized you were lost.

Nestled amid the boulders a blue car, riddled with bullet holes, lay flipped over on its roof. How, he wondered, had anybody gotten a car to that particular spot? But he didn't pause to ponder that. Resisting the impulse to do some target practice of his own, he pressed on. He'd taken Pop's .22 and a box of shells.

After a while the terrain leveled out again. He came to an open glade and stopped. There in the grass, a rust-colored doe grazed peacefully, obliviously. Slowly he lifted his rifle to his shoulder. Her head came up; she stood there, ears pressed back, motionless and alert. Calmly he took aim. She leapt just as he pulled the trigger, but the bullet caught her nonetheless, and as she completed the graceful arc of her leap, she fell motionless to the ground. He walked over to where she lay on her side, one black, liquid eye staring up at him. No blood was visible, not a mark on her. As he looked at her, a flicker of movement out the corner of his eye caused him to turn. Two more does stood facing him. Strangely, they seemed utterly unalarmed by the report of his rifle. Hardly believing his luck, he aimed and fired. Fired again. Both sank to their knees, and he fired twice more.

And now, amazingly, he saw a fourth deer, a buck this time, its rack of antlers majestic in the dim light. It was moving off into the trees—a tricky shot, but he tried it, and his aim must have been perfect. Two chattering squirrels that had been chasing each other around a tree trunk stopped dead still, and he picked those off as well.

His firing seemed to have attracted attention from all over. A fox loped into view, gazing his way with wary, intelligent eyes. He shot it. A possum balanced in the crotch of a tree. A black bear was rooting at a fallen log. A family of raccoons appeared at the mouth of a boulder pile. He fired and fired again, barely bothering to aim, but his bullets never missed their mark. He kept reloading as fast as he could; he brought down dozens of creatures. He felt giddy and hot as the woods discharged their bounty. Goats and lions and zebras and giraffes came toward him. Buffalo and antelope and radiant white polar bears. He was covered in their warm blood, it steamed off him, thick and intoxicating. In the trees a pack of monkeys jabbered and howled, their faces almost human, and he thought how once you started you couldn't stop, but it was impossible to kill all of them, there were just too many, and too many different kinds, and so he'd never be done with it.

He woke with a start. Kyle was over at Leanne's tonight. Jesse had the bedroom to himself.

There were things you'd never say. How the room without Kyle in the middle of the night felt all wrong, a boat come unmoored and now drifting in black water far from any shore.

He lay still amid the humid, sour-smelling sheets of his bed as both the dream and his hard-on faded away. Already he could only remember that sensation of amazement when all the animals had started to fall beneath his bullets, then only the vague feeling that he'd done something illicit but highly pleasurable, finally nothing but a squeamish pang that got tangled up in a stray memory of how much he used to hate Michelle de Hulter. How Kyle would lie in the bunk above him and nightly chart his slow, agonizing progress toward that one sweet goal he had in mind, supplying plenty of ripe details to give his younger brother a hard-on he couldn't help but put his fist around, silently, silently, don't make the bed shake, till finally Kyle made it with Michelle one Friday night out by the cement quarry. "Man, it just slipped right in," he reported. "For a minute there, I was afraid my damn joint was gonna slip right back out." Hearing it all made Jesse feel useless, sick, excited. And when he'd see Michelle and Kyle at school, leaning into each other by the lockers, a feeling of amazement and rage would go through him.

Michelle de Hulter was practically a million years ago, long since replaced by probably a dozen girlfriends. He had no idea why he should be thinking of her—or even why, once upon a time, he'd hated her so much. He didn't hate Leanne, for example, except when she'd come out with something stupid—"You and Donna are such a cute couple" being one of her favorites. That stung, and he wondered if, behind her smile of gleaming teeth, she knew it.

Sleep, he could tell, was past him. The clock by his bed said three-twenty, though that wasn't entirely dependable. The damn thing was always either fast or slow. But at three-twenty, who cared?

He briefly considered finishing the job his dreaming brain had set him to, but jacking off, he knew, would just depress him. Adjusting his boxers, he rolled out of bed and went over to the open window. The air was still and heavy. He wasn't sure what he expected to see, and there wasn't anything except an elongated rectangle of light cast from a downstairs window, which meant the kitchen light was on.

He debated whether he should just crawl back in bed or go down and see if by some chance Kyle had come back home. Without turning on the light in the hall, he made his way down the narrow stairs and emerged into the brightly lit kitchen.

His mom sat at the table, smoking a cigarette and staring off into space. In front of her, a half-empty glass of water, her macraméd cigarette case and lighter, an open magazine. He stood in the doorway, and for the longest time she didn't see him. It surprised him how worn-out she looked, but maybe everybody looked that way in the middle of the night.

Out of nowhere the sad thought came to him: she'd washed their clothes and fixed their meals and packed them off to school in the mornings—but it was Pop they'd longed for when they came home in the afternoons. It was Pop who scooped them up, when they were little, and rode them around on his shoulders; or later, took them tramping through the woods on cold November mornings, their breath steaming all around them like they were cows or horses or some other big beasts.

He wondered what she was thinking, sitting there all alone. He worked to make out the upside-down headline on the magazine article she'd been looking at. "Is Ricky Martin Gay?" it asked.

Well, duh, as Donna would say.

"Jesse, honey," she mentioned, looking his way at last. "What are you doing up at this hour?"

"I could ask you the same thing," he said, suddenly aware of his near-nakedness.

"Well, don't. And don't just stand there. You're making me nervous. Is it your brother's snoring that's keeping you up?"

"Kyle ain't here. And he don't snore."

"Well, somebody does. Drives me crazy. I hear it right through the walls."

"It ain't me either."

"Them that snore are the lucky ones," his mom said. "Anyway. What do you want?"

"Nothing. I just came down."

"Well, sit. I'd offer you a cigarette, but . . ." She shrugged. "Funny how they hand out the vices around here."

"You blame Pop, don't you?" It made him nervous to say such a thing to his mom.

"It's a lousy life. What can you say? That's why I believe in God."

"Then why're you wanting to sell the house?"

"I know Kyle's taking it hard." She stubbed out her cigarette in the little metal ashtray and shook another from the case. He noticed how the pink and white macramé was stained from handling. "But he's got to understand. You both got to understand. I know this place has memories for you. I know it goes way back, and some people put a whole lot of stock in old things just because they're old. I'm not like that. Your daddy was. That's why he hardly ever let anything go. He hated for anything to change. And I put up with that because, well, because I was his wife, and that's what I owed him. But not even your daddy, bless his heart, could keep things from changing. I know, the two of you think you're gonna be around here forever. But you won't. You're gonna want to settle down on your own somewhere, raise your own family. That's the way it is. I just wish you boys had more business sense." She paused to inhale deeply on her cigarette. Jesse wished he hadn't come down. He didn't like to hear his mom talk like this. She really did blame Pop after all.

He wanted to love his mom like he was supposed to. Like Pop would've wanted him to.

"If I had a hundred thousand dollars," he told her on impulse, "I'd give it to you in an instant. Then you could go and fix this place up any way you wanted."

She laughed. "A hundred thousand dollars. And just where's that going to come from?"

"I got prospects," he told her. "This guy I been working for. He's helping me buy a new truck."

"How do you mean 'helping'?"

"He's giving me some money."

"You mean *lending.*"

"He's giving it to me."

She looked at him skeptically, and he rebuked himself for not having the wits to keep quiet. Cameron, it seemed, was one of those topics that just wanted to spill out, no matter how you sealed your lips against it.

"What kind of a fellow is this?"

"He's got money. Pop was gonna do work for him before he got sick. That's how me and Kyle came into it."

His mother made a pulled-down expression. "Well," she said, "I'm sure you know what you're doing. A fellow's known for what he does. Your daddy had his schemes too. They never came to nothing. You just might want to remember that."

He hit the table with his fist. It made her jump. "Why do you always, always talk against Pop?"

"I don't talk against him. But you boys always idolized him—beyond sense, if you ask me. I don't see nothing wrong with trying to put some sense back into it all. I know you and Kyle don't like to hear that. Kyle especially. Well, I'm sorry. Your daddy wasn't a bad man. I did some

211

idolizing of him too, back when. A dreamer and a schemer. Now there's a combination to beware of. Sometimes I wonder what you boys took from him, but I guess time'll tell on that one." She put out her cigarette and stood up. "Good night. Turn out the light when you're done down here. Somebody leaves these lights on all the time. Thinks we got money to burn." At the door she paused and turned back to him. "I didn't mean to say anything to hurt your feelings. It's just late-night talk, is all. I love both my sons very much."

I love you too, he should have said, but he wasn't very good at saying that kind of thing to anybody. He sat in silence as his mother's footsteps creaked up the stairs. "Is Ricky Martin Gay?" asked the upside-down headline.

"Who the fuck cares?" he said under his breath, reaching across impatiently to shut the magazine so he wouldn't have to look at the stupid question any longer. In his dream, he recalled, he'd been hunting, he'd been slaughtering animals, and it had felt powerful and exhilarating. It'd pumped his dick full of raging blood.

TWENTY-ONE

He hadn't really thought this day would come, he realized, pausing to survey the line of cars that overflowed his driveway and stretched along both sides of the road, almost to the cemetery. Lying in his hospital bed, contemplating the Catskills in the distance, the lovely world that would so casually outlast him, he'd commanded himself, Let it all go. But life continued to shower him with possibility after possibility.

The sky was a deep, dazzling blue, the sun hot but the humidity refreshingly low. It would all be perfect were it not for the on-again, off-again complaint of a chain saw somewhere in the distance.

"Your garden looks truly beautiful," Elliot enthused. "A work of art." Dressed all in white, wearing a Yankees baseball cap and sporting a chic shadow of beard stubble, he looked uncommonly handsome. They were on their way to becoming friends; nonetheless, Cameron couldn't quite banish the feeling he was keeping a guilty secret he should have disclosed by now.

"Thanks," he told Elliot. "And thanks for coming. Drinks are over there. And tons of food." He motioned to the table set up in the shade of a catalpa tree, where two handsome lads, clad in nothing but combat boots and white Speedos, tended the bar, doling out the mint juleps Cameron had decided, as a last-minute whimsy, were to be the afternoon's featured drink. Already he was regretting that impulsive choice. Only Perry would get the joke, and Perry was still at the train station in Poughkeepsie fetching arrivals from Manhattan.

"They look delectable," said Elliot. "Do I know them?"

"Probably. One of them was our waiter the other night—Bryan I-forget-his-last-name."

"Of course. How could I forget?"

"They're Max's contribution to the festivities. Do you think it's too vulgar? I'm not sure I want to know how Max talked them into those outfits."

"Oh, I'd say the trick was talking them *out* of their outfits. Anyway, it's a nostalgic touch. All we need now is some disco music."

Cameron supposed Elliot was right; at the moment, though, the lads looked more comical than anything else. He'd treated them to a fortifying couple of shots of Stoli before the first guests had arrived. Now he hoped they'd remembered their sunscreen. On the beach at Ölüdeniz he'd lotioned Toby's freckled back till Toby looked at him over his shoulder and said, with a grin, "You pervert, you've given me a hard-on."

For a sweet, disconcerting moment, that image muscled out everything else. Then Elliot was before him again, saying, "I think I'll go have me a nibble. I'm so happy you're throwing this little shindig. Plus, I love your hat." He caressed the straw brim affectionately, familiarly—as if they were the oldest of friends; as if, perhaps, they'd long ago been lovers and survived all that to enter into this mellow, supportive companionship.

If Toby had lived, might they one day have ended up just this way? The thought was too melancholy to contemplate. For here was Cameron's whole life—or what remained of it. From Manhattan, Lucien Davidoff and Daniel Corsair, his partners from the days of playgrounds and urban nooks, had arrived in a chauffeured car they'd sent away, commanding the driver, "Don't come back till the sun sets." Robert Angstrom, whom Cameron wouldn't have invited had he known Dan wasn't planning to come, had ventured up by bus. Matt, Stan, and Julian had rented a car and gotten lost; they'd had to phone for directions from Rhinebeck, on the wrong side of the river.

From Stone Hollow and environs came the bulk of the guests: Irving Fischman, a good-looking man who worked in the Development Office at Columbia and drove up from Brooklyn every Friday to spend the weekend in a dreary little house trailer on a piece of property where he planned one day to build a house; Andrew Hackett, the antique dealer who'd cheerfully raided the Vanderhofs' yard sale; Morgan Hayes, who restored old furniture by day and, according to Dan, who should know, by night prowled the Internet looking for hookups in the area; Billy Koslowsky and Matt Blane, fresh from finishing renovations on their third Victorian wreck in Kingston, and ready to sell and move on to a fourth ("The day we stop working is the day we part company," they joked in all seriousness); Phil Haas, New Paltz florist and fellow sufferer; Daniel of Daniel's, a hair salon in Poughkeepsie; Abe and Lillian Gorecki, he a well-known painter of colorful abstract canvases, she a largely unknown sculptor of strangely pleasing, quasi-organic forms (Cameron had bought one of her sculptures, nestled it among dwarf hinoki cypress and spreading juniper where, alas, no one ever noticed it); Jorge Varo and his mysterious, mysteriously beautiful wife, Sula, who, in Cameron's presence at least, seldom uttered a word; the fiercely pierced and tattooed Damien of Liberation!, at the moment comparing body decoration with Daryl Dahlheim; Chuck Haze and Peter Lippmann, a quiet, dignified older couple who'd met while serving on the USS *Missouri* during the Korean War; and four young fellows Cameron barely knew, who lived in a handsome old house they'd dubbed Sodom on the Schneidekill.

And more were arriving; it was as if a whole flock of tropical birds, blown off course by some storm, had landed amidst his garden, coloring it with their laughter and gossip. Only one person seemed left out; he sat alone on a bench out by the shed, watching everything with that slightly glazed, altogether impenetrable look he sometimes got. He'd come dressed in his usual uniform—workboots, tight white T-shirt, those camouflage pants that in this particular crowd attracted rather than deflected attention.

Aware he'd been neglecting his reluctant guest, Cameron forsook the high chatter of the aviary and wandered over.

"You don't care for my party," he said.

"It's fine," Jesse told him, cracking his knuckles in either boredom or anxiety. "It's just, I don't know nobody here."

"Then I'll introduce you," Cameron offered, suddenly conscious how few women were in attendance, how many queers. This was his family, for better or worse, but why had he wanted—or needed—Jesse to experience them firsthand? Had he hoped, in some perverse way, to punish this clueless straight boy?

But what on earth for?

All this was troubling, suddenly, as they both searched fruitlessly for something more to say to each other.

"You'll be happy to see I didn't make good on my threat to line the tree trunk with candles," Cameron said valiantly.

Jesse glanced toward the fallen oak and nodded. It had been a terrible mistake to invite him. How could he be expected to feel anything but contempt for the nonsense that passed for Cameron's life? Candles on a tree trunk indeed.

But Jesse seemed to be thinking other things. "You'd never tell there was a drought on," he observed with a quiet laugh.

"What do you mean?" Cameron asked, the conspiratorial tenor of Jesse's words having sent a thrill through him.

"It was all that mulching I done. Whoever thought I'd be much for working a garden like I did?"

They watched the flower heads nodding in the warm breeze, crimson bee balm and black-eyed Susan and purple echinacea, goose-necked loosestrife and midnight-dark spikes of salvia, the silver-gray sea holly otherwise known as Miss Wilmot's Ghost.

With hardly a bit of warning they'd turned a corner, Cameron thought, entering into some wonderful precinct of their own, a garden beyond the garden, cool and fragrant and green.

"Paradise, the Persians called it," he said, but Jesse didn't follow, and Cameron wondered if he risked ruining the unexpected gift of this moment. "Paradise. The Persians' word for garden was *paradise*. The blessed oasis in the desert. The thirst-quenching place of life."

A sudden, angry spurt of noise from the woods across the street interrupted their fragile communion. In the real garden before him he could see heads turn, people uncertain what the commotion meant. He'd been half-aware of a dull whine in the distance, the approaching sound of ATVs. Now they were revving aggressively, somewhere just out of sight, just beyond the yellow-and-black NO TRESPASSING signs he'd posted.

How dare people trespass on his land?

"Indian attack," yelped one of the young men from Sodom on the Schneidekill. "Quick, girls! To the barricades!" Everyone around laughed, and Cameron thought how he envied those young men, peroxided and bitchy and in full embrace of their faggotry. At the same time he was conscious of the cold look Jesse directed their way.

With a powerful roar, the marauders erupted from their cover of vines and bushes onto the road's weedy shoulder. There they paused uneasily, two young men seated on their ATVs, for all the world like a scouting party taking stock of a vulnerable settlement, its innocent festivities arrested midgesture.

"My brother," Jesse said.

"So it is." Cameron laughed, relieved—for a moment he'd thought it might be Crazy Jamey on a rampage—though at the same time disappointed his and Jesse's mood of almost spiritual accord had been so rudely shattered. (And who knew? Maybe the young man on the ATV beside Kyle was, in fact, his phantom caller. Now that would be rich . . .)

"Did Kyle know you were coming to my party?"

"He knows now. He sees me." For a moment Jesse seemed lost in thought; he shook his head silently.

"He and his friend are certainly welcome to join us."

"You don't know my brother. Nor Brandon neither."

"Well, I do know Kyle a little," Cameron protested.

"Not the way I know him. Not the way he knows me."

The ferocity of it took Cameron aback, and for a startled moment he remembered how Toby, from the poignant safety of his Manhattan refuge, had on rare occasion actually wept to recall his awful, precious Oklahoma childhood.

It was like the minute hand of a clock got stuck and couldn't push forward. What the fuck was Kyle thinking? It wasn't a crime to be riding around on a Saturday afternoon, but what had brought him out here of all places? And what was Brandon saying to his brother as they sat on their quads and surveyed Cameron's party? They leaned their heads in close; he could see them both laughing. But they made no move to approach, just rested there on the edge of the woods, engines running. This wasn't right, he thought. It wasn't playing kosher, somehow. Kyle raised his hand, a gesture of salute meant just for him. Was it to mock him—or something else?

With no warning, the minute hand came unstuck, jolted forward; the two turned and thundered off the way they'd come. Jesse watched the wall of green swallow them up. But everybody had seen them. There was a stir all around.

"I guess the answer's no," Cameron said with way much too much cheerfulness. But how could he know anything? You think I'm your friend, Jesse thought. Right now he was nobody's friend. Not Cameron's; not Kyle's either. The admission startled him, but it was true; he didn't much cotton to Cameron's brand of foolishness—and why did the guy insist on wearing that ridiculous straw hat all the time?—but neither was hanging out with Kyle what it used to be. Partly that was Brandon, but Brandon was nothing new; Brandon went way back. Something else stood in their way. His brother didn't trust him: that was Jesse's sneaking suspicion. But what was there not to trust? He wouldn't be here unless Kyle wanted him to. He wouldn't be doing any of this, he didn't think, without his brother's urging.

Once, when he was a kid, he'd been having this dream: he was in a car arguing with Pop, and in that dream the argument was giving him a splitting headache. Then he woke up—or something woke him up. The bed was shaking. *Hey, stop it,* he'd yelled up to Kyle's bunk, but Kyle said, *It ain't me, man.* The whole house was shuddering; a little earthquake had rolled through, and he thought, That's what was giving me that headache.

That was how he felt these days with Kyle. Sooner or later there was bound to be a rumble somewhere; already, hidden fault lines were making their presence clear.

And on top of that—all this. He looked around at the mess he found himself in the middle of. That poor excuse for a human being who'd yelled "Indian attack!" for instance. You really couldn't stir them with a stick, could you? He tried to feel superior—they were only fags after all. Still, something nagged at him, like everybody around him was speaking some tongue he'd never quite understand.

Why would he even want to understand their fucking twisted language?

"Somebody walking on your grave?"

"What?"

"The way you just shivered," Cameron said.

Get away from me, Jesse thought. Just let me be. Though of course he was the one who was trespassing; he understood that. Maybe the best thing to do was just walk away from it all while he still had the chance.

But at that very moment, as if to block his way, Perry came strolling up the driveway crowded with expensive cars. He had two fellows with him.

"Finally," Cameron exclaimed. "I thought they'd never get here."

Perry spied them and headed their way, his two friends following close behind like they didn't know anybody here either. Jesse was interested to see they weren't too much older than him. Normal, nice-looking guys. It gave him some faint glimmer of hope.

"The train took forever," Perry said, kissing Cameron on the cheek. It no longer jolted Jesse so much. Still, he thought, Perry better not try anything like that with *him*.

And Perry didn't. He just smiled, said, "Hey, Jesse," and stuck out his hand while one of the two fellows who came up behind him had folded Cameron in a big hug, saying, "Marvelous to see you, honey. You're looking really well."

"Flattery will get you everywhere," Cameron told him.

"Charlie Morse," Perry said, "Jesse Vanderhof."

Jesse was surprised Perry remembered his last name—or even knew it in the first place; certainly he had no idea of Perry's. But then, something about Perry sort of focused right in on you. It was hard to squirm out of his sights.

That worried him a little, but he hadn't time to worry too much because Charlie had stepped forward and caught him in a hug just like the one he'd given Cameron. Startled, Jesse tried to step back, but then found it easier just to give in and let himself be held tight for several seconds.

"Jesse's a little reserved," Cameron said. "He's been helping me with my garden."

"You've done a fantastic job," Charlie said. He reached out and grabbed the other fellow by the arm and dragged him into their circle. "Both of you, this is Tracy Parker."

Jesse could still feel the stubble of Charlie's cheek where it had rubbed against his.

"The one I've heard so much about," Cameron said.

"Charlie's new boyfriend," Perry explained, like Jesse would be interested in anything like that. They hadn't looked all that much like queers

219

from a distance, but wouldn't you know? Tracy followed Charlie's lead in trying to give him a hug, but this time Jesse managed to fend it off.

"We need some drinks," Charlie announced. "I couldn't help but notice the bartenders back there. Sexy."

Jesse of course had noticed them too. Who wouldn't? The thought of a guy showing himself off like that was scarcely believable, though he supposed girls did it all the time. Kyle and Brandon faked their way into the topless lounge in New Paltz now and again, reporting everything back to him in gory, magnificent detail.

He wondered if Donna'd think two guys prancing around in the buff except for their Jockeys was something sexy, but the thought of his girlfriend made him suddenly queasy.

He made up his mind to mention the fact of Donna to these fellows, the first chance he had. But they didn't seem all that interested in him. It was the new guy, Tracy, they all wanted to talk to. Well, fine, he thought; he didn't have anything special to say to them anyway.

Still, when they moved toward the bar, he followed. What else was he going to do? Stand around by himself waiting for some queer he didn't even know to go hitting on him?

He watched as Charlie casually draped his arm around Tracy's shoulder, and Tracy made no move to shrug him off. No way he felt anything about them but disappointment at two nice-looking guys having gone queer like the rest of the crowd. It was a damn shame.

And what if Gary Dunkel was to turn up next?

"You've got to be kidding!" Perry said. "Mint juleps?" He reached out and yanked the brim of Cameron's hat down over his face.

"Hey," Cameron told him. "At the time it seemed like a good idea."

"I'll definitely have a mint julep," Tracy said. He turned to Charlie. "Arthurina would want us to, I think."

"Absolutely," Charlie agreed.

It all left Jesse out. He tried not to stare at the bartender's bare chest, the little gold ring through one of his nipples. Didn't it hurt? There'd been a few guys back in high school who'd thought putting a stud through their ear was cool, but this was something else entirely.

"Want one?" Cameron asked. He was holding out a glass of what looked like iced tea.

Not knowing anything else to do, Jesse took and sipped the sweetish, off-putting concoction.

"Don't let him make you drink that if you don't want to," Perry advised.

"This is a mint julep?" Jesse asked. Just one swallow and he could feel its kick.

"Definitely an acquired taste," Cameron said. "There's plenty else to drink if you don't like it. But now you can't ever say you never tasted one."

"It's a southern thing," Perry explained. "Only nobody in Dixie really drinks that shit. Only southerners who go north and want to impress—like Cameron here."

"Go ahead. Make fun," Cameron said. "Who's the one who insisted on cooking chitlins that time?"

"Aren't those, like, intestines or something?" Charlie asked.

"Exactly," Cameron told him, touching a finger to the tip of Charlie's nose.

Seeing how Charlie didn't even flinch, Jesse took another sip of his drink, then another. Way too sugary, and he could do without the mint, but otherwise it wasn't too bad. He had the vague sense he was in some kind of trouble with his brother, but he told himself that couldn't be. It wasn't like he was actually enjoying himself, though he'd definitely relaxed a bit—and he was interested to see that Perry poked a little fun at Cameron. Maybe he was a little relieved to see nobody took his employer too seriously.

"It's so strange being back here in the Hudson Valley," Tracy was saying. He shook his head and made a strange face. "I taught school for a bit down in Middle Forge, I guess three years ago now. Other side of the river, of course."

"It's very different over there," Cameron told him. "We're much funkier here. It's why I like it."

"I heard Kate Moss moved up here," Charlie said.

"And Robert De Niro and Willem Dafoe. It's getting a little *too* trendy, if you ask me. It wasn't like this when we moved up here. There I go again. *We.* I'm still not used to the singular."

"Cameron's just getting over a nasty breakup," Perry explained.

"Oh, it wasn't nasty at all," Cameron said. "That's the worst part. It was perfectly amicable."

"Where *is* Dan?" Perry asked. "I thought he was coming. I was planning on throwing a drink in his face."

"You're out of luck. He called me at the last minute and said he'd decided to go to South Beach. I guess he got some offer he couldn't refuse."

"What a despicable little shit," Perry said.

All this chatter dazed Jesse a little, but he was content to sip his drink and listen. He kept glancing from Charlie to Tracy to Perry. Maybe it was the mint julep going a little to his head, or maybe the afternoon's bright sun, but he felt a hollowness that wasn't exactly unfamiliar. The way Charlie'd let Cameron tap him on the nose stayed with him, like the afterburn of Charlie's stubble grazing his own cheek. He wondered where Kyle and Brandon had gone to, and if he should go find them, be with his own kind.

But that was crazy. Brandon, he told himself, would never be his own kind.

The little group was starting to break up. Somebody took Cameron by the arm and told him how well he was looking. Charlie and Tracy drifted off to look at the garden. He found himself left alone with Perry, who touched his elbow lightly and said, "Here, let me get you another. Or maybe you want a real drink."

Jesse knew he probably shouldn't, but he said, "I'll have whatever you're having."

"And what *am* I having?" Perry wondered, putting a finger to his chin in thought. "I know. Bryan." He addressed the fellow with the ring through his nipple. "Make us two cosmos. Can you do that, honey?"

"Absolutely," Bryan said.

"Ever had a cosmo?" Perry asked Jesse. "They're all the rage in the city."

"I don't get into Kingston all that much," Jesse told him.

"That's funny," Perry said. "Cameron told me you had this dry wit."

Jesse just looked at him.

"Two cosmos," Bryan announced.

Jesse took the bright red drink—a faggot drink if ever there was one—and sipped warily. It tasted fruity, but what did he expect? He wondered if it had occurred to anybody here he wasn't yet twenty-one. The free booze was something Kyle would definitely appreciate, though only a handful of days remained to separate him from the magic line. Jesse was counting down those days as eagerly as anybody. They'd be free of needing Sean. It'd be one less thing to worry about.

"What do you think?" Perry asked.

Jesse shrugged. "It's okay." He was suddenly conscious he was stuck here alone with Perry without a clue what they were supposed to talk about. In vain he looked around for Cameron, but he'd disappeared into the crowd. Who would've guessed his employer had all these friends? It made Cameron seem larger, somehow, no longer the lonely fellow with nothing to do but fuss around in his flower garden. Funny, Jesse had never considered Cameron might be somebody who mattered to people. He wondered if that had ever occurred to Kyle either.

"Let's go for a little walk," Perry suggested. "Let's go look at your shed."

They'd just been up there, of course, but maybe Perry for some reason wanted to inspect it a little more closely. Jesse followed, aware of the slap of Perry's sandals on the flagstones underfoot. He took a long, cooling swallow from his cosmo, but it didn't help much.

From the shed's vantage, the party looked more like a movie than anything real, and he told himself that was how he'd think of it when it was all over: some long, boring movie he'd watched in a nearly empty theater, untouched by whatever commotion flew by on-screen.

"That's better," Perry said. "Far from the madding crowd."

Jesse couldn't think of a thing to say—but Perry didn't seem to mind. He sat down abruptly on the grass and crossed his legs Indian-style. Jesse followed suit. All that standing around, he realized, had been wearing him out.

Perry patted the pocket of his white shirt, then pulled out a slightly crumpled joint. "Here." He straightened it out. "This'll cool you down. You seem kind of uptight."

"It's just, I don't much know nobody here," Jesse told him.

Perry lit the joint and inhaled, then passed it over. Jesse associated the sweet smell with Brandon's basement. He'd pretty much gotten off that stuff once he met Donna.

"That was hardly enough to buzz a chipmunk," Perry said, so Jesse took another, deeper drag. "That's more like it, guy." Perry reached over and took the joint from between Jesse's fingers. For just a second their hands touched. Jesse thought about saying, Guys don't touch me—but didn't. He watched as Perry sucked down a load of smoke and held it in his lungs.

"Aah," he said in a long exhale. "This is more like it. You know—I love Cameron, but I sort of hate his parties. So he tells me you've got a girlfriend."

It took Jesse a second to make that leap. He guessed he should be grateful for the opportunity, but somehow he wasn't.

"Mnn," he said, staring into his empty glass. A bug was crawling around the rim and he flicked it off with his finger.

"So tell me about her. What's her name?"

"Donna," he said reluctantly.

Perry seemed vaguely amused. "Donna what?"

"DuBois."

"Let me guess. High school sweetheart?"

Why were these guys always so curious? Or did he know why? "We been going out two years. So, yeah, we started when we was in high school. Probably get married too." Was he spoiling something by saying that? He'd wondered that when he talked to Cameron too. But a strange, even brilliant idea was occurring to him. "How about you?" he asked. "You got a girlfriend?"

Perry grinned a grin full of dimples and perfect white teeth. "Like you wouldn't believe," he said. "But then, you've met Max. We weren't exactly high school sweethearts, but we've been together so long it sometimes feels that way."

Jesse experienced a little what he did when he danger dived. It was one thing to talk to Cameron, something else to be sitting here with Perry, who wasn't part of any scheme he could shelter behind. If he was talking to Perry, it was because he was choosing to talk to him.

"You're not saying anything," Perry said. "I'm not shocking you, am I?"

"I don't get shocked so easy."

"Well, you never know these days."

"What somebody wants to do, it's their own business," Jesse told him.

He wondered if Perry sucked Max's cock. If he let Max fuck him up the ass. There was no condoning any of that.

Perry was smiling that faraway smile pot smokers got when they smoked. Jesse wished he'd taken a bigger hit, now that his drink was all gone. On the other hand, he was kind of glad he hadn't.

"Ever been tempted?" Perry asked.

"You don't got to go down every road you see."

"Fair enough." Perry nodded to himself like he'd figured something out, though Jesse knew from experience that whatever you figured out on pot usually wasn't worth much of nothing the next day.

"You're not such a talkative one, are you?" Perry said.

"I don't got too much to say."

"Then tell me more about this Donna. What's she like?"

Jesse gazed out to where Tracy and Charlie were talking to a tall, bald black man. It occurred to him he really didn't know what his girlfriend was like. It was was like trying to catch a scent—the more you try, the more it goes away. "She works down at the Family Market. Likes animals. Has a whole collection of stuffed ones, all kinds."

"You mean taxidermy? She *shot* them?"

Jesse had to laugh. "Like little kids have," he explained.

"Beanie Babies. I get it. What else?"

"She spends most of her time at the mall with her girlfriends. When she's not working."

"The one in Kingston? She drag you along?"

"Tries to."

"Personally, I hate the mall. I wish they'd tear it down."

But Jesse knew at least three people who worked there. "It's jobs for a lot of folk," he reminded Perry. Patti'd worked there from time to time to help pay for school.

"I always forget those inconvenient facts. Max says I'm too much of a hothead."

"Is he really running for mayor?" Jesse asked. If anybody was to ask why he'd been here, he could always explain it that way. Spy in the enemy camp. Top secret mission authorized by Uncle Roy.

"Beats me. He's certainly talking like it. Me? I don't know if I can take being first lady. I'm not too good at ball gowns." Perry laughed a high, giddy laugh. "Maybe I *am* trying to shock you a little. You're very new to all this, aren't you?"

"I wasn't born yesterday."

"No, I guess you probably weren't. I could tell about you."

"What do you mean, tell about me?" Cameron pushed a little, now and then, but never like this. Maybe he liked a little pushing, Jesse told himself guiltily. Nobody would ever have to know. Nobody that counted, anyway.

"Oh," Perry said, "you seem like a pretty adventurous guy. You're in good shape. You've got a great body. Does it bother you if I say something like that?"

Jesse made himself shrug. He remembered Cameron's comment about somebody walking on his grave. Maybe Perry was walking on his grave.

"You ever thought of modeling?"

It was another of those stoned leaps Perry was making, and once again it gave Jesse pause. But this time he just had to laugh. "You got to be kidding."

"You're very beautiful."

"And you're so full of shit."

But Perry only smiled, his eyes all bright with the dope. His lips were big and luscious like a girl's—but Jesse had noticed that before. He tried not to think too much about it.

"Will you at least consider it?" Perry coaxed. "I might have you all wrong, but—I think you're kind of interested."

The guy was trying to flatter him, of course. He knew that old trick. Still, it felt strangely exciting to be caught in Perry's focus like that. It wasn't too often he was in anybody's focus except Donna's, and Donna's focus was, well, pretty different than somebody like Perry's.

He refused to meet Perry's look, that bright gaze riveted on him.

"You really want to take my picture?"

"I'm actually a pretty well-known photographer. At least in certain circles out there. I'm in books and galleries. You should stop by someday, check out my slides. I'd be more than happy to show you what I do. I live right down on Main Street, the white house with the big porch just past the post office. You really should feel free to drop by anytime."

"You're not gonna want me to take my clothes off or nothing, are you?" he asked warily.

Perry tapped his knee lightly. "You won't have to do a thing you don't want to. I can promise you that."

There wasn't any particular harm, he supposed: he wasn't committing to anything. Despite everything, he sort of liked Perry—the way he sort of liked Cameron. They weren't anything like any other people he knew, but they weren't like what the people he knew made them out to be either.

It was one more thing nobody else needed to know.

"Maybe I'll think about it," he said. "But I ain't promising nothing. I'm pretty busy these days. I got a lot going on."

"Of course." Perry smiled again. He was all smiles now, and suddenly Jesse didn't like him so much anymore. I could beat your ass to a pulp, he thought, imagining the quick work Kyle and Brandon would make of somebody like that. Though he didn't want to beat Perry to a pulp, not in the least. But what did he want?

I sure don't want *that*, he assured himself, even as the image stole into his head—him and Perry down by the cement mine, wrestling on the shore of that strange blue water, laughing and wrestling, buddies who could share anything. Maybe it wouldn't be too bad, getting to know him a little better. Letting him take a picture or two. See what happens, anyway.

"I got to go now," he said, standing up abruptly and brushing some stray bits of grass from his pants. "Nice talking to you."

Instantly he regretted admitting that, but what was said was said.

"Same here," Perry told him, though he made no move to get up. "Hope I'll see you around."

Don't hold your breath, Jesse thought, though what he said was, "Who knows? Maybe I'll surprise you."

Certainly he'd already surprised himself—and he wasn't, he reminded himself, too much of one for surprises.

Across the way, he could see Elliot seated on a teak bench, conversing animatedly with Irving Fischman, to whom Cameron had introduced him some ten minutes ago. There was something cheeringly civilized about the sight of two adult homosexuals striking up an aquaintance at a garden party, Cameron thought. He watched their apparent ease with each other, Elliot resting an arm comfortably on the back of the bench, Irving dangling a loafer from the end of a languidly crossed leg. Cameron remembered how, in grade school, only fags crossed their legs that way, and he'd been extra careful never to be caught in such a pose.

Now, at least in his little world, the tables were turned entirely. He watched Jesse wander, alone and rather lost-looking, down from the vicinity of the shed. He was failing, utterly, to mingle—probably had not the slightest idea how. Cameron felt both sorry for him and, unaccountably, annoyed at the complete absence of social skills. How could you ever manage to know someone like that, seriously, for the long haul?

"Cimcifuga racemosa," he told Lillian Gorecki, whom he was taking around the garden, his seventh or eighth tour of the afternoon. "I really love its flower spikes, though they do have a rather peculiar smell to them. And next to that, with the huge leaves, *Ligularia 'Desdemona.'* It's looking a little ragged. The bugs have been having a field day, but I refuse to use pesticides anymore. I used to *drench* gardens in them, back in the bad old days."

There were those who noticed and those who didn't, and of course different people noticed different things—still, he thought, attention mattered. In a perfect world, everything would be noticed, everything would be appreciated.

At least where his garden was concerned, Lillian was gratifyingly appreciative.

"That's *Eryngium varifolium,"* he explained in answer to her query. They paused before a clump of subtle, silver-blue blooms. All at once he felt a warning twinge in his gut. He forced himself to go on. "Also called Miss Wilmot's Ghost. Miss Wilmot was so fond of *Eryngium*—sea holly—that she carried its seeds wherever she went. Dropped them in all her friends' gardens like calling cards. Not a bad way to be remembered, I'd say. I actually got these from a very old friend of mine, a gardener in England. The person who introduced me to the world of gardens. I've had them forever. They tend to migrate around the garden from year to year, but I like them wherever they pop up."

Mrs. Waddeston's benign, wandering ghost.

"I don't see how you manage," Lillian said as another spasm tweaked him. "I can barely keep the weeds out of my little flower patch by the patio."

"Actually, I have excellent help," Cameron explained, gesturing Jesse's way across the crowd. Some at his party would instantly recognize a vigorous weed flourishing among delicate exotics ("So who's the hot little number?" Matt Blane had asked), and some, like Lillian, casting a perfunctory glance in Jesse's direction, would remain happily oblivious.

"I should really have you over for a drink sometime soon," she told him. "I could definitely use some of your gardening genius."

"It's a date," he said, suddenly stung by a fiery surge in his bowels. "Now if you'll excuse me, I'm afraid I have a little emergency to attend to."

Screwing up his contempt, Jesse made his way toward Bryan with the pierced nipple and said, in a flat voice, "I'll have another of them cosmos."

Bryan looked at him from under arched eyebrows and rolled his eyes. What're you looking at? Jesse wanted to say. He felt a hand take him by the elbow. "So," said the pink-faced fellow by his side, "this is an unexpected surprise."

He moved to free his elbow from the thick fingers that clutched him.

"You remember me, I hope. I'm Craig. I was out at your house the other day. Craig Hallenbeck."

Of course, Jesse thought. Makes perfect sense you'd be a fag.

But then it occurred to him: maybe Craig was thinking the same thing too. He had that kind of grin, that was for sure.

"One cosmo," Bryan announced, handing over the bright red concoction.

"Looks delicious," Craig said. "What is it?"

"Here," Jesse told him. "You can have it."

"What're you going to drink?"

"I thought I was thirsty. Turns out I'm not."

"Well, thank you. Now what's your first name again? Vanderhof's your last. I know that much."

"Kyle. Kyle Vanderhof. I got to be going now."

"So soon? Hey—call me sometime. It'd be fun getting to know you. I've got my card here somewhere."

But Jesse wasn't waiting on any card. Before Craig had even managed to pull his wallet from his pocket, he'd strode away into the crowd. How long was he expected to stick around this place, anyway? He scanned the garden for Cameron but couldn't see him. More and more people had shown up: there must be nearly a hundred now. Their chatter filled the garden, nonstop noise—which if you stopped to listen to would drive you crazy. He had a moment like that, then found himself focusing in on a single voice. It was Max, Cameron's friend. Perry's . . . he wasn't sure what to call it. It wasn't something he particularly wanted to name, but words seethed in his head anyway. Boyfriend. Lover. *My husband,* he could hear Perry say in a strange, mocking sort of voice.

He wished he hadn't given his cosmo away.

"We're right on the cusp," Max was saying. "Demographically, I mean. Of course, so many of us being weekenders handicaps us a little. If it wasn't for that, we'd have this town. Still, it's only a matter of time. The Vanderhofs know that as much as you or I. Roy and his ilk—their days are numbered. It's a fact of life. Things change. The Village of Stone Hollow is well on its way to becoming the People's Republic of Stone Hollow." He smiled broadly behind his wire rims and gray mustache. Jesse didn't understand for an instant how you could go with a guy like that. Perry must be a good ten years younger, if not more. Was he in it for the money, then?

He had to admit he had no idea what gay guys did together—not in bed, that wasn't hard to figure out, but the rest of the time. How they lived their lives together day after day after day. How did they even know what to do from one minute to the next? It was hard enough, even with a nice girl like Donna, to know what was expected of you.

"The People's Republic of Stone Hollow. I like that," said the bald black man. "Could it be a campaign slogan?"

"No, no. This has got to be a bit of a stealth campaign. You don't want to scare people off."

"I hear the other side is going to run on a Save Our Town platform," said another man.

"Yes," said the black man. "But what they don't know is, it isn't their town to save anymore. It's our town now."

"Now, now. It's everybody's town," Max said. "I'm the candidate for all the people. People's Republic of Stone Hollow—that's just a throwback to my radical youth."

"But how are you going to address the gay question? Everybody knows Roy Vanderhof and his crowd are a bunch of homophobes."

"If they want to bring it up, let them. Otherwise . . ."

"I'm sure they'll bring it up. I'm sure there'll be a whisper campaign against you."

"I can whisper as well as the next person," said Max, seeming to look straight at Jesse. Or did he? Jesse had turned away before he was quite sure. Still, he thought he'd seen a merry glitter in Max's eye.

Feeling all at once defenseless, he decided to look for Cameron one more time before hauling out. Perry, he could see, had rejoined Charlie and Tracy, and the three of them were deep in conversation. Craig Hallenbeck, still nursing his cosmo, was chatting animatedly with a couple of elderly gentlemen. The fellow who'd yelled *"Indian Attack!"* earlier was sitting by himself, concentrating on a plate of food, occasionally dropping a bit to the little black cat that had appeared out of nowhere and kept rubbing itself up against his ankles.

Jesse counted exactly six women in the whole crowd. The host of the party was nowhere to be seen.

At the hors d'oeurves table he paused to sample a couple of the fancy-looking little sandwiches. They're weren't half-bad, though there was no telling exactly what was in them. Probably better not to know. He told himself he could always stop by the D & Dee for a hot dog on his way home.

Cigarrette stubs floated in half-empty plastic cups. Paper plates overflowed the trash can. The lawn chairs he'd directed Jesse to set out in carefully composed groups had all reconfigured their alliances.

"Can we have music?" asked one of the young men from Sodom on the Schneidekill. "We were snooping in your CDs."

Cameron wanted to protest that they weren't really his, either Toby or Dan had bought most everything in the collection, but why would this beauty with his fabulously peroxided hair want or need to know any of that ancient history?

"If you want to set it up, sure," he told the young man whose name he'd surely known at one point or another during the afternoon.

"Excellent," said the young Sodomite, delicately fluttering his eyelids.

Cameron wondered where Jesse had gone. In the gathering dusk that settled over his garden, his young redneck was nowhere to be seen. Surely he hadn't slipped away without saying good-bye? But then, Cameron had spent a good twenty minutes exiled to the upstairs toilet, followed by a change of underwear and trousers. Any number of people had drifted away in his absence.

He was sort of ready, as a matter of fact, for everyone to go home.

"Wonderful gathering," Lillian told him, affectionately rubbing his arm. "Are you feeling okay now?"

"Much better. My pills and I don't always agree. I think it's this new antiseizure medicine the doctor's started me on."

She made a sympathetic face as Abe shook Cameron's hand manfully, saying, "Don't be a stranger, now. Hopefully we'll see you soon."

"Yes," Cameron told them both, "I'm trying to get out more these days. This party was a good start, I think."

In the distance, Max walked among the party's detritus, picking up cups and napkins and paper plates and stuffing them in the garbage bag he trailed at his side. Charlie and Tracy sat on a low stone wall talking intently, intimately, Tracy reaching out now and then to pat Charlie's thigh, Charlie in turn caressing Tracy's shoulder, and Cameron felt a gust of lonely yearning sail through him. But I'm not in love, he told himself with a smile. In fact, far from it. Still, he rather wished Jesse hadn't left without saying good-bye.

From a window of his house, where a stereo speaker now perched, feverish anticipatory chords led to a full-throated black woman exclaiming in rapturous disbelief, as the song took flight, *It's raining men!*—and all at once the Ordu Caddesi was crowded with vendors selling melons, cucumbers, bowls of chickpeas and rice, in Istanbul's humid night, and a boom box in a T-shirt stall (those T-shirts with bizarre English-language slogans like DIFFERENT ALLEY DRAMA and RESINOUS WOOD) blared the Weather Girls hit that he and Toby had danced to six months before in New York, and that now followed them like a stray everywhere they went, the Ottoman Pansiyon in Antalya and the outdoor Disco Nympheum in Side and a truck stop in Anamur where they'd eaten the most glorious grilled fish in a room garish with fluorescent lights and, of all things, Christmas decorations in the middle of summer—all to the ebullient refrain of *Hallelujah, it's raining men!*

The boys from Sodom had spilled from the house and were dancing on the lawn. They danced as if dancing meant everything to them, as if it were an element they left only at their own peril. He did not envy them, really, though he thought he should perhaps get to know them better; perhaps he'd invite them to dinner sometime, the whole gang. One could do that, after all; they were one's own kind.

Then why would he so much rather sit on the stoop and drink a beer with Jesse still sweaty from his exertions in the garden, his beer bottle sweaty too, beads glistening on the brown glass bottle he tilted to his mouth now and then, throwing back his head to swallow, Adam's apple rising and falling, and in between nothing but a silence more comfortable than awkward these days.

Hallelujah! insisted the anthem to giddier, vanished days (and that RESINOUS WOOD T-shirt Toby'd bought and worn for months afterward still hung upstairs in his closet).

"We're off, I think," Charlie told him, touching his arm.

"Great party," Tracy said.

Cameron hadn't even noticed their approach. "Won't you dance?" he asked them. "It seems to be where we're headed."

"God, this song takes me back to closeted junior high," Tracy said, swaying a little to the beat. He was certainly a dreamy-looking young man, and Cameron was happy for Charlie, happy for the two of them. It had caused Max quite of lot of temporary grief, five or so years ago, when Perry'd taken it on himself to initiate Charlie Morse, then a student at Bard complete with beautiful girlfriend and incomplete desires, into what Perry liked to call "the mysteries of man love."

A persimmon smudge of a moon had climbed into the hazy sky. The music shifted, another ancient band broke the surface. Was that Bronski Beat? Charlie and Tracy danced together, loose-limbed and gorgeous. Max and Perry sauntered up—holding hands, Cameron was touched to see.

"If you boys've had enough gyrating for the time being," Max said, "maybe we should go."

"You're not taking the train back tonight?" Cameron asked. He'd miss the lovely postmortem he and Dan always undertook after their garden parties—who'd arrived with whom, who'd left with whom. Why else give a party, really? He'd seen Daryl depart with Damien. He wondered who else might have found each other.

"They're staying with us," Perry said. "Come have brunch tomorrow."

"Maybe I will."

"Come spend the night," Max said. "Looks like your party can take care of itself."

"How do I get them to leave? I'm exhausted."

"Don't worry," Max said. "I'll let them know the party's over on our way out. If I'm going to be mayor, I have to get used to that sort of thing."

Quiet filled the garden, though noises still abounded. The sheen of crickets, an owl's throaty murmur from the woods. The faint stream of traffic from the Thruway several miles distant, audible only in the still of night. And from even farther away, along the shore of the Hudson, the lonely chord of a freight train's whistle. As if his party had been a scrim temporarily laid over the real life of the place.

He sat on the back steps, Casper napping in his lap, and sipped the Stoli and orange juice left over from his handful of pills. He'd drunk more than he should, exerted himself a little too much, though he didn't feel drunk at all, only tired and a little headachy, the effects of sun and his inconvenient bout with diarrhea.

He wondered what Dan was doing right now, down in vulgar, exciting South Beach. The root of all suffering is desire, said the Buddha, and that was undoubtedly true. At the same time he found himself remembering the words of a Catholic cardinal whose recent death had been in the news: the mystery of suffering deepens who we are.

The noise of a truck roaring down the road interrupted his musings. Traffic this late at night was rare, and this truck was going way too fast for an hour when deer were in the habit of leaping without warning from the underbrush, when possums and raccoons and the occasional stalking cat found themselves, too late, picked out in the glare of oncoming headlights. He waited for the truck to pass him by, but it didn't. Instead it slowed, then seemed to come to a stop. The motor cut off.

He realized his house, at midnight, was still ablaze with lights, a signal of sorts—but to whom, and of what? A little alarmed, he rose from the steps as Casper slid from his lap and vanished into a flowerbed. He heard a truck door slam, and suddenly he felt a rush of exhilaration. How extraordinary, he thought. Jesse, who'd slipped away without a word, had returned to say good-night. There were moments like this when the world you imagined and the world that was came together in a single, perfect coincidence.

The first time he'd ever kissed Max Greenblatt had been such a moment.

Hearing someone knock briskly, he crossed through the brightly lit house. Past the screen door, he could see Jesse's familiar form; his white T-shirt glowed.

But it wasn't Jesse.

"Mr. Barnes," Kyle said.

"Hey, Kyle." Cameron's voice was reflexively deep and assertive.

"Sorry to bother," Kyle apologized. He seemed a little unsteady as he held the screen door open. "Saw your lights still on."

Had there been an accident? Was Jesse hurt? Already Cameron was rushing to the hospital. Already he was hearing the terrible news. (In high school, as if wanting to test the difference between grief and love, he used to imagine Mitchell Johnson dead in a car crash.)

"Is everything okay?" he asked a little breathlessly.

But Kyle had his own question. "Enjoy your party?"

Apparently the young man was quite drunk.

"You and your friend should've stopped by," Cameron improvised. "You'd certainly have been welcome." He realized he was still holding his half-empty glass of Stoli and orange juice.

Once again, Kyle didn't particularly seem to be listening. His eyes scoured the bright, empty room behind Cameron. "Jesse ain't here, is he? I was looking for Jesse."

Cameron glanced unnecessarily at his watch. "He left quite a while ago. Hours ago. Why?"

"I can't find him nowhere, is all. I saw your lights on. I thought maybe he was still here."

Cameron heard the sound of a truck door slamming down by the street, and an unfamiliar male voice call up, "Hey—Kyle?"

"He ain't here," Kyle called back into the darkness. His eyes traveled one last time around the room. "Sorry to bother you, sir," he said with that redneck formality that made Cameron cringe. "You have a good night, now."

"You too," Cameron told him. "And drive carefully."

Kyle turned to go, but then paused to smile at him dead on—an extraordinary smile, Cameron thought, amusement and contempt and threat all vying in equal measure there on that handsome, all-too-familiar face.

PART THREE

Gethsemane

TWENTY-TWO

A small bundle lay in the road. For a second his heart clutched. Those annoying brown spots swam before his eyes. Setting aside the cup of coffee he'd brought out onto the front porch—the morning was pleasantly cool; yesterday's party had left him with only the whisper of a hangover—he raced down the steps and across the lawn. But the body, he realized as he drew breathlessly near, was neither Diva's nor Casper's. It was only a possum. As if dozing peacefully, oblivious to danger, it lay curled on its side, draped across the yellow center line.

Extraordinary, he thought, how often you saw animals who'd been hit and killed but had not a single mark on them. Their cat Brutus had been that way. They'd carried him into the house, still warm and limp, and laid him out on a towel on the kitchen table, stroking his fur as if that might wake him from his stubborn slumber. A trickle of warm urine had spilled out onto the table. Brutus's eyes, wide open, were glazed and dry. Still, even when they lowered him into the hole they'd dug under the lilacs, Cameron couldn't resist the horrified feeling that they were being far too hasty in consigning him to a grave.

The world was dazzling, all sun-dappled and at peace. Crickets throbbed in the grass. A pileated woodpecker hammered noisily at a tree trunk somewhere in the woods. And amidst all this, a life had ended.

From the shed he retrieved a shovel. He tried to slide the blade under the dead creature, but only succeeded in half-pushing, half-rolling the body along the asphalt. He felt bad manhandling the poor thing. On his third try he managed to work the shovel under it. A car coming down the road slowed, giving wide berth to this middle-aged man standing in his blue bathrobe and slippers and balancing a dead possum on his shovel. He watched the New Jersey plates disappear around the curve that led to the cemetery, then carried his burden over to the edge of the woods that had, over the years, become another kind of cemetery. Squirrels, skunks, raccoons: all told, he must have laid a dozen creatures to rest, not counting the several deer he'd had to call the county road crew to come and pick up.

He supposed none of them mattered. They were just animals, after all, and accidents happened. Still, anybody with half a conscience would have long since refused to countenance anything so brutal as their systematic slaughter. Living with moral Toby, he'd pretty much given up meat altogether, but then Dan had turned out to be such an avid carnivore that he'd swept Cameron right along with him. Well, perhaps the time had come to change. For better or worse, he couldn't use Dan as an excuse for anything anymore.

Then he remembered that Max was expecting him for brunch. Nobody, alas, made tastier bacon or fluffier scrambled eggs and cheese than Max Greenblatt.

Hoisting his shovel over his shoulder, he started to turn back to the house when he noticed that someone had ripped down the yellow-and-black NO TRESPASSING signs he'd posted across the road. He felt a puzzlement that turned to quiet outrage. They'd been there yesterday—he was sure of it. Someone must have come by in the night, after the party, and torn them down.

Half past noon, and somebody'd been squeezing his head in a vise. At least that was how it felt. He was trying to eat some cereal, thinking a little nourishment in his stomach might help, but each bite made him want to throw up. Patti and his mom weren't helping too much, either. In fact, he could almost think they'd set out to torture him. They'd come home from church to settle around the table for coffee and cigarettes, starting up a conversation that crawled around in his head like cockroaches in a sink full of dirty dishes.

His mom must've noticed he was struggling. "You don't look so good," she said, peering at him through a blue haze of smoke. "You and your brother have a late night?"

Kyle was out even later than me, he felt like telling her. He hadn't even heard when Kyle came in. His brother was still upstairs, happily unconscious in a way Jesse, at the moment, could only envy. He ate another spoonful of Froot Loops and pushed his bowl aside.

"You got a couple messages from Donna on the machine," Patti mentioned. "You listen to them?"

Wearily he shook his head.

"When're you and your brother thinking about doing the septic?" his mom asked. "I see somebody brought over a backhoe."

He hadn't noticed any backhoe. "Kyle must've done that," he said. And sure enough, when he went over to the window to look out, there the yellow machine sat under the shade of a tree.

I'll fucking die, he thought, if we got to do the septic this afternoon. But it would be just like Kyle.

"The sooner the better," said his mom. "Mr. Hallenbeck says August's a prime selling month. So I'd like to get us on the market—"

"I *know*. Jesus. I'm not stupid."

"All I'm saying . . ."

"I wonder what's got into him," he heard Patti say as he walked out of the kitchen into the bright, aching sunlight. Poke, snoozing on the porch, barely raised his head. Jesse'd never interested him much; all his attention had always been focused on Kyle, the only human on the planet willing to spend half an hour at a stretch scratching the stupid animal behind the ears.

Feeling at a total loss, he wandered down toward the pond Pop had dug from the swamp. Last night, he was sorry to say, was something of a blur. From Cameron's party he'd been supposed to go straight to Donna's, that was the plan, but he hadn't done that, and he still wasn't sure why. Maybe he'd been afraid she'd be able to smell it on him, some skunk odor he himself couldn't detect, being in the middle of it, but that somehow would straightaway mark him out. He didn't know. All he knew was, he'd stopped by home first, taken a long, hot shower. He'd put on some fresh clothes. Then, unable to go any further, he'd just sat on the edge of his bed, holding his head in his hands, for the longest time.

Once you're with Donna, he'd told himself, you'll feel a whole lot better. What was Donna for, if not to make him feel a whole lot better?

241

Still, for all his urging himself, he hadn't been able to move.

She'd be sitting on the sofa, likely as not, watching TV with Sean, eating popcorn and those red licorice twists she liked. He could picture the smile she'd shine his way. She wouldn't know where he'd been; he'd kept all that from her, his afternoons with Cameron, the schemes he'd made, figuring at first it wasn't worth mentioning, then one day realizing it was way too late to start.

He felt a little sick when he thought about that.

Out on the pond's still water three white geese floated side by side. In the weeds by shore, an old aluminum rowboat nobody ever used lay overturned. He heaved it upright. The pond was way down, lower than he'd ever seen it—a skirt of muck edged the water and a little island had emerged in the middle, a sandy hummock where weeds already sprouted, those purple flowers he didn't know the name of, but that were taking over the fields and ditches everywhere you turned.

Cameron would know the name, he thought as he threw in the oars and slid the boat into the water. Cameron would be more than happy to tell him. A sort of floating slime covered the pond's surface. The wary geese steered clear of him. He sort of hated Cameron, the way he hated anybody who seemed to know everything.

He rowed some yards out, then stuck his oar down into the soft mire to pause the boat. It was peaceful enough, he guessed, though green flies buzzed, and tiny insects floated all around him like gauze. At least he'd kept himself out of trouble yesterday. It wasn't too much consolation, but better than nothing. After he'd left, he'd driven around for a while, rolled down Main Street past Perry and Max's, where the lights were on, the shades up, where he could see them with their friends from New York, everybody sitting around drinking wine. It made him feel so hollow, like he'd tasted something that hardly agreed with him but he found himself wanting more, maybe just to make sure, only it wasn't being offered again. He'd driven past half a dozen times, each time fearful the noise of his motor was somehow going to give him away, then taken himself back home, stoked up the three-wheeler, headed off down the rail trail to the cement mine. For what seemed like hours he'd sat on an outcropping of rubble, watching the hazy half-moon, sipping from a pint of Kyle's whiskey he'd kidnapped.

He slapped at a mosquito pestering his ear, but the bug was too quick for him. From the middle of the pond the sky looked huge. Mushroom-shaped clouds sailed over. He'd given both his brain and his liver one hell of a workout last night. How he got back home, and when, exactly, he wasn't too sure.

From the shore Kyle was calling to him, "What the fuck are you doing out there?" His brother had come down barefoot, shirtless, just in his jeans. Poke in tow. "Get the fuck outta there. You and me got a shitload of work to do."

Reluctantly Jesse poled his way back to shore. Kyle grabbed the prow and pulled him in.

"Where'd you find the machine?" Jesse asked, trying to miss the muck but managing to put a foot down in it anyway.

"Friend of Uncle Roy's. But he needs it back first thing tomorrow, so we gotta get a move on."

"Fine."

"So you want to tell me about it?"

His brother's voice arrested him midstep. "Tell what?" He tried to sound innocent—but then, he *was* innocent.

"I was looking all over for you. Donna said she hadn't seen hide nor hair. Nobody else either. Me and Brandon even went back to check if you were still at the party, but everybody'd taken off by then. Just our friend there alone. Shitfaced and horny." Kyle paused to snicker. "Not a pretty sight."

"You went there looking for me?" Jesse asked. He couldn't really, at the moment, imagine a worse thing—Kyle and Cameron talking about him.

"You seemed to be having a pretty good time when last I saw you."

"I was doing my business. Like we agreed. It wasn't about having a good time. But, yeah, if you want to know. All in all it was a pretty good party," Jesse said, a little surprised he sounded so defiant all of a sudden.

It seemed to back Kyle off. He grinned a little. "Tried to wake you up when I finally come in, but, man, you were fucking unconscious." He rested his hand on Jesse's shoulder, but his grin faded. "Hey—I was just worried maybe you fell in the wrong hands back there."

Jesse didn't like it. He removed Kyle's hand from him. "You know me better than that, I hope," he told his brother coldly.

But Kyle didn't answer. He gave Jesse that searching look you didn't turn away from, no matter how long it decided to search you for.

At the foot of the drive a horn bellowed. Only then did Kyle look away. "Let's get going," he said. "Brandon's here with the honey truck."

Max and Perry lived on Main Street in one of those big, dilapidated houses that had so charmed Cameron and Dan when they had first driven through Stone Hollow that fateful winter afternoon. A boardinghouse for cement miners in the boom times of the last century, it wasn't a building Cameron would ever have made his own—the interior was gloomy, neighboring houses hemmed it in on both sides, there was no property to speak of, only a narrow backyard that ran down to the melodious Schneidekill. But Max and Perry loved its every shortcoming.

Perry had mixed a pitcher of Bloody Marys. "We're sitting out on the patio," he announced when Cameron entered. "Max is banning all observers from the kitchen while he works his magic."

"Yes. Now get!" Max said with a mock scowl. But then he called after them, "Hey! Don't I get my drink?"

Perry scowled back. "You *are* looking a little worse for wear," he teased—though if Perry was hungover as well, Cameron thought, he certainly didn't look it. But then Perry had that rare capacity to emerge unscathed from just about anything.

The table on the new patio had been set for five. A gather of alert-looking black-eyed Susans stood in a blue pitcher.

Promising himself a limit of one, Cameron sipped with gratitude the Bloody Mary Perry had offered him. "And the guests?" he asked.

"Sleepyheads," Perry said. "We were up pretty late last night, and I gather the boys were up even later. I went right to sleep, but Max said they kept him awake half the night. He said they were making the whole house shake, and who can blame them?"

Cameron tried to imagine. "Lustrous youth," he told Perry.

"Lustrous youth indeed. And speaking of such, I had quite a little chat with your own lustrous youth yesterday. What a hottie. I'd love to do a photo shoot with him sometime."

Cameron thoroughly believed in being generous—without generosity, after all, and especially among friends, what was there? Nevertheless, Perry's tone made him wary. It still smarted, a little, that Jesse had fled his party without a word of farewell, though he tried to convince himself it was nothing. Parties were like that: you inevitably came away more confused than sated.

"Jesse?" he said. "I wouldn't exactly hold my breath."

"I never hold my breath. You know me. I breathe deeply, evenly, calmly. At least I try to. You'd be surprised what comes your way if you just breathe evenly."

"I don't doubt it. So did you propose this photo shoot to him?"

Perry laughed. Who wouldn't fall for someone like him? "Of course," he said. "We'll see what happens. Besides, I'm not so sure he's all that straight."

Cameron felt his heart clutch just the way it had when he'd first glimpsed the possum in the road. But why did he hear Perry's words with such a sense of doom?

"Trust me," he said. "Jesse Vanderhof's about as straight as they come."

"Well, you'd be the one to know, I guess. It's too bad." Perry gazed out at the glittering Schneidekill. "I don't know," he said after a few seemingly pensive moments. "Some guys like him are just waiting. All you have to do is touch them and they come bursting out of the closet with a vengeance."

"He's got a girlfriend," Cameron said, rather wishing at the moment that Jesse and Perry had never crossed paths.

"They all have girlfriends. Charlie Morse had a girlfriend when I first met him. He'd never even considered being with a man. Anyway"—Perry poured himself another drink—"I suppose you're right. Alas. But it's always fun to fantasize."

"Okay, fellas," Max said, pushing the screen door open with his shoulder while balancing three plates. "The bacon's a little too crispy, sorry about that, but everything else is just about perfect. And look who the cat dragged in."

For a second, Cameron half expected Jesse to walk through that door. But it was only Charlie and Tracy, both looking radiant and rested in chinos and white T-shirts, their hair still wet from the shower.

As Cameron stood to be embraced, first by Tracy, then Charlie, who went so far as to graze his neck lightly with his lips, he reminded himself that Perry's seductions could have entirely felicitous endings for everyone concerned. How delicious, after all, to have Charlie Morse put his arms around you. How stirring to feel the warmth of comradeship, seasoned just a little with the spice of eros, permeate the entire patio. For here they were, five men who loved men making of this bright moment a stand against the hostile world. Wouldn't they happily welcome a newly minted homosexual like Jesse into their ranks? But that happy thought died almost instantly. Recalling how wretched Jesse had been at his party, Cameron couldn't begin to imagine the young man ever joining this crowd to sip Bloody Marys at brunch. And what was even more surprising—or, on second thought, perhaps it wasn't surprising at all—he found he didn't long for that one bit. No, he wanted Jesse to remain just as he was.

But how was that? He didn't begin to know Jesse, only what he'd made of him based on a few meager conversations, feeble rays of light cast down into an immense obscurity.

"Sleep well?" Perry was asking the boys.

"Perfectly," Tracy said. "I hope we didn't snore."

"Not a bit," said Max as he poured Bloody Marys.

"Your party, by the way, was so much fun," Charlie said, lightly touching Cameron's knee. "It's amazing how something like that creates its own space—like the ordinary rules are suspended. For a few hours some other god holds sway. The Dionysian influence."

"Speaking of which," said Tracy. "Perry was telling us last night how you'd traveled a lot in Greece and Turkey. We're thinking of going there this fall. We've both got two weeks off in October."

"Go," Cameron said. "By all means."

"Want to come? We invited Max and Perry. They're going to think about it."

"Are we?" Max asked. "Unfortunately, I think that was just inebriated exuberance talking last night. I've got an election to win this fall."

"Spoilsport. What about you?" Tracy asked Perry.

"I'd love to, but, I don't know. Max'll need me by his side."

"Aargh. You're such responsible adults," Tracy told them. "It'd be such a blast. The queer battalion does Istanbul in the spirit of Dionysus. What do you say, Cameron? I bet there're all sorts of secret places you could show us."

"It's years since I was there," he said. "I'm sure it's all changed beyond recognition."

"You wouldn't be interested in seeing it again?"

"It'd probably kill me."

Tracy looked concerned. "You mean, healthwise?"

"Yeah," Cameron said, even as he realized that wasn't at all what he meant. There was a little emerald cove, completely deserted, he and Toby had found. A half dozen columns lay in the clear water, a bit of ancient wall jutted into the sea. Could he even remember where it had been—the Mediterranean coast or the Aegean? That he'd lost its location troubled him. But then came a far worse realization: Charlie and Tracy were fine, they were delightful, they livened up one's life immeasurably. But he never wanted to find his way back to that secluded cove without Toby Vail.

"Sweetie, you should see what Dr. Vishnaraman says," Max urged. "Phil Haas went to Thailand last year, and he had no problem at all."

"It can't hurt to ask," Charlie said. "Besides, we'd really love to have you along."

Istanbul. Only last night, hearing that song, he'd remembered it all so vividly. Still: all that had been dead for such a long time.

"We're serious," Tracy said.

He'd be the odd man out, of course—unless he did something like invite Elliot Shore along. But he dismissed that thought out of hand, feeling bad that he'd rather neglected Elliot at the party, though of course there was always the excuse that, as host, he'd had a million things to attend to.

Then another thought occurred to him, so absurd he couldn't help but entertain it. Forget the truck, he imagined himself telling a surprised Jesse Vanderhof. How about October in Turkey? It'll change you forever. Change both of us.

Yes. He'd take Jesse to Turkey. All bets would be off. So far from home, in surroundings so utterly strange and foreign, he'd be able to convince the skeptical young man that nothing that happened there between them had any permanent reality, it was only a beautiful dream where nothing at all was forbidden. They'd swim in a secret cove where the water was emerald and warm, he'd be miraculously returned to health, hope, the lost body of his youth. Everything would once again be before him.

He didn't like to admit it, but Perry's plans for the young man had sparked something in him as well. He stood in imminent danger of being unable to get Jesse out of his head.

Gingerly guiding the backhoe's bucket, Kyle probed the ground. He scooped up rocky mouthfuls of soil.

Brandon stood on the edge of the growing pit and directed. "Whoa," he shouted over the noise of the machine. "We're hitting paydirt here."

They'd had a hard time even finding the damn tank. Now they inspected planks the backhoe had uncovered.

"I'll be damned," Kyle said. He jumped down in the pit and kicked at the boards with his boot.

Black liquid oozed up from the gaps in between.

"Careful," said Brandon. "Don't let it splash on you."

"Man, somebody could've fallen right through here." With his toe Kyle showed them just how springy with rot the boards laid across the open mouth of the tank really were. "This is one ancient shithole. Looks like the baffle's totally rusted out."

"Come on the fuck out of there," Brandon said. "Man, that shit stinks."

"What do you expect? I'm sure you've contributed your share." Kyle climbed out of the pit and stood wiping his boot soles on the grass. "All right," he said. "I'm gonna bust on through. Everybody stand back."

He climbed up into the cab and put the machine in gear. The bucket came down hard. There was a splash, a big burp of liquid. The smell took your breath away. Jesse resisted the impulse to gag.

"That'll do it," Brandon said. "All clear."

Jesse approached the hole and peered in. Pieces of shit bobbed in the black water. Here and there sheets of toilet paper floated on the surface. The whole mass heaved slightly, like it harbored something alive, ready any moment to come welling up at you.

"Don't go breathing the fumes, guy," Kyle warned.

From his cousin's truck, Brandon uncoiled the pump hose; he snaked it across the grass and fed it into the cesspool. "Man, I don't know how Jimmy stands it, doing this for a living," he said as he switched on the pump.

"You get used to anything," Kyle told him.

CLEAN PROMPT PROFESSIONAL promised the words written in green along the side of the truck's white tank, though around the disposal vent a splatter of brown matter soiled the white. The sight turned Jesse's stomach. His face felt hot, his forehead sweaty. He hated himself for having gone and gotten drunk last night on top of everything else. He blamed Perry for that.

He watched Brandon vacuum the muck, the hose slurping like a straw at the bottom of a soda cup. What was his old enemy thinking, he wondered—or did Brandon ever do much thinking about anything? It wasn't natural, of course, to do as much thinking as Jesse did. It led you all sorts of poisoned places. It let you look at a splatter of brown on a white tank—

He turned and took three or four quick steps before doubling over and letting it all come out—Froot Loops, chunks of hot dog, a pint of borrowed whiskey, one cosmo, one mint julep, a couple of fancy sandwiches whose contents he couldn't identify either then or now. The whole sorry history of the last twenty-four hours.

He retched again and again, till there was nothing left but a little clear liquid dribbling from the corner of his mouth.

"Hey, little brother, you okay there?" Kyle asked.

"I must've ate something didn't like me much." Jesse wiped his mouth and tried to catch his breath, but the reek from the tank was too ripe to deal with. "I gotta get out of here. I'm sorry, man. I ain't got the stomach for this."

Kyle just looked at him for a minute. "Funny," he said finally. "This particular shit don't bother me none."

Muzzy-headed after too many Bloody Mary refills, a little intoxicated by the oriental fantasy he'd indulged and just as quickly abandoned, though not without promising Charlie and Tracy he'd take their proposal seriously, he wandered around his garden with a trash bag, picking up here and there a stray plastic cup, a napkin, a half-empty bottle of beer he'd missed the night before. White butterflies flickered among the coneflowers and bee balm his assiduous watering had managed to keep looking lovely. But beneath all that, the drought still worked its ruin. By next year he'd have lost any number of plants, even some that still appeared perfectly healthy, even flourishing.

My last garden party. The words came to him, almost as if he had spoken them aloud—a reminder of what he could not afford, ever, to forget. Whom was he kidding when he entertained notions of going to Turkey in the fall? Or when he imagined, even for an instant, that he'd ever again find the kind of love he'd had with Toby Vail. No, it was all over for him. This prospect of a new life was nothing but a cruel farce.

Up the road a truck came slowly, haltingly. There was no mistaking that truck. Cameron listened as it wheezed into his driveway and its driver mercifully put a stop to its misery.

Had you shown up last night, it might have made all the difference, he silently addressed the young man who strode toward him across the lawn, his innocence still intact.

"Hey, man. How's it going?" Jesse reached out his hand, and Cameron gratefully let himself be held by its firm grip. Was it really possible Jesse Vanderhof was gay? For the last month Cameron had entertained that notion in only the most automatic of ways, his imagination running virtually every attractive young man he met through that particular mill, a process he knew meant nothing beyond the momentary, speculative pleasure it provided. Now he tried hard to find in that handsome face some clue—but there was nothing.

"Did you have a good time last night?" Cameron asked. "You kind of slipped away there."

"I had to go over to Donna's. We had plans. But, yeah, I had a pretty good time. It's just, I guess I don't have too much in common with your friends."

So there, Cameron thought with a twinge of satisfaction. He wished Perry could hear his hopes dashed so easily.

"Sometimes I have to wonder how much even *I* have in common with my friends," he volunteered. "But what can you do when you've known certain people practically forever?"

"I hear what you're saying," Jesse said. "There's lots of folks you get all tangled up with and then can't seem to shake loose."

"Well, as long as you avoided any snares at my party." Cameron found himself trying to imagine Donna; he wanted her, suddenly, to be everything a young man like Jesse might want. He hoped, most of all, Jesse was getting regularly laid. It might save them all a certain amount of grief.

"Oh, there was a few snares here and there," Jesse confided, but clearly he was naming no names, and Cameron thought it best to change the subject.

"Your brother ever find you? He stopped by after everybody'd cleared out." He wondered whether he should mention that, for a single mad moment of hope, he'd thought it might be Jesse.

"I apologize," Jesse told him. "Kyle had no business. I hope he didn't cause you any inconvenience."

"Not at all. He seemed sort of anxious to find you."

"I guess we just got our wires crossed. He must've thought I was going over to Donna's. Anyway, I thought maybe you might need help cleaning up, but looks like you made out just fine."

Cameron realized two things at once: he was still holding a trash bag, and, more unaccountably, he seemed to have caught Jesse in a lie. Why say he'd gone to Donna's if he hadn't? What did that conceal?

"All done," he said, lifting the limp plastic.

Did Jesse too realize his mistake? All at once he looked around, as if scanning the horizon for something. He scratched his head along the back rim of his baseball cap. At last, hesitantly, he said, "You know, I was thinking." He paused, searching again the corners of the garden. Cameron was astonished to find how powerfully erotic that pause suddenly felt to him. It was as if the mystery of Jesse's lie suddenly bound them to one another. Then Jesse spoke. "I meant to speak with you at your party, but it wasn't the place. You remember we were talking once. Well, I got my eyes on this truck. Al's holding it for me down at his shop: 1992 Dodge Ram. Four-by-four. Reconditioned V-8. She's pretty nice looking. He's asking sixty-five hundred but'll probably come down if it's cash. Maybe you want to take back what you were offering. It's a bitch of a sweet deal, though. I was thinking maybe you and me could drive up there. Al said he'd be around this afternoon if I wanted to stop by."

"Yes," Cameron said, fending off a sudden onslaught of despair, "by all means let's go have a look at that truck."

He'd expected they'd take his car, but Jesse had a better idea. "Al tells me he'll give me two hundred for my wreck. So's we could just take it there and leave it. I mean, if you like what you see and give me the go-ahead."

The young man avoided obsequiousness, though perhaps just barely— a curious mixture of tact and persistence that looked like it might just be about to pay off for him.

Cameron had never experienced Jesse's truck up close. Acne of rust pocked the surface, daubs of Rust-Oleum here and there attesting to the futile attempt to stem the rot. The passenger door resisted him. Inside, the seat had gone all to tatters, but the cavernous cab had a stately austerity, so unlike the plush comfort everyone seemed to demand these days, even in pickup trucks. It took him back to the days when he was seven and mortified whenever his dad would drive him to school in his old black Plymouth.

Jesse pulled out the choke, stomped down on the clutch, and began the tricky process of starting the engine. It coughed, turned over once or twice in its grave. Jesse adjusted the choke and tried again. The motor stirred promisingly, then gave up. Jesse was undeterred. He smiled patiently. So here we are, Cameron thought, wondering at the man that seven-year-old had in the end become.

With a shudder of protest, the motor gave in to Jesse's coaxing. He grasped the knob of the long, naked-looking stick shift and jerked the truck into gear.

"You really do need a new truck," Cameron said, but Jesse merely grunted, and Cameron tried in vain to think of something more to say. For a long mile they rode in silence. He watched the Shawangunks in the distance, how brown patches were appearing where trees, shallow-rooted along the rock ledges, were starting to die. Above the ridge, the sky blazed blue. He could barely make out four or five black specks, turkey vultures lazily searching for anything promising down below. Then, as always happened whenever he gazed too long at the sky, the brown spots started to interfere, and he looked back at the road.

Jesse cleared his throat. "That friend of yours. Perry."

He'd been rehearsing that sentence for some minutes now, Cameron realized. His heart sank. He turned and looked at the young man's profile, but Jesse gazed straight ahead as if he'd not uttered a word.

Cameron waited a moment, then said evenly, "What about Perry?"

"He takes a lot of pictures, don't he?"

You have no idea, Cameron wanted to say. But who was he to venture a single word? There are traps set everywhere in this world, he reminded himself. Even I am a trap—the trap whose jaws refuse to snap shut.

And indeed, he desperately liked having Jesse in range like this, even if he chose never to spring.

"Yes," he said. "Perry's quite the shutterbug. I take it he asked you to do some modeling? Whenever he meets somebody he likes the look of, it's practically the first thing out of his mouth. We're all used to it by now."

Jesse had no reaction to that, and Cameron wondered whether he'd taken the wrong tack. But then he really shouldn't take any tack, one way or the other. Stay aloof, he told himself, and watch from the safe distance. It has nothing to do with you. For you it's all off-limits. Anyway, who could resist Perry once he'd got you in his sights? It was practically inevitable.

"I don't know that I care for him all that much," Jesse said, but they'd all at once reached their destination and, Cameron noted with regret, the apparent end of their fledgling conversation.

Bosco's Garage looked deserted. BEWARE OF DOG warned a hand-painted sign. From within a criminally small chain-link enclosure, a listless black dog raised its head to look them over, then went back to its slumber.

"There doesn't seem to be anybody here," Cameron observed, feeling all at once out of place amid some fifty or so automobiles in various states of decrepitude. It was, as Max might say, enemy territory.

"If I know Al, he's probably upstairs drinking beers," Jesse said. "He told me he'd be here for sure." Without any hesitation, he mounted a flimsy-looking set of stairs that led up to a little plywood-and-tarpaper addition perched on top of the garage. Rapping several times on the door, he stood, hands slipped in his back pockets, and grinned down at Cameron, who smiled back. "You drunk in there or what?" Jesse yelled. The door opened, and fat, unshaven Al Bosco peered out.

"I said I was coming by."

"Yeah, I remember. I see you brought your fellow with you. He making good on you?"

"I think so," Jesse said, lowering his voice but not enough to prevent Cameron from hearing. He tried to look as if he weren't listening. It felt awkward to be talked about like that—and oddly thrilling. In Bergama he and Toby had been approached by a handsome teenager who'd offered his services; Necmit had taken them around to all his cousins who owned restaurants, carpet shops, stalls in the bazaar, showing off these Americans who were all too willing to part with their money. He too had carried on as if they weren't there. He'd even, at the end of the evening, eager to squeeze the last few drops out of his new friends, offered himself for sale—$200, which quickly eroded to $20, then to nothing as he pulled them inside the abandoned shell of an old mosque, kissing first one, then the other, as bats darted about noiselessly in the dim dome overhead.

Now Cameron gazed with frank longing at this young man who was talking about him as if he weren't even there. Who triumphantly descended the steps with Al Bosco in tow, pointing to the red truck parked in the far corner of the lot like a rose among thorns. Jesse didn't have a price, at least for him—Cameron was as sure of that as he was of anything. He'd have detected the least glimmer of it by now. Still, he followed the two gamely across the lot, reflecting how much around here depended on a pickup truck. He'd see young men at the convenience store admiring one another's rigs, sweetly covetous. Jesse was no different. He circled his prospective truck carefully, appreciatively. He hungered to take possession, to be the new man the truck would make him. And it was all up to the faggot. Cameron knew he'd been foolish and sentimental with his offer. Even so, he thought, he didn't regret it.

"So what do you think?" Jesse asked.

"Well," Cameron said, "it certainly looks in good shape."

"She looks fantastic," Jesse corrected him.

"Well then, does she run?" he asked, happy enough to sex the hunk of metal before them.

"I took her out for a spin the other day. She's so smooth, she practically purrs."

I bet, Cameron thought. (Would Donna know enough to be jealous?) He only nodded, though, trying hard not to expose too clearly how they would always be worlds apart. But Jesse seemed happily oblivious to all that. He ran his hand along the shiny hood as if to brush away a speck of dust.

"I'll throw in a used cap for free," Al offered, awfully eager to close the deal. "I got one back there. She's a pretty snug fit. Keep the weather out for you."

"What do you say?" Cameron asked Jesse. "It's your call. I'm more than happy to put the money down."

"You don't want to see how she runs?"

"I trust your judgment. Really. You certainly know trucks a whole lot better than I do."

"Just down to town and back," Jesse pleaded, and Cameron realized, suddenly, Jesse *wanted* them to go for a drive. Maybe, he thought, the boy was as eager as he was for their interrupted conversation to resume.

"Go ahead," Al urged them. "Try to run off—you won't get too far."

It gave Cameron pause. "You wouldn't trust this truck for long distance?"

Al grinned. "That ain't what I mean."

Cameron wasn't entirely sure *what* he meant, but he climbed into the cab anyway as Al handed Jesse the key in through the window.

"Listen to that," Jesse said at the engine's smooth turnover. "Sweet."

They drove, once again, in silence, Jesse strangely cautious, as if he'd been given a new toy he was afraid he might break. He surprised Cameron by taking a left onto the old post road.

"The scenic route?" Cameron asked, though he regretted instantly the irony in his tone. "Actually, I always liked this road. Dan and I, when we first moved here, used to get in the car and just drive around, getting hopelessly lost, then suddenly finding ourselves somewhere unexpected. It was nice."

Jesse nodded, but said nothing. From the beginning he'd had a disconcerting way of making Cameron feel utterly fatuous.

Ancient maples shaded the road. A stone wall ran beside them. Beyond, a pasture had grown up in goldenrod and Queen Anne's lace.

After a country mile Jesse broke the silence. "Can I ask you something?"

"Of course. You know you can ask me anything." Some things, it seemed, you had to take the back roads to talk about at all. Well, he welcomed that.

"Something I've been wondering. It's been bothering me." Jesse hesitated.

"Yes?"

"What I mean is—that guy, the one you sucked off."

Cameron found himself savoring both the sound and the surprise of that phrase in Jesse's mouth. "You mean Tommy. What about him?"

Jesse glanced Cameron's way just for a second, then looked back intently at the road. "What I've been meaning to ask is, if you hated it so much, why didn't you just say no? Why'd you keep coming back? That's the part I don't get."

"I never said I hated it. I mean—you're right. I did hate it. But I also didn't want to give it up. I wish I could explain. You had to have been there."

The truck lurched, a jolt that sent Cameron forward. He put out a hand to the dashboard.

"Sorry. I ain't trying to kill you. I used to have to stomp the brakes in my old truck."

It seemed they were destined always to be interrupted—as if some life-changing conversation was perpetually just over the horizon, and they journeyed toward it steadily, received tantalizing hints, but then just as they seemed poised to arrive, it receded before them.

Up ahead, Cameron could see the orange highway department vehicles that had made Jesse hit the brakes. A bucket truck and a dump truck trailing a wood chipper. A bare-chested young man, dangerously tanned, fed branches into the machine's maw. Out the chute, into the back of the dump truck, fell a rain of wood chips. Several large maples had been shorn to their sturdy trunks, and another young fellow in the bucket lift was beginning to have a go at one of the trunks.

Jesse pulled up slowly and leaned his head out the window. The guy loading branches shut off the chipper and came over to them.

"Rusty. How's it going, man?"

"Same old same old," Rusty told Jesse. Highway crews were full of guys like Rusty you never looked at twice, generic figures in the landscape. He gave the driver's door a pat. "Nice rig. Who'd you steal it from?"

"Nah, man. I picked this up from Big Al."

There was something both heady and distressing in seeing Jesse among his own kind. This was the world as he'd never know it, Cameron realized; do what he might, the gulf was unbridgeable.

"You gotta tell me how you're making your money these days," Rusty said.

Jesse clenched and unclenched, just once, his fists around the steering wheel. "I'm making it honestly. Ask anybody."

"Who's your friend?" Rusty squinted into the cab. "Hey there, mister."

It bore in on Cameron how his gesture of generosity was at worst suspicious, at best absurd.

"This is Mr. Barnes," Jesse said. "I been doing a bunch of work for him."

"You paying tip-top wage, or what?" Rusty wanted to know.

"We try," Cameron told him.

Rusty gave him what seemed like a friendly wink. "Well, she's a beaut. Your brother still got dibs on Leanne?"

"Don't even think about it," Jesse said with a grin. He touched the gas pedal and the truck leapt forward.

The motion startled Rusty. "Careful there," he called out.

"Sorry. Don't know my own power."

Once more in control, Jesse eased the truck past the rest of the crew, honking twice to acknowledge them. It occurred to Cameron that it was a Sunday afternoon. What was a road crew doing out on a weekend? Then he remembered what Max had claimed—that Otto Vanderhof was working his crews overtime to "improve" as many rural roads as possible before being voted out of office in the fall. Hyperbole, Cameron had thought at the time. One of Max's incendiary exaggerations. But here it was, plain as could be. They were chopping down stately old trees with abandon.

Jesse seemed to see nothing amiss in the wounded landscape. Other things were clearly on his mind. "It don't make me uncomfortable taking a gift from you," he volunteered, though at the moment he seemed distinctly uncomfortable. Still, he looked at Cameron with a flicker of defiance. "Like I said, everything I got, I got honestly. Aren't I right?"

"Absolutely," Cameron had to admit, though the admission seemed one of failure more than anything else.

"Well then," Jesse said, "I guess we better get on back and pay our money. Al'll think we eloped or some damn thing like that."

He said it casually, not looking Cameron's way at all.

TWENTY-THREE

It was his tenth pass or so, and he was starting to feel a little ridiculous. Nonetheless, he slowed his bitch of a sweet deal to a crawl and, from behind the wheel, studied the big white house. It could use some work, starting with a paint job, and for a few seconds he half-considered whether he should make that his excuse for stopping by. But who was he fooling? If he pulled his truck to the curb, if he knocked on that door—

Perry stood on the porch, his back to the street, pulling mail out of the box by the front door. Jesse eased to the curb and cut the engine—but Perry wasn't noticing a thing. It's not too late, Jesse reassured himself. Then Perry turned around. A look of pleasure crossed his face. He's got me, Jesse thought with a spurt of anger. And I let him.

Still, he didn't have to make it easy on the son of a bitch.

"Hey there," Perry told him. "This is a nice surprise." He wore blousy white pants tied up with a drawstring, a tight white muscle shirt. Jesse saw he was barefoot. That disturbed him, for some reason.

"I was just driving by," he explained. "I happened to see you there on your porch."

"Yes. The mail. High point of my day. That is, till now. You got a few minutes? Want to come inside?"

Jesse was aware how, one by one, he was letting any chance of escape slip away. He said, "I don't got to be anywhere else right now."

Perry smiled that dangerous smile of his. "I was just finishing up some developing. I'd love to take a break. Show you some of my work."

Disappointed, a little, that Perry hadn't seen fit to compliment him on his truck, Jesse followed him into the dark house. A narrow hallway led to a cluttered kitchen. It surprised him how messy the house was. Not at all like Cameron's.

"Can I get you anything to drink? A beer or something?"

"I'm fine."

"I sort of feel like a beer myself. Sure you don't want one?"

Jesse felt the old, familiar misery settle in the pit of his stomach. "Okay, sure," he said. "I'll have one if you are."

Perry opened the fridge and handed him a bottle. Jesse twisted the cap.

"You got to use this, dude." Perry held up a bottle opener, tossed it Jesse's way.

Jesse looked at the label. Pop had been loyal to Pabst Blue Ribbon. Foreign beer's for queers, he used to say.

"Come on back here," Perry told him. "I'll show you what I'm up to these days."

Once again Perry led and Jesse followed. He'd never been in a darkroom before. All the windows were covered over. From a tray filled with liquid, Perry fished out sheets of black-and-white photos. With the squeamish sense he was looking at things he maybe shouldn't, Jesse took in the images. Some guy leaned against a tree trunk, grinning for the camera. He figured he should've guessed: it's what Perry was going to want him to do. In the next picture, the guy had already taken off his shirt and undone the first couple of buttons on his jeans, and Jesse realized he recognized him. That little metal ring in his nipple.

"Bryan's such a great subject," Perry was saying. "Really comfortable with his body."

Jesse nodded. For some reason his hand that held the pictures was trembling a little. Both he and Perry could see that. By the fourth picture, Bryan was buck naked. Jesse winced to see that woodie pushing up there, but he didn't look away.

"Pretty hot, don't you think?"

"Where?" Jesse said, hearing a strange little choke to his voice. He remembered he had a beer to swig. "Where, I mean, did you taste this? *Take* this," he corrected himself.

"Recognize it? That old oak you took down for Cameron. Pretty priapic if you ask me. I'm always photographing Cameron's garden. It's sort of like a holy spot for me."

Bryan had somehow gotten himself up into the crotch of that tree. Jesse felt a little offended. He hadn't spent a morning sawing up all those branches just so some smart aleck could cavort around with his woodie on show.

"So what do you think?" Perry stood close by, their shoulders nearly touching.

"I think that fellow needs to cool down a little," Jesse said.

"Oh. Bryan was just goofing around. He's very high-spirited. You wouldn't have to do anything like that."

"I don't have to do anything," Jesse reminded him.

"Spot on, dude. But enough of these. They're just play. Let me show you some ones I'm prouder of."

Jesse let the prints slide back into the tray. Strange the things you couldn't ever take back, even if it was just goofing around. And there were so many things you wouldn't want a picture of; things you'd want to be able to explain away if you had to.

They went into the living room. From a stack of books on the coffee table, Perry hoisted a large volume. "This came out a couple years ago. German publisher. They did a really fine job with it, I think."

Jesse held the heavy book, paging past an Arab boy squatting and smoking, two teenagers in microscopic swimsuits, one with his arm around the other. He paused at a dark-eyed boy who stared out at him. That time he and Kyle gave the once-over to Cameron's house, how could they have known in advance all there'd be to see? But the difference between them was—Kyle just shot a glance and moved on, while he'd gone and let himself get stuck like a wasp in honey.

Of course, that had been the plan all along—though he saw now it wasn't a plan. They hadn't either of them had a clue what they were up to. And yet it wasn't an accident either. That was the part that rested like a heavy stone in his gut.

"You took all these?" he asked, knowing the answer but sensing that any kind of talk was probably better than silence. "You must travel a whole lot."

"Every chance I get. There's a lot of pretty fantastic stuff out there in the world to look at."

Jesse didn't answer. He turned the pages briskly and pretended to study what they offered, but already Perry was touching his arm.

"I'm just wondering, Jesse," he said in a quiet voice. "Do we have some unfinished business between us, you and me?"

"I ain't sure what you're talking about," Jesse told him as Perry took the book from his hand, and he remembered Brandon saying, that long-ago afternoon they'd been goofing around, stupid and bored, *Hey, Jesse, I'll give you a dollar if you suck my dick.*

"You're one hot guy," Perry said. "And I could really get into making it with you." He paused like he was waiting to see what would happen, like he was expecting the worst. Jesse thought he should probably give him the worst too, but something paralyzed him. "I think maybe you're not averse to that," Perry went on. "What do you say, guy?"

But Jesse couldn't say a word. It was like the ability to speak had completely left him. He'd been expecting to say no when Perry asked him to pose with his shirt off. He'd expected to see how it went from there. But here Perry'd gone and bypassed all that.

"We'll take it real slow and easy. I've got a feeling you're probably new to all this. But don't worry. They say I'm a great teacher." Perry's voice was calm and soothing, and he just kept smiling that fascinating smile of his, kept looking right into you with those ice-blue eyes, and Jesse felt some dam give way just like it had when he'd found himself reaching, in what would forever seem like slow motion, for that dollar bill Brandon held out, not quite sure where the goofing ended and something completely different began, and Brandon not knowing either by the serious look on his face as he let Jesse take the dollar bill from between his fingers.

"I ain't doing nothing with you," Jesse warned.

Perry looked at him strangely; only Brandon had ever looked at him that way. They'd been in the basement searching for an old race car set Brandon thought was down there. All afternoon there'd been some kind of queasy charge between them, like before a thunderstorm.

"Are you sure?" Perry asked.

"No," Jesse heard himself say.

He always thought Brandon should've known better—Brandon, who was a year older, his brother's best buddy—but none of that stopped him. *I've done it before,* Brandon had said. *Once you get used to it, it ain't so bad.*

Perry's fingers grazed his cheek. "Come on. Let's you and me go upstairs."

Hurry, Jesse heard Brandon say, then Kyle's voice calling down the stairs, "Hey, you guys, what's taking so long down there?" He'd pulled away in alarm and Brandon in the same motion had stuffed his thick rod of flesh back in his jeans and the whole sorry thing was over nearly as soon as it began.

Only—once it started, it wasn't ever over. He knew that as Perry took him by the hand and led him up the steep, narrow stairs. Once, twice a week: *Feel like a dollar?* Brandon would say, and Jesse'd be on his knees. Why'd he do it if he didn't like it? And he didn't like it, he hated it—and every time Brandon sidled up to him with his low-voiced proposition, his stomach turned over and his heart was in his throat and he found himself nodding silently with dread and excitement.

At the top of the stairs they halted. "Why don't we take the guest bed-room?" Perry said. "I just washed the sheets. We had guests last weekend."

"I know," Jesse said in that strange-sounding voice that seemed to have replaced his own. "Them guys—I met them."

"So you did. Let's hope they didn't break the bedsprings."

"I told you about my girlfriend."

"I remember that."

"Then what the fuck do you think you're doing?"

Perry squeezed Jesse's hand. "I could ask you the same question. But I won't." Perry touched his finger to his lips. "There's plenty of time for talking. But right now, let's just be quiet. I have this feeling our bodies have both got plenty of talking to do to each other."

Jesse realized he was still holding a cold bottle of beer in his hand. "I'm not the kind of person you think I am," he said.

"I have no idea who you are, Jesse. That's what I'm dying to find out. And I think maybe you're dying to find out too. I think that's why you're here right now." Like it was the most normal thing to do, Perry pulled his muscle shirt over his head and dropped it on the floor. He'd been working out; he had an athlete's pecs, a firm, rippling stomach. He was the kind of guy you saw in underwear ads. Undoing the drawstring of his pants, he let them fall to his ankles, then stepped right out of them.

Jesse stood frozen. He tried not to look, even though it was hard to avoid with Perry standing directly in front of him.

"See?" Perry said. "I don't have a thing to hide from you. You've got me all turned on. What can I do? Or maybe the question is, what do you want to do?"

"You're really one pretty fucked-up dude," Jesse said. "You know that?"

Perry didn't answer, just smiled with his pouty girl's lips. Jesse tried to imagine kissing those lips. He found he could imagine all too well—one long kiss down that chest, that stomach, the trail of neat black hairs below his navel. Who ever guessed Jesse had such a truly sick imagination? Surely not Brandon, who'd never undressed, never kissed, just slid himself between Jesse's lips, at first warning, *Watch the teeth, man, watch the teeth,* till after a few times he didn't have to mention that particular concern anymore, his only other one being to say *I'm gonna shoot* so Jesse wouldn't have to swallow.

"I'd love to give you a blow job right now. I give amazing blow jobs. You'll see. How about it, guy?"

If he'd hated it so much, why did he sometimes swallow anyway? What kind of sick monkey did that make him? And why did it take him nearly a year to work up the courage to say, *We got to knock this stupid shit off*?

"I gotta go." Jesse gripped the beer bottle in his fist so hard he was afraid it was going to break. Or maybe he wished it might. Some shattering glass might feel good about now. Brandon had told him once how his dad used to draw blood when he hit him.

"Relax," Perry told him. "Come here. Everything's gonna be okay. And you'll feel a whole lot better. I guarantee."

"Look. I think I made a bad mistake coming over here. I'm sorry if I inconvenienced you."

Perry laughed—sort of a wild laugh, like he didn't exactly credit what he was hearing. "Are you kidding? This is the best move you ever made, coming here. You got to trust yourself on that one, Jesse."

Jesse shook his head: Perry had no idea how wrong he was on that one. In the same instant—"Oh, fuck," he heard himself moan—he flung the beer bottle with all the force he had in him against the far wall. It hit with a loud thump, not shattering, just rolling to the floor with beer foaming from its mouth.

Perry seemed hardly fazed. His look was more concern than surprise. He didn't even glance down at the bottle that rolled to a stop against his bare foot. "You're free to walk out of here," he said quietly. "I'm not keeping you."

But something was keeping him, and if it wasn't Perry, then what was it? "I didn't mean to do that," he apologized. "I . . ."

Perry's smile was so sympathetic—Jesse thought maybe he'd been waiting his whole life for a smile like that. More than anything else, he wanted to take that face in his hands and kiss it for all it was worth. But that was craziness itself. He'd never be able to live with himself if he did something like that, though the terrible thought occurred to him that maybe what he'd been doing all along hadn't been living anyway.

In all the excitement, Perry'd lost his woodie. In fact, the whole moment seemed to be fading—in no time at all everything'd be lost, like none of it ever happened. But that's what he wanted, wasn't it? For none of it to have ever happened? Not just now, but going back years, all the mess he'd been holding inside.

Go on, he pleaded silently, trying to beam his thoughts into Perry's head. Try something, dude. Please. Try anything.

And, like a wish come true, Perry did. He moved in steadily, warily—and why not?—but when he opened out both arms in a big embrace, Jesse just allowed himself to be enfolded, the way you might wrap some hurt, trembling dog in a blanket to try to calm it down. He'd never kissed a guy's neck, and he let himself do that. He let his lips graze the stubble of Perry's jaw, and when Perry's open lips met his, when Perry's tongue came calling, even though he knew that was worse, in a way, than what he and Brandon had ever done, which was just getting off, no different, really, than animals, he didn't resist letting a man's tongue roam at will in his mouth.

He'd been hungry and thirsty a long, long time. He could feel Perry's revived woodie nudging his thigh, and he reached down boldly to seize that prize. Perry wasn't as big as Brandon, but still Jesse could feel the shiver that went through him, and he shivered too as Perry flexed his pelvis against him and his tongue renewed its liberties.

The instant they stopped, Jesse knew, everything else was going to come flooding back, worse than ever. He could already see that. The farther he went, the worse it was going to get. If there was just some way for this to happen but afterward not to have happened—if they could just go to some place where time stopped for a few minutes, where they could step outside of everything and do what they wanted with each other and then step back in and nobody'd ever be the wiser. He'd used to wish that down in Brandon's basement too, but it hadn't worked that way then and he knew it wasn't going to work that way now either.

"Let's get you out of these things," Perry murmured, starting to roll Jesse's T-shirt up his torso.

But Jesse was having none of it. "I can't," he said. "I got to go. I don't wanna do this shit."

He knew Perry wasn't fooled; he knew the guy'd felt his woodie poking up in his pants.

"I said, I got to go." He pushed Perry's hands away from him, maybe a little rougher than he meant. Still, if it got his point across—

"Okay, okay." Perry sounded out of breath. He held up a hand, palm out. "I hear you. I'm just, like, getting these mixed signals, you know." Jesse was aware his T-shirt was still riding high across his chest; he yanked it down.

"You had no right," Jesse said.

"It was an honest mistake, okay? We'll just forget about it."

Jesse was surprised to see he was making Perry nervous. Surprised and a little satisfied. Maybe fear would keep him from talking. *You ever say a word,* Brandon always told him, *I'll fucking ruin you.* Maybe fear was the one thing could open that space up, where for a minute you were free.

"Come here." Jesse beckoned. "You wanna blow me, dude? Then go ahead. You say a word, I'll fucking ruin you to everybody."

He could see he was really surprising Perry now.

"Come on, do it," he said. "Before I decide to hate you or something."

Perry shook his head. "You're too fucking crazy. I should just let you go." But he didn't. He took a couple steps forward and went to his knees. His hands were expert in getting what he wanted out in the open. His mouth could teach Donna a whole new world.

The thought of Donna made him so sad he wanted to cry, only crying wasn't something he did—but he felt scarily close as Perry worked him to the root. In no time he was there, then more than there. "I'm gonna shoot," he said, because that was what Brandon always said, and it was what he told Donna as well. Fair warning was just good manners, and Perry took heed. He held Jesse's dick against his cheek as it spurted, then rubbed the head around in the deposit of goo. He kissed the tip but didn't put it back in his mouth.

Jesse's heart was pounding like a jackhammer. Perry had a blank look on his face like he was far away and dreaming. A driblet of come hung off his chin. "I got to go now," Jesse said, stuffing himself back in.

It seemed to call Perry back to earth. "If you feel like it," he said, "call me sometime. Okay?"

Jesse paused at the door. "This didn't never happen. And I sure wouldn't bet on it happening again."

TWENTY-FOUR

Someone had been pounding on the door downstairs, demanding to be let in; Cameron was sure of it. But now, as he lay jolted awake in the dark, there was only silence, or what passed in the country for silence: the August crickets, the faint perpetual river of traffic on the Thruway. Whatever it was hadn't wakened Casper, who continued to sleep soundly in his favorite spot at the foot of the bed.

Should he turn on the light and betray his presence? But surely whoever was knocking knew he was there, and that's why they were knocking in the first place. Maybe it was Jesse, distraught and confessional, perhaps half-drunk. Or Crazy Jamey, crazy to get laid, having snuck out of his parents' house in the Hasbrouck Estates down the road. Or Kyle and his thuggish-looking friend on some mysterious, slightly unhinged mission.

Whoever it was, now that he was awake, they made not a sound.

About once a week he woke to that heavy, urgent pounding on the door. He wondered—might it really be nothing more than the sound of his own heartbeat that startled him awake? After Toby died, there'd been a time when he'd actually hoped a ghost might visit. He'd wake in the night to ask, Are you there?

He'd had a few dreams, it was true—Toby would show up, curiously diminished in size, though no one else in the dream ever seemed to think it odd that he'd shrunk, or even that he'd come back. His eyes were bright; his face looked wizened, like a turnip. In one dream he'd gotten a new wristwatch and was annoyed it didn't work properly. After a while he stopped appearing at all. It had been years since Cameron had seen Toby in a dream.

He'd always wondered if the dead continued to exist in some way. It just seemed too impossible for a presence as vivid as Toby's simply to cease without leaving any kind of trace in the universe. But he suspected that that was precisely what had happened—to Toby, to everybody. All the rest was just wishful or desperate thinking.

Out in the dark something substantial went thump. Then, hard on its heels, a hollow crack. All Cameron's senses went alert, but nothing followed except tense, unwelcome silence. For whatever reason of their own, the crickets had paused in their incessant music, fading back into the night as some intruder made its way among them. But what was out there?

Without turning on the light, Cameron slipped cautiously from bed. In faint moonlight, he groped his way down the stairs. Stupid not to keep a flashlight by the bed—but he found one in the kitchen, the big rechargeable one he kept plugged in by the sink. He paused, peering out the window at his moon-silvered garden. Nothing stirred, and slowly, one by one, the crickets resumed their measured cacophony.

From the back stoop he shined the flashlight into the dark. Its beam made the outlines of his garden dramatic, even garish. He saw what had fallen. Someone or something had overturned the birdbath. Its heavy platter, cracked in two, lay on the flagstones. He swung the beam in a wide arc, alert for the bright twin disks of an animal's eyes, but could see nothing. Perhaps a thirsty raccoon had tried to pull itself up for a drink and its weight had tipped the bowl. That was certainly a reasonable explanation, certainly more reasonable than any other he might entertain. Hooligans had never vandalized his garden, though it had always seemed a possibility.

He didn't feel like venturing out into the dark; he'd inspect the damage in the morning. Double-locking the door just in case, he remounted the stairs to find Casper still asleep at the foot of his bed. But innocent sleep had left him. He lay on top of the humid sheets, waiting for some other sound to betray whatever was out there. Of course nothing was out there, he told himself—just the world. The wide, busy, treacherous world.

He wondered where Jesse was at this moment. Asleep, surely—but he realized once again how little he knew. Did he sleep over at his girlfriend's, for instance? Odd, wasn't it, that he'd never met her—or was that odd at all? He barely knew Jesse, though the thought that they were now bound together, however tenuously, was something of a comfort. For the rest of Jesse's life, Cameron would occupy a space, however meager, in his history. He would always be the friendly guy who'd helped him out when he needed a new truck. The guy who, inexplicably, had asked nothing in return.

But didn't everybody exact something in return? Had that freaked Jesse out, on reflection? Cameron realized he had no idea what Jesse made of any of that, or even if he bothered to make anything of it at all.

This faggot I got friendly with.

As clearly as if they'd been spoken, Cameron heard those words. Heard also the low, self-congratulatory snigger that followed.

His imagination was playing tricks, old fears talking from way back, when he used to worry that Mitchell Johnson somehow suspected his secret. He'd left all that behind years ago. Still, he thought he'd feel more sanguine about everything if he'd heard from Jesse since they'd parted, a scant two days ago—with a firm handshake, a frank "Sir, I can't thank you enough." On the best of terms, he was sure of that.

Jesse wasn't the kind to cut and run, was he?

Into his head, unbidden, wandered Perry's idle talk about putting the moves on Jesse someday, should the opportunity ever present itself. He wondered if he should have been more explicit in warning Jesse, but of course it wasn't any of his business. And if Perry did try—it wasn't possible, was it, that Jesse could really be seduced? And if it *was* possible, then was he himself a hopeless fool for never having tried?

But that was absurd. He'd given all that up. To even try to seduce somebody like Jesse was folly and worse. What kind of life could a doomed faggot ever hope to give a healthy young man like Jesse anyway? Hadn't he been down that dead-end road already with Dan?

A secondhand truck, sadly, was as far as he could go, the best he had to offer.

And to think there was a time when everything had seemed possible. What would have happened, he wondered, if this disease hadn't come along? What would his life have been like? Hard to imagine that Toby would be nearly forty now. How would his career have turned out? Would he have been famous on the stage, would he have gone to Hollywood?

Would success have wrecked their relationship? He used to worry that he was just a passing phase in Toby's charmed life—when instead, it was Toby who'd turned out to be the passing phase in his own.

Usually he kept all that at bay. Now, for some reason, there was Toby, lying in a bed in what he used to call the Doom Ward at St. Vincent's, seizures coursing through his unconscious body, terrible gusts that threatened to lift him right off the bed. They'd tied him down to prevent that—also to prevent the half dozen tubes feeding into him from being yanked out. He looked like an old man, cheeks sunken, lips pulled back in a ghastly grin. He looked in unimaginable agony. Just for a minute Cameron had left the room—it was two-thirty in the morning, the same hour as now; he'd gone down to the nurses' station for some coffee to try to keep himself awake. When he got back it was over. With no one looking, Toby had slipped away.

He told himself it wouldn't have made any difference if he'd been there. He'd been telling himself that for thirteen years. It still hurt. And what a mistake it had been to think he could ever be that intimate with anyone again.

At the back of his photo album, in an envelope, were some photographs Perry had taken perhaps a half hour after Toby'd died. He and Max had come as soon as Cameron called them. They both said Toby looked incredibly peaceful in those pictures, all the agony wiped off his features and replaced by a kind of serenity. Cameron had never opened that envelope. He hadn't wanted to remember Toby that way. He wanted to remember the bright, athletic boy with brown hair dyed blond for his role in an off-off-Broadway play whose title Cameron had long since forgotten. He wanted to remember the young man who wrote incomprehensible poetry (he still remembered the title if not the exact text of "Holy Elm Under the Shadow of Blood"). Whose years working as a caterer had given him the ability to turn any random batch of ingredients rummaged from cupboard and refrigerator into an astonishing feast. Who called his mother in Tulsa every Sunday afternoon. Who used to proclaim, in the midst of lovemaking, "Oh, man, I so *love* getting fucked!"

Cameron sat up and turned on the light. He'd had the most surprising idea, the sort of idea that only comes to you in the middle of the night, and unless you do something about it then and there, it'll never happen, the sober light of morning will evaporate it straightaway.

Mrkgnao, said Casper, looking at him curiously. He went to his desk and located the folder that contained his will. There it all was, in black and white, the document he and his lawyer had drawn up when he first got sick. He went through and, in bold strokes, crossed out Dan Futrell's name wherever it appeared and wrote in its place Jesse Vanderhof. There. It was done. Something a little in the spirit of Toby, a foolish thing, no doubt, and in the morning he'd probably feel abashed and change it all back, but for now it felt strangely satisfying to have done this in the middle of the night. Everyone would be shocked; they'd shake their heads at his secret, inscrutable life. Well, too bad. He'd have to call his lawyer first thing tomorrow and make it all legal.

Wide-awake now, he went downstairs to look for that photo album. When he pulled it from the bookcase, the envelope fell out onto the floor. He retrieved it and sat on the sofa, the album open in his lap, and scrutinized the sealed envelope. No, it didn't tempt him. He wouldn't recognize that Toby. Much as he'd vowed to keep him alive forever in his heart, like all the dead, Toby had faded. There'd come a time, sooner rather than later, when no one would even remember Toby Vail had ever lived on the planet at all.

For a long time Jesse remained motionless, amazed the roving flashlight beam had failed to expose him crouched among the rhododendrons. Why he'd thought that sitting silently in Cameron's garden in the middle of the night was going to solve anything, he didn't know. But he'd left his new truck at the cemetery entrance and walked down the deserted road to Cameron's dark house. The highway department hadn't mowed in a month, and weeds were blooming, the disks of their flowers ghostly in the powdery moonlight.

He envied the weeds their blooming. And the question throbbed in his head: What the fuck had he been thinking? Because he couldn't tell himself he hadn't been thinking. He'd been doing way the fuck too much of it.

It'd be funny to consider what a trick it all was. Sex. The hunger and need for something that an instant later seemed to vanish into thin air. He wasn't even out Perry's door before the hollowness set in. Going in there, he'd been so full of something—nothing could have pushed away his resolve. He'd felt powerful, intent; he'd felt certain in a way he only did in dreams, the predator after its prey. Ridiculous to consider how the simple act of squirting a little seed could change all that, till what had looked so logical and necessary just a minute before suddenly turned to ashes on you, a fire all burnt out in an instant.

He wished he'd made it clearer to Perry what would happen if ever he spoke of what had never happened. Brandon had his honor, after all; you could count on him to keep mum. But could you trust a faggot to keep a secret?

Was that what he wanted to ask Cameron? Not directly; there was no asking directly—but maybe, he'd thought, sitting in Cameron's garden in the dark in the middle of the night might suggest answers actual words couldn't begin to say.

So he'd sat there on the bench for a good hour, gazing out at the flowers and shrubs palely sprinkled with moonlight, his heart in his chest racing unnaturally, just like it had all the panicked afternoon and evening long, pounding so loud he was afraid it would wake the dead. But nothing woke. Except for the static of crickets, the garden was silent, the dark house was silent, Cameron long asleep, dreaming whatever dreams faggots dreamed.

But then he was afraid he knew exactly what dreams faggots dreamed. He had them all the time. He was just kidding himself to pretend he didn't.

"Fuck, fuck, fuck," he'd murmured, taking off his baseball cap and running his hands through the bristles on his head. Then he saw the bear.

For a moment he thought it was a big, shaggy dog. Somehow it had shuffled near without him hearing it. So all that talk had been true. There really was a bear, and now it looked at him and huffed, a kind of warning bark, then turned and ambled off the way it had come. Though not without taking down the birdbath, which fell with a thump and crack onto the bluestone flags. Jesse'd bolted as well, in the other direction—and none too soon, it turned out, as Cameron swung a flashlight's beam out over the garden from the safety of the back porch.

He'd had to resist the urge to call out. What would Cameron have thought, to find the crazy kid who worked for him hiding in his garden late at night? There was no explaining, and besides, Jesse was already way more tangled with Cameron than he wanted. He didn't blame him, exactly, though he'd left the truck unlocked, thinking what a hoot it'd be for somebody to go and steal it, take it off his hands, erase the whole damn summer from the slate. But he knew everything that was written there remained, and it was all connected up like a bundle of twisted-together wires you'd never succeed in untangling. Best just to throw the whole thing away and start over, only the whole thing was all there was, there wasn't any starting over.

He should never have listened to his brother. He should never have taken the job. He should never have let Perry talk to him like he did at the party. He should never have taken a dollar from Brandon, even as a stupid joke. He should never, he should never, he should never—but when did it stop?

His thighs ached from crouching down—the way they used to ache after endless minutes on his knees in Brandon's basement. Getting to his feet, he decided the coast was clear. The garden had given him whatever it could. He wondered if he'd really seen a bear—but the broken bowl of the birdbath lay on the ground in silent proof. The shameful, never-to-be-lived-down realization came over him. Back at Perry's, he wished he hadn't turned and run. He wished he'd stayed to do to Perry exactly what Perry had done to him.

In the upstairs window—Cameron's bedroom window—a light went on. Jesse decided it was best to take a long detour around through the woods and head up to his truck before anything else happened in that dangerous garden.

TWENTY-FIVE

Hot sunlight streamed in through the bedroom window. He lay in a drowse, sweating lightly, not unpleasantly. The world by daylight didn't seem half-bad, though the interval of forgetting quickly faded, and with a groan, remembering the house on Main Street, he was right back inside his stupidity again.

Still—a single mistake wasn't enough to kill you, was it? Weren't you supposed to learn from your mistakes?

He'd just about convinced himself of that when a sharp rap on the door made him jump. Without a word, Kyle strode across the room. He squatted down beside Jesse and roughly palmed the top of Jesse's skull like you would a basketball.

"Hey," Jesse said, "what're you doing? You're hurting me. I just woke up."

"Get your clothes on." Kyle leaned in close, smelling sweetly of booze. Jesse fought back alarm, even as he thrilled to Kyle's touch. He feared he might have his own reek to him—get too close, and anybody'd be able to sniff out what he'd been up to.

"What's up?" Jesse asked as Kyle released him.

"You and me need to go up to Pop's grave."

The alarm turned to full-scale panic. Had somebody seen his truck parked at the cemetery entrance last night? He scrambled to come up with an explanation, but Kyle didn't press for one—if that was even what was on his mind.

Jesse was conscious of being watched as he slipped into jeans, a T-shirt. He looked around for his baseball cap. It was like Kyle had never seen him get dressed before. He half-expected his brother to follow him into the bathroom when he went to piss, splash a little water on his face, run a wet finger along his gums to get the furry feel of sleep out of his mouth.

Outside, he headed intinctively for his truck.

"We ain't taking yours," Kyle told him.

They drove the whole way in a silence that let each thought lead to a worse one and then to a worse one still. Jesse remembered the way Pop would march one or the other or sometimes both of them down to the edge of the woods and cut a switch from a birch branch.

The cemetery was deserted. They cruised slowly past the tall monuments moldering in the shade of old trees and then out to the lawn where the neat new stones sparkled in the sun.

Pop's plot was off to itself, just a little metal plaque planted in a brown stretch of lawn, though when Jesse climbed down from the truck, he saw it hadn't been neglected, exactly. A small pile of coins, a few shotgun shells, some colored marbles: somebody'd been tending things. A full whiskey pint stood watch.

"You been coming here," Jesse said. His own neglect of Pop's memory hit him hard. Here he'd been practically next door, at Cameron's, day after day, yet he never thought of coming by. Or no—he had to correct himself—he thought about it every day, but he just couldn't do it. What did he want with a bare rectangle of earth some weedy grass was trying to fill in? But Kyle must've been by a lot.

You couldn't see Cameron's place from here—the trees hid it—though in winter, with the leaves fallen, you'd have a perfect bead on the white house with green shutters and a wisteria vine pulling down the front porch.

Kyle said nothing. He lit a smoke and stood gazing down at the lonesome little shrine. There were times you should definitely say something, Jesse knew, but those were always the times you couldn't for the life of you think of a single thing. Over in the distance, a car had pulled up beside a gravestone. He watched a stooped old lady carry a watering can to the geraniums she'd planted. Had their mom been out here even once? Had Patti? Pop had been a hard man lots of the time, no doubt about that. Already, Jesse could see, most everybody was shedding his memory the way a snake sloughs off its old, constricting skin. Only Kyle had stayed loyal. Only Kyle had kept watch on the barn after all the horses had slipped away.

"It looks nice," he said. "You been keeping it up nice."

Kyle gazed out across the graves. He threw his cigarette down, let slip a last spume of smoke from his nostrils. "I been thinking about some things," he said.

The way he said it made Jesse jump a little. "What things?"

"How you and me need to powwow here." It had been Pop's way of sitting them all down when things got serious.

He tried to tell himself he was jumpy for no cause. When would Kyle ever cross paths with the likes of Perry? And surely Brandon wouldn't go and tell his brother some damn lie after all this time. He was safe, he told himself. What could Kyle possibly have on him?

"Fine," he said with a sense of doom nonetheless. "Shoot."

"I just got a question for you," Kyle said. "That house down there. You ever go through it?"

"What d'you mean? You and me went through it together, remember? Kind of seems like it was your great idea at the time." That all seemed so long ago, some other, barely recognizable life he'd mislaid for this new, itchier one. It shocked him, a little, how far they'd all traveled these last couple of months. Like Pop underground, they'd been changing too—and not necessarily for the better.

"You ever take anything of his? You got plenty of chances, right? He goes off, he leaves things lying around. That time you and me had a look around—don't tell me it didn't make you curious. His checkbook, maybe. Credit cards. Papers. He gives you pretty much free run of the house, don't he?"

"What're you getting at? I never took a thing. Why're you asking that?"

"You ever take Donna over there with you? Introduce her to your man?"

They stood looking at each other—Kyle's steady, watchful gaze a challenge.

"What's that got to do with anything? And, no, I didn't. It ain't none of her business. It's between him and me."

"You're keeping stuff from me," Kyle said. "I don't like it."

When Kyle studied you like that, you were powerless to look away. You were afraid something might snap, and the recoil would knock you right to the ground.

"I'm worried," Kyle went on, "you might of gotten yourself in deeper here than you planned on. I want you to tell me about it."

"I don't know what you're talking about," Jesse said. "You and me had this plan from the beginning, right? Go along and see what happens. You sounded pretty happy when you heard about the truck. So I don't know why you're suddenly pulling out on me."

Kyle shook his head slowly. A bitter sort of grin passed across his face. "Sometimes," he said, "you look back on everything you planned, and it just seems like so much shit. It's like you were fixing to bite into this beautiful ripe piece of fruit, and once you bite, once you get a mouthful, you realize it's all fucking rotten."

Jesse felt a whisper of a shadow race across them both, faint as a breeze, perilous nonetheless.

"You tell me what I should do," Jesse said. "Tell me what to do, and I'll do it. You want me to give the truck back, I'll do that."

It hadn't occurred to him before, but maybe it wasn't the worst idea. Maybe there was still time to back out of the muck he seemed to have waded into.

"Go over to my truck," Kyle told him in Pop's old voice—quiet but meant to be obeyed. "Take a look in the glove compartment."

Across the way the old woman was getting in her car. Jesse watched the late-model sedan pull away slowly and head down the drive toward the entrance. It was like hope itself had decided to abandon him there. He scanned the cloudless sky where nothing but the silver mark of a jet opened up a seam in the blue. Kyle's truck ticked in the heat. Feathers of rust spread around the wheel wells, Jesse noticed. Maybe he *had* been selfish, grabbing up Cameron's offer when it came his way. Maybe in his brother's eyes . . .

He clicked open the glove compartment and saw in an instant what Kyle had meant him to see.

Impossible, he thought, blinking involuntarily—like that would make it go away. It's not what you think, he was already telling Kyle in his head, though to no avail. It was the worst possible thing that could have happened. He glanced back at his brother; Kyle stood where he'd left him, hands in his back pockets; every once in a while he'd dig a little pebble out of the soil with the tip of his boot, bend over, and pick it up and then pitch it in the direction of Pop's grave. Like he was bored. Like he couldn't care less. Jesse looked again at the magazine's glossy pages, those incriminating images he'd only glanced at once or twice, and then only out of sick curiosity. Two buzz-cut marines in camos and T-shirts, then in nothing but their dog tags as they did together things no dogs would ever do. It made him dizzy and empty inside with revulsion or longing or whatever it was that choked him up.

It was like somebody had reached into his chest and gripped his heart in their fist. He'd picked at random from the shelf in Cameron's closet. He'd almost completely forgotten its existence, tucked under his mattress, unstudied for weeks.

Why the fuck had he done it? What had he been trying to prove? And worse—how could he have left such a damning piece of evidence lying around, even in hiding?

It's not what it looks like, he rehearsed despairingly. And what the fuck were you doing going through my stuff? You had no right.

It was his brother. He had every right.

He walked back slowly to where his brother stood. Kyle's face was expressionless, that invulnerable look he'd perfected so long ago, the look Jesse so envied and had never been able to master.

Kyle said not a word. All he did, when Jesse came in range, was land a punch squarely in the center of Jesse's chest. The thud it made was startlingly loud, and Jesse stepped back not so much in surprise—hadn't he seen this coming?—as to try to keep his balance under the impact. Then Kyle was on him, a flurry of punches catching him all over—his stomach, his chin, the side of his head—crazy, flailing, barely aimed punches raining down. There was something satisfying in those blows. One caught him just under the ribs and he let out a low moan, he couldn't help himself. But he wasn't crying out for Kyle to stop. No, he rejoiced in the sickening contact of fist on flesh, and he knew Kyle did too. This had been a long time coming, but now that it was here, he welcomed it. He used to watch with a kind of envy the way his brother and Brandon fought, their teasing, playful wrestling. It'd been ages since he'd fought anybody that way, and this wasn't like that, this was different, this wasn't playful but to hurt, to punish. These were grieving blows, a whole summer of sorrow with no way out but this. He understood that. Give it to me, he thought. Give me everything you've got.

He richly deserved it, every last blow his brother showered down on him.

But Kyle's punches had lost their heart. "Oh, fuck," he yelled. "Shit." It was almost a wail. He flung himself off Jesse, staggering around in a half circle like he was the one who'd been pommeled. Then he collapsed onto the ground, his breath coming in what sounded almost like sobs. Jesse was breathless too, the wind knocked clean out of him. He bent over, resting his hands on his thighs, and tried to suck air into his lungs.

"Don't fucking do this to me," Kyle said. "You can't fucking do this, Jesse."

Jesse couldn't have spoken if his life depended on it. He gasped but no oxygen connected with his lungs. He ached in a dozen places, already bruising. Then all at once a painful breath took, then another.

Kyle's knuckles had opened up a cut under his eye; Jesse felt at it with his fingertips while blood ran down his cheek, stained his T-shirt with bright blotches.

"I ain't a faggot, Kyle," he said as soon as he could speak. His sentences came out broken. "I swear that to you. On Pop's grave, I swear it. Lightning strike me."

It wasn't that he expected lightning to strike, but he waited there—they both did—for a bolt from the blue sky. But nothing happened except a faint, dry breeze.

"If I could explain it to you, I would," Jesse said, though the explanation, to him, had unfortunately never been so clear. "You got to believe me."

"I ain't calling you a faggot. Here." Kyle held out his hand. "Help me up, buddy." He staggered to his feet, a little disoriented from all the punishing he'd done. "But I ain't forgetting this neither. You got your fucking truck. How, I ain't gonna ask. It's none of my business. And I ain't saying nothing, either. So you don't got to worry about that. It's between you and me, little brother. But I just want you to know—I'm watching you, man. I'm watching you like a hawk. So just remember that from now on."

Once more Cameron had waited most of the morning for Jesse to stop by. Once more no Jesse had appeared. A film of anxiety shrouded every-thing—the bleakly powerful sunlight, the flowers dozing in the heat. The young man's schedule had always been a bit informal, prone to occasional lapses—but nothing had been said to alter the general rhythm they'd both grown accustomed to. It wasn't as if, now that the garden party had come and gone, the poor garden itself had outlived its usefulness. And yet, as Cameron strolled among the flowerbeds, he had a mournful sense that that was exactly what had happened.

Surely there was an explanation, a misunderstanding that could be cleared up instantly. Yet he hesitated to call; he told himself everything would be fine, even as he once more decided to forgo for the fourth straight day his usual latte at Zanzibar in the hope of seeing Jesse show up in that bright red truck that was already costing Cameron more, at least inwardly, than he'd bargained for. By midmorning, however, he had to be on his way. Nothing ever changed. He'd felt the same waiting for Mitchell Johnson to call when he'd said he would. Or for Toby to show up at the apartment at any reasonable hour.

At the Rudds', he was relieved to find that Barbara was out. He'd not invited his clients to his party—something Jorge had lightly chastised him for. There'd been a time when he'd have considered it a professional obligation.

The garden itself, he feared, betrayed similar lapses. For some reason—midmorning, midweek—the crew had deserted the site, as if some great calamity had happened out in the world and no one had bothered to tell him about it. Despite the absence of workers, the work, he saw as he strolled about the grounds, was coming along nicely. The stonework was essentially done—the terraces and retaining walls and steps. The garden's backbone. If the whole looked, at the moment, awfully severe—the walls too imposing, even fortresslike for the overall scheme (especially as a sin-gle cloud, intent on altering the mood, passed across the sun)—he reminded himself that plantings would soften the effect.

But in the light suddenly gone flat and lifeless, how absurd gardens were. What grotesque expenditures of time, energy, hope—and for what? Still, at times he imagined himself walking alone in a walled garden—

stuccoed walls of luminous white, austerely planted, perhaps some stands of graceful, long-legged bamboo, in the center a low, murmuring fountain surrounded by black river stones, overhead a pale blue sky of evening—and he understood the image as nothing less than a rendering of his deepest soul.

No one else walked there. Perhaps that was his secret, unalterable doom and joy.

Through the leaves of the aged maples the sun, reappearing, tossed coins of gold onto the lawn. All summer, for some reason, he'd been thinking about Derek Jarman's garden at Dungeness, that simple black fisherman's cabin set amid desolate shingle decorated with magic circles of white flint, gray pebbles, red bricks smooth-washed by the tide; sculpture devised from driftwood, old tools, cork floats, anything the stormy surf cast up. No daffodils bloomed there, or roses—only sea kale and horehound and viper's bugloss and rue.

On the side of the house, Jarman and friends had painted the text of "Busie old foole, unruly Sunne," that scolding paean to love's fine lassitude that Cameron had learned by heart when he was at Oberlin and disconcertingly in love with Max Greenblatt, but which he could no longer, alas, recall in anything like its entirety.

In all his successful, fatuous career of nearly twenty years, he'd never designed anything half so brave as that strange little garden.

But up the drive came a red pickup truck, and for a moment his heart leapt. The certainty flashed through him: he had something urgent to tell Jesse—or perhaps to ask him. But what? Like a fish in water, the notion shimmered, then disappeared into the depths. The truck, he registered almost instantly, wasn't Jesse's at all, but instead a dull, rust-splotched thing belonging to Dave the stonemason—who emerged, with a friendly smile, fiendishly scratching at the silvery toupee he persisted in wearing, even though hardly an acquaintance of his hadn't, at one time or another, seen it knocked comically askew by his manual adjustments and readjustments, each posing as a persistent itch to be perpetually scratched. He wore jeans and a denim shirt both chalky with stone dust. A fragrant halo of pot smoke engulfed Cameron as he reached out to take the chalky hand Dave offered. Cameron had subcontracted to him for years; no one in the business was more reliable or adept at puzzling stones together.

"Looks great," Cameron told him.

"We got to finish laying down by the reflecting pool. Then that'll be it. We should be out of here by the end of the week. Jorge's got us on a job up in Rosendale. But you probably know that."

Cameron didn't, in fact, though he nodded nonetheless. Jorge ran Paradise Designs more or less independently these days, much to Cameron's relief.

Seated on the shaft of a fallen column, Toby smoked weed he'd bought from some Germans in Antalya. *It's not the greatest,* he said. *But it sure beats going without.* He wore that day the olive green, sleeveless T-shirt that was a mainstay of his austere itinerant wardrobe; very short khaki shorts that rode up, when he sat, to reveal nearly the whole of his taut thighs; sandals that disclosed his shapely toes. His chestnut, sun-saturated hair fell past his shoulders as he looked out over the ruin of yet another ancient city. Which one, which one? It was too long ago; they were all too much alike in the end.

"I'm real pleased," Dave said, "about the way the curve down by the first landing came out. I didn't care for the massing effect on the first pass, so I had the boys redo it. What're you thinking of putting in down there?"

"Grays and aromatics. To fend off the deer. Massed lavender, artemisia, stachys, sea holly. It should have a soothing effect."

"It's a good thing I work in stone," Dave said. "It'd drive me crazy to go to all this trouble, then have a bunch of deer come through and tear it all apart."

Cameron remembered, all at once, the thing he had to tell Jesse. Beware. Stay away from Perry. Come with me to Turkey in the autumn.

Was it too late? Had something already ruined the delicate, nearly invisible filament that so improbably connected the two of them?

An unfamiliar car was parked in front of the house. A Saab, a car nobody Jesse knew would drive. Their mom came strolling down the lawn, talking with two men he'd never seen before; they walked one on either side of her, flanking her like she was the belle of the ball. Then Jesse saw that Craig Hallenbeck brought up the rear. For an instant he thought Kyle was going to throw the truck in reverse and get them the hell out of there, but Kyle didn't. He spun in next to the bright red pickup and slammed the brakes on hard. The three men and their mom all looked up in alarm. Poke too, snoozing in the shade, raised his head, then stood and shook the sleep from himself. Kyle detoured out of his way to give the mutt a scratch behind the ears before approaching the house.

"What happened to you?" cried their mom when they were still at some distance. "You get in an accident, or what?"

"Fell off his high horse back there," Kyle told her. "He'll be all right now. What's going on here?"

"Jesse, honey, you got blood all over your shirt," his mom pointed out when they'd closed in. He'd stripped his T-shirt off and was using it to try to stanch the bleeding, not with too much success. "These are my two boys," she paused to explain to the two strangers. "This is Kurt, and this is Luke. And of course you know Craig."

The three men looked him up and down. He guessed he probably was a bit of a sight.

"We were just telling your mother how much we love this place," said Kurt. He was maybe forty, his face all pocked with acne scars he'd grown a scraggly beard to try to hide. The sentence wasn't half out of his mouth before Jesse knew the worst of it.

"It's a dream of a house," Luke agreed.

"Kurt and Luke are from Manhattan," Jesse's mom explained, politely blowing the smoke of her cigarette away from them. They wore sandals, and matching Hawaiian shirts.

"We'll treat this place with tender loving care," Kurt said. "We intend to bring it back to its former beauty."

"Not that it isn't absolutely beautiful now," Luke hastened to add. "But old houses like this take a lot of work to keep up. More than most people think is worth the trouble."

"She'll be in good hands," Kurt assured them all.

Why wouldn't they just shut up? Jesse wondered.

Craig had sidled up to him. "Good to see you again," he purred as Jesse continued to hold his T-shirt up to his cheek. "That's a pretty bad cut there. You want to put something on it? I've got a first aid kit in my trunk." He touched Jesse's arm, and Jesse automatically pulled away. That didn't faze Craig. "Sorry we didn't have more of a chance to talk at Cameron's. Wasn't it a fabulous party?"

Jesse just looked at him.

"What party was that?" his mom asked.

"Cameron Barnes's," Craig said—like Jesse's mom would know. She only shook her head. "Well-known garden designer. Does wonderful work." He turned to Jesse. "Don't you agree?"

Jesse only shrugged. "I wouldn't know."

"I thought you were doing work for him. I thought—"

"I wouldn't know," Jesse repeated, though less certainly. Still, it was enough to shut Craig up, at least for the moment.

He'd had a thought, coming down from the cemetery, past Cameron's house. The BMW wasn't in the driveway, and for just a moment, daubing a rag to the cut under his eye and surveying that empty house, he'd thought, There'll come a day when Cameron's gone. That would solve things, wouldn't it? If Cameron went away. If he died. It would wipe everything clean.

Of course the thought had lasted only an instant, because in the next instant Jesse knew too well how that prospect still left Perry and all his crowd. It left the homegrown traps like Brandon. It left Craig Hallenbeck, who wasn't stupid, who had, already, half a clue. Everywhere he turned, it seemed like one trap or another lay waiting to snare him the instant he let down his guard. And it was going to be like that from now on.

Cameron, Jesse understood with a hole gaping wide in his heart, had never been the problem at all.

Kyle, in the meantime, was taking matters into his own hands. "Get the fuck off our property," he said.

"Excuse me?" said Kurt.

"Get the fuck off our property." Kyle's voice wasn't a bit angry; it was calm and matter-of-fact, which Jesse knew from experience was a whole lot worse. "I don't want you the fuck here. Far as I'm concerned, you're trespassing. Now get the hell out."

"Wait a minute," Craig said, flushing crimson and sweat breaking out along his brow.

"Honey," said their mom.

"I think there's definitely some misunderstanding," Luke said. "Craig's showing us this property. Your mother here—"

"Fuck off."

"Honey, stop it," their mom pleaded.

"Who's making me? Do I see anybody here?"

"Kyle," said Craig. "You are way out of line. These gentlemen have signed a binder. They have legal rights. Your mother—"

"She don't know half what she's doing."

"Don't talk that way, Kyle," said their mom.

Kyle turned and gave her the Vanderhof glare. "Pop's heart must be fucking breaking right now" was all he told her, in that same quiet voice Pop used to lay down the law. Jesse realized he couldn't blame his brother for a thing. Without Pop around, they'd all gone to pieces. That was the real story of the summer. But Kyle had known. Who else had been looking out for them but the one who'd hurt more than any of them, who'd taken Pop's death hardest because he knew exactly what it was they'd all be losing by it?

Some pitch in Kyle's voice must've carried down to Poke, some hint the tide had turned; suddenly he lunged against his chain, a dog all at once wanting to do somebody serious harm. The air swarmed with his barking, and in the midst of it Jesse heard their mom explaining, "My boys lost their daddy this summer. They've been under an awful lot of stress."

"Maybe we should come back later," Luke suggested.

"We certainly don't want to cause any difficulties," Kurt agreed as Craig began pushing the two, as discreetly as possible, in the direction of their car—taking care to give Poke, who was still flinging himself against the limits of his chain, the widest berth he could.

"Don't worry," Jesse could hear Craig trying to assure the two. "We've got a binder on this place. It's all in the mother's name, anyway. That fellow there has no legal title whatsoever. I know Kyle Vanderhof. All he's got is a big mouth, and nothing but."

Car doors slammed. The Saab pulled away. Poke looked with longing after the prey that had got away and tried, with the occasional fitful bark, to lure it back. The three Vanderhofs likewise watched the empty road.

"Kyle, just what do you think you were doing there?" Their mom brushed a tear from her eye—almost, Jesse thought, like she'd been laughing to herself at the sight of grown men so easily routed.

Kyle looked at her and grinned. Maybe he too had a tear in the corner of one eye. Maybe only a speck. "How the fuck should I know?" he told her. "All I can say is, I don't think Pop would mind one bit. Now let's get

Jesse cleaned up before he goes and dies of blood loss. He's looking a little pale. Ain't you, little brother?"

"Jesse, honey." Their mom peered at him with concern. "Maybe we better take you up to the emergency room. That cut don't look good at all."

In the Family Market, Cameron came upon Max raiding the lettuces. His shopping cart held a half dozen heads each of romaine, red leaf, and Boston.

"Hey there." Cameron tapped his friend on the shoulder. "Save some for me."

"Isn't this ridiculous? I'm reduced to scavenging. We didn't get our shipment this morning."

Cameron couldn't help but ask, "Are we sure all this is organic?"

"Who'll fucking know the difference? It's all shit anyway."

"You're in a mood," Cameron said. "I can tell."

Max held a head of romaine whose tips were delicately edged with black. He smiled. "I will not let the world defeat me." He dropped the lettuce into his cart. "I will not, I will not, I will not. It's just lettuce, after all. So what are you doing here?"

"Don't get the wrong idea, but in a weak moment I invited Elliot over for dinner." Cameron held up his shopping basket, as if to illustrate with its contents—a bag of small red potatoes, two fillets of scrod, a lemon—the simple meal he'd planned.

"Don't apologize. I'm glad our friend's finally making some progress with you."

"Don't get your hopes up. It's just—well, he's nice. And I have this bad feeling I haven't been treating him very well."

"Oh, then—a guilt dinner. My favorite kind."

"No, no," Cameron protested, though of course Max knew him too thoroughly. Would he have to end up in a relationship with Elliot out of sheer politeness? "I do genuinely like him."

"You're hopeless."

"But you've always known that." Cameron wondered why he couldn't bring himself to confess the simple truth to his oldest friend in the world—that the only soul who preoccupied him in the least these days was an entirely feckless young redneck. And yet that, unfathomably, was the one thing, of all the things he held in his heart, that he wanted to savor in secret. He knew the private tangle they'd gotten themselves into over the truck crossed lines best left uncrossed, but the trespass was delicious nonetheless.

As for his will, that document of such promise and doom, daylight had tempered the previous night's dark celebration, but only a little. He'd visited his lawyer, and in the venerable gloom of his office in Kingston's old stockade district, they'd worked through the finer details. The result, his conscience assured him, treated Dan with thorough decency, and for feckless Jesse there remained what would no doubt be the surprise of his life. That such stupendous generosity, arriving one day without warning, might well seem as much ambush as surprise was not lost on Cameron, so that when he imagined that moment—and how many ways there were to imagine it!—the pleasure he felt was tinged with a guilt that turned out, on inspection, to contain its own bittersweet traces of pleasure.

In the meantime, however, and for perhaps years to come before that fatal moment, his life would continue apace. There were gardens to finish, friends to entertain, a dinner to cook for Elliot Shore. At the register, he laid out his items, then reached into Max's cart, which crowded him from behind, to remove one of the less blighted heads of romaine.

"Hey." Max slapped playfully at his wrist.

"I forgot salad makings. Please. Just one."

"Well, okay." Max adopted his queenliest voice. "For you, my dear, and in the interests of romance, *anything.*"

Across the cashier's face, Cameron noticed, there passed the flicker of a grimace. That kind of disapproval still made him wince, and he judged her ruthlessly as she, in turn, rang him up: one of those cowish, depressing young things just out of high school—if she'd even managed to finish— and longing, no doubt, to be pregnant as soon as possible. Well, good luck finding a boyfriend, sweetie, he thought with idle malice.

"Paper or plastic?" asked the bag boy, in contrast a cute kid with spiked hair and little gold hoops in both ears.

Do we have a secret? Cameron wondered idly, telling the boy, "Paper, please," even as he registered, simultaneously, two things: that the name tag pinned on the cashier's rather generous bosom (the term *udder* came to mind) proclaimed HI, MY NAME IS DONNA, and that Roy Vanderhof had just joined them in the checkout line.

For a moment Roy ignored them, picking up a colorful tabloid from its rack and briskly perusing it ("Is Ricky Martin Gay?" the headline inquired. Who the fuck cares? thought Cameron). Then Roy slid the paper back in its place and observed, in that languidly garrulous way he had, "I see somebody's shopping for their bunny rabbits."

Cameron recognized the tone of banter he and Dan used to enjoy in the Main Street Luncheonette, that slightly volatile mix of boastful threat and surly good humor. He also knew Max thought such humor small-minded and depressing, one more reason to despise the way rednecks navigated their diminished world.

He waited for Max to fire off some tart response or other. But instead Max said, without deigning to cast a glance in the mayor's direction, "What's happening out on the old post road, Roy? Can you tell me that? Or do you and your brother want to talk to the lawyers?"

Roy shrugged—affably enough, it seemed to Cameron. Roy was buying a box of coffee cakes. He'd set them down and was fishing for his money. His hand groped about in the pocket of his worn work pants in a faintly obscene way. Finally he withdrew a money clip thick with bills.

"Always had me a sweet tooth," he mused, as if to no one in particular, perhaps only to himself. "Sugar diabetes runs in my family, so I suppose I'd best be careful. There's so many things to watch out for in the world. You can't hardly keep them all straight, now can you? Howdy there, Donna."

Of course, Cameron thought, only now making the connection. It made perfect sense. With curiosity, sadness, despair, he looked at this Donna who'd known Jesse in ways he could only imagine.

She had not a clue who Cameron was. *He's this sick faggot who's sweet on me,* he could hear Jesse explain to her. *He's my ticket on the gravy train, the goose that's gonna lay me a golden egg.* Not that poor Jesse had any idea what a splendid golden egg had already been laid. For one miserable instant Cameron permitted himself the hopeless fantasy of getting fucked by Jesse Vanderhof, perhaps of fucking him in lovely return.

It wasn't about that. He told himself it never had been. But then what, exactly, *was* it about?

"Talk to me, Roy," Max demanded. "You know perfectly well Otto's got his guys out overtime. Cameron here saw them firsthand, working Sunday afternoon—didn't you, Cameron?"

Roy seemed not to care. "Donna," he said, attempting to reach across Max with a fistful of bills, "let me pay for my sweet rolls here. I got to be on my way."

"Are you planning on answering my question, Roy?" Max had raised his voice. "And don't touch me," he warned as Roy flung down several singles on top of the lettuces on the counter.

"Let me on by here. Keep the change, Donna, keep the change." Roy's bulk made it hard for him to squeeze past Max and the shopping cart, hemmed in as they were between the counter and racks of candies and tabloids. Roy's elbow snagged a display box. Chocolate bars spilled onto the floor. Donna said, "Oh!" and Cameron wasn't sure what happened next, only that Max's shopping cart suddenly shoved him from behind, propelling him past the register and Donna and the bag boy, who continued to grin at the whole scene. Cameron caught his balance as the empty cart rolled slowly to a stop against a shelf stocked with bags of dog food and birdseed. When he looked back, he saw that Max and Roy and the whole rack of candies and tabloids had fallen together in the narrow aisle, and that Max and Roy were pawing at each other in an attempt to clamber to their feet.

Max was the first to stand, exclaiming, "He attacked me. The fat bastard attacked me. Did everybody see what happened? Did you see?" His voice shrill and unsteady, he appealed especially to Donna, who looked flustered, and the grinning bag boy, who did not.

"Whoa, there," Donna said, as Roy hoisted himself up with the help of the grocery counter. "Is everybody okay?" The commotion had attracted the few other customers in the store: an obese woman in soiled pink sweats, the friendly lady with a crew cut who worked in the post office, an old man Cameron always saw trundling up and down Main Street on some unknown or unknowable mission.

While Roy examined, with a thoughtful look, the crushed box that held his coffee cakes, Max walked back and forth agitatedly. "I will not be harassed by this man," he said to the group at large. "I'm filing charges. I'm calling all of you as material witnesses."

The memory came to Cameron: Oberlin, a dorm corridor, Max launching a well-aimed, vicious kick at Glenn Watkins's butt as Glenn walked away from a completely obscure argument they'd been having about Theodor Adorno and the Frankfurt School.

"I'll do that," Donna told the bag boy, who, still grinning as if at a private joke, had retrieved Max's cart and was busily stowing the lettuces there. She pointed to the carnage. "You clean up *that* mess." She was bossy, Cameron noted. Demanding. She craned her head around to ask in a petulant voice, "Where's Mike gone to? He's never around when you need him."

"The manager?" Max said. "I think I'd like to see the manager. Definitely."

"Sir, I'll call him if you wish." She was, in fact, rather a bitch.

"Please," Max told her.

"I'm going," Roy announced. "Max. Sorry I tripped over you there. My big clumsy self."

"You can't go," Max said. "You just assaulted me. Everybody here can give testimony to that."

Roy looked around—at Donna, at the bag boy. Neither said a word. He fixed a faintly humorous, distinctly long-suffering gaze on Cameron.

"Max," Cameron said, "I really think it was an accident."

Max stopped his pacing. "Whose side are you on here?"

"Let it go." Cameron touched Max's shoulder. "Really."

Roy shrugged and began a stately amble toward the door. "Good day, everybody," he said without looking back, waving one hand vaguely in their direction.

"Let the man go," said the old man. "He's the mayor. He don't mean harm to nobody in this town."

"Isn't you the one that's running for mayor too?" asked the woman in pink.

"I'm asking you all to vote for me this fall. Even you," Max added, turning to Cameron.

"Sir," said the bag boy, his voice vaguely familiar (but from where?) as Max, triumphantly, headed for the door. "Don't forget your groceries."

TWENTY-SIX

"Come on, come on," he told her. "We're gonna be late."

"I told Mike I'm not leaving till seven." Donna made a big deal of looking at her watch. "It's only six fifty-five."

He hated her when she was like that—a stickler for detail. Who cared about five minutes one way or the other, except when they were going to make you late?

"Kyle's waiting out in the truck," he reminded her.

"So? He can wait. Anyway, how're four of us supposed to fit? And what's that cut under your eye? Honey, you hurt yourself. You gotta bruise coming on."

"Yeah, yeah. A little accident. Leanne ain't coming."

"Oh," she said warily. When Kyle and Leanne were on the outs, you were extra careful, you treaded on eggshells. Donna knew that as well as anybody. She peered at Jesse more closely. "You got stitches. What happened?"

"Just a fucking scratch," he said, remembering how there used to always be some busybody teacher at school asking the same after a rough weekend had rumbled by. And really—now as then—it was only a dull throb, nothing he couldn't get used to. If anything, it'd serve as a useful reminder lest he was tempted to forget himself.

"You get hurt more than anybody I know," Donna said.

"I'm still here, ain't I? And what're you looking at?" he asked C.J., who was grinning that stupid grin he always wore.

"You shoulda been in here earlier," C.J. said. "You missed all the excitement."

"What the hell's he talking about?"

"You know this town," Donna said. "Never a dull moment."

"That's why I'm starting to hate this place. I'd be thinking of leaving if there was anyplace else to go."

"Soon as I graduate," C.J. volunteered, "I'm moving to New York. Gonna go to art school there."

"You fucking would."

"Jesse, your language is totally outta hand today," Donna pointed out.

"That's not the only thing. Now fucking come on, will you, before Kyle loses his patience out there."

They'd brought the last of the wine out onto the front porch. To the west, salmon clouds painted the sky. Supper had not been an unmitigated success.

"Nothing with a central nervous system," Elliot had delicately explained as Cameron set before him a plate with a nice filet of scrod poached in lemon juice.

There'd been a time—years ago, in New York—when, at Max's urging (but then, how much hadn't he done at Max's urging?), he'd gone with some regularity to a dim but well-meaning therapist; this was exactly the kind of pointless thing he and Sydney Rothenberg, Ph.D., might have talked about—had he really forgotten his guest was a vegetarian, or was some subconscious aggression making itself known?

Elliot, as usual, seemed entirely forgiving, making do happily, as he insisted several times, with a spartan alternative of potatoes, salad, bread. Now he sipped his chardonnay, pausing to remove, by touching the tip of his little finger to the surface of the liquid, some small winged insect that had landed there, whether by mistake or ill-conceived design. He blew a gentle breath to dry its wings, then shook it free.

"That was kind," Cameron told him.

"All things considered," Elliott mused, "I'm probably a Jainist at heart."

"Remind me who the Jainists are."

"Respect for all life. Tread as lightly as you can in this world."

"Oh. Right. The ones who won't kill a fly. We used to laugh at the notion of that when we were kids. I don't know why we found it so funny. Kids are cruel, I guess."

He'd really hoped, when he got home this afternoon, to find a note, a phone message, anything.

For a moment they sat in companionable silence. He had to admit: there were times when being with Elliot was entirely pleasurable in its own quiet way. Still, some restlessness swarmed in Cameron. All evening, Max's encounter with Roy had been on his mind. It was the first thing Elliot had reported on his arrival; he'd heard about it from Irving Fischman, who'd heard about it from Daryl. Already the incident had blossomed into full-blown fisticuffs; Max had had to go to the emergency room for stitches—six of them—under his right eye.

"Do no harm," Cameron said. "It's not possible, is it? I mean, I think about my own life. What has it been, really, but a long, way too long, trail of damage? It's not that I've ever intended to do damage, not in the least—but I'm afraid, when I look back, what I see is an awful lot of wreckage. Just this afternoon I was thinking about how Dan and I once had a fight over whether Ceylon and Sri Lanka were one and the same. Isn't that depressing? But when I think about our relationship, especially the last couple of years, that's exactly the kind of thing I remember."

"And who turned out to be right?"

"Actually, I was. I went and looked it up in the atlas."

"So there," said Elliot. "You should never argue about factual stuff. Those arguments are way too easy to lose."

"You know what his response was? He told me, 'You always have to be right, don't you?'"

"Changing the terms of the argument. An infallible strategy."

"I got a postcard from him today. I don't know whether I'm disappointed or relieved. We haven't talked since he blew off my party. Sometimes you just want a clear end to everything. But that's not how it usually works, is it? Things just go on and on."

From the woods, three white-tailed deer sauntered leisurely out onto the road. A doe and her two fawns, their summer spots just beginning to fade. Halfway across, they stopped, pausing motionless, alert. He and

Elliot watched in silence. Cameron held his breath; he waited for the sound of a car approaching around the curve. The deer too seemed to hold their breath. Of what were they aware? Could they sense two humans sitting on the front porch of an old farmhouse? Did they care?

From up the road came the whir of an engine. Cameron could hear it clearly; he knew by the sound the vehicle was speeding, as cars and trucks often did on that lonely stretch by the cemetery. Still the deer hesitated. The doe took a tentative step forward, but the fawns remained frozen. It had been that same spot exactly, hadn't it, where a deer had gone down his and Dan's first morning in the house. An omen, he'd always thought. Slaughter Alley, Dan used to call their bit of road.

As if responding to some secret, agreed-upon signal, all three creatures, in the same instant, sprang into motion, bounding gracefully across the other lane and into the safety of the woods. Traveling much too fast, a black muscle car barreled around the curve and roared past the house.

"I should tell you," Elliot said in the silence that followed. His tone was quiet and serious; something in it made Cameron sit up. "I've been seeing a lot of Irving Fischman this past week. Since your party. It's just sort of happened. The chemistry and all. Funny how that is. But I'm eternally grateful to you. If it hadn't been for your party . . . Well. I just wanted to tell you." Elliot paused a moment, contemplating his wineglass, then said, looking at Cameron with a rueful smile, "I hope you're all right with that."

"Well, why not?" Cameron said, a flicker of not-quite-identifiable emotion vanishing as quickly as it arrived. "Why shouldn't I be? I like Irving. He's nice. I've known him for years."

"He's very nice," Elliott agreed.

So there. He'd had his chance, which he'd assiduously refused to take. He told himself he begrudged the two men nothing at all.

"I firmly believe," Elliot went on, as if it were something he'd rehearsed, "if you're not in love with somebody, then you're not living; you're just surviving."

"Absolutely," Cameron told him, wondering if Elliot meant it, in part, as a reproach.

"I was of course up-front with Irving about the health." Elliot leaned forward earnestly, and before he said a word, Cameron already knew. "Between you and me, he's positive. Asymptomatic so far, knock on wood. He'd rather keep it quiet. He's on an excellent regimen, has got a great doctor down in New York. He's one of the lucky ones. People like us just missed by a few years, didn't we?"

It was a line of thought Cameron never liked. "I always thought we were luckier than we had any right to be. Considering."

"True enough. But now I want you to tell me one thing. Are you ready for it?"

"Well, I suppose."

"You have to be honest with me now. Who are you in love with?"

Cameron laughed nervously. It was one of those questions—*What're you looking at?* was another—that had always alarmed him.

"What's funny?"

"You know, the boy I had a crush on back in high school used to ask me exactly that. Usually after he'd been singing the horny praises of some hot girl or another. So, of course, I could never tell him."

Toby used to ask it too, he remembered—years into their beautiful ordeal together, trying to pry from Cameron something, anything, to assuage his own guilt or failure or regret. But Cameron, alas, had had only the same answer all those years.

"So are you not going to tell me?"

Cameron wondered what he could possibly tell about Jesse Vanderhof that would make any sense. That they'd had a couple of conversations in a hospital room, that he'd offered some financial assistance Jesse had reluctantly but, finally, willingly accepted. That that was about the whole of it, except—

What it was, exactly, he could scarcely put his finger on. The summer had been, in a sense, the sum of everything. No one else looking at it could see that. It was a secret sense—the way all his realest, truest loves had been secret—because how could you ever begin to express qualities that were, by definition, ineffable? But he sensed them nonetheless, their presence suggestive, bright, bewildering all at once.

In spite of everything, it brought out, at the moment, the worst in him. Finishing off his wine, he found himself wondering aloud, as if idly, "Didn't Gandhi think love for particular human beings is wrong, since it gets in the way of our general love for humanity?"

"Gandhi, I'm sure," said Elliot with surprising energy, "could probably have afforded to get laid a little more often than he did. God, you frustrate me, Cameron. I've tried, I've really tried, but I don't get you one bit."

Cameron was silent for a moment. "I haven't treated you very well, have I?"

Angel Face was finally mixing it up. After letting himself get taken down half a dozen times, then cowering on the ropes, he'd decided to come out swinging. It took the Animal by surprise. Before he knew it, he was flat out on his back. Angel Face did a few mincing little steps before throwing his full weight on the Animal, who looked down for the count with the referee calling out, "One! Two!"—then the Animal heaved Angel Face off him like he was nothing more than an old pillow. The crowd in the Mid-Hudson Civic Center loved it, Jesse too—the rush of adrenaline, the hisses and catcalls from the audience when Angel Face did his pathetic little victory dance, the roar as the Animal surged back from defeat.

You knew in the back of your head it was all a fix, but that still didn't take away the excitement once things got all stirred up. Besides, Angel Face was getting the drubbing he deserved.

On the other side of the ring, a fellow hoisted a sign he'd spent some time on. NO FAGGOTS IN THE HOUSE it spelled out in big, angry letters. Jesse read it and felt everything shift to slow motion. The blood rose to his face; his cheek ached where Kyle had struck him. The Animal pushed the faggot's pretty face down on the mat. Almost playfully, he swatted Angel Face's butt. Donna loved that. "Hoo!" she shouted. "You go there, Animal."

For a few minutes there he'd been able to forget, but now it all swarmed in his head again. What did Kyle see when he looked at that sign? You'd have to be blind to miss it.

On the other hand, this was kick-the-faggot's-butt night. It was hard not to get into the spirit.

He saw an opening and took it. "Don't Angel Face look a little like C.J." he said, nudging Donna with his elbow.

"What?" Donna's face was all red with shouting.

"I mean, if C.J. got himself all pumped up on steroids," he said, practically shouting to make his words heard.

"You're weird. What's this thing you got about C.J.?" Donna wanted to know as Angel Face slithered between the ropes trying to get out of the Animal's reach—but to no avail. No place to run, no place to hide. The

Animal followed him out onto the floor. Angel Face's white-blond hair was spiked just like C.J.'s. Anybody could see that.

"I don't got nothing about C.J.," Jesse yelled over the roar of the crowd.

"You're always talking about him."

Donna's words gave him pause. "No, I'm not always talking about him," he told her. "When's the last time I ever said a word about him?"

"Whatever," Donna shouted, craning to see the tussle on the floor. Angel Face had broken away again. He leapt onto the ropes. Somehow he'd managed to grab a bright blue feather boa along the way, and he taunted the Animal with it like he was a bullfighter or something.

"What're you two on about?" Kyle asked.

"Nothing," Jesse said, making himself concentrate on the wrestlers in the ring, but what they were doing all of a sudden seemed completely depressing and pointless. He tried to reassure himself he had never had a second thought about C.J. one way or the other, but the reassurance was longer in coming than he'd have liked.

Angel Face whipped his boa around his neck and struck a pose while the crowd jeered. "Heaven may have kicked me out, but I'm proud of what I am," he proclaimed, sashaying back and forth. "Go to hell!" somebody yelled, and soon everybody was chanting, "Go to hell! Go to hell!" Kyle especially. He pumped his fist in the air and screamed like Angel Face had gone and stolen something from him. It was that personal. He'd been swigging whiskey nonstop ever since he'd come back from Leanne's without Leanne.

The emcee was whipping the crowd into a frenzy; not a single person in the auditorium didn't hate Angel Face. Jesse hated him too—perhaps most of all. "Throw him down, tear him up!" chanted the crowd. Jesse yelled along for a while, but all the yelling he did wasn't keeping at bay the one thought that kept muscling its way back in. *Kyle knows*. No matter what Jesse said, no matter what he did or how he made up for his lapse, Kyle would still always know. Till the day he died.

With a great roar, the Animal rushed the ropes and Angel Face and his feather boa were history.

Two blond chicks in bikinis—twins as near as Jesse could make out—took the Animal by his elbows and paraded him in a victory circuit around the ring. The mooks were going wild. "Hail to the Animal," they shouted, stretching out their arms and bowing down to him like he was their king and master. The Animal made his famous face. The two blondes just smiled, like they were having the time of their lives strutting with the hero.

"What'd you think of that, little brother?" Kyle asked as they all pushed out into the humid streets of downtown Poughkeepsie. Streetlamps lit everything in an orange glow. Kyle was flushed and breathless, like it was him personally who'd won the fight, but without Leanne to hold on to his elbow. "The Animal rocks," he said, jabbing at thin air. "Or was you rooting for Angel Face?" He skipped ahead, then stopped dead on the sidewalk. "Come on, Jesse." He walked backward in front of them. "Tell us who you was rooting for."

"You're too much," Donna told him.

"He thinks he knows better than the rest of us," Kyle said.

"Don't listen to him—my brother's drunk," Jesse countered, grinning to show Donna it was all in fun.

"True. I'm fucking drunk as a damn skunk. And why not? Life sucks. Everybody dies. And now my brother's lining himself up with the faggots."

"There's a low blow," said Donna.

Everybody, it seemed, was having fun.

"You heard him. He just admitted it." Kyle was beside them now, walking like a puma on the prowl for anything to bring down. Whiskey without Leanne was a mean recipe.

"If you knew your brother like I know your brother," Donna told Kyle, "you wouldn't say nothing like that."

"Hey, Donna." Kyle all at once sounded serious, even deadly. "You know what? I don't wanna know my brother the way you know him."

"Donna, that's gross," Jesse joined in. Still, the picture was there in his head—for a moment it must be in all three of their heads.

"I know what I know, is all," Donna said with a smirk. Hooking her foot around, she kicked Jesse lightly on the butt. She was sticking up for him. He was proud of her—and to show it, he draped his arm over her shoulder.

But she ducked him. "You're all sweaty."

"No, come on." He tried again to get an arm around her.

"Get off me," she said, pushing him away. It made him angry: What right did she have? But they'd come to his truck. Gleaming even in the low light of the parking garage, she sat high and proud. Despite everything, a thrill of possession seized him as he unlocked the door. They set-tled into the wide cab, Donna in the middle.

Kyle fiddled with the AC controls, then sat back to admire the cool air that breathed across them. "Jesse tell you how he come by this beauty?" he asked Donna as they headed out toward the bridge.

"You're poking me with your finger."

Kyle shifted himself in the seat to look at her full on. "You got no idea how Jesse got this truck, do you?"

"I don't ask too many questions. I never have been one to do that. So what're you saying? Jesse, did you steal this truck?"

"I didn't steal nothing," he said, instantly regretting the lie.

But Kyle didn't seem to care about that little, unforgettable detail. "Go ahead and tell her how you got it," he urged. "Your girlfriend should know."

"You tell her, since you're so interested," Jesse said, already as good as doomed. "What's your story of how I got this truck, Kyle? I'd be pretty interested to hear that."

"I'm all ears," Donna said, like she still thought it was all some joke she wasn't in on yet.

"You ain't gonna like this," Kyle said.

Jesse concentrated on the road. They'd crossed the Hudson, back to their side of the river, where he knew all the shortcuts, the back roads and dark lanes, for whatever any of that was worth. There was nothing he liked more than driving fast on country roads at night. Probably he got that from Pop, who used to take them riding on summer nights back when they were kids, to cool them off. But there was no going back to any of that.

"He tell you about Cameron Barnes?" Kyle asked.

"I don't think I've heard that name." Donna touched Jesse's shoulder. "You ever tell me about that person, hon?"

Jesse bit his lip and looked steadily ahead of him. There'd been a mil-lion chances to mention Cameron Barnes, so why hadn't he? And how did Kyle know he hadn't? Did he just guess? Jesse hadn't thought anything of it at the time, but now he saw how it must look kind of odd.

He hated having to explain Cameron. "He's this guy I been doing some work for. I don't tell you everybody I work for. I'd bore you to death if I told you everybody."

"Yeah, he's been working steady for this gay dude," Kyle said. "And guess what, this gay dude decided to reward Jesse for all his help. Help for, well . . . whatever. So he gave him the money to buy a truck." Kyle slammed the dashboard with his palm. "This truck. Which reminds me. I got more booze around here somewhere." He fiddled with the glove compartment and finally cracked it open. "Handy little hiding place for stuff, don't you think?" He brought out a nearly full pint and offered it to Donna. "Want a bite?"

"I could do that," she said, to Jesse's disappointment. She swigged, then handed it his way.

"I'm driving," he told her.

That made Kyle laugh. "We're driving our new truck. We got to be careful driving our new truck."

Jesse turned onto the old post road that the highway department had been improving in the last couple of weeks, only to remember, too late— but what did it matter now?—that he'd brought Cameron this way, before everything went as dark as the fields and apple orchards that lay on either side of them. To the northwest, heat lightning flickered. He remembered riding in the backseat, warm summer nights, Pop humming a tune at the wheel, and it used to scare him, those distant sheets of light with no thunder, no rain, just a kind of menace in the air.

"You're jealous, is all," Jesse decided to say. "This baby could of been yours, only you didn't go earn it like I did. You just had a thought, then you forgot about it. Left me to do the legwork. Well, I did the legwork. And so I got my reward."

"So that's how it is," Kyle said. "No more to it than that?"

"I don't really know what either of you're talking about," Donna said, taking Kyle's bottle from him and helping herself to another swallow.

"I don't either," Jesse said. "And I don't think Kyle does either, so let's just forget it, okay?"

"Fine with me," Kyle said. "You make your choices, you live with them. Like Pop always said."

"Pop's got nothing to do with this."

"Now I'm really confused," Donna said.

"Donna," Kyle said in a quiet, even voice. "Why don't you find something on the radio we can listen to. You can do that, can't you?"

Jesse could feel Donna stiffen next to him. He'd always figured it was a good thing, somehow, that Kyle made her nervous. Now he wasn't sure. But then, he thought as Donna obediently raced the radio up and down the dial in search of something good, pausing on one station for two seconds, then another, he'd stopped being sure about anything anymore.

"Drop me off at Leanne's," Kyle commanded as they came into Stone Hollow. For the last few days Jesse'd been avoiding Main Street every way he could. He remembered how Main Street used to be deserted at night. Now there were little shops he'd never set foot in, there was that café with the weird name. Through the big windows strung with little white lights, he could see people in there. A chalkboard set up on the sidewalk advertised LIVE JAZZ. With a stab of misery he remembered the house with the darkroom at the other end of Main Street.

"She expecting you?" Donna was asking Kyle.

"If she ain't, she's got a surprise coming."

Jesse hated it that he wondered whether Perry was home right now. It was like a kind of madness trying to shoulder its way in. They turned off Main Street, onto the road that led back to the little neighborhood of house trailers where Leanne lived. Out of the dark a gust of grief struck Jesse's heart. He only wished he could have Kyle back on his side.

And it was just like his brother to know once again, miraculously, what he was thinking. "No hard feelings now, okay," Kyle said, climbing down from the cab. "I love you, man. Whatever. Take good care of this boy tonight," he instructed Donna.

"Don't I always?"

"I worry about my little brother, is all. I want the best for him. Know what I mean?"

"Get the fuck out," Jesse said, relieved and grinning. They were having a good time tonight, weren't they? Just like they used to. Just like they always did.

Lit by the TV's flicker, Sean was passed out on the sofa, an empty beer bottle cradled between his thighs. "Shh," Donna whispered, though it seemed to Jesse they could probably shout "Fire!" and Sean wouldn't come to his senses. Head thrown back, he breathed in big, irregular gulps.

Jesse gazed on him with pity and envy. At least they weren't using him anymore—not since Kyle turned twenty-one. That was one shameful thing, at least, Donna was never going to have to know.

She held on to him, a little unsteady, as they crossed the living room. From experience Jesse knew she got horny when she had a couple drinks in her. Not being the least bit drunk—or horny, either—he almost wished he'd taken a few himself.

She closed the bedroom door behind them and smiled, her eyelids half-shut in a way he knew she thought was sexy.

"So what kind of mood are you in?" she asked.

"I don't know. I'm tired is all."

"You want to lay down on my bed?"

It was either do that or leave, so he cleared a space among the pile of stuffed animals and reclined on the soft mattress.

"There." Donna sat down beside him. "Ain't that better?"

He had the absurd notion he was about to burst into tears—but for what reason? He took up at random a little monkey and started idly to twist its head.

"So what was Kyle on about back there?"

"The fuck if I know."

"There's stuff you're not telling me. That I know already."

"What stuff? I been working for this guy, that's all. He loaned me some money for my truck. What else Kyle's got going on in his head, beats me."

"Your brother's got you pissed off about something. I don't know what it is, exactly. Here, give me that before you break it." Donna plucked the little monkey from his grasp and set it on her nightstand.

"I ain't gonna break it. Jesus. And don't talk to me about my brother. That's between me and him."

She peered at him like he had some suspicious odor about him, some giveaway look in his eye. "You got nothing to prove with me, you know."

"What's that mean?"

"You just ain't." She touched a finger to his lips.

It wasn't what he expected. It made him flinch. He took her wrist and steered her touch away from him. "I told you, I ain't feeling much in the mood tonight."

"Seems like you're never much in the mood."

"What does that mean?"

"You keep asking what everything means. I don't know what it means. Just what it sounds like, I guess. You're supposed to be my boyfriend."

"I *am* your boyfriend."

"It don't feel like it sometimes. You make me feel lonesome when I'm with you. That's a shitty feeling, Jesse. That's not the way you're supposed to feel when you're with somebody."

"Well, I feel lonesome too. If that makes you feel any better."

"No. It don't. What's *happening* to us?" The way she said it, with a little wail at the end, it sounded like a line she'd been wanting to use for a while now.

"There ain't nothing happening. Everything's the same as it's always been. You just need to trust me on that."

He was angry at all of them, he thought, and hard to say who he was angriest at. Donna for trusting him like she did. Brandon for bringing him down and Perry for spying him out. Or maybe Kyle, who delivered him to the lion's den in the first place and then left him there to fend for himself. Your own brother shouldn't do that, and why he did—well, that was the mystery.

If there was anybody at the root of his troubles, it was Cameron.

"I gotta go," he said, rising up abruptly. "I can't be here no more tonight."

"Suit yourself," Donna told him. He'd hurt her feelings, he knew. He was sorry about that. But she wasn't the one he needed to talk with face-to-face.

Her voice stopped him at the door. "When you get it all sorted out," she said, sounding angry as well as hurt, "why don't you come tell me about it?"

TWENTY-SEVEN

Cameron stood at the sink, hands wrist-deep in soapy water, and searched about for a last fork or spoon. He'd apologized to Elliot as best he could for having been so reluctant a friend, though he'd been able to see, even in the midst of apologizing, that he remained as recalcitrant as that piece of silverware that eluded his searching fingers. (But there it was; he rinsed the salad fork and stuck it in the dish rack.) The evening had ended in a fond hug, no bad feelings, an affirmation of what Elliot insisted was their ongoing spiritual connection. But Cameron had to wonder: Would Elliot find any reason to continue their friendship now that Irving Fischman was in the picture? He tried to imagine inviting the two of them to dinner sometime, but the prospect made him feel indescribably weary.

Let them visit each other in their dreary little houses and cook gourmet meals of spaghetti squash and talk about radiance and the soul and life on meds.

He rather despised himself for his thoughts.

With a thump the cat door swung open as Casper glided through. "Oh, hello there," Cameron said as the cat nudged his calf. "Hungry?"

Casper gave a sprightly meow.

"Okeydoke. Have I got a treat for you." From the refrigerator Cameron removed a nicely poached fillet of scrod. Unlike Elliot, Casper went after the delicacy with a blissful little growl. "Now where's your sister? Out catting around?" How Dan used to hate it when he talked to the cats. But then Dan had never heard Toby Vail sing snatches of opera to *his* beloved Cleopatra.

From its magnet on the fridge door, he plucked Dan's postcard. The front featured a buff young man in Speedos posed against the trunk of a palm tree: GREETINGS FROM FABULOUS SOUTH BEACH! "It truly is fab here," Dan had written on the back in his sloppy scrawl, "but, you know, I miss you a whole lot. I wish you were here, tho' I know how much you'd hate it! Much love."

Cameron barely wanted to register that last phrase. He wanted Dan to move on; really he did. On a winter's afternoon they'd let themselves get lost on lonely roads to find this house they'd made their home. Then, unaccountably, they'd let themselves get lost all over again.

And yet Dan had written him those words. He felt all at once completely at the end of everything. Dan, Toby, all the rest of them. Now Jesse too was gone. Somehow he knew that—had known it for days but had kept avoiding the sickening certainty. He couldn't be angry with the young man, exactly. Hadn't he suspected all along, down in the cobwebbed basement of his heart where all the bodies would eventually turn up, that Jesse was only after something or other? For a mere fantastical flicker of a moment he'd thought his young redneck might be, if not gay, then at least fascinated by something he saw there. Now he recognized his mistake: he'd attributed to Jesse only the baffled motives he himself possessed, when in reality Jesse's desires had turned out to be entirely straightforward. Who knew the high point of everything would turn out to be a trip to Big Al Bosco's, an exchange of a few thousand dollars? There was still the will, of course, which he'd conceived as a sort of superfluity, a staggering above-and-beyond-all-measure, but which now turned out to be merely an extension of the obvious.

Sated, Casper licked one paw and rubbed it in circles over his nose, his forehead, a flexible ear. Now, no doubt, he'd find one of the Persian carpets to throw up on.

Past the kitchen windows, a glimmer of heat lightning to the west caught Cameron's eye. As a boy, he used to sit with the adults out on the wisteria-clad porch of his grandmother's house in Tupelo, waiting for the stifling heat to abate so they could all go inside to sleep. Their talk bored him; all that ever seemed to interest them was material things and their cost—how tomatoes were on sale this week at the Cee Bee Grocery, how little his mother had paid for the blouse she was wearing, how much his grandfather had gotten for the set of old chairs he'd sold—while out in the dark, beyond the porch, beyond the suffocating banality of the world, fantastic intimations of some other life lit up the sky.

Those flickers, restless as intelligence itself, still spooked and thrilled him.

Noticing the light on the answering machine was blinking—someone must have called when he and Elliot were out on the porch—he pressed PLAY, hoping against hope for the sound of Jesse's voice, even though he realized he'd never once actually spoken to Jesse by phone.

"Hey there," said Perry. "It's around nine. Just calling to see how dinner with Mr. Right went. Along those lines, I have a little story I think you'll be amused by. So call me when you have a chance. Oh, and thanks for looking out for Max this afternoon. What would I ever do without you? Good night, sweetie pie. And Max says the same."

He hoped Perry's story wasn't *too* amusing. Ever since brunch, he'd felt vaguely wary of his friend's sense of adventure—but why should that be? Whatever escapade Perry had been up to, it was sure to be scintillating. He'd call him first thing in the morning; it was too late now, just after midnight. Casper had already headed upstairs for his usual perch at the foot of the bed, and he should follow, but he felt desperately unready for bed. Against his better judgment, he opened another bottle of wine and took a glass out onto the back stoop. A late-summer drone of crickets spread itself over the garden. Somewhere in the woods beyond the road an owl's low-throated call answered another farther off. Meanwhile, the lightning had grown nearer; now a suggestion of thunder rolled with it over the horizon. In the still air he thought he detected the faint, delicious scent of rain—and at the same time, even fainter, a memory, almost a kind of déjà vu, something from long ago. He tried unsuccessfully to place it—all that remained was a feeling, a radiant sense of surprise, as if he'd made, once upon a time, a sudden unexpected but perfectly simple discovery that even now, years later . . .

A noise out past the lilacs interrupted his reverie. Cameron sat very still, waiting for the faintest rustle to betray itself. A possum or raccoon on its nightly rounds? A deer browsing among what was left of the ravaged hostas? The rampant bear people were talking about?

The animal moved, a pale splotch of white, and he realized it was no ordinary animal. "Who's there?" he said, feeling the old panic of being completely alone out in the country at night.

For a long moment there was no response. Then the figure stepped forward. He was dressed in camouflage fatigues and a white T-shirt. He wore the baseball cap he never seemed to take off.

"What's up?" Cameron asked, caught off guard but feeling a fierce rush of elation. "Where's your truck?"

"Up the road," Jesse told him, stepping reluctantly into the porch light's glow. "I'm parked at the cemetery."

Cameron saw that a nasty-looking cut marred Jesse's cheekbone, just under his left eye. The flesh was plum-colored and swollen. He appeared to have gotten stitches.

"Is everything okay?"

"Yeah, everything's fine. I mean, I guess everything's fine."

"What on earth happened to you?"

Jesse touched his cheek as if he'd somehow forgotten. "Oh. Me and Kyle was just fooling around."

"I see. I'd really hate for the two of you to get serious sometime."

"Yeah." Jesse turned aside as if to have a quiet laugh at his own expense, a rueful gesture Cameron loved.

"Want a beer?" he offered. "Or wine? I'm having a glass of wine."

"Man, a beer. I could use one," Jesse told him, seeming all at once to relax from some invisible tension that had held him rigid till now. "I'm glad I found you. It's been some kind of crazy evening."

"Tell me all about it," Cameron said. Almost giddy, he stepped into the kitchen, chiding himself for finding Jesse's distress more erotic than was either decent or prudent.

When he returned, Jesse had sat down on the porch steps; in the interval, a kind of defeat seemed to have settled on him. He took his beer with a mumbled "Thanks, man," as Cameron sat beside him and poured himself another glass from the bottle he'd brought out. He was flirting with a hangover, but the risk seemed worth it. As long as he didn't forget to take his pills before turning in.

This is really all I want from life anymore, he thought with surprised acceptance as they drank in silence. To sit with someone whose human mystery interests me. It was sexual but not sexual. It was a kind of tender curiosity, its own species of compassion. Why Jesse Vanderhof, of all people? Even now, he had no idea. But he honored the bewilderment, he bowed before the mystery with respect.

"I'm not a faggot," Jesse said. The young man's vehemence jolted Cameron from his contentment. "Everybody seems to want to think I am. *You* probably think I am—but I fucking swear I'm not."

Cameron hesitated, torn between disingenuousness and the truth. "I never thought about it one way or the other," he said finally, adding, "You are who you are."

"That ain't good enough. What I come here for was to offer you back your truck."

Cameron felt a vise clamp around his heart. This was worse than he'd feared. "That's crazy," he said. "Why on earth would you do that?"

"You wouldn't know the half of it."

"Try me."

But Jesse had run out of words. He swigged his beer, nearly finishing the bottle in a couple of determined gulps, and Cameron was afraid the young man meant to leave. Had he been drinking before? Cameron couldn't tell, but he felt a kind of tension in the air. Redneck Alcohol Danger, Dan used to call it.

Jesse rolled the bottle between his two palms. "I'll be honest with you," he said. "It don't look right, me accepting a gift from somebody like you. I don't know why I didn't think of that before. People're bound to take it the wrong way."

"What people?" Cameron asked, conscious he didn't much need to know; he only wanted to make Jesse have to name names. Had he known all along the truck might get the kid in trouble? Surely that couldn't have been any part of his aim.

"My brother," Jesse said. "My girlfriend. The folks who matter to me."

The admission made Cameron wince—but when had he ever had any illusions about where he stood? And yet he'd made his will out to this wretch. What an amazing, unfathomable thing to have done.

"They don't want you associating with a faggot like me. Is that it?"

Now it was Jesse's turn to wince, he noted with satisfaction. It felt like some sort of victory, though he hadn't, till now, quite understood there might be a war on.

"You gotta know how it is," Jesse said, turning to him with a miserable smile. "You've lived in this town long enough." With a savage flick of his wrist he pitched the empty bottle into the dark. The bright sound of its shattering on the bluestone flags startled them both. The gesture seemed both impotent and strangely satisfying. Had Max and Roy felt that this afternoon, as they fell to the floor in a murderous heap?

"Sorry, man. I didn't mean to do that. I don't know why I did."

"Maybe nothing else suggested itself," Cameron said. "Don't worry about it. I'll clean it up in the morning. Go get yourself another one if you want."

"Do you mind?"

Are you kidding? Cameron thought, though all he said was "Of course not. Go ahead."

Jesse stood up, turned to go into the house—but then he stopped. "You ever . . . I mean, what I want to ask is . . ." He stood there tongue-tied, bursting, it seemed to Cameron, with everything a shattering beer bottle couldn't relieve. "Ah, forget it," he said, and lurched into the house.

Cameron downed his own glass and poured another. He was definitely going to be hungover tomorrow—but the intoxication he was feeling had nothing to do with alcohol. It was adrenaline and desire and the scary, joyous sense that the whole summer was coming to fruition exactly here.

"I have to ask you a question," he said as Jesse settled back down on the steps beside him. "If you were planning on giving me the truck back, why'd you park up at the cemetery?"

"I didn't know I was going to talk to you till I seen you."

"You mean, till I caught you out there?" Cameron knew he was taking a risk, but he went on with it. "How many times've you been out here, Jesse, waiting to get caught? And besides, why give me the truck back? Why not just sell it? Keep the money. Is it because it's too late? The damage has already been done?"

A grumble of thunder seconded all that series of questions.

"It's gonna rain," Jesse said, as if desperate to turn the conversation aside. But Cameron was pretty sure he didn't really want that. It was just the reflexes of a lifetime talking.

"Anyway," Cameron continued, "what am I supposed to do? Put up a billboard saying Jesse Vanderhof never had a thing to do with that faggot Cameron Barnes? Cameron Barnes personally guarantees to everybody who might be interested that Jesse Vanderhof's no fag—cross my heart, hope to die? Look," he pressed on, "what were you and Kyle fighting about?"

"You." Jesse flung the answer back at him. "We was fighting about you. So there. That's why I can't see you no more. After all you done for me, I got to wash my hands of you."

"Am I really that dirty, Jesse?"

"It ain't that."

"Then what? There's a whole lot I'm not getting here."

"Look, man," Jesse half-shouted. "What the fuck do you want from me? Tell me you're no different from any other faggot out there who just wants to suck my cock."

Cameron had to laugh. "Please. I wouldn't touch you even if I could. But I also have to tell you—I wouldn't be here right now if it wasn't for you. I'm not talking about seizures and fainting spells. I'm talking about everything else. So what do I want from you? What do people *ever* want from each other? I don't know, Jesse. After all this time, I really have not the faintest idea. So I thought we could be friends, and just leave it at that."

Jesse had set down his beer; now he put his head in his hands. Cameron resisted mightily the urge to reach out and touch his shoulder, quite certain if he did such a thing, the young man would explode with even more force than a random bottle slammed against stone.

"You don't understand," Jesse practically wailed. "It don't work that way around here." He stood abruptly, fists clenched in front of him, his jaw working angrily. "I feel like I walked into some kind of a trap when I met you."

"I didn't set any traps."

"No, I know you didn't. You couldn't ever of known beforehand what kind of trap you were gonna be for me."

And with that Jesse leapt up from the porch steps and was off. Cameron hardly had time to call out after him before he'd rounded the corner of the house. His own heart pounding, he crossed through the kitchen and living room and came out onto the front porch in time to hear the crunch of Jesse's soles on asphalt as he sprinted up the dark road—as if his very life depended on precipitous flight. With an uneasy sense of elation Cameron stood looking in the direction of the cemetery. He wasn't sure what he'd gained, but he knew he'd touched something that had been waiting a long time to be touched.

Would he see Jesse again? He told himself it didn't matter, but of course it mattered very much. For all the young man's health, his youth, that rough sexiness he seemed so completely unaware of, Cameron found he didn't envy Jesse one bit. His life was going to be hard, perplexed, incoherent—to the very end. Would he ever know anything like the simple happiness that doomed faggot Cameron felt at this very moment as fat, lazy raindrops began to fall on the parched ground? All around him rose that saturated smell, as if the earth really did have secrets to give up to the rain, the night. Slowly he walked down the front steps. He spread his arms wide. There was no wind, not even the trace of a breeze. The lightning and thunder had moved their show to another part of the sky. He moved aimlessly across the lawn to the driveway, feeling with a shiver of delight the weight and coolness of each raindrop as it touched him.

Headlights swung round the curve from the cemetery. All these rednecks insisted on driving way too fast. Jesse was no different. Cameron watched the truck barrel down the straightaway; he was prepared to wave as Jesse sped past in his great urgency to get—where? Home? His fat bitch of a girlfriend's lair? For a moment he allowed himself to picture the poor kid driving in a panic all night, how dawn would find him farther from home than he'd ever been.

The shriek of tires surprised him. For one terrible second he imagined Diva had darted into Jesse's path, but then he saw that the truck had abruptly swerved into the driveway. It came toward him at full speed. The glare of its headlights blinded him. Surely Jesse saw him, he thought, taking a step back and shielding his eyes even as he heard the skid of tires and the scatter of gravel.

"Hey," he called out with a jittery laugh as the truck's bumper came to rest barely inches from his knees.

"I didn't even see you there," Jesse told him. Cutting the headlights, he hopped down from the cab. "Honest. I wasn't meaning to scare you."

Though Jesse did scare him, a little—the way Tommy McCalla used to scare him when he'd come up behind him between classes and clap a hand on his shoulder and whisper with hot milk breath in his ear, *See you after school, buddy.* If it was fear, though, it was delicious fear, thrill-of-being-alive fear he hadn't felt in years. Between that brand of fear and the miserable fear of death lay all the world.

"You're back," he said, as nonchalantly as possible.

Jesse looked around as if hopelessly lost. "Yeah. I'm back. Don't ask me why."

"So what *am* I supposed to ask?"

"Don't ask nothing."

Cameron sighed, and ventured the question anyway: "Then am I right to be thoroughly confused right now?"

"I could leave if you wanted me to," Jesse said, sounding all at once annoyed—as if his gesture were in danger of being taken the wrong way. "I don't know what the hell I'm doing coming back here."

"I don't know either," Cameron said. "I wish I could tell you."

"Fuck." Jesse gave the epithet its full, fecund weight.

"Yes," Cameron agreed. "What *I* always say when in doubt."

But he wondered whether he should be joking with the young man. That sprint to the cemetery had hardly cleared Jesse of what seemed so pent up inside. If anything, he appeared more desperately conflicted than ever.

"Look, I ain't gonna beat around the bush with you. Can I stay here tonight? I mean, I'm fucked if I do and fucked if I don't. I got no other place to stay right now."

There was a propulsiveness to his words Cameron scrambled to make sense of. "Of course you can stay," he said. "Why not? I've got a guest bedroom nobody's used in ages."

"I wasn't thinking of going to bed."

"Oh," Cameron said. "I see."

"What the hell," Jesse cried out, throwing his arms around Cameron, who wasn't sure whether he was being attacked or embraced.

"Wait a minute," he warned, feeling the young man's chin dig into his shoulder. Then he realized Jesse was sobbing. He could actually feel tears soak through his shirt—all that with the rich scent of rain, as if some invisible bloom had opened in the night. More shocked than surprised, he allowed himself to put his arms around Jesse in return, holding him cautiously, then with more assurance as the young man made no move to break away. Never, he felt, had he been so tightly clutched, so hung on to for life itself. He let his hands explore, tentatively, through that white T-shirt, the forbidden territory of Jesse's muscular back. What was sym-

312

pathy, what was eros? It was a moment he hadn't dared imagine—yet he realized there hadn't been an instant all summer when its absurd possibility hadn't lurked somewhere in the shadows.

But this was crazy. This threatened the ruin of every delicate bit of balance he'd pursued. He didn't quite dare, but what he wanted, under the circumstances, was simply to laugh out loud—with wonder, amazement, sheer terror.

"I'm fucked, man," Jesse repeated into Cameron's shoulder. "You don't know how fucked I am."

"How, Jesse? How are you fucked? You've got to tell me. I can't help if I don't know what it is. We can talk, right? We talked back when I was in the hospital. I cherished that."

Why not say whatever he felt? He'd waited for this disease to change him for the better—to free him into some bolder sense of life. But it hadn't happened. Staring death in the face—that impassive, indifferent face he knew so well by now—he'd remained trapped in exactly the self he'd always been. Funny. For an instant there, as the truck roared toward him, he'd almost wished Jesse wouldn't stop. He'd almost wished it could end right there.

And maybe Jesse hadn't stopped. Maybe this was the actual collision, right here and now.

Loosing Jesse from him, he spoke briskly. "Let's go inside. I'll make us both a nice cup of tea. We'll sit down and talk this thing through."

Jesse's first thought as Cameron disappeared into the kitchen: he should bolt outright. "I ain't no good at talking," he warned his invisible host.

"Not to worry." Cameron poked his head back into the room. "We can sit on the sofa in absolute silence, if that's what it takes."

So he was in the faggot's lair. That was the image that came to him, and though he tried to shake it, it persisted. The faggot's lair. He heard that exact phrase in Kyle's voice—as if his brother stood there in the room with him.

But of course his brother wasn't there. Jesse was completely on his own.

And for the moment, the faggot's lair seemed strangely tranquil. The blue walls warmly held the light. The little white busts regarded him coolly from their perch on the mantel. Every antique or expensive-looking thing sat confidently in its place. Then the black cat walked carefully and silently across the room. His mom was superstitious about black cats; Pop always used to tease her about that, calling them the devil's own luck.

"Hey, Blackie," he said to the devil's own luck as Cameron came back into the living room. He carried a tea tray just like you'd expect a damn faggot to. Jesse's heart sank. He tried to stave off the thought that he had to get the hell out of here pronto.

"Her name's Diva. The white one's Casper. He's upstairs asleep. I never introduced you properly, did I?"

"I've seen them around," Jesse said, aching to land Diva a good kick to show her what was what.

"Alas, it looks like our rain's petered out for the time being. All blow and no show. The tea's lemon balm, by the way. From the garden. It's quite settling."

Jesse thought, all things considered, he'd rather have a deep swig of whiskey. He wondered if you could ask for something like that from a guy like Cameron. Instead, without pausing to consider just how deeply crazy he could be, he said, "So, do you want to give me a blow job?"

He decided he really liked the look on Cameron's face at that moment. *All blow and no show.* Well, that would show him. The poor guy stood frozen, still holding his tea tray. He didn't smile, but his eyes were smiling. Smiling and bright and shining—like maybe now it was Cameron's turn to cry, thought Jesse, remembering with humiliation how, for a second or two, he'd lost all control back there.

"I thought we already had this discussion," Cameron said. "So I presume you're joking." He set the tray down on the coffee table like nothing in the world was out of the ordinary. In response, Jesse slid down a couple of inches on the sofa and opened his legs a little—just to make a point. Inside his jeans, he could feel his cock take on some serious weight.

"I told you I'm fucked. That's why I'm here. So why not let's just fuck it all up good."

"Jesse, Jesse." Cameron sat down next to him on the sofa, but made no move to touch him.

Still, Jesse felt his heart quicken. He'd close his eyes, lie back, and let it all happen.

"Do you even know what you're saying?" Cameron was asking him.

"Of course I know," Jesse said. "What do you think I am—stupid?" He wanted to say, *Your friend was happy enough to blow me,* but he didn't; he wasn't sure how that would go over. He had the distinct sense his three minutes with Perry had made everything that much worse. But what could be worse than exactly this—sitting here expectantly on the sofa of a faggot who really seemed not to have a clue he could go ahead and put his lips around your cock?

"Go on, man," he urged. "I swear I'll let you."

"I haven't tried to get into your pants," Cameron told him. "I hope you don't think that was ever the case."

"Then what was you trying to get out of me all summer?"

It seemed to exasperate Cameron. "Jesse, I like you. That doesn't at all mean I was trying to get something out of you."

For one terrible moment, Jesse could almost believe what Cameron was saying was true. "You're so full of shit," he said, "it makes me fucking crazy."

"So what're you going to do? Beat me to a pulp? Ransack my house? Isn't the real question here, What do *you* want from *me?*"

So Cameron knew, then. It was that simple. The guy wasn't stupid—he'd known all along what was up.

"You're supposed to want to give me a blow job," Jesse told him. "That's how it was supposed to work."

"It?"

"The plan. The one me and Kyle put together. You were supposed to get interested in me."

Was there any use in hiding anymore what was plain to see?

"I don't believe this," Cameron said, but he sounded like it amused him more than anything. He didn't seem angry in the least. "This is just too rich." He shook his head. "The two of you, thick as thieves. It's priceless."

A disturbing thought occurred to Jesse. "You didn't know?"

"I could've figured it out. Sure—if I'd wanted to."

"It don't change nothing," Jesse said. "You can still touch me if you want. I don't mind. Give me your hand." He took Cameron's hand and laid it halfway up his thigh. "Go ahead. Don't you want to?"

"Why do I still have this feeling you're just waiting for me to put a move on you and then you'll haul off and let me have it?"

"You don't get it, do you? Here, look, I'll prove to you." Jesse reached over for the zipper to Cameron's slacks, but Cameron's fingers circled his wrist and held him back.

"You really don't want to blow me, Jesse. You don't want anything to do with me that way. I don't think you have any idea what you'd be getting yourself into."

"AIDS don't matter," Jesse said. "It's in my future already. There's no way around that." So there. He'd gotten that out in the open. What an incredible relief.

"But that's crazy," Cameron told him. "Why would you even think something like that?"

"Look at you."

"Well, yeah. Look at me. What exactly do you see when you look at me, Jesse?"

"I been trying to figure that one out all summer. Crazy, huh? All I seem to think of is Pop laying there in the hospital. That's what I can't get out of my head. If it ain't AIDS, it's gonna be something else. There ain't no stopping that."

Only now did Cameron let go of his wrist. "This is insane, Jesse. You don't have to go through any of this with me. If you want to know the truth—I've already made out my will. And guess what? You're getting a whole lot of money from me."

The taunt enraged Jesse. "You're such a fucking liar," he said. "Why would you think about doing anything like that?"

In answer, Cameron only threw his head back and laughed. Jesse watched his Adam's apple that a karate chop could so easily crush.

"Why would I?" Cameron asked. "Hilarious, isn't it? Absolutely one hundred percent mad if you ask me."

Jesse couldn't think of a thing to say. Then Cameron looked at him, suddenly serious, all laughter gone. Their eyes met and held in a challenging stare. Jesse dared himself not to look away. He and Gary Dunkel used to play that game, once upon a time. Gary's pupils were two shades of blue set in a clear field of white. Cameron's eyes were all bloodshot, his pupils, nearly black around the edges, fading to the color of that sourwood honey Pop used to slather on a biscuit for breakfast, then lick off his fingers. They were sitting so close he could feel Cameron's warm breath. Surely they could say something, either one of them, and break this contest that wasn't a contest exactly—but what was it? He had the awful, lonely feeling that what he most wanted was to stretch out on that sofa and ask Cameron to lie on top of him and just hold him tight. How did you ever tell a guy you wanted something weird and stupid like that? He used to think about Gary Dunkel doing something similar, back when he and Gary were still friends and maybe, just maybe, he liked to think, that wouldn't have been impossible. He used to wish Brandon would want something along those lines too, but Brandon only ever wanted the one thing.

He used to wonder—even now he still fucking wondered sometimes, when he was temporarily out of his mind—what would happen if Kyle, coming home late one night and a little drunk, mistook the bottom bunk for the top.

Of course Donna lay on top of him like that all the time on that bed of hers with the stuffed animals, but that was just the dead weight of sorrow suffocating your chest, same as every other day. He didn't hate Donna DuBois. He didn't have a molecule of feeling about her except maybe shame. She'd want to kill him if ever she found out, and there was nothing he'd deserve more. Probably he'd hand her the knife and say, Go ahead, carve me up good.

Then Blackie walked through the room again, this time toward the kitchen, intent on something but not showing the slightest bit of interest in either of them. Still, looking away from Cameron's unwavering gaze for that single split second, Jesse knew he'd lost.

"It's very late," Cameron said, the spell mercifully broken (how ridiculously long could it have gone on?). "We're both of us, I suspect, totally confused. And I, for one, am exhausted. I'm going up to bed now. I have to take my pills. Look." He reached out and boldly touched the tip of a finger to Jesse's chin (you'll live to regret all of this, he thought—though whether the doing or the not doing he wasn't sure). "You're very beautiful. Handsome, I should say. You sort of break my heart. But there's a limit, alas, to everything."

Jesse hardly flinched. He seemed vaguely stunned—but then they both were, weren't they? A little reluctantly, Cameron stood. Go for it, you fool, he could hear Max urge him. You've earned it. You've got nothing to lose.

Poor, brilliant Max: after all these years he didn't understand a thing about his foolish friend.

Jesse had stood as well, but seemed utterly uncertain what to say or do next, waiting motionless as Cameron turned off a light here, locked a door there, poured himself a tall glass of springwater (he didn't dare raid the Stoli, though the idea of offering Jesse a nice stiff drink at this point did occur to him briefly).

"So make yourself at home," he told the young man. "The guest bedroom's upstairs on the left; there're towels in the closet."

"I'll be fine," Jesse mumbled, though he hardly sounded fine.

"Well, then. Good night."

With great melancholy joy Cameron climbed the steep steps of the house he and Dan had so lovingly nursed back to life. Hard, even impossible, to fathom what had just happened. Equally impossible to imagine where it could go from here. Odds were, the morning would find Jesse long gone—and just as well. He carried more trouble than Cameron had either the stamina or audacity for.

Stepping into the bathroom, he doled out his pills and capsules from their many bottles. Then he began the task of swallowing one after the next, each rewarded by a gulp of cool, delicious water. When he looked up, he saw that Jesse stood in the bathroom door watching him. He hadn't heard him come up the stairs.

"Give me one of those," Jesse said.

"What on earth for?"

"I want to take one."

Perhaps this had been fun and provocative, but now Cameron thought he just wanted Jesse to go. Max's altercation with Roy, his own fatiguing dinner with Elliot—really, it had been too long a day. It must be well after midnight by now, and the young man's exciting animal energy was beginning to wear on him.

"I don't really think it'd be good for you."

Jesse held out his palm. "It won't hurt. It's just medicine. Give me one of those there."

Cameron hesitated, unnerved a little by Jesse's intent look. "Well, here," he said. "Try this. It's Zoloft. An antidepressent. I guess it can't hurt."

Jesse took it without water.

"I'm going to brush my teeth now," Cameron said. "See how exciting life is around here?"

He took extra care, even cleaning the back molars he often missed. He spit in the basin. As always, there was a little blood.

Jesse watched him in silence. As soon as he was done, Jesse said, gesturing for the toothbrush, "I need to brush my teeth too."

Cameron knew all about bug chasers; he found them both pitiable and despicable, fucked-up club kids, for the most part, whose hip suicide pacts he absolutely refused to indulge. He hardly expected such a thing from someone like Jesse, though at the same time he registered a perverse thrill at the thought that Jesse would want to share everything, even a deadly disease, with this man he hardly knew. It wasn't love, then, but something much vaster, an ocean in which they both hoped to drown . . .

"Forget it," he told Jesse. "Even without AIDS, sharing a toothbrush is just plain unsanitary. Don't they teach you kids anything nowadays? Anyway, I think I've got a new toothbrush somewhere here." Cameron opened the medicine cabinet and pulled out a brush still in its box. "Use this. I'm going to go to bed now. I'll see you in the morning, okay?"

He could hear Jesse brushing methodically, spitting, brushing some more. Crisis averted, he sat on his bed and began pulling off his shoes and socks. Though he couldn't help but wonder, Had he held Jesse *too* much at bay? Was he a fool not to have at least given him a blow job, which after all was a fairly safe activity for both parties, as such things went.

As if in answer, Jesse came and stood in the doorway. Excited and at the same time sick in the pit of his stomach, Cameron pretended to ignore him. He stood to undo his trousers. Folding them as he always did, he laid them on a chair.

"I don't know what you're looking at. This old body's not a particularly pretty sight these days."

"That don't matter." Jesse pulled his T-shirt over his head, wadded it, and tossed it on the floor.

"Thank you," Cameron managed to murmur, his long-dormant cock beginning to stir. "You have no idea what that means."

"What?"

"Doesn't matter. Not in the least." So this was where his renewed potency had brought him. It had all been an exquisite trap laid by the wily, unruly god of the garden, that nameless dread that overtook one alone, in a grove of ancient trees, or at the edge of a meadow, among flowers and silent butterflies and loudly chattering birds, the threat of disorder lurking in the very heart of the principle of order itself.

Awkwardly, Jesse balanced on one foot, then the other, to remove his workboots. Unsnapping his camos, he tugged them off. He wore gray boxerbriefs, with a white band of elastic at the waist. Cameron could see the upturned curve of his cock outlined there. He unbuttoned his own shirt and folded it and laid it atop his trousers. He considered stepping out of his plaid boxers but decided not to. He'd never liked sleeping completely naked; he wasn't about to begin now. And sleep was what he intended, he told himself nobly—no matter what disturbances Jesse might be up to.

Pulling back the sheet, he said, "I don't know what you're planning. All I'm doing is going to bed. As you can see."

The night was warm but not stifling. Even on the hottest nights he slept with a sheet over him; otherwise he woke with an ache in his shoulder. He tried to make himself comfortable. "You might want to turn out the light," he said.

Then Jesse was beside him in the darkness. He felt the sheet lifted up, the mattress sag as the young man slid in next to him.

"Don't say nothing," Jesse said. "We don't need no more talking right now, okay?"

Cameron lay motionless as Jesse's hand crept across his chest. He felt the young man snuggle his head into his shoulder. The hand explored freely, testing a nipple, ruffling the hair of an armpit. Cameron could feel Jesse's erection blatantly poke against his thigh.

"We're just going to sleep," he reminded his bedmate.

"Shh!" Jesse said. "Just lay on top of me, okay?"

"Isn't it a little warm for that?"

"Then I'm going to lay on top of you."

Cameron didn't resist. He was too curious to see what confusions Jesse needed to work through. Anything too compromising, he'd put a stop to in an instant. The young man's innocence both charmed and puzzled him. All he wanted, apparently, was some very basic intimacy. And he couldn't get that from his girlfriend? Still, Cameron knew all too well how there were times when only the arms of another man around you would do.

"Oof," he said. "You're crushing me."

"Sorry. Just let's lay like this a minute, okay?"

Cameron put his arms around the firm young body that was so pleasantly smothering his. He hugged tight, and Jesse returned the embrace, which evolved into a kind of slow-motion wrestling. Cameron found his hands massaging Jesse's narrow buttocks through the cotton of his briefs; his dry lips brushed a salty shoulder. He felt a fist clasp, briefly, his own fired-up cock, which had managed to steal through the slit in his briefs.

"Okay," he cautioned sadly. "Let's cool down here. We're going to sleep, remember?"

"Yeah, man," Jesse said, reluctantly releasing him from his grip. "I know. We're just going to sleep."

Sleep, though, was more easily courted than caught. The cut under his eye throbbed. By the faint light that seeped through the bedroom window, he lay propped on his elbow and studied the unconscious form next to him. Cameron snored, his mouth fallen slightly open. Jesse fought back a twinge of repulsion. It seemed he just kept crossing one line after another—but if there was a point of no return, where was it? And how would you ever know for sure once you'd reached it?

This, he was afraid, was pretty damn far. He practically never spent the night with Donna. Once or twice back in the beginning, but then he came up with the line that he couldn't get a good night's sleep unless he slept alone. Maybe that was true. He sure wasn't sleeping now—though he did feel strangely at rest, if that was possible with all these feelings churning through him. He knew what he'd done was off-the-chart crazy. He knew Cameron was a walking death sentence. What he also knew was that he could've gone all the way if Cameron hadn't called him off; he wouldn't have cared a bit. But could that be true? How could you be so scared of dying and at the same time court it like that?

He kept coming back to that notion of some point of no return, a place he'd sail past and be on the open sea. It wouldn't be in this town; he knew that. Not even here in Cameron's house shut away from everybody's eyes. But where?

If it wasn't for his snoring, Cameron would look like a corpse lying there beside him. His face had gone slack, there was this gauntness to him. It wasn't a body he longed for; he could see that easily enough. It wasn't Gary Dunkel, or even Brandon Schneidewind. Still, he was glad they'd done what they'd done. He replayed their slow grappling in his head. It didn't have to have ended. It could've gone on and on.

Careful not to wake Cameron—but he was out like a light—Jesse got up from the bed. He hesitated a moment, then slipped off his briefs. His cock, still half-hard, sprang free.

Moving through the dark rooms felt like trespassing, even more out of line than that day two months ago when he and Kyle had taken their measure of the place. They hadn't known what they were looking for then, and he wasn't sure he had any better clue now.

He wandered down the softly creaking stairs. Were the cats around? It'd be just like him to step on one and let loose a ruckus to raise the dead.

Because there were dead here, weren't there? Or was the joke on him, and he was the dead one, a ghost haunting these darkened rooms?

The whole house lay open to him—completely at his mercy. There was a time when Kyle would've given anything to see this. It would've been his dream come true. But now all that was changed. Standing in the middle of the living room, Jesse suddenly realized—he couldn't go back to Kyle. Or even if he did, his brother wouldn't have him anymore.

Was that the point of no return, then? If it was, it plunged him into emptiness, it forced him to sit down on the sofa like all the air was knocked out of his lungs. There was no way Kyle would have him back. Not after this.

Jesse wouldn't have to breathe a word of it. Kyle would still know. And Kyle would cut him loose forever.

The dark of the room spooked him. He flicked on the nearest light. The lamp on the end table revealed the living room he was starting to know too well. On the coffee table in front of him, a stack of books. Perry's beautiful book, he saw with distaste. Beside it, a photo album Cameron must have dragged out to take a look at. He'd never thought of a guy like Cameron keeping a photo album—but why not? Curious, he flipped the pages. Cameron looked so much younger, fuller of face, healthier. In one picture, he had his arm around this long-haired dude who flashed a certain heart-stopping smile, not unlike the one Gary Dunkel used to shoot his way across the crowded school cafeteria.

Page after page, Jesse followed the owner of that smile. He crouched on a city fire escape crowded with pots of red geraniums. He contemplated what looked like a fat joint while a black-and-white cat sat on his shoulder and rubbed its forehead against his earlobe. Wearing nothing but a tiny, olive green Speedo he cavorted in surf and napped on a sand dune. In very short cutoff jeans and a white wifebeater, his feet clad in sturdy hiking boots, he clambered over rubble, broken columns, crazy heaps of debris. For a moment you could almost imagine it the ruins of an ancient castle built by Iroquois kings. Was that a coffin carved out of rock? It sat precariously, its heavy lid partially ajar. The sun was bright up there in those mountains that were by no stretch of the imagination New York mountains. The sky was a velvety blue. Cameron and the fellow sat shoulder to shoulder, both smiling at the camera that captured them there so many years ago in such a faraway place.

Each page was six months, a year. Jesse recognized Max with no mustache and a lot more hair on his head; he recognized Perry in a kid not too much older than himself. With consternation, fascination, finally a kind of awe, he watched the long-haired dude lose his silky hair, his build, even his captivating smile. He watched him turn into a pair of bright, haunted eyes. So that was how AIDS dwindled you down. Pop on his deathbed hadn't been even half so wasted as that.

Interleaved between the album's last two pages was a sealed envelope. Inside, it seemed, were three or four more photos, but Jesse didn't need to see them. The end of something great and exuberant and enviable, he knew, lay hidden from all the world inside that envelope. Hidden, but for all that not quite vanished.

The night was humid, even oppressive; still, he had to suppress a shiver. Never had he felt so completely alone—the aloneness the dead must feel, stuck inside coffins, in sealed envelopes never to be opened, fading fast in the memory of the people who knew them so well, or at least thought they did, when they were alive.

TWENTY-EIGHT

The palpable sensation, as you come out of sleep, that you are not alone—in the bed, in the world. Could he have said, in those first half-waking moments, who it was, other than that whoever it was was *there?* For a long time he used to wake next to Dan and for a single bittersweet instant believe it was still 1982, that light-filled apartment on East Fourth Street, with Toby very much alive and well and no hint of the terrible future anywhere in him.

Jesse slept on his stomach, his face turned toward Cameron. He breathed lightly through his mouth. The cut under his eye looked ripe, ready to burst. A trace of crusty, golden ooze had seeped around the black stitches. Cameron had never noticed the barely visible splatter of freckles across Jesse's cheeks and nose. A couple of small acne scars by his mouth; faint stubble of overnight beard growth; whorl of a downy ear. A single mole on an otherwise smooth shoulder.

Last night's promise of rain had come to naught, alas, but happily so had his anticipated hangover. A front had passed through and the air was cooler, drier—almost with a whiff of autumn in it; his head likewise felt remarkably clear.

He didn't want to wake Jesse. He very much feared what a conscious Jesse Vanderhof might think or say or do on waking to find himself in a strange—no, impossible—bed. There was no excuse of drunkenness.

There was no excuse, period. Only the consequences, whatever they might be.

In the doorway, Casper crouched and glared at the trespasser who'd claimed his usual spot on the bed.

Cameron dressed quickly, without showering or shaving. In the bathroom he took his pills and brushed his teeth. Then he headed downstairs. One of the cats had brought in a field mouse and laid it on the kitchen floor.

"Was that you?" he asked, stooping to fill the food bowl for Casper, who'd followed him down. "You lethal beauty, you." He hated it when his cats killed things, yet at the same time he felt their pleasure.

Sweeping the mouse into a dustpan, he examined for a moment its delicate body, unmarked by any visible wound. Then he deposited it outside, beneath the lilacs that grew near the back stoop.

He was just stirring the pancake batter when he heard Jesse's heavy tread on the stairs. "So," he said without looking up, "I thought I'd make us some breakfast. Are you hungry? There's coffee."

Jesse said not a word, though Cameron could hear him pour himself some coffee.

"How do you feel?" he asked his overnight guest.

"How do you think I feel?"

The words brought a not-unanticipated chill to his heart. Cameron turned to face him. "Gee, Jesse. I don't know. I have no idea."

"This was in your closet." Jesse touched the faded flannel shirt he'd put on. "It's a little chilly this morning."

Cameron had worn that shirt only once; he remembered how comfortably it had fit, how soft against his rain-chilled skin.

"Funny to see it hanging in there with all your stuff."

"You should take it back if you want it."

"Take it back where? Nothing's changed since last night. I still got no place to go." Jesse's tone rebuked him.

"Well, so let's talk about it. What happens from here? You're not thinking of leaving town, are you?"

"Where the hell would I go? I ain't got nowhere else."

"You can certainly stay here. I mean, for a while at least."

"What'm I supposed to do? Hide out in the attic? Besides, every other frigging person in Stone Hollow's probably seen my truck out there by now."

"I'm still not entirely sure what you're hiding from, Jesse. Since I seem to be right in the middle of all this now, you've got to tell me. You're having girlfriend problems. Your brother seems to think you're gay, but you're pretty insistent that you're not. Yes? But just to complicate things, maybe you *are* having some confusions of your own. Am I on the right track?"

It seemed vaguely shameful to interrogate someone so miserable, but at least, finally—maybe—they were getting somewhere.

"Keep going," Jesse told him.

Cameron poured roundlets of batter onto the griddle. "I'm not exactly clairvoyant, you know."

"What you talked about that day in the hospital."

Cameron tried hard to remember what that might be. He had the sense he'd rambled over all sorts of topics while Jesse had sat and listened.

"When you was in high school," Jesse prompted.

It came to him with a kind of wonder. "Tommy McCalla. Of course. Now it all makes sense." Pausing for a moment to take it all in, Cameron flipped the pancakes with his spatula. "So. Are you still seeing this fellow of yours?"

The pancakes were done. He eased them off the griddle and onto plates.

"See him? I see him all the time. Every time I fucking turn around I see him. But I cut out all that shit with him a while back. I was supposed to get over it, you know? Like when you give up smoking—after a while the craving goes away." Cameron watched as Jesse poured syrup liberally. He was dying to ask who this fellow was. The absurd thought occurred to him that the fellow in question might be Kyle. But surely not? Even if it made a certain wild sense, he knew by now that life never managed that intense a dramatic economy.

"That friend of yours. Perry," Jesse said with badly feigned nonchalance. "He's some customer, ain't he?"

Cameron felt quiet footsteps of dread in his soul. "You keep bringing him up," he said. "I thought you didn't care for him much."

"I don't much think I do." Jesse stared at his pancakes. He hadn't so much as touched them. "Sorry. I guess I ain't all that hungry. Me and

Perry kind of tangled with one another a few days back. I ain't too proud of that fact."

So that was the little story Perry had been calling to amuse him with. Cameron was surprised only by how little the news surprised him.

"These things have been known to happen," he said—aware, all at once, of standing at a great distance from everything. "Especially when Perry's around. My impression is, though, it always takes two to tango. Or tangle, as you say."

"You must think I'm a fucking asshole," Jesse told him. "I never wanted to tangle you in all this. I swear."

"Don't worry about it."

"No, man. Don't you see? I'm gonna get you in big trouble if I stay here." Jesse hit the tabletop hard with his fist. "What the fuck am I gonna do?" he cried out.

"Come away with me," Cameron said. "We'll go to Turkey. I'm already supposed to go in October with friends of mine—Charlie and Tracy, you met them at my party. Think of it. Istanbul in the autumn. Cappadocia. The Mediterranean coast. I haven't been there in twenty years, but it's fabulous, let me tell you. It's the most beautiful place you'll ever go. I swear, you'll forget all about all this once you're there, like it was some bad dream that never happened."

Jesse only looked at him blankly. "You must be crazy," he said.

"No, seriously. Think about it."

"I gotta get out of here." Jesse stood abruptly.

"Where're you going?"

"I don't know. Just—out of here."

"Will you come back?"

"Like I said, man, where else do I have to go?"

But Jesse didn't move to go. Just as he had the night before, he fixed Cameron in his unfathomable gaze. There should be a special language, Cameron thought, reserved for moments when two human beings stared at each other like that, some syntax beyond anything ordinary speech could manage—but wasn't the stare itself, moody and questioning, wasn't the heavy silence painfully ready to burst open but incapable of doing so, wasn't all that already exactly the language he craved?

Then, without a word, Jesse had gone.

327

The logical thing would've been just to walk in like nothing had happened. Make himself some coffee, sit down at the kitchen table, wait for Kyle to come down, barefoot and hungover and sullen. They'd grumble a hello, maybe cast a suspicious glance at each other, then get on with it. But he couldn't do it. Kyle would smell his betrayal on him, a reek stronger than any whiskey or blood. He'd catch its sheen in Jesse's eyes, hear it crack the normal tone of his voice.

In a high state of unreasoning fear, he'd driven past the house a dozen times in that conspicuous truck of his, waiting for the coast to clear—and finally it had. First his mom's Crown Victoria, then Patti's Mustang, then at last Kyle's pickup—all disappeared from the parched lawn where they were parked in familiar disarray.

Poke raised his head listlessly to watch him cross the porch. He had to tug at the front door, which always stuck. Why did he feel like a damn thief entering his own house? Once inside, though, the ordinariness of everything struck him. The comforting smell of stale cigarette smoke, their mom's well-thumbed magazines stacked in a precarious pile, the crescent-moon-shaped wall shelf that held an assortment of glass figurines handed down from their Grandma Bondurant, the television set running with the sound off like it did nearly all the time, whether anybody was there or not. If he thought things through halfway calmly, he could see that the world hadn't changed overnight. What he knew in his own head wasn't what everybody else knew. To his mom, his sister—to nearly everybody he might come across, he was exactly the same Jesse he'd always been. Even Kyle remained mostly in the dark. Except for that stupid misunderstanding about the magazine, what did his brother know, really? Even now, Jesse found he could squint and half-pretend that episode had never happened; already he could imagine some time in the future when the embarrassing memory had faded away completely.

Then the bleak reminder: Kyle would never forget.

But about everything else—about Brandon, about Perry, even the madness that had transpired last night—the only person who knew the whole story, who could connect the dots, put everything together into one clear, undeniable picture, was Cameron.

If only Cameron could somehow be persuaded to vanish into thin air, that would solve nearly everything. He'd chattered on and on about wanting to go to Turkey (and who the fuck in their right mind would want to go to Turkey?). But maybe that meant he was itching to leave Stone Hollow; maybe that meant he could be induced to clear out for good. Then everything would be the same as it used to be.

Except there'd still Brandon, there'd still be Perry, there'd still be all those land mines out there that could blow up on him at any moment. That was what made it all so intolerable: never for an instant anymore would he have any peace; as long as he lived, everywhere he turned there'd be another reminder of doom waiting for him, the same doom he'd felt in the hospital room with Pop, when he'd realized some diseases were accidents but others were genetic, how in those cases your number was written from the instant you were born, your own particular death lying in wait for you all along, just biding its time. Every day of your booby-trapped life was another day it could happen.

He was halfway up the stairs when the sound of a vehicle coming up the drive made him freeze. It wasn't Kyle. From all those nights lying awake, waiting for Kyle to get home safe and sound, he was acutely attuned to the rhythms of Kyle's truck.

A glance from the bedroom window showed it to be their mom. Was it only yesterday Kyle had run off those fellows she wanted to sell the house to? He watched as she unloaded two bags of groceries from the trunk. Never before had he minded what his mom and Donna might say to each other in the Family Market's checkout line. Now he heard a tiny distressing voice inside remind him of the astonishing fact that he and his girlfriend had broken up last night—well, sort of broken up, like they only sort of did everything. Surely Donna wouldn't go around announcing such a thing before he'd had a chance to patch things up.

And why had they broken up, anyway? It all seemed blurry, without consequence. Still, the troubling realization swarmed all over him: he didn't have a girlfriend anymore. For two full years he'd had the incredible luxury of not having to think about that, the way you never thought about the roof over your head till it started leaking. Everybody knew a guy without a girlfriend was about the sorriest case in the world, and he'd congratulated himself on having successfully avoided that plight.

He remembered the secret kick in the pants she'd sent his way last night, outside the Civic Center, just to show she was with him. Boy, he needed that from time to time: that reassurance. Without it, he was too perilously close to nowhere.

He'd had the vague notion that he'd come home to grab some clothes and a few other things, but now the absurdity of that move dawned on him. Unless Donna was willing to take him in, he still had nowhere to go except back to Cameron's.

Hadn't she told him to come tell her when he got things sorted out? And wasn't he doing that right now?

The thought of sleeping in her bed piled high with those stuffed animals made his chest tighten. Still, what else was left? He'd given Cameron too many ideas; he couldn't spend another night there without feeling duty-bound to initiate another bout of wrestling, and by the unforgiving light of day he didn't feel so good about those shenanigans.

Then it occurred to him: maybe he should just go ahead and ask Donna to marry him. Wouldn't that put everything to rest once and for all?

The idea didn't seem too far-fetched. In fact, the more he considered it, the friendlier it looked. With a satisfying slap it'd swat down those fat, ugly rumors buzzing against the windowpane. It'd make a clean break, once and for all, with Cameron and all his dangerous crew. It'd give Kyle the proof positive he was looking for.

Best of all, Pop in his grave would grin with pleasure. It was the one thing Pop had asked of him—to marry Donna and give him seventeen grandchildren.

He wasn't sure he could do seventeen, exactly, but one or two—he could probably manage one or two. Why hadn't he thought of it earlier? It seemed so simple, such a sure thing, now that he turned it over and over in his mind. He'd propose, he and Donna would get a little apartment of their own, he'd be clear of this place. For all he cared, their mom could go ahead and sell to any clown that came down the pike. And if Kyle needed somewhere to stay, well, he was always welcome to stay with him and Donna—whether she liked it or not.

That last thought darkened, a little, his mood that had just begun to lighten. Nevertheless, it seemed urgent to put the question to Donna as soon as possible. Till he'd done that, the whole happy solution looked as fragile as a spider's web.

"Jesse? That you?" asked his mom as he pounded down the stairs.

"Hey," he said. "I gotta go."

"Where was you out to last night? Kyle was worried you didn't ever come in."

"Donna's. I spent the night at Donna's."

He saw her frown and immediately regretted the recklessness of his lie. He was acutely conscious that he wore Pop's old shirt, and he thought she must be too. Hadn't she seen him give it away to Cameron once? But she didn't mention it, though for a moment she touched his sleeve—like somebody who knew the whole of his sorrow, if not any particular shape it took.

"That cut's still looking ugly," she told him. "You take care of it. Don't let it get infected."

"Don't worry. Everything's under control."

"That's what your brother always says."

"And he's usually right, ain't he? We're Vanderhofs."

Her smile was tired, even exhausted; she released him from her touch. "Yes, my boys are Vanderhofs. That's very true."

He hated thinking about things too much, especially things that didn't concern him, but he carried the expression of her face with him to the truck. He'd never realized it before: unlike the rest of them, their mom was a Bondurant. Always would be. The rest had just been pretending, years on years of it. No wonder she'd been so eager to get out from under Pop once she'd done her duty by him. Who was he, of all people, to blame her?

He wished he had anything else to drive to the Family Market, but he didn't. First thing he'd do after Donna said yes was sell back to Big Al Cameron's damn truck, which was more trouble than she was worth. He might have liked to drive her into the quarry, let her sink among the bodies Pop always insisted were down there, but he needed the money. If nothing else, it'd cover apartment rent for a goodly number of months. And in the meantime, he could always drive Donna's crummy little Malibu till he got a real job and started to make money to live on, not that any so-called real job was going to be half as lucrative as working for Cameron had been. But he couldn't think about that now. Nor could he think about the ugly pleasure of slow-wrestling (why did it keep sneaking up on him like it did?). The two of them both frankly stiff and showing it, neither saying a word, almost like dreaming, like some delicious agonizing duel to the death. He could have put his hands around Cameron's throat and slow-choked him right there. Or better yet, Cameron could have reached out and done the same to him. He'd have welcomed that, wouldn't he?—just as much as he'd have been happy to swallow the man's poisoned come.

He couldn't really have wanted that, could he? But his throat was suddenly full with a sob he choked back, realizing, as he pulled into the Family Market's treacherously potholed parking lot, that from now on he'd always know he'd once offered to go down on a guy full of virus.

She didn't see him as he came in. She and C.J. were talking; C.J. had that stupid grin he always wore. There was something about that grin too, Jesse realized, that he would never quite get out of his head.

"Hey." He touched Donna's shoulder blade, taking her—he could tell—by surprise. "Catch a break, okay? I wanna talk to you."

She turned and looked at him. Looked right through him.

She slapped him hard across the face.

"Okay," he said. She'd caught him across his stitches; it took his breath away. "You and me still should talk."

"Dude, you're bleeding," C.J. told him with a nervous chuckle.

"Please," he begged. "This is really important. You're gonna want to hear what I have to say."

"I ain't in the mood for your apologies," she said as a customer approached the register—Mrs. de Hulter, whose daughter he'd hated, for a while, with such lightning intensity. She began to lay out her groceries on the belt. "Could you stand off to one side while I'm working?" Donna asked him coldly.

He was furious with her. Why had he ever, even for an instant, thought he could stand to be married to her? Touching his cheek, he examined the smear of blood on his fingertips. Busy bagging Mrs. de Hulter's groceries, C.J. beamed at him.

Jesse glared back. "What the fuck're you looking at?" he hissed.

"Have a nice day," Donna told Mrs. de Hulter. Then she turned to Jesse, arms crossed over her breasts. He hated her breasts; he hated her dull, lank hair, her fat wrists, her slobbering mouth when it kissed his; he hated everything about her. Her voice, though, had softened. "Honey, I opened your cut. I'm sorry. You just have me so mad right now."

"Can we go outside?"

"Two minutes. Not a second more. I ain't letting you get me in trouble."

"Fine," he said.

They stood under the front awning; he sensed C.J. was probably watching them through the plate-glass windows.

"You been using me all along," she told him. "Just like you and your idiot brother were using Sean."

"What?"

"Don't think I didn't know all about that one."

"We didn't use—"

"Don't fucking deny me. Low-down piece of shit."

He'd never heard her curse before. And he couldn't believe she'd dared call Kyle an idiot.

"I was gonna ask you if you wanted to marry me."

She just looked at him for a few long seconds. "Jesse," she said, "are you the biggest moron on the planet, or what?"

"So," Perry told him. "You'll be very interested to hear about my visitor the other day. None other than our luscious youth. He stormed right into the house, and practically before I could say Friend of Dorothy's, he was throwing himself at me. What choice did I have? I dropped right to my knees and gave him a blow job I trust he'll never forget. The poor puppy pretended to be totally freaked-out, but that's the name of the game, isn't it? He'll be back, I'm sure."

Cradling the receiver against his ear, Cameron listened in silence to the news that was hardly news. But of course Perry couldn't know that. Cameron considered what he might tell of his own strange adventure, but decided not to say a word. It wasn't that he feared jinxing anything; the whole episode was already thoroughly jinxed.

Still—surprisingly—he allowed himself a single flicker of hope. After all, for the briefest of moments, a drowning soul had clung to him as to a last, bleak bit of flotsam in the heaving ocean.

Of course, anything could happen. He'd no doubt been way too hasty in mentioning the possibility of Turkey. That could only frighten off somebody who'd hardly ever left the county before. But there were plenty of other ways of escaping Stone Hollow's shadow; young men escaped their hometowns all the time. Jesse too would learn the lessons of exile, if he dared.

Perry was still talking. "Let's just admit it. I'm such a hopeless connoisseur of cock. Nothing gets me going like a shapely, young, fully aroused penis. I had to call Max up at Zanzibar right away. Elvis has left the house, I told him. He knew immediately what I was talking about, God bless him. I mean, not Jesse per se, but, well, you know Max. He's so cool about everything. So compassionate. That's why our marriage is going to last forever."

Did he feel in the least bit jealous? He knew Max suffered Perry's escapades philosophically—"Thank Zarathustra for all that Nietzsche I imbibed at Oberlin!" Max would exclaim. As for Perry—despite all his predatory satisfaction, he could have no inkling what sweet agony it was just to be clung to, for a few plangent minutes, by Jesse's drowning soul.

"Well," Cameron said, "your news is certainly delicious. Thanks for sharing. I wouldn't have thought it likely, but there you go. I keep forgetting how unlikely a place the world turns out to be."

"You're not pissed, are you?"

"Why should I be? I think it's all rather, well, as you said, *amusing*. Comic, even."

"Good. I'm so glad you think so. Come to dinner soon. Bring Elliot. We'll grill swordfish or something."

"Sounds lovely. Talk to you later, Romeo."

So it would be all over town—at least a certain segment of the town. Every queen from here to Kingston would be in the know. Poor Jesse. He had no idea how marked he was—another piece of local trade, once possessed and now forever, at least potentially, available to anyone with the gumption to try for him.

No wonder the occasional homosexual gentleman had a nasty encounter from time to time with the locals.

The thought made him quail: Had he himself been far too reckless for his own good? He tried to calm himself on that score, reasoning that it hadn't, after all, been a sudden thing in the least, but rather the secret logic of the long summer finally revealing itself.

Not only a summer, but the breadth and length of a life itself. That, it seemed to him, was its dark and fateful elegance.

That said, he still felt restless, uneasy, exhilarated—an unnerving mix. Though the heat had held off, the morning's brave blue sky had given way to a dull sheen of clouds and haze. The quiet of the cemetery called to him, a leisurely circumnavigation of its grounds promising just the antidote to his unsettled state. Who knew?—he might even pay a visit (whether contrite or quietly victorious, he wasn't entirely sure) to poor Bill Vanderhof's grave.

He crossed the lawn, stopping at the mailbox to extract and examine the afternoon's arrivals—an appeal from the American Foundation for AIDS Research, a self-serving update from his state senator, a circular for the Family Market advertising, "Tuesday is Meat Day"—all of which he slid back into the box to retrieve after his walk.

Along the margin of the road, so far spared the highway department's noisy mowers, late summer flowers bloomed among the tall grasses: pale blue flax, Queen Anne's lace, wild bee balm. Several large lemon and black butterflies poked lazily among them. A dragonfly, fantastically double-winged, hovered nervously. In the woods a mockingbird poured out its delirious chatter.

A car went by, swinging leisurely into the other lane to avoid the solitary walker, a woodchuck, startled at his approach, retreated into the undergrowth, two brilliant goldfinches sailed from cover in bounding flight, heading, perhaps, for the feeders in his garden, and all at once Cameron felt seized by that same déjà vu that had flickered last night as he sat out on the steps, and that now left him, for a moment, without any bearings at all. Then the spooky disorientation passed, and he was walking home from the bus stop after school, his heart suddenly, without warning, full to bursting with Mitchell Johnson, not any specific image of his friend, only the luminous promise that, by loving the boy who played trumpet and was good at math and ate, every day for lunch, a bologna sandwich on white bread, the baffled fifteen-year-old who was Cameron Barnes could somehow succeed in transforming himself into someone more beautiful, more wise, more kind than he'd ever imagined he might be. It was an early Memphis spring, dandelions ran riot in the unmowed lawns, and as he walked, schoolbooks nestled in the crook of his arm, in no hurry to arrive anywhere at all, the sensation was so pleasant, the remarkable discovery he'd just made, as if his heart were a pouch he'd never looked in before, of whose priceless contents—even the possibility that it might contain any contents at all—he had, up to this moment, been totally unaware.

He walked at the same leisurely pace, no different at forty-six than he'd been at fifteen, still baffled, still borne aloft by that shimmering promise.

With a roar, an ATV burst from the woods up ahead and came to a halt at the edge of the road, amid the weeds and flowers and butterflies, the rider gunning his engine directly beneath one of the new NO TRESPASSING signs Cameron had angrily stapled to a tree trunk only days before.

"Hey," Cameron called out, waving both his arms. He knew the rider couldn't hear him over the roar of his engine—but he saw Cameron's gesture, and instead of turning tail and disappearing back into the woods, he waited for Cameron to approach.

"That's private property there," Cameron said a little breathlessly. "Can't you read? There's no trespassing."

The rider wore a helmet that obscured his face. He sat there, engine idling, just staring at him—undoubtedly with a mix of resentment and contempt. Cameron knew what these locals thought—the woods belonged to them, to do with as they pleased. They cared not a bit that they trampled ferns and lady's slippers and mowed down beech saplings and left empty beer cans everywhere. That times had changed, they didn't register at all. What's the good of nature, one fellow he'd accosted a few years back had complained, if people don't get to use it? Well, their stupid swagger didn't frighten him. He'd learned over time that the local rednecks were mostly cowards when you got right down to it, their biggest crime a kind of endemic thoughtlessness.

"I don't want you riding over there, tearing the place up," he said, suddenly furious at the whole benighted crowd of them. "I'm giving you a warning this time around. Next time, I won't hesitate to call the police. Okay? And tell your buddies—these woods are off-limits to ATVs."

He might as well have been talking to a stone, the figure before him showed so little reaction.

"You hear what I'm saying?" he shouted, needing a response—anything at all to show his words had some effect.

Without warning, the machine spurted toward him.

"Hey," he said, "what the hell are you doing?"

The rider took off his helmet. For one terrible instant, Cameron recognized in that thin, attractive face and those merciless eyes the Jesse who'd almost run him over in the truck last night, now returned to finish the job. Then he saw it wasn't Jesse at all, but rather that old original confusion he'd thought the summer had long since resolved. A thrill of fear went through him.

"Oh," he said, feeling both foolish and alarmed. "Kyle. I was just saying—that land's posted. No trespassing. I'm trying to give nature a chance to heal."

Kyle regarded him indifferently. Cameron thought he could smell whiskey.

"Seems like you don't mind trespassing too much when it suits your own purposes," Kyle said over the hum of his idling machine.

"Excuse me?"

"I said, keep the fuck off what don't belong to you."

"I have no idea what you're talking about," Cameron said, though the accusation, however baseless, still stung.

"What're you doing with my brother?"

"I'm not doing anything with him. What do you mean?" He felt, nonetheless, the same bolt of adrenaline he'd felt when Kyle had first shouted up to him on the front porch that lambent evening at the beginning of summer.

"Why'd you give him that magazine?"

"I'm absolutely clueless here, Kyle. I haven't the foggiest notion what you're talking about."

Sometimes in dreams—nightmares—he tried in vain to make himself understood to the wolf crouched before him, fangs bared, menace in its eyes and utterly beyond the reach of human language.

"That truck's pretty nice," Kyle said, sounding suddenly reasonable. But at once his tone turned again. "What else you been giving him? You ain't been giving him AIDS while you're at it, have you?"

"This is absurd," Cameron told him.

"Why'd he spend the night at your place last night? Why didn't he come home? His truck was in your driveway all night, I know, so don't tell me otherwise."

"You always keep tabs on Jesse like that?"

"Sometimes my brother ain't the brightest bulb on the tree. No sense of what's good for him. Always been that way. Maybe you noticed."

"He seems pretty clever to me," Cameron said, angered by Kyle's admission of spying.

"Stop pulling the fucking wool over his eyes," Kyle snarled.

Cameron could only laugh in disbelief. He resisted the urge to tell Kyle everything; that would only enrage him further, and Kyle felt very dangerous at the moment.

"You got to be smarter than anybody else," Kyle went on. "You and your buddies. Coming in here, treating this town like you own it. Declaring the woods off-limits. Buying up people's houses that's been in their families since shit knows when. I don't know if you know it yet, but word's out on you guys. Your faggot asses are fucking toast."

Cameron was uncomfortably aware how lonely a stretch of road this was between his house and the cemetery. In all their encounter, not a single car had passed by. But what was Kyle going to do? Run him down in broad daylight? Of course not. It wasn't so much the present as the future he had to fear, all the dark country nights that would never again feel entirely secure.

He tried to sound conciliatory. "There's an election in November. Everybody'll get to have their say in the ballot booth. It'll all shake itself out one way or another, I'm sure. Live and let live is my philosophy. But you've got to let your brother live too, Kyle. Like it or not. He's got to be able to live however he chooses."

"He don't fucking know what he's choosing. I don't know what you did nor how you did it, but I got to congratulate you. You've gone and got him screwed royally. All I got to say is, it ain't fair to them he belongs to."

So that was how it was. All at once Cameron saw clearly. What held Jesse back wasn't an intangible muddle at all—no, what gripped poor Jesse by the throat and held him so ferociously possessed an entirely palpable form after all.

Cameron aimed his blow carefully. "You made a mistake, didn't you, Kyle? Jesse told me about the little scheme you two had. But you messed up. You weren't paying enough attention; things got out of hand. That's what happened, isn't it? Your little brother slipped right out from under you, and now you're furious. You're determined to get him back. Well, I think maybe it's too late for that, Kyle. I think maybe Jesse's gotten away from you for good."

338

With an angry hiccup Kyle's machine leapt forward. It was strange—almost as if Cameron knew what was coming the instant before it happened.

He felt himself fall.

Had he actually been struck? He didn't think so. He felt nothing, no shock or blow to the body. But he was lying flat out on his back, he was sure of that. He'd only had the wind knocked out of him. He lay still and waited to return to himself. Somewhere off in the woods a mockingbird warbled excitedly, running through half a dozen different voices. When had he last lain on his back like this? The sky above him was aqueous, milky, opaque. He waited for the brown spots that had plagued his vision all summer to start swarming before his eyes, but wait as he might, no flaws appeared.

Of course, Jesse thought as he drove away: Donna was absolutely right. He *was* the biggest fucking moron on the planet. He saw that now, just as he also saw that the one person who understood why he was acting like a moron was Cameron. Who'd have ever thought it? But Cameron knew. He'd been there, he'd lived through all that. And somehow he'd found his way out.

But to what end? Those pictures in the photo album last night haunted Jesse: that guy with the long hair and beautiful smile wasting away before his eyes.

He wasn't sure what he was going to say to Cameron. He dared himself to take up that offer of Turkey. Hell—he didn't even know where Turkey was; the only thing he knew was that joke Pop used to tell, about how Greece cooked Turkey while Italy gave Greece the boot. He saw a strange dirty town in an ugly desert, a crowd of jabbering foreigners surrounding him, gesturing rudely, sticking their fingers in his face, and his heart panicked, he was pulling out a gun, he was shooting his way through that crowd but they just kept surging forward along with a horde of camels and donkeys and stallions and goats, all practically indistinguishable from each other.

No way would he ever go to Turkey or the Greece that cooked it or the Italy that gave Greece the boot. There had to be some better idea. He and Cameron would talk. They'd come up with a plan. He was sure of it.

He'd just rounded the curve by the cemetery when he saw the flashing lights—a cop car pulled up behind another car on the side of the road. Flashing lights always made his heart clutch a little, even when he knew he wasn't the one in any trouble. He slowed, saw the officer was Kenny. His stout cousin stood talking to a man and a woman who'd both gotten out of their car. Kenny looked his way, and Jesse raised a hand in acknowledgment. Then Kenny motioned him over.

That was odd. Kenny on the job was focused and no-nonsense—so professional, most of the time, if you didn't know better, you'd think he hardly knew you. Only Kyle seemed to bring him out of his work shell.

Jesse parked on the shoulder. Insects ticked in the tall weeds. The pulled-over BMW had New Jersey plates—stupid weekenders caught speeding. The man and woman both had the leathery tans Jesse associated with rich people who wasted too much time on beaches and sailboats.

"Hey, man," he said to Kenny. "What's up?"

Kenny looked pale and flustered. "We're just waiting for the ambulance. We've got a body here."

"What?"

Kenny pointed toward a form lying half-obscured in the weeds. "Don't ask me what's up. It's a mystery."

Jesse didn't wait. He sprinted across the road, knowing even before he got close. Cameron lay on his back, staring straight up into the sky. Except for his open eyes, it was hard to believe he wasn't just napping.

"He's having a seizure," Jesse called out. "He had one like this before. We got to get him to the hospital."

Kenny was by his side. He put a hand on his elbow. "Steady. He ain't going anywhere. Poor guy's DOA. I checked him out. There's nothing to be done. You know him?"

Terror breathed all through Jesse. "Yeah," he said after an instant's hesitation. "Yeah, I know him. Cameron Barnes. I did some work for him this summer."

The man from New Jersey joined them. "Phil Bridges," he said. "You know, I sort of half saw it lying there, out the corner of my eye, thought it was a deer, but Kendra, she's the sharp-eyed one, she swore we needed to go back. 'It's a person,' she said. Good thing I listened. We couldn't get a pulse or anything. I tried calling on the cell phone but zip, nada. Coverage is really lousy up here. You guys need to put up more towers. I ended up going down to that house there to try to get some help. Car was in the drive, place was unlocked, but nobody home. I used the house phone to dial 911."

"He lived in that house," Jesse said.

"That's what Officer Vanderhof here just told me. I wonder what happened. Heart attack or something."

"There'll be an autopsy to determine all that," said Kenny. "I wouldn't speculate."

"He was in the hospital earlier this summer," Jesse volunteered, struck by just how eerily matter-of-fact he sounded. "He had a seizure. He was sick. I think he had AIDS. No, definitely, he had AIDS."

Kenny looked at him curiously. "Really?"

Jesse shrugged. Had he gone too far? Did Kenny have any reason in the world to be suspicious—of anything? "That's what he told me," he said.

It was like lightning from heaven had struck, the worst possible thing that could ever have happened. Jesse felt weirdly empty; he felt sheer, overpowering relief. He tried not to burst into tears.

What would they do if he bent down and kissed the dead man on the lips? He'd earned that right, hadn't he?

Though nobody would ever know.

"Did I hear you say AIDS?" asked Kendra. She was face-lift beautiful, if you went for that sort of thing. Jesse tried for half a second and failed miserably. "Honey," she said, putting her hand on Phil's arm, "it's a good thing you didn't try mouth-to-mouth."

"He was way too gone for that," said Phil, shaking his head and sounding genuinely apologetic. "Wasn't the faintest chance of bringing him back."

A second police car and an ambulance, lights flashing, sirens off, appeared around the curve. Jesse watched a green fly crawl from the edge of Cameron's lip up to the corner of his eye. It seemed obscene to stand there and let that happen—but it just showed how dead Cameron was.

Nobody would ever know with what strange thoughts Jesse Vanderhof had lain in a bed propped on his elbow watching that face for long minutes in the dim light. All of that was a dream now, all in the head of the dreamer. What you'd only dreamed, no one could charge you with.

Still, he couldn't shake the notion that Kenny was going to put him in cuffs right then and there because, face it: Cameron wouldn't have gone

341

for a walk when he did if it hadn't been for Jesse leaving the way he did. He wondered, had his friend been upset? Whatever the poor guy had been thinking those last minutes, nobody'd ever know. It was all erased just like that.

Dream or no dream, Jesse was glad he'd given Cameron what little he had. That, at least, could never be undone. He thought maybe it was the only thing he'd ever given that he felt that way about.

Kenny was talking to him. He'd put a weighty hand on Jesse's shoulder. "Buddy, I'm sure glad you happened by when you did. Some things you just never get used to. Hell, I have a hard enough time when I get a call somebody's hit a deer needs to be put down. But to see a person lying by the side of the road like that makes you wonder. It could kind of freak you out if you thought about it too much, you know."

"I know what you mean. Am I, like, a witness or anything? Do you need me for that?"

"Nah." Kenny patted Jesse in a reassuring way on the shoulder—they were family, after all. "This doesn't have anything to do with you. You're one hundred percent free to go."

TWENTY-NINE

Rain had been falling for three days straight, a drumming downpour filling up the emptied-out ponds, flushing full the creeks and rivers. All the stunted corn was drowned in its fields.

The number of cars in the parking lot of the de Hulter Funeral Home surprised him, the same way he'd been surprised to see the road lined with them the afternoon of Cameron's party, that long-ago day barely a week past. He'd made up his mind not to come to the memorial service Perry had somehow found his number to call him about: no way was he going to show up with that crowd. He wanted nothing more to do with them. It was a clean, heaven-sent break he'd been offered—why tempt his good fortune?

Still, he'd circled around five, eight, fifteen times in the truck he hadn't had the heart to let go of. He tried hard not to think of it as blood money, but the color was too perfect not to think that. Wouldn't it always be on his mind now?

He hadn't done anything wrong. Not a thing.

Music played, brash, bustling stuff he could hear from the lobby—hardly music for a funeral. As soon as he entered the chapel, the noise faded abruptly. Max had turned down the volume on a boom box.

"Petrushka," he said, speaking loudly, theatrically, "was Toby Vail's favorite piece of music. And so, of course, Cameron's as well."

It meant nothing to Jesse, though some people laughed, which seemed a strange thing to do at a funeral. He looked around in vain for the casket; there was nothing but the lectern Max stood behind, and a couple of blown-up color photos propped on music stands on either side of him.

"Cameron *always* had a tin ear," said a man seated in the front row. "Believe me, I tried."

"Dan should know," Max told everybody.

Jesse stared hard at dark-haired Dan. Dan wore a lime green, short-sleeve shirt. He had his legs crossed at the knees; his dangling leg fidgeted like he was nervous. Jesse tried to remember what Cameron had told him about this Dan.

"Well, again, thank you all for coming," Max went on. "A few of us are going to say some words about Cameron. And then anybody else who wants to share a memory should feel free. He'd have hated this memorial, I'm sure—but of course, it's not really for him. It's for us. Which is something he'd have understood completely. At some later date, we'll organize a little gathering to scatter his ashes. That is, if it ever decides to stop raining. I think Cameron's using his newfound influence up there to make sure all his gardens get a proper watering."

There was another murmur of laughter. Jesse rocked back and forth on the balls of his feet and tried to decide whether to stay or go. Probably a hundred people were there; lots of them he recognized from the party. He prayed Perry, in the front row next to Dan, wouldn't have any reason to turn around and see him. He wished Perry's profile, when he shifted in his seat to whisper something to Dan, wasn't so damn agreeable looking.

"I knew Cameron for a long time," Max said. "Longer than anybody here. Richard Nixon was still president when I first knew that shy boy from Tennessee. You wouldn't believe how thick his accent was back then. He lost it so gradually down through the years; then one day it was just gone, and he was one of us. So to speak. I don't think he liked me very much at first. He'd never met a Jew before, and I think I scared the pants off him."

The people in that room seemed ready to laugh at practically anything. Max leaned forward on the lectern and looked out sternly over the crowd. "That's *not* what I mean." Then he grinned. *"That"* was later. And I have to say, once Cameron came out, he was out and proud for the duration. For many of us he was a role model that way—he showed us how to shed our old fears, the self-hatred we grew up with. In his quiet, courageous way he taught us to join our comrades in the struggle."

Jesse hardly listened. He studied those photos he'd seen before. That heart-stopping smile made his heart stop all over again. The two of them looked completely happy, perched among big, chaotic blocks of stone without a care in the world while behind them mountains soared into a flawless sky.

"This summer was a time of renewal for our friend," Max was telling everybody. "He'd suffered a lot, but he was moving on gracefully from the past into the future. He was making new friends—Barbara and Bernard Rudd, Elliot Shore. He was more engaged in his work than ever. He'd been at death's door more than once—he joked he was going to get picked up for loitering if he didn't watch it. But every time, he came back. I guess some of us grew to expect that. But the other day, sadly, it was different. The autopsy found that he had a greatly enlarged heart. Well, it doesn't surprise me. Cameron *did* have a greatly enlarged heart. He was the most generous person I ever knew. Generous, and open for change, the potential for change. How many of us in this room realize that the Stone Hollow we know and love today is a direct result of Cameron Barnes? He'd be too modest to admit it, but if it wasn't for his vision of what a great town this could be, Perry and I would never have moved up here in the first place. He saw a house on the verge of ruin and he thought, 'We can renovate this, we can bring it back.' The same with this community we all love so much. Wasn't it John F. Kennedy who said, 'Some men see things as they are, others see things as they wish them to be'? That was Cameron. And if you ask what we can do in his honor, I would say this: let us all work together to make change happen in Stone Hollow, to build together the kind of community—the kind of civic family—that would make our dear friend proud."

The photo was Turkey. Suddenly—terribly—Jesse knew that. The realization punched him hard. So that was what Cameron had offered him: the place in the world where he'd once been happy. And what had Jesse said, practically the last words he ever spoke to the dead man, words he'd never be able to take back?

You must be crazy.

What was *crazy* anyway? To be where you weren't supposed to be? If that was so, then why was he here? Here being the de Hulter Funeral Home on a rainy afternoon in August. Here being Stone Hollow itself.

For the dozenth time in the week since Cameron died, Jesse willed those thoughts back into the depths where they belonged.

"A lot of us in this room loved Cameron down through the years," Max said, "and in a lot of different ways. And he loved us back. I don't know if there's a heaven—if there is, I hope it's a lush, gorgeous garden, and he's walking there right now with Toby and Roger and Larry and Mike, and all the others we've lost along the way. To tell you the truth, I don't think Cameron ever thought he was going to see any of them ever again—but I hope he's wrong. I hope he's in for the biggest surprise of his life.

"That's all. Thank you, everybody. Now Perry is going to say a few words."

"So," Kyle had said. The sound of that voice had made Jesse jump. He spun around. Kyle stood in the kitchen doorway. Jesse hadn't heard him come in, even though he'd been all ears, nervous as hell to be one last time where he didn't belong. It was a risk, for sure. But he'd needed to come back, if for no other reason, he told himself, than to make sure Cameron's cats were fed.

The cats, though, were nowhere to be found. Did animals know, somehow, when to jump ship?

He stared at Kyle. No words came.

"I thought you might be here." Kyle leaned against the doorframe, arms folded across his chest.

"Did Kenny tell you what happened?"

Kyle seemed to think about it for a minute. "Yeah," he said—almost tenderly. "Kenny told me all about what happened. Me and Brandon was sitting in the D and Dee eating ice cream when he walked in. We been out painting all day."

Kyle paused again, unable to resist casting his eyes about the room. Jesse realized, with a mix of pride and regret, that he knew the house a thousand times better than his brother.

"I figured you might be here," Kyle said.

"None of it's what you think."

"Don't matter. It's over now. All that shit I got you into."

"You didn't get me into anything," Jesse said, though he wondered whether letting Kyle tell the story wasn't maybe best for everybody. He was surprised Kyle could take the shocking news so casually—but then, Kyle had hardly known the guy.

"No," his brother went on, still subdued. "I fucked up. I should've known better. Now I *do* know better. Look, Jesse—I'm sorry as hell about some of the shit I said yesterday. I was just playing you rough, man."

"I see," Jesse told him.

Kyle sort of laughed. "You know me. Not the most stable type. But I'm still your brother. Whatever happens, brothers gotta love each other. You know that, don't you?"

Jesse felt strong arms circle him and hold him tight. There was no resisting. His brother smelled of whiskey and sweat.

"I know," he said, speaking into Kyle's shoulder, his lips practically grazing the faintly sour fabric of the T-shirt.

Then Kyle released him. He didn't know when Kyle had ever hugged him like that. It left him breathless.

"Little brother, I only want what's best for you," Kyle said.

But hadn't Cameron also wanted what was best for him?

It didn't matter. In that instant, Cameron—like his cats—vanished without a trace. What did any kind of loyalty to a dead man matter, if giving him up meant you got your brother back? Could anything be happier or more necessary than that?

Kyle must have smelled victory. "Look, we should get outta here," he said. "This place ain't good."

"So where're you parked?" Jesse asked him. "You stole up on me like a damn coyote."

Kyle grinned. Jesse knew it was the kind of compliment he liked to hear. "Up at the cemetery. I thought maybe we should go pay our respects proper. Not like yesterday. What you and me could use right now is a roaring drunk. Don't you think?"

Jesse looked his brother carefully in the eye, persuading himself there was no hint there, not the least trace, of suspicion or reproach or disgust, nothing but the blood trust they'd always had between them.

"Sounds like a fine idea to me," he'd said, and though it had taken him half a week to get over the hangover, now he was glad for every minute of it.

347

Gripping the sides of the lectern with both hands, Perry gave a toss to his dark curls as he surveyed the crowded room. How many other guys, Jesse wondered, had Perry managed to talk into one thing or another? Well, he was immune to all that now, the way patients injected with just a trace of virus were inoculated against the larger disease. He guessed he should be thankful for the lousy summer, the future it had shielded him against. He wouldn't have stopped by the funeral home, wouldn't have risked the nagging sense that he was somehow betraying Kyle's trust, unless he was absolutely certain he was over all that.

But just then Perry looked directly his way. For a single second their gazes met; in that instant of fear he thought Perry was about to speak his name out loud. But Perry didn't say a word. He looked stricken—like he, and not Jesse, was the one the moment had decided to nab. He peered down at the lectern like he was searching for notes that weren't there. Everybody waited for him to speak. You could feel the whole room holding its breath.

All that came out was a single long sob, more horrifying than any words Perry might've said. That was something Jesse knew he wasn't going to forget—that cry of somebody choking back too much ever to recover from. It nailed him dead on.

Without a second's hesitation, he left that place. He left quickly, stopping his ears and not daring once to look back.

PART FOUR

Under the Shadow

THIRTY

They'd all gathered in the kitchen to bring out the cake Patti'd bought. To the Greatest Mom in the World, testified a pink scrawl of icing. Uncle Roy cut slices for everybody—Donna, Leanne, Aunt Doty.

It was a rainy afternoon in October, and their mom was celebrating her fiftieth birthday. Jesse sat squeezed in next to Donna and Leanne on the short wooden bench in the corner. Leanne was sexy in black spandex and a loose flannel shirt. Donna wore her favorite pink sweats with the tea-colored stain on one thigh that never seemed to come out in the wash.

"What a crowd," their mom said, handing around the plates. "This kitchen's always been so small."

"This kitchen's just fine," Kyle told her. "It's a frigging beautiful kitchen." These days he had Pop's old whiskey glow about him most of the time. Could their mom tell? At Kyle's insistence, she'd pulled the house from the market. It hadn't made Craig Hallenbeck happy—in fact, he'd been an asshole about it—but what could he do? As Patti'd said with a hoot when she'd heard about that afternoon, "It's like Jesus throwing the money changers out of the temple." For several whole weeks it raised Kyle up to new heights in her estimation, and when he heard what she'd said about him, he'd returned the favor.

The fall had been cool and wet. Leaves fell early. In front lawns throughout Stone Hollow campaign signs had sprouted. You saw Max Greenblatt's grinning face everywhere you turned. ISN'T IT TIME FOR A

CHANGE? asked his slickly printed signs. PROGRESSIVE GOVERNMENT FOR THE PEOPLE.

"Those fellows sure have deep pockets," Uncle Roy grumbled. He'd paid Jesse and Kyle twenty bucks to drive around one Sunday afternoon staking up his own hand-stenciled signs. "People ain't stupid. They know when outside money's trying to buy an election."

Still, Jesse thought it must be a little disheartening for Uncle Roy to see how many GREENBLATT FOR MAYOR signs there were. At night, sometimes, Kyle and Brandon would rip a few down and toss them in the Schneidekill, but the next day they'd spring right back up, twice as many—in front of houses old and new, in the windows of nearly every business on Main Street.

The only sign in front of Cameron Barnes's old house was a FOR SALE sign, courtesy of Hallenbeck Realty. For several weeks Jesse'd gone out of his way to avoid that road, but then at some point he'd started using it again. All that stuff of the summer seemed so long ago; there were times when he'd wake in the morning and for the space of a few blessed minutes it was like none of it had ever happened.

It was when he woke in the middle of the night that he remembered everything.

He'd been damn lucky, he supposed. From Perry he'd heard not a peep, nor had he run into him anywhere, as he was sure would have to happen sooner or later. Only once had Jesse caught a glimpse of him, standing on the sidewalk in front of Zanzibar, chatting with two guys he didn't recognize. Whether Perry had seen him as he drove by in the truck that would never really belong to him, he had no idea.

He told himself he didn't care. That world was behind him now. Since that epic healing drunk in the cemetery, things had never been better between him and Kyle. Things had never been better all around, it seemed.

"Let's see that ring of yours," Uncle Roy was saying.

Donna held out her hand.

"Nice," he told her. "Nice," he said again, looking straight at Jesse with a congratulatory wink. "Your daddy'd be proud." Then he turned to Kyle and Leanne. "Now when're you two heathens tying the knot?"

"Hell ain't frozen over yet," said Leanne.

Uncle Roy laughed. "Well, winter's coming," he told her. "Sooner than you think."

"I ain't got this filly quite broken," Kyle said. "Though she's near enough about broken me."

For that, Leanne gave him a peck on the cheek.

Donna was still admiring her ring, though the attention had passed elsewhere. She turned her hand this way and that, and Jesse felt a rush of— what was it? Tenderness? Pity? Disgust? He knew he'd done the right thing. She might have called him the biggest moron on the planet, but when you got right down to it, being with a moron was a hell of a lot better than being alone. There'd been enough of feeling lonely for everybody this past summer.

Patti must've been watching that measly ring too. She leaned close to Donna and said, "Just about the last thing I ever heard Pop tell Jesse was, he wanted seventeen grandchildren. He'd be a real happy man right about now, if he could see the two of you."

A knock on the front door interrupted their party.

"That's funny," said their mom. "Did we invite anybody else? I didn't hear nobody pull up."

Down in the yard, Poke was barking up a storm. Uncle Roy went to the door. Jesse could hear him down the hall, cursing under his breath as he struggled to pull it open. It stuck worse when it rained.

Then he was back, squeezing his bulk into the cramped kitchen. "Jesse, son. Mailman's got a letter needs your John Hancock," he reported,

The mailman wasn't their regular one. A stout little fellow, he looked pretty put out at having to traipse up to the house in the rain. "I hope that dog of yours down there don't ever get loose," he said.

"Poke's harmless. He just don't like the rain."

"Who does?"

"He's got a nice doghouse he don't ever use," Jesse added, but the mailman wasn't too interested.

"Now sign here," he told Jesse. "Registered letter."

Jesse had never gotten a registered letter before. Schenkewitz, Murphy and Tannenbaum, Attorneys at Law. What kind of trouble was he in for lawyers to be writing him? For weeks there, he'd been half convinced Cameron had died because of him—but of course it wasn't so. The poor guy's heart had just failed. That was all. To think he was in any way a part of that was sheer craziness.

Standing in the open doorway, he skimmed the letter, then read it through more carefully, comprehending just enough to feel a queasy dread unfurl itself inside him.

It wasn't really possible, was it?

"What you got there, honey?" asked his mom, coming up behind him. "And shut the door. You're letting the damp in."

"It's nothing," he said, though his hand that held the letter was trembling. "Just some stupid business I got to take care of."

He felt everybody scrutinize him as he threaded his way through the kitchen and toward the stairs.

"Jesse?" Donna reached out to grab his wrist. "Everything okay? You're missing out on some delicious cake."

"I'll be right down," he told her, conscious of shaking himself loose from her grip. Crumbs had caught on the ledge of her breasts.

"Now who's for seconds?" asked Uncle Roy.

"I'll have another little piece," Jesse heard his fiancée mention as he stumbled up the stairs.

He sat on his bed and read the letter through once more. His first thought was that it must be some kind of a joke—Perry, maybe, was messing with him. But in his heart he knew he wasn't that lucky. A hand had reached out from the grave and tapped him on the shoulder. So Cameron Barnes had been as good as his word. Who could've known? At the time his response had been "You're such a fucking liar," and Cameron hadn't said a word to contradict him. Afterward, in all that followed, he'd forgotten—or not forgotten, no, he hadn't forgotten a thing about that night, he'd just shoved it so far back in the shadows he'd have thought nothing could ever drag it out to the light again.

Had Cameron somehow known, his last evening on the planet, that he was going to die? Not in the way anybody with half a sense of things could grasp the inevitable, but with some special foreknowledge that was precise and awful and complete, the kind Pop too must've had those last days in the hospital. Had Cameron planned his leaving down to the last detail? Because you could see a kind of beautiful completion to it, like the hand of somebody—and Jesse didn't believe for one instant you could either praise or blame God in anything—had gone and arranged it all to perfection. But no, he reassured himself. Cameron Barnes was only one very sick man, and between one breath and the next he'd given up the ghost. Simple as that.

In any event, he'd said his silent prayer of thanks to that invisible hand and moved on, his single nod to the summer's recklessness being one afternoon's decision, after he'd sucked down a good part of Kyle's whiskey stash, to go down on bended knee before Donna there in her pink bedroom where she sat crosslegged on her bed among all her beloved animals and ask if she'd have him, the biggest fucking moron on the planet. For the longest time she'd looked at him from under half-closed eyelids, her face gone slack with thought, till finally she burst out, "Oh Jesse, you're gonna make me cry."

It was the best and hardest thing he'd ever done. He was sure of that.

And now this. He couldn't think of anywhere to hide the letter he held except that ill-fated spot under his mattress. But already it was too late.

He looked up to see his brother in the doorway. "Hey, man." Kyle lounged against the doorframe. "What you got there?"

"It's nothing," Jesse repeated, wishing you could say something and make it true.

"Don't lie to me."

Jesse handed his brother the document.

Kyle's lips moved silently while Jesse studied the dirty trickle of water that made its way down the inside of the bedroom wall by the window. He and Kyle had been up to the roof twice with the tar gun, but the leak wouldn't go away. They'd laid some rolled-up towels along the baseboard to try and soak up that persistent rivulet.

"Whoa," Kyle said. "You know what this means?"

Jesse found he couldn't say a word.

"Oh man," his brother moaned. "It's a motherfucking fortune you got here." Clutching the letter, he did a sort of war dance halfway around the room. "This'll set you up sweet, Jesse. Hell, this sets us all up."

"No," Jesse said.

Kyle stopped mid-stride and looked at him. "What do you mean, no? It's yours, man. Free and clear. You earned it. I don't know what you did back there or how you did it, but I gotta hand it to you. This is fucking awesome."

Jesse hated the triumphant grin that had spread across his brother's face.

"Don't you see? It's Pop smiling down on us. It's the lucky jackpot he was always looking for. He must of figured out some way to work them controls up there in heaven."

"I didn't want him to die," Jesse said.

"Hell, none of us did."

But Jesse didn't mean Pop. How even to begin to say what he meant?

He reached out and took the letter from his brother's hand. Without looking at it again, he slowly tore it into little strips. They both watched the scraps of paper flutter to the floor.

"That don't do nothing. It's still all there. It's all in the bank waiting for you. It's got your name written on it."

"I ain't touching it," Jesse said.

Kyle scrutinized him fiercely. "Man, I can't fucking figure you out. We go to all this trouble, we get what we want—what we fucking deserve—and now you're telling me you don't want it?"

"I never wanted it," Jesse said. "It was your bright idea, remember? It just fell to me to do all the dirty work."

"I'd say you fucking earned it, then."

Jesse felt he had to say something like the truth. "It wasn't ever about the guy's money."

"Then what the fuck did he do to you?"

The anger in Kyle's words took Jesse aback.

"He didn't do nothing to me."

"You're a fucking liar. You wasn't like this before you knew him. Something happened to change you. Whatever it was, I don't like it. I ain't standing for it."

"Nothing happened. I swear." But even as he said it, he saw how there was no longer any retreat. His brother was dead right. Jesse could go on like nothing was different. He could continue to hang around Kyle and Leanne, he could avoid the likes of Perry on the one hand and Brandon on the other, he could marry Donna all he wanted: none of that was going to take him back to where he'd been. He'd thought he'd put the summer behind him, but it would never be behind him. He stared at the curls of paper on the floor, half expecting the ripped-up letter to knit itself back together before his eyes. He could go on shredding that reminder forever, but to no avail. Above his head, rain tapped unrelentingly on the roof, and closer, water dripped inside the walls. Some forces, once they wanted in, could get in anywhere.

From downstairs came a burst laughter—Leanne's high-pitched whinny, Uncle Roy's belly-deep guffaw. They were having a good time down there—though Jesse was oddly relieved not to catch Donna's voice in that spirited concord. She was the one who'd end up taking it the hardest. She was the one, when you got right down to it, he'd hurt the most.

He spoke as bravely as he could. "You don't know me like you used to," he told his brother. "I don't know how it happened. I'm not lying there. But you just don't know me anymore."

"The hell I don't. Jesse, man, you can't fucking betray me like this. Not after what we been through. I don't know what the fuck you're thinking—you're right about that. But you're gonna come around, Jesse. You can't *not* come around. Think about it. You and Donna are gonna be needing that money. And this house—don't you think it could use a little cash infusion right about now? Think how happy Mom would be for a roof that don't leak. A new stove. Money to help Patti with that school of hers. All the stuff Pop would of wanted for this family, only he never got to see any of it. You really gonna let our old man down that like? Turn this money down, whatever sorry-ass reason you think you got, you're turning your back on everybody you're supposed to care about. Don't you see the self-ishness in that? Don't you see what it means?"

"It never was my money," Jesse told his brother, "and it ain't now."

"You're just talking," Kyle said.

But it was more than just talking. Jesse remembered that look Pop had got when he'd started to wander far off into those woods he never found his way back from. How he must've sensed each of them, Kyle and Jesse and Patti and their mom, fall away one by one from his side till it was just him alone there in the dark woods, and glimmering somewhere in the shadows, barely discernible but you knew with a kind of blood fever they were out there, all the fabulous animals that dream-forest teemed with.

"You gotta listen to me," Kyle pleaded. "I know some deep shit went down back there. We both know it. Stuff neither of us is too proud of. Me as well as you. But it's past. It's over now. We're free and clear, both of us. With the money we got, we can practically buy ourselves a little para-dise. Why do you want to go ruining that?"

Without warning he lunged at Jesse, seizing him by both arms and pulling him into a thrilling embrace. With just such a hug Kyle had reclaimed him from danger that August afternoon in Cameron's kitchen. Brought him back safely into the fold.

Now Kyle spoke like a lover might, his warm breath lush with whiskey's afterburn, his words low and urgent in Jesse's ear. "What I done for you, little brother, you got no idea. Nobody can ever know what I done. But life's gonna be a whole lot better around here. Everything'll be like it once was."

With a sob Jesse threw off his brother's embrace. "Don't you see?" he cried. "We can't never be like we used to."

They stood apart, both panting a little, but neither made a move. To grapple and jab and pommel: that would have been fine, it would have made something happen. But they couldn't fight like that anymore. They stood motionless in the narrow room where they'd dreamed alone and traded stories and hatched schemes, where for all the years of his boyhood Jesse had longed for nothing as much as that perfect, punishing, unattainable figure lying in the bunk above him. Now he shed all that. Kyle too must have seen how things were. For the longest time he gazed at Jesse with the stricken look of someone only now discovering what he might have lost—though the full extent of that loss, its incalculable sum, neither brother could yet even begin to know.